A Timeless Romance Anthology

A Yuletide Regency

SIX ROMANCE NOVELLAS

A Yuletide Regency

SIX ROMANCE NOVELLAS

Regina Scott
Sarah M. Eden
Jen Geigle Johnson
Annette Lyon
Krista Lynne Jensen
Heather B. Moore

Mirror Press

Copyright © 2018 Mirror Press
Print edition
All rights reserved

No part of this book may be reproduced in any form whatsoever without prior written permission of the publisher, except in the case of brief passages embodied in critical reviews and articles. These novels are works of fiction. The characters, names, incidents, places, and dialog are products of the authors' imaginations and are not to be construed as real.

Interior Design by Cora Johnson
Edited by Kristy Stewart, Jennie Stevens, Kelsey Down and Lisa Shepherd
Cover design by Rachael Anderson
Cover Photo Credit: Arcangel

Published by Mirror Press, LLC

ISBN: 978-1-947152-52-6

Table of Contents

Always a Kiss at Christmas
BY REGINA SCOTT

A Yuletide Match
BY SARAH M. EDEN

The Forbidden Duke
BY JEN GEIGLE JOHNSON

Mistletoe at Willowsmeade
BY ANNETTE LYON

Follow the River Home
BY KRISTA LYNNE JENSEN

The New Earl
BY HEATHER B. MOORE

MORE TIMELESS ROMANCE ANTHOLOGIES

Winter Collection
Spring Vacation Collection
Summer Wedding Collection
Autumn Collection
European Collection
Love Letter Collection
Old West Collection
Summer in New York Collection
Silver Bells Collection
All Regency Collection
Annette Lyon Collection
Sarah M. Eden British Isles Collection
Under the Mistletoe Collection
Mail Order Bride Collection
Road Trip Collection
Blind Date Collection
Valentine's Day Collection
Happily Ever After
A Yuletide Regency
Kissing a Billionaire

Always Kiss at Christmas

Regina Scott

*To all those who hold Christmas in their hearts, and to the
Lord, the author of Christmas*

Chapter One

Rose Hill, Surrey, Christmas Eve, 1802

IF SHE COULDN'T win an offer at Christmas, there was no justice in the world.

Mary Rose tied the final red satin ribbon on the kissing bough and stood back with a nod of satisfaction. Mr. Cowls, their grey-haired butler, pulled on the chain, and the circular evergreen bough climbed with the brass chandelier until it was high overhead, framed by the white of the entry hall ceiling.

"Very nice," her mother said from her wheeled chair at the foot of the stairs. "I'm certain Mr. Godwin will approve."

Mary kept her gaze upward. It didn't matter whether Chester Godwin or any of the other friends, neighbors, and family expected for her mother's annual Christmas Eve party approved of her efforts. She didn't even care if Julian Mayes approved. All she needed was for him to stand under the bough long enough for her to kiss him. Surely one kiss would convince him that they were fated to be together.

Everything had been planned to that end. She'd arranged for the guests to be greeted in the entry hall rather than on the front steps so she'd have a chance to address him directly.

She'd asked Cook to bake gingerbread, one of his favorites, and the rich scent wafted through the house even now. She'd worn her best winter dress, a white velvet trimmed in swan's down, which called attention not only to her curves but also her raven hair. And now the kissing bough was as ready as she was to see this done.

"Mary?" her mother murmured. "You will be kind to Mr. Godwin, won't you?"

As Mr. Cowls hooked the chain against the wood-paneled wall, Mary went to join her mother. It seemed every morning Mama looked a little thinner, paler. She had tried to hide her malady today by having her maid curl her greying hair into fashionable ringlets around her face and wearing one of her brightest gowns, a ruby velvet with white lace at the neck and puffed sleeves. But Mary saw the changes.

"She's wasting away," she'd told the local physician. "Can nothing be done?"

"Nothing that need concern you," Doctor Parkins had said, patting Mary's shoulder. "A pretty young lady like you should be focused on balls and teas."

If he truly thought such trivialities more important than her mother's health, he must consider Mary's head to be distressingly empty and her character singularly flighty. Yet no matter how severely she dressed for his visits, no matter how straight she stood and how directly she engaged him, she had not been able to disabuse him of the notion that she was too young and untried to be involved in her mother's treatment.

He wasn't the only one. Her father's will gave guardianship to an old friend of the family, but the aging Lord Farley always said he had complete faith in her mother and saw no need to intrude on their domestic arrangements. Mary had tried writing to him; his return letter merely reassured her she had no need for concern. The vicar in the nearby village of Weyton said the same.

They were all mistaken, but they would not listen to her. She had observed that only three things gave a woman standing here in Surrey: age, consequence, or marriage. The first two were denied her; she could not make herself older or elevate her family's standing.

But when she married Julian, she would be the wife of a rising solicitor. Then the physician would have to listen to her, for fear of her husband if nothing else.

"I will be considerate of all our guests, Mother," she promised her now. "I want this Christmas to be perfect."

Her mother's lavender-colored eyes, so like her own, glistened with unshed tears. "So do I, dear." She held out a hand, fingers cramped by her illness, and Mary took it gently. How brittle, how fragile. She had to convince Julian to marry her, for her and her mother's sakes.

But Julian was not among the first guests to arrive that afternoon. Her mother had had Mary send invitations to their neighbors—the Mayes to the north, the Garveys to the west, the Godwins to the south, and even the mighty Duke of Wey to the east. Friends Mary had made at the finishing school from which she'd recently graduated were also invited, as was her odious cousin, Nigel.

"He is family," her mother had replied when Mary had protested.

And so, God willing, would be Julian.

Perhaps because Nigel was the last person she'd hoped to see, he was the first to arrive. Short and fleshy, with tiny dark eyes and a pursed mouth, he tended to walk quickly, fingers curling and uncurling, as if always reaching for something beyond his grasp. Mr. Cowls ushered him into the entry hall and accepted his greatcoat with barely a twitch of his long nose to show his displeasure at handling the worn, stained material. Nigel was less kind.

"That wood wants polish," he proclaimed, eying the Jacobean paneling instead of Mary's mother, who sat ready to greet him. "And there's a stone missing from the bottom stair outside. This house looks more ruinous every time I see it."

"Then perhaps you should see it less often," Mary said.

He turned to Mary with a frown, as if he could not decide whether she'd intended to insult him.

"What my daughter means," her mother said in her soothing voice, "is that if you visited us more often you might come to love Rose Hill as much as we do."

"Alas, I am terribly busy," he said with a sniff from his bulbous nose. "My current circumstances do not allow for a life of luxury." He turned his gaze to her mother at last. "And how are you, Mrs. Rose?"

"Quite well," Mary said before her mother could answer. "We have hopes Mother will live to see her grandchildren and great-grandchildren play at Rose Hill."

His smile barely lifted his pudgy lips. "How . . . charming."

Her mother reached out and squeezed her hand. It was a warning to behave. Some in the area considered her too proud, too confident because she was tall enough to look them in the eye for all her mere sixteen years. She'd heard the comments after services and at the assembly.

That Mary Rose, so outspoken. I fear she's been terribly spoiled.

Nigel likely agreed. She was just glad the knocker sounded then, forcing her cousin into the great hall on their right so they could greet the newcomers.

Who were also not Julian Mayes.

Mary smiled and curtsied and nodded to welcome

various guests who arrived over the next half hour. Most had known her family for years and were quite solicitous of her mother. Even Dr. Parkins wished her well, even though his look was assessing. The only other person who gave her any trouble was Chester Godwin.

They had associated as children, but since he had gone off to Eton, he had decided he was far too sophisticated for the Surrey countryside. His amber-colored hair was cut short on the sides and left longer on top to curl over his brow. His shirt points were so high they likely poked his ears. He walked with the mincing gait of a dandy, wasp-waisted coat boasting improbably broad shoulders and calves suspiciously bumpy in his white stockings. If he wasn't careful, he would spend his entire fortune on padding.

"Mrs. Rose, Miss Rose," he greeted them with the barest of bows, likely because his tight clothing prevented them. "How kind of you to rescue me from the sea of boredom that is Surrey in winter, or any other time of the year actually." He smiled as if he'd been particularly witty.

"We would not dream of entertaining without you, Mr. Godwin," her mother assured him. "In fact, I believe Mary planned the decorations with you in mind." She glanced up at the kissing bough.

Mary's stomach dropped. Kiss Chester? No, no. That was assuredly not the plan.

She needn't have worried. The high collar on his coat prevented him from looking about. His gaze reached no farther than the swag of evergreens on the landing behind them. "Ah, yes. Very pretty. But then, so is Miss Rose."

"You must see what we've done with the hall," Mary said, pointing him in that direction and giving him a little nudge. He wandered off.

"You said you'd be kind," her mother scolded.

"Trust me, Mother," Mary said. "That was kind."

Among the last to arrive was her friend Lady Eva. They had met at finishing school, where the beauty had taken first in every course. The daughter of a duke, Lady Eva had pale hair that glimmered and blue eyes that shined. Today her slender figure was draped in cerulean velvet trimmed with ermine. As Cowls helped her chaperone with her wrap, Lady Eva took both of Mary's hands for a squeeze.

"Thank you for inviting me. Things have been so busy since we left school. I have missed our talks."

"I don't know how much time we'll have to talk," Mary confessed as her mother greeted the round-faced little chaperone. "But I wanted to wish you happy in person. To think, you'll be marrying the heir of the Duke of Wey!"

Lady Eva's smile was as cool as her looks. "Yes. Some consider him quite the catch. Find me later." With another squeeze, she turned and led her chaperone into the hall.

Mary's mother sighed, shoulders sagging as if she'd endured much. "That should be all of them. Would you wheel me in, Cowls, so we can start the festivities?"

Mary caught her breath. The time for greetings had ended, and he hadn't come. Why?

Laughter rang from the great hall. Her guests expected her to lead them in the games and activities planned for the day and evening. How could she leave this spot? She hadn't caught Julian.

"I believe there is one more, madam," Mr. Cowls said, standing with his head high by the door.

Her mother frowned. "Who?"

As if in answer, the knocker sounded on the big front door. Her mother nodded to their butler to answer.

Mary clasped her hands together to keep them from shaking. It had to be him. She'd worked too hard, prayed too long, for it to be anyone else. Mr. Cowls swung open the door, and winter's wind swirled through the entry, sending snow-flakes dancing. As if borne on their wings, Julian Mayes stepped into the house.

Under a top hat touched by white, his red-gold hair curled naturally around his handsome face. Warm brown eyes welcomed all he saw. Those shoulders and calves required no tailor's art or artifice for improvement. He moved with a grace that said he feared no one and nothing. He was, all in all, perfection.

Mary drew in a breath and stepped forward to meet her future.

◇◆◇

He was late. Fashionably late, his friends at Eton would have teased him. In some circles, he would have been praised for the trait—such ennui, such polished sophistication. He'd certainly cultivated the veneer. When one was only the son of a country squire, one needed something to stand out against all those titles, that wealth. Yes, he could have strolled insouciantly into the hall as if he owned the place.

Only it was Mrs. Rose and Mary, and they deserved better.

He almost hadn't come. His parents had been unwilling to brave the snow. They were getting on in years now. And it wasn't as if he and Mary were the friends they'd been as children. It had been months since he'd last seen her. That hadn't stopped his mother from adjusting his top hat before he'd left the house.

"May I hope for good news?" she'd asked, brown eyes eager.

"I am in no position to seek a wife, Mother," he'd reminded her.

Her mouth had dipped, but he could not satisfy her

longings. A fellow ought to be able to offer a lady a home, an income to support it. He had only just landed an apprenticeship with a highly regarded solicitor in London. And while he had always enjoyed Mary's company, she was several years his junior, having only recently left the schoolroom. Surely she had plans for her debut in London this coming Season. He certainly had plans for the next step in his life, and that did not include taking a wife.

But one look at the beauty regarding him from across the entry hall nearly changed his mind.

Her raven hair was swept up high, secured by pearl-headed combs. The gleam in her lavender-colored eyes could only be called challenging. And the white velvet dress betrayed curves he hadn't remembered.

If he hadn't been so determined to play the peer, he might have stared.

As it was, he strode forward. "Mrs. Rose, Miss Rose, thank you for your invitation. Happy Christmas."

"Happy Christmas, Mr. Mayes," her mother said, forcing his gaze to her. The change in her was even more pronounced. He remembered her round-cheeked smiles, the brambleberry pie she'd encouraged him to gorge on, her laughter at his stories. Now her lamp had dimmed, her body thinned, until she was a shadow of her former self.

As if to hide this fact, Mary darted in front of her mother. "Happy Christmas, Julian." She looked over his head expectantly.

Had someone else come in behind him? Julian turned but saw only the elderly butler, whose gaze was also high over his head. What had he missed?

"Miss Rose." The whining voice made her name sound like a complaint. Chester Godwin wandered out of the great hall. He too had changed since their childhood, but Julian could not admire the new look. Already one shoulder pad was slipping backward, making him appear lopsided.

"Miss Rose," he repeated as if he hadn't noticed Julian standing there. "Do come in and save me from these country nobodies."

Funny. Godwin had been raised among these country nobodies. It seemed Julian wasn't the only one trying to appear above his station.

Mary took the interruption more pointedly. Her eyes flashed as she lowered her gaze to skewer her guest. "I shall be along in a moment, Mr. Godwin."

"We'll both come," her mother said. "I believe that's all, Cowls. Join me, Mary."

Julian could almost feel the tension in Mary. She seemed rooted to the spot, her gaze veering from her mother to him and back again.

The butler moved in behind Mrs. Rose, and Julian realized she sat in an invalid chair. The butler managed the wheeled contraption toward the great hall. Godwin fell in beside it. Still Mary didn't budge.

Julian offered her his arm. "If I may."

She sighed as if giving up, then put her hand on his. "Thank you. But we must speak at your earliest convenience. Privately."

Interesting. From his observations, ladies generally only wanted a private word with a solicitor for two reasons: to get themselves out of trouble or into it. Surely Mary had no need for legal representation. If she had, her mother would likely have hired a more seasoned advocate.

That meant she must have something planned for this party. It appeared he wasn't much changed after all, for he could hardly wait to learn what mischief was coming and how he could play a part.

Chapter Two

ANY HOPE OF a tête-à-tête Mary might have had was doomed the moment she and Julian moved into the great hall. She simply had too many guests congregated in the space. Like the entry hall, the walls here were covered in squares of dark wood paneling. But the massive white stone fireplace, the lintel carved with scenes of harvest, brightened the long, low-ceilinged room, as did the brass sconces affixed to the walls. The crimson carpet in the center of the polished wood floor matched the chief color of the tapestry over the hearth. With everything draped in holly and ivy, she could not have asked for a more festive setting.

Now her guests stood or sat in groups, members flitting back and forth, conversation ebbing and flowing like waves. Her mother had positioned herself just inside the door, her gaze darting to Mary and a frown marking her brow. Did she suspect her daughter was ready to ignore everyone for one special man?

"May I have your attention?" For all his regal and calm bearing, Cowls could certainly make his presence known when needed. Around Mary, voices quieted, people stilled. He stepped back, and her mother stood. Mary hoped she was the only one who noticed the tremor in that gentle voice.

"Thank you all again for joining us in our Christmas

tradition," she said, gazing around at the assembled group. "I know we generally celebrate outdoors, but some of us have made the acquaintance of a warm spot by the fire on a cold day and found it pleasing."

Several of the older guests chuckled.

"Never fear," she continued. "My Mary and our staff will be hosting the outdoor activities while I hold court here in the great hall. We have ice skates for the pond and warm robes for the sleigh ride, and I believe some gentlemen are particularly eager for the snowball fight."

"Not just the gentlemen," their neighbor Mrs. Garvey called while her husband rubbed his hands together in anticipation. The pair regularly trounced their neighbors at the annual event.

"Remember there will be hot cider, roasted chestnuts, frosted sugar biscuits, gingerbread, and other treats here in the great hall," her mother finished, "along with a roaring fire and good company to warm you when you tire of chasing winter. Mrs. Pomfrey and her sisters have agreed to regale us with songs of the season later. Please enjoy."

Everyone began moving then. Some closed in on her mother to settle themselves for a long talk. Others hurried for the entry hall, where the footman and Mr. Cowls were helping people back into their coats and hats. She would never manage a moment alone, much less a kiss, with Julian. But she didn't have to abandon him entirely.

"What do you prefer?" she asked him.

His look would ward off any chill. "To be at your side."

Mary nodded. "Outdoors, then."

She went to don her winter cloak, a voluminous scarlet wool with a black velvet hood and trim. She turned to allow the footman to slip it over her shoulders, and a breath brushed her ear.

"Allow me," Julian said.

A shiver went through her as he draped the cloak about her shoulders. Despite the crowds around them, she glanced up once more at the kissing bough. But Julian had turned to help another lady.

And Mary had a duty.

The snow had stopped falling, she saw as she ventured outside. Like muslin, white sheets draped tree and field. Their gardener had swept the snow off the pond, and the ice glittered darkly under the heavy sky. She pointed one group toward the sleigh that stood waiting, the horses' breath fogging the air, and another group toward the lawn, where two industrious youths were already fashioning snowballs. Though he remained at her side, Julian kept glancing toward the pond. Skating, then. Gliding along, arm in arm, their steps matching as they used to do when they were younger. How romantic. Another shiver went through her.

"Cold?" Julian asked, taking a step closer.

Not with him so near. Those eyes were all encouragement, his mouth turned up and head cocked as if he were ready to listen to anything she cared to impart. He was going to be an excellent solicitor. Already she wanted to confess her hopes.

"It will pass," Mary assured him. "Would you care to skate?"

"Delighted." He offered her his arm, and they walked over to the wrought-iron bench overlooking the pond. Already another couple swept past on the ice. Grooms stood by to strap the steel blades onto footwear. In moments, Mary was out on the glassy surface with Julian at her side. The cool air nipped her cheeks as they set off.

Oh, to always feel this free. It took the merest pressure to sail along. The evergreens alongside the pond flashed by, dusky against the silver of the pond and sky. Julian matched her stride, though he kept his hands behind his back, as if for balance.

"Was it last year you raced me to the end of the pond?" he asked, a twinkle in his eyes.

"And won," Mary reminded him.

"You've changed since then," he said.

Perhaps not as much as she'd thought, for the urge was impossible to resist. "I could still beat you."

"You're on." He glided to the closest end of the pond and turned.

"Ladies and gentlemen," he called, warm baritone cutting through the cold air. Everyone else in the area turned to listen. "I have challenged the current skating champion of this fair acre to a race, and she has graciously agreed. Kindly clear the way."

Other skaters pushed for either side of the pond, leaving the center empty. The artificial waterway ran along most of the front of the white stone house and into the garden, perhaps fifty yards. She'd raced the distance dozens of times over the years. This time, the thrill was sharper, deeper.

She glanced at Julian, who grinned back.

"I would be delighted to start you," Lady Eva said from the edge of the pond.

"You are too kind," Julian acknowledged.

She raised one arm. "On my mark—three, two, one, go!" She dropped her arm, and Mary pushed off as Julian flashed past her, greatcoat billowing.

She pushed harder, digging into the ice. She had to catch him, prove to him she was his equal. Head down, legs pumping, she matched him, passed him. His laughter chased her down the pond to the scratch of metal on ice. People called her name and his, encouraging. She reached the farthest bank and whirled just short of the rhododendrons clustered there. Julian skidded to a stop beside her.

"Still the reigning champion," he declared, taking her gloved hand and holding it high. Cheers and applause echoed around her.

She drew in a breath and closed her eyes as Julian lowered his head toward hers.

One kiss. One kiss, and he'll know.

"I suppose I should congratulate you as well."

Mary's eyes snapped open in time to see Julian straightening to regard her cousin, standing next to the rhododendrons, the green framing his round face. Nigel's eyes were narrowed, his mouth a thin line. Oh, why now!

"I don't believe I've had the pleasure," Nigel said. "Introduce us, Cousin."

Propriety rather than his demand suggested she comply. "Mr. Julian Mayes, may I present my cousin, Mr. Nigel Rose."

Julian inclined his head. "Mr. Rose."

Her cousin barely nodded. "Sir. Why are you monopolizing my cousin?"

Mary drew herself up. "Mr. Mayes is hardly monopolizing me. We were enjoying the ice together."

Julian drew closer as if to protect her. "I'm sure your cousin spoke only from concern. You have no need to worry, sir. Miss Rose and I are old friends."

With the possibility of becoming so much more if Nigel would just leave be.

"Mr. Mayes." Lady Eva waved at them. "You are so good on the ice. Would you assist me?"

He glanced at her and back at Mary, and she could feel his indecision. He wanted to stay with her, but a gentleman did not refuse a lady help, especially when he must know she was affianced to his closest friend.

"I'll rejoin you shortly," Mary promised.

With a last look at Nigel, Julian skated over to help Lady Eva.

Her cousin frowned after him. "Interesting fellow. A solicitor, I understand. Why would you need one?"

So she had him worried. If only the physician would react the same way. "As Julian said, we are longtime friends."

Both his chins jiggled as he turned to look at her. "Julian, is it? I must have a word with your mother. You are far too young to be calling gentlemen by their first names."

Before she could stop him, he strode toward the house. She couldn't very well follow without removing her skates and leaving Julian behind. Well, let Nigel tell tales. The important thing was to bring Julian up to scratch. She had to remember that.

She turned and spotted him at the other end of the pond now, helping an older lady gain her balance. Lady Eva glided in beside her, as confident on the ice as she was on land.

"So that's the gentleman you spoke of at school," she said with a nod in Julian's direction.

Mary sighed. "I used to dream of him proposing, but not today, it seems."

Lady Eva made a moue. "You can't expect him to go down on bended knee under these conditions. You need a more congenial setting."

"I agree. I designed the kissing bough in the entry for his benefit."

"Bold." Her friend looked suitably impressed. "You need only encourage him to return to the house with you. The entry hall should be empty. Perhaps you should grow faint from the cold."

"I've never fainted in my life," Mary informed her. "Besides, he'd think me weak."

Lady Eva shook her head, pale curls bright inside her ermine-lined hood. "Catching the attention of the right suitor requires subterfuge, cunning."

Mary stared at her. "Is that how you became engaged to Lord Thalston?"

"That and other approaches," Lady Eva said. "Make no mistake—one does not become betrothed to a duke's heir without careful planning." She glanced at Julian again. He was applauding a lad's first attempt on the ice, to the youth's red-cheeked delight. "Though perhaps a solicitor needn't be so exacting in his expectations for a wife."

She felt as if she'd slipped through the ice on the pond. "You sound like my cousin."

"Well, you needn't be unkind," Lady Eva said, turning to her again. "I was only trying to help. Here, watch me." She threw back her head and gave a husky laugh, as if Mary had said something tremendously witty. Everyone in the area, including Julian, glanced their way.

"Mr. Mayes," Lady Eva called. "When next do you expect to see my intended, Lord Thalston?"

Julian excused himself and came to join them. Their race had brought the color out in his cheeks, and his brown eyes showed to advantage over his charcoal-colored greatcoat. Mary raised her head and fluttered her lashes.

He was focused on her friend. "On Boxing Day," he said. "Thalston and I hope to ride before I return to London, if the roads are clear enough. But please allow me to offer you my congratulations. He has spoken of you in the most glowing terms."

"Indeed," she said. "I am the most fortunate of brides. I wish all my friends to be as happy." She smiled at Mary.

Mary smiled at Julian.

He examined the middle button on his greatcoat.

"You look cold, Mary," Lady Eva said. "You should go inside and warm up. Mr. Mayes, I know I can count on you to see she reaches the house safely."

She made it sound as if the fifty or so feet were a great distance filled with gaping chasms. But Julian offered Mary his arm, and they skated to the edge of the pond, where he took off his skates and helped her with hers.

Large hands, capable hands. Hands that held her future.

He glanced up at her. "Something wrong?"

"No," Mary assured him. "Shall we?"

As Lady Eva had suggested, the entry hall was empty as they came through the door. Heart pounding in her ears, Mary drew him to the exact spot with the kissing bough overhead, then tipped up her chin. "Julian?"

"Miss Mary?"

Mary held back her puff of vexation as she turned to the footman who was approaching. Some of what she was feeling must have shown on her face, however, for he drew up short.

"Your mother wished a word," he said before swallowing.

Would she never have her moment? "Excuse me," she said to Julian before heading into the great hall and her mother's side.

༄༅

Julian shook his head. What was it about Mary today? He had the feeling he ought to follow her.

To the ends of the earth.

The door opened, and Lady Evangeline swept in. They had met once, at his friend Thalston's instigation. After all, as the daughter of a duke, Lady Evangeline had no need to make the acquaintance of a lowly solicitor, unless he happened to be friends with her betrothed. Then as now, she was ethereally beautiful, but she appeared as cold as the weather outside. The current duke and his wife had chosen her to marry his friend, so Thalston didn't have much choice. Though at times he envied Thalston his position and wealth, at least Julian could marry whom he liked.

"Has Mary left you alone?" she asked, moving closer.

"Temporarily, I'm sure," he answered. "Her mother had need of her."

"I'm certain she's eager to return to your side. She is very clever, our Mary. She'd never leave a gentleman like you alone for long."

She almost made Mary sound like a fortune hunter. The only problem was, he had no fortune.

Just then Mary came out of the great hall, and Lady Evangeline waved her closer. "What a dutiful daughter you are," she said as Mary joined them. "I was sorry to see your mother so unwell. Will this illness pass soon?"

Mary glanced back toward the great hall. "Not soon enough, I fear. Already she's tiring."

"Ah. Pity. Perhaps Mr. Mayes can advise you." Her gaze brushed him as she turned toward the doorway herself. "If you'll excuse me, I'll cheer her. It is only my duty as the future duchess." She moved off.

"Will she speak to any of us once she's wed?" Julian mused with a shake of his head.

"I imagine she'll be too busy for visiting," Mary answered, watching her friend. "Her new position will have many responsibilities, and she is trained to perform them well. Lord Thalston must be delighted to be marrying such a paragon."

Scared out of his wits, more like, but Julian couldn't tell her that and betray a confidence. "Their families account it an excellent match."

She turned to glance up at him through raven lashes. "And what of you, sir? What do you look for in a wife?"

Julian laughed. "I don't look for a wife at all."

She put her hand on his arm as she stepped closer. "What? A handsome fellow like you? Surely the ladies must be sobbing into their tea in London."

With those lavender eyes gazing up at him so adoringly, he found it hard to remember there were any other ladies on the planet, much less London. "You've grown up."

She fluttered her lashes. "You noticed."

Was this show purely for his benefit? Why did he feel like preening?

"You'll have your pick of suitors when you go up to London this Season," he predicted.

"And if I've already made my pick?"

Just as he had on the pond, he found himself leaning closer. "He is a very fortunate fellow."

Those rose-colored lips inched higher. "Ah, if only he would speak, convince me of his devotion."

Dangerous territory. She might not have a father or brother to demand to know his intentions, but she was a lady through and through. He had no right to dally and no consequence to offer more.

"Perhaps he has reason to remain silent," he said.

"What could I say, what could I do, to convince him otherwise?"

The door blew open, and Chester Godwin tumbled into the entry hall. Shaking melting snow off his greatcoat, he started forward.

"Ah, Miss Rose, Mayes, you are an island in a sea of tedium." He glanced at each of them as if awaiting praise for his turn of phrase.

"If only I could find you a boat," Mary said with an unconvincing smile.

Godwin missed the sarcasm. "I have another conveyance in mind. Miss Rose, might I convince you to ride with me in the sleigh?"

Mary linked her arm with Julian's as if to anchor herself to his side. "And abandon Mr. Mayes? I would never be so cruel."

Godwin made a sad face. "Thoroughly bored, are you, Mayes? Can't blame you. It's not like these country affairs can hold much interest for men of the world like us."

Julian was ashamed to admit a similar thought had crossed his mind that morning. Had he truly become so jaded?

"There is something endearingly sweet about the quiet of Surrey," he said with a look to Mary.

Her nod was approving. But over her shoulder he spotted her butler approaching. Julian detached himself as the grey-haired fellow bent to murmur something in Mary's ear. She excused herself to follow him into the great hall. Godwin moved to take her place next to Julian.

"Sweet little thing, ain't she?" he drawled.

Julian kept his look respectful. "I have only admiration for Mrs. Rose and her daughter."

"Oh, to be sure," Godwin said, hitching his greatcoat closer. "I am considering offering for her."

Every muscle in his body tightened, and he had to stop himself from grabbing the fellow by his pretentiously tied cravat and giving him a shake. What was wrong with him? Godwin was well heeled, with an estate nearby, so Mary would be supported in surroundings she knew and loved if she married him. With her will and intelligence, she might even be able to guide Godwin into less boorish behavior.

Yet the idea of this creature marrying his Mary raised bile in the back of his throat.

"Only considering?" he asked, careful to use a nonconfrontational tone.

Godwin shrugged. The movement must have caused his shoulder pads to slip, for he began to grow a hump on his back. "She is lovely, of course. Her mother is well known in the area." He lowered his voice and ducked his head. "But she hasn't a feather to fly with. When her mother dies, which sadly appears to be soon, she won't even have a home. Her cousin inherits everything."

Julian glanced to where Nigel Rose was scuffing his toe against the carpet as if to determine how much nap remained. He vaguely remembered his parents discussing how Mrs. Rose had the house only during her lifetime. If she passed before her daughter wed, what happened to Mary? He couldn't see her cousin being particularly openhanded.

Was Mary's future in danger?

Chapter Three

MARY WAS JUST heading back to the entry hall—after addressing Mr. Cowl's question as to whether to put the candied gingerbread house out on the refreshment table and asking him to add more cinnamon sticks to the cider—when Lady Eva drifted to her side. She had greatly admired the older girl in school. Lady Eva was regal, composed. Her full name—Evangeline—was wonderfully romantic. Mary had always wished her name was more colorful—Meredith, perhaps, or Melisandre. In school, Lady Eva could do no wrong. That she'd pursued an acquaintance with Mary had seemed an honor. Mary was a little taken aback by her friend's calculating comments today.

"Well?" Lady Eva asked now. "Are you making progress?"

"No," Mary admitted. "I was bolder than I've ever been, and all he did was wish me well."

She wrinkled her nose. "Disappointing. You may have to resort to more drastic measures. He is honorable, I take it?"

Mary frowned at her. "Certainly. Why would you ask?"

"Because only honorable men propose when they think they've ruined a lady."

Mary gasped. Several guests glanced their way. Cheeks heating, she drew Lady Eva closer to the window overlooking the pond, where couples skimmed along arm in arm.

"Ruined?" she murmured. "Julian Mayes would never compromise my reputation."

"Not without encouragement," Lady Eva agreed.

"I couldn't . . . I wouldn't . . ." Mary sputtered.

Lady Eva put her hand on her arm. "There, now. I've shocked you. Forgive me. But you said you wanted to marry him. Some gentlemen take considerable persuasion beyond our beauty, wit, and talents."

"Not that kind of persuasion," Mary insisted.

"It depends on the gentleman." Lady Eva dropped her hold. "And how badly you wish to wed."

Mary glanced at her mother, who seemed to have slumped lower. "It is imperative."

"Then only you can decide how far you're willing to go," Lady Eva said. "I will give you one more piece of advice. If you love him, if you want to marry him, don't wait to tell him. Circumstances may force you to make another, less satisfying choice."

The conviction in her voice could only have come from experience. Mary's heart softened. "If you truly don't want to marry Lord Thalston, cry off."

Her gaze went off into the middle distance. "One does not cry off from marrying the heir to a duke. I know my duty."

Several of the older women approached then, to offer Lady Eva their congratulations, and she smiled graciously and thanked them. Her composure never cracked once. If Mary had been forced to wed a man she didn't love to meet her mother's and Society's expectations, she would be raging at the sky.

Or thinking of a way out of it.

Surely that's where she needed to put her energies now. She had lost her initial opportunity with Julian under the kissing bough and been thwarted on the ice. Her responsibilities to her guests would make additional contact challenging, but she refused to follow Lady Eva's advice about compromise. That was no way to show her feelings for a fellow.

And she did have strong feelings. She'd admired Julian since she was a girl. Whenever he and Lord Thalston were home from Eton, they would ride past Rose Hill nearly every afternoon, and she'd run to the gate at the end of the drive to watch for them. At times, she was certain that anyone looking would wonder which was the duke's son and which the son of local gentry. She'd imagined riding with them, talking of important things, being recognized as their friend.

Then one day Julian had arrived at the door, accompanied by his parents. While his mother and father visited with her mother, she had been given the task of showing him about the estate, a groom following dutifully behind them. Her words had tripped over each other as she'd tried to talk to him, and he'd nodded and listened as if taking her as seriously as he would the prince. From then on, he visited whenever he was home, taking her riding, driving. They skated arm in arm in winter and picked berries for her mother's famous pie in the summer.

When she'd turned fifteen, he'd even accompanied her to the local assembly, where she was allowed to dance even though she wouldn't be considered out until she went to London for her Season. Some of the local ladies whispered that he was besotted. Mary didn't believe it. Their activities were too companionable, their discussions more philosophical than romantic.

"Why do you come so often?" she'd asked him one day after he'd eaten no less than two slices of the brambleberry pie her mother loved to bake while Cook was busy with other matters. "Surely you have better things to do."

"Better than spend time with you?" he'd challenged.

When she'd stared at him, he'd grinned. "Besides, your mother makes the best brambleberry pie in Surrey."

Mary had puffed out a sigh. "I'm sure she'd be happy to give your mother the recipe."

He'd leaned forward. "Ah, but then I wouldn't have an excuse to visit."

Slippery then and slippery now. She could not be sure of him, only that she needed his strength to protect her mother. He'd be home through Boxing Day, just two days away. And she wouldn't go up to London for her Season until after Easter. Her mother needed help now.

She squared her shoulders and turned for the entry hall. Though only a short distance away, she had to stop and commiserate with Mr. Fallman over his gout and compare stillroom recipes for chafed hands with Mrs. Pomfrey. She joked and laughed and listened and praised her way forward, inching ever closer to where Julian and Chester Godwin were standing in the entry hall, deep in conversation.

Funny. She'd never thought Chester particularly deep. What were the two of them talking about so earnestly?

Through the door to the great hall, Julian watched as Mary moved from group to group, leaving smiles in her wake. She'd always known how to talk to people—when to cheer, offer advice, or show compassion. She would have made an excellent solicitor.

And a miserable wife to Chester Godwin.

He nearly winced at the realization. If Godwin was right and Mary would be in dire straits should anything happen to her mother, marriage might be her best security. But surely she could do better than Godwin!

"A dowry isn't as important as the woman you marry," he told the fellow now. "But I doubt Mary Rose would make you happy."

Godwin stopped in mid-scratch and stared at him. "Truly? Why?"

"Highly opinionated," Julian confided. "And not afraid to share those opinions. Why, I remember not so long about she called my horse a cob."

Godwin reared back. "She criticized your horse?"

With good reason. When he had last visited, she'd pointed out that, since leaving home, he had come back each time with an animal of poorer quality. She was quite right. The nags were all he could afford at the moment. He'd beg a better mount from his parents before returning to London.

"And she once told me the fold in my cravat was disgraceful," Julian added for good measure.

Godwin goggled.

"Because it was," Mary said, joining them. "It was his first attempt, you see, Mr. Godwin. He wouldn't even allow his father's valet to help him. I fear it was a crumpled waterfall by the time he reached the assembly hall."

His consequence had been equally crumpled, until she'd laughed and found a footman to help him. He couldn't see Godwin appreciating such intervention.

"Still, Miss Rose," the fellow protested now, "to insult a man's attire. It just isn't done."

"Which would you prefer, sir?" she asked. "That I speak up and prevent a friend from looking like a fool or that I remain silent and ensure he will look foolish?"

"Well, I . . ." He adjusted his cravat, then hastily dropped his hand. "I believe it wiser to be silent."

"Then I shall cease speaking to you," Mary said. "Since you value silence so highly."

He opened his mouth, shut it, then cleared his throat. "I beg your pardon. I'm sure I never . . ."

Mary had pity on him. With her sweetest look, she lay a

hand on his arm. "There, now, Mr. Godwin. I never meant to put you to the blush. Like Mr. Mayes, you are one of my oldest acquaintances. Are you enjoying this year's party?"

His smile eased into sight. "Yes, thank you." He seemed to recall he was supposed to be above such country pastimes, for he straightened, causing the shirt points to drop below his earlobes for once. "That is, I find it quite tolerable for Surrey hospitality."

"Such praise. I'm sure Mr. Mayes's presence has helped. What an interesting conversation you two were having. Whatever prompted you to discuss every silly thing I did as a girl?"

"He did it," Godwin said with a nod at Julian. "I would never discuss a lady's foibles."

"Of course not." Her gaze veered to Julian. "And you, sir?"

As if he saw a fight coming, Godwin excused himself and fled.

Julian chuckled. "Well, that's one way to be rid of him."

"You haven't answered my question," Mary pointed out.

"Perhaps I've learned the value of silence as well."

She laughed. "Oh, come now, Julian. Tell all. What possessed you to drag out our past?"

"I find it a commendable past," he said. "Neither of us has ever shied away from direct conversation. We both enjoy riding, skating. We share a concern for our neighbors."

Her smile softened. "We have much in common." Her gaze drifted upward again, but he saw no reason to look to the heavens.

He took Mary's hand. "And my concern now is for you. Admit it—you are working too hard at your own party. You refused Godwin's offer of a sleigh ride. What if I should offer myself in his place? You indicated you wanted a private conversation." And, at the moment, so did he.

Her gaze came down, and she nodded, then motioned to the footman to bring them their wraps once more.

Julian tucked her hand in his arm as they moved toward the door. It was a gesture of courtesy, one he'd employed countless times. Why was he suddenly so aware of it and her? Her skirts swished against his boots; her gloved fingers brushed his sleeve; her sigh whispered past his ear.

"It appears we missed our opportunity," she said as they stopped outside.

He forced his gaze from admiring her creamy skin to the empty drive, where two other couples awaited the return of the sleigh. "Perhaps a stroll through your kingdom then, your majesty," he teased.

She put her nose in the air. "I am used to more sycophantic attendants, but I suppose we can contrive, sir."

With a laugh, Julian led her across the drive and into the garden. Their gardener must have cleared the path, for the snow was mounded on either side of the meandering flagstone walkway. A shriek of laughter from the pond told of frolics. Shouts from the lawn beyond promised the beginning of the snowball fight. Snow was falling again, drifting down to sparkle like stars on her lashes.

"What would you tell me, Mary?" he asked.

In answer, she stopped by a tree, put her back against the bark, and gazed up at him with lavender eyes so filled with hope he wondered if there was a dragon he could slay for her.

"Oh, Julian," she murmured.

He leaned closer to hear what else she might say, but that only meant he was closer to those rosy lips. One kiss, to celebrate the day? One kiss, to show her he would always care?

One kiss might not be enough.

Something white flashed past his face, and Julian jerked upright even as Mary gasped.

Chapter Four

MARY HAD BEEN waiting, hoping, praying, for Julian's lips to meet hers. Against all odds, they'd found a moment of quiet during the party. Then—smack! Cold exploded against her cheek, and white obscured her vision.

She blinked away the snow as the rest of the ball tumbled down her cloak. Julian had straightened away from her and was scowling in the direction of the lawn.

"Godwin," he growled. "I can see those mismatched shoulders attempting to skulk away. We cannot allow him to escape."

Much as she could wish Chester to the depths of the Canadian wilderness at the moment, she had to agree. Such behavior called for retaliation. She accepted Julian's hand, and they ducked out from under the tree and ran in pursuit.

The lawn was a battlefield. Mr. and Mrs. Garvey and their sons were lined up with backs to the pond as if to defend the skaters, while others advanced from the far side, using the trees on the east and west as cover. White balls streaked through the air. Laughter vied for supremacy with cries of vengeance. Chester stood at the edge of the melee, both hands up and calf pads knocked to the front so that he appeared to have four knees.

"It was an accident," he declared. "I meant to hit Mayes."

"Such things happen," Mary allowed, bending to scoop up a handful of snow. "But turnabout is fair play."

Chester stiffened his spine and faced straight ahead. "I will endeavor to take it like a man. Do your worst."

Mary packed the ball, but Julian put his hand over hers. "Allow me. I was his target, and I cannot abide a slight to a lady."

Mary intended to refuse. She was perfectly capable of hurling a snowball, accurately and with sufficient force. But Chester paled, turned, and ran.

Mary snatched her hand away from Julian's. "After him!"

They darted between the lines, ducking under balls, dodging combatants. She was hit in the shoulder, the thigh. Her cloak was soon clumped with snow. Julian's hat went flying. She was laughing so hard she could scarcely remain upright.

On the far side of the lawn, faced with the line of trees that edged the property, Chester turned and held up his hands once more. His face was red, and every part of him was askew, but the air of haughty sophistication had gone, and he grinned like the boy she remembered.

"Pax!" he pleaded. "I've been hit a dozen times in penalty for the one I threw. Can we call a truce?"

Julian glanced at Mary. "What do you say, Your Majesty? Mercy on the enemy?"

"On the enemy, never," Mary declared, and Chester's face fell. "But on a friend, always."

Smiling sheepishly, he came forward and shook Julian's hand, then bowed over Mary's.

She twitched her cloak to dislodge some of the snow. "What are our chances of returning to the house unscathed?"

"Ten to one," Chester said, eyeing the battlefield beyond. "In their favor."

Julian looked from one to the other. "There's only one thing for it—a full assault, all guns blazing. Arm yourselves well. And may I say it is an honor to go down at your sides."

※

They made it to the house only slightly the worse for wear. Mrs. Garvey had quite an arm and an eye for accuracy. Godwin had managed to rescue Julian's hat, which had a good-sized dent in the crown. He could only hope his father's valet could reblock the thing, for he had no money to replace it or to hire his own valet as yet.

Godwin was still grinning as they entered to divest themselves of their snow-covered garments. He must have caught sight of his shoulder in the process, for he glanced from one slipping pad to the other and sighed. "If you'll excuse me, I should see to my toilette."

Mary caught his arm as he started past, and he looked at her askance.

"Remember who you are, Mr. Godwin," she said. "Manners may make the man, but I have ever thought character and kindness more important. You are blessed with both."

Cheeks turning rosy, he nodded and hurried off.

"You care about him," Julian said.

She turned to him. "He is a longtime friend who seems to have lost his way. In such cases, I believe it a lady's duty to help."

"You assume he is displeased about the matter," Julian pointed out. "Perhaps he doesn't wish to find his way."

"Well, better to find his character than to be forever looking for his padding," Mary returned, and Julian laughed.

She shifted beside him, and suddenly she was closer, head tilted back to send her gaze over his head. Was she too concerned about how his hat would turn out? Or was she appealing to heaven, concerned about her future?

"Did you know he was considering offering for you?" Julian asked.

Her gaze dropped to his, brows up. "No. Don't be ridiculous. We would never suit."

Why did his heart lift to hear her say it? "I agree. You need someone more established."

She eyed him. "Are you implying I need someone older and wiser to guide me?"

He felt his cravat tightening. He refused to touch the thing. "Not at all. You have always been advanced for your age. I merely thought you might be happier with a man more mature than a freckle-faced youth. Someone who can match your wit and vitality."

She grinned. "Or at least fashion sense."

"That too," he agreed.

She cocked her head, a raven curl teasing her cheek. "So you told him those stories earlier to scare him off?"

Julian shrugged. "It was a calculated risk. You deserve better, Mary."

She stepped closer, skirts a swirl of white velvet, like a snowstorm about to envelop him. "Do I? Who do you have in mind, Julian?"

Me.

The thought was so strong, he marveled everyone in the house hadn't heard it. But, in a sense, he was no better a choice than Godwin. He might have a polished presence and some sense of fashion, but he had no income to support a wife. And his years at Eton had proven to him that only hard work and the support of his friends would ever earn him the consequence that approached what they had been granted at birth.

"Who do *you* have in mind?" he replied in challenge. "You mentioned you'd made your pick. I'm told many a young lady can describe her perfect groom."

"Several of the girls at the finishing school could," she allowed. "Some wanted dark hair or flashing eyes. Some had their heart set on a duke."

Or a duke's son. He could not help remembering Thalston and his cold bride.

"I thought it rather foolish at the time," Mary continued. "Why not let fate lend a hand? Why not let love find you? I'm coming to understand that sometimes you must give fate a nudge."

He nodded. "Such as in the case of the estate going to your cousin on your mother's death."

She started. "What? Who told you that?"

She didn't know? How could her mother have hidden it from her? Did the servants not dare to speak of it?

"Your mother sought advice from my father years ago," Julian explained, "and he mentioned the matter in passing."

"He must have misunderstood," she said, but the fingers plucking at the nap of her gown belied the certainty in her voice.

"Perhaps," Julian allowed. In another situation, he would have let the matter go, but Mary needed to understand what she faced. "But Godwin mentioned the same thing earlier."

"No." She stepped back from him, stiffening. "No, you're wrong. A moment with my mother will prove as much." She turned and stalked back into the great hall, straight for her mother's side.

Chapter Five

HER HOME LOST? It couldn't be. Mary hurried past Mrs. Pomfrey and her sisters as they sang Christmas carols together, altos blending with sopranos. But one look at her mother sitting and listening made her rethink her questions. She could only hope for the sake of her mother's pride that few noticed the fingers trembling on the arms of her chair, the brittle smile. Mary slipped in beside her and wheeled her back a little way from the quartet.

"You didn't have to do that," her mother murmured with a sigh. "I'm all right."

"But you will be better for a moment's rest," Mary said. "I am so proud of you, Mother. You are still the perfect hostess. I just don't want you to overtire yourself."

"You are good to me." Her mother unlatched her grip on the arm of the chair and patted Mary's arm. "Are you enjoying the party?"

More than she'd expected, despite her inability to maneuver Julian under the kissing bough. What was it about Christmas to raise such hope, such joy? To remember all the things she treasured from her childhood—family, friends, fun. Yet how much more glorious it would have been to announce her engagement to all those who had known her growing up. She could imagine Julian looking so adoring as he declared his love in front of them all. But she couldn't confess her dreams to her mother.

"I'm enjoying it well enough," Mary said.

Her mother nodded toward the hearth. "Mr. Godwin looks as if he could use some company."

Mary shook her head. "You are unaccountably devoted to Mr. Godwin."

"He has potential," her mother said, and Mary thought she might be one of the few to reach that conclusion.

"Perhaps," Mary said. "But I must speak to you about another matter. There is an ugly rumor circulating. Tell me, Mother. Are we beholden to Cousin Nigel?"

Her mother fussed with the lap blanket Mr. Cowls must have draped over her skirts, the blue and green plaid of the wool dark against her white gloves. "Not at the moment."

The room felt colder. "But someday."

"When I die," her mother murmured. Then she straightened and went on in a stronger voice. "Should I die, your cousin inherits the house and all its contents. My dower arrangements last only that long."

Mary could not catch her breath. "And if I outlive you?"

Her mother's smile was as tremulous as her fingers. "You will be happily married in your own home, so the matter need not concern you."

Mary swallowed. "And if I am yet unwed?"

"If you are younger than one-and-twenty, you will have to have a guardian. If Lord Farley allows, you could stay here as your cousin's ward, under his protection."

"Under his thumb, you mean," Mary said.

Her mother nodded. "As his ward, you would have to do what he says."

It was impossible, unthinkable. She had five years until she reached her majority. How could she survive five years under Lord Farley's benign neglect or, worse, with Nigel pecking at her like an angry rooster?

It wouldn't happen. It couldn't happen. Her mother would be fine. She just needed rest, the right physician.

"That's why I've been encouraging you to choose a groom, Mary," her mother explained. "I want to know you'll have someone dependable at your side should the worst happen."

Mary squeezed her mother's hand. "I understand, Mother, but you'll pardon me if I doubt Chester Godwin is all that dependable." She did look his way then. He was trying to wiggle his shoulder pads back into place, making it appear as if he was jigging to the tune of "God Rest Ye Merry, Gentlemen." Perhaps he would make a good husband someday, but not for her.

Her mother shook her head. "He has a reliable income, and he lives in the area. With you beside him, he could go far. I know he may seem common to you, but there are no perfect gentlemen."

Now her gaze strayed to Julian. He had returned to the great hall and was speaking with an older couple, his look engaging. Others drifted closer to hear what he had to say.

"Not even Julian Mayes," her mother said.

Mary started, then gave her a wry smile. "Sorry, Mother, but I will have to disagree with you there."

Her mother sighed. "Oh, Mary. I have always liked Julian. He's bright and charming, and he's grown into a fine-looking man. But he has ambitions far beyond Surrey. I'm not sure he'd be willing to put them aside for you."

Mary drew back. "And why should he? He has every ability to make his mark on the world. I don't intend to hinder him; I want to help him. You said I could be the making of Chester Godwin. Why not Julian instead?"

"Because," her mother said with a look his way, "Julian Mayes thinks he needs no one's help, least of all yours. Set your sights on someone who will put you first. I fear he lacks that capacity."

Mary was set to argue. Julian loved her. He must love her. He just hadn't realized it yet. But Dr. Parkins was approaching, and her mother rallied to sit higher.

He did not appear to notice as he lay a hand on her shoulder. "Mrs. Rose, I'm not sure this party was well advised. Perhaps you should rest."

"Perhaps you should find better treatment," Mary countered.

"Mary," her mother admonished.

The physician straightened. An angular fellow, with sandy hair and a neat beard and mustache, he had a way of looking at Mary that made her feel as if she were a child again.

"Rest assured I am doing all I can for your mother," he said. "Enjoy the party." With a nod, he moved on.

"You deserve better, Mother," Mary said. And so did she.

༼୨ଓ༽

Funny. Julian's neighbors were all fine people, but he remembered them as bigger, wiser. They seemed to have shrunk, or perhaps he had grown. He would never want to be like Godwin and decry them as country bumpkins. He just had other matters on his mind now than the timing of the frost on the fields and the size of the new bell in the church tower. His mentor would expect him to consult on cases of merit— larceny, criminal conversation, even murder. He would have to settle estates, arrange dowers, confirm inheritances. He'd help pen new laws, revise old ones. He would be working with some of the most titled, wealthy, and famous members of the land.

But first he had to make sure Mary was all right. The revelation of the estate's future had to have left her reeling. She needed to know she could count on his support, even if he could offer nothing more at present.

He turned his steps in her direction and found her cousin blocking his way.

"Good of you to come, Mayes," he said as if he had had anything to do with the party. "Despite the unusual circumstances."

"Mrs. Rose has held her Christmas Eve party since before I was born," Julian reminded him. "I don't find it so unusual, sir."

He clasped his hands over his bulging belly. "To be sure, to be sure. What I find unusual is that she should insist on hosting it when she is clearly unwell. What is the point of such an extravagance when the money should go to her care?"

"Begrudging her even this moment of cheer, are you?" Julian couldn't resist saying.

He stiffened, hands falling. "Certainly not. All things come to those who wait. Rose Hill will be mine soon enough. I merely wished to save you the trouble."

"Trouble?" The man was impossible. "What trouble should I find in the transition?"

He sniffed. "Well, your neighbors were glad to relate how many times you have paid my cousin attentions in the past. Best to steer a wide berth now, if you take my meaning."

Julian drew himself up. "Not in the slightest, but I will warn you, sir, of the inadvisability of slandering the lady in my presence."

Rose held up both hands, betraying reddish stains on the palms of his gloves. "I only speak the truth. Surely you've noticed she's too high in the instep. She is due for a fall. As a gentleman, I would not like to see you caught up in it."

"As a gentleman, you should be doing your best to prevent it," Julian argued. "She is a member of your family, sir, and you are the titular head. It is your duty to protect her."

He sighed. "Would that that were so. According to the local magistrate, the terms of my late uncle's will give Mary and her mother far too much responsibility. It has bowed them, I fear. I would step in if I could, but my hands are tied." He moved closer, eyes brightening. "But you are a solicitor. You would understand such things—how inheritances work and how they can be . . . managed."

Julian fixed him in place with a look. "Are you suggesting I attempt to nullify a legal document?"

"No, no, nothing so difficult." Rose spread his hands. "But if another magistrate could be persuaded to offer a different interpretation, or perhaps appoint a different guardian over Mary given her mother's ill health, it might suit all involved. As it stands, the old family friend who was appointed in the role of guardian rarely even visits. I'm certain Lord Farley would find it a relief if I were to serve the function instead."

And give this miscreant more reason to trouble Mary and her mother? Over Julian's dead body.

Mary didn't need this oily creature watching over her. She was doing perfectly fine on her own, if the flawlessly executed party was any indication. And if she did need help in the future, she should turn to someone who respected her, wanted the best for her, cared about her.

Like he did.

Once again, the force of his feelings overwhelmed him, and he thought the very floor was shifting under his feet. He'd tried so hard to be more, yet one look at Mary and all his pretensions were undone. Why hadn't he seen it before now? Mary was his to protect, his to encourage.

His to love.

"So?" Rose asked, oblivious to Julian's tumultuous thoughts. "Is such a thing possible? Would you be willing to undertake it, for a fee, of course?"

Julian smiled at him. "Such an undertaking is illegal, the attempt punishable by death or transport. I could have you up on charges even for suggesting it."

Rose stepped back, eyes widening. "I'm sure I never..."

"But you did," Julian said, keeping his voice pleasant. "The exact legal term for falsifying a will is forgery. Trying to enlist my aid is akin to bribing an officer of the court. And I shudder to think how our local magistrate, the Duke of Wey, will react when he hears you tried to circumvent his decision. Shall I go on?"

Sweat trickled down the side of Rose's face. "No, no indeed. It was only idle speculation, sir. You mistake me if you thought I would suggest anything---"

"Untoward?" Julian offered. "Larcenous? Treacherous?"

Each word sent him back another step. Julian closed the distance.

"If I hear that you have spoken of this plan to another person, I will have you hauled before the magistrate. Inflict your presence on someone else before I lose my temper."

Rose rallied, head coming up. "You have no right to order me about. I am the one with the power here. I will not allow you to marry my cousin. I will tell Mrs. Rose that I forbid it."

"You may tell her what you wish. Like your preposterous attempt to negate your uncle's will, nothing you do will stand. Now, leave off, or I will be obliged to call you out."

He gasped. "You wouldn't dare!"

"Swords or pistols?" Julian challenged. "I prefer the sword myself. A fellow can bleed to death from a dozen cuts. A ball in the chest ends things far too quickly."

"You're mad." Dragging out a handkerchief, he mopped his brow, then turned and hurried away.

Julian looked for Mary. She had been standing near her mother, but she must have moved while he was arguing with her detestable cousin. She must be warned.

But she wasn't near the iced gingerbread house gracing the refreshment table or overseeing the installation of the Yule log to cries of delight. He angled his head to peer out the closest window. The snowball fight had dwindled, a few stray white puffs shooting through the air. He couldn't spot a crimson cloak among the combatants.

How had she disappeared from her own party?

Chapter Six

"It was very good of you to join us, Mr. Godwin," Mary said as they waited by the front door. He was the third to take his leave so early; Lady Eva and her chaperone had excused themselves, her friend with a look that warned Mary to do all she could to secure Julian's regard. Her mother had wished them well, but she had insisted that Mary see Chester out personally. Now if only Mr. Cowls would bring the fellow's greatcoat quickly so Mary could return to Julian.

"My duty," Chester said, head up with pride and shoulders once more on straight. "I'm considered a leader in the area, you know. As such, I must be kind to widows and orphans. See? You've already inspired me to improve my character."

Perhaps not enough if he thought to brag about the matter, but it was a beginning. "I'm glad I could be of assistance."

"Of course, I had other reasons for attending," he said, glancing down at his shuffling feet. "I can't have the other fellows moving in on my girl."

She could not have heard him correctly. "Your girl?"

He glanced up and about as if to make sure none of the other guests were approaching, then moved closer until his shoulder pad brushed her cheek. "You must know I admire you, Mary."

Mary took a step back. "Thank you. And you must know I look on you as a dear friend of the family."

He frowned. "You needn't posture. There's no one about."

If Cowls would move a little faster, there would be.

"I am not playing coy, sir," she informed him. "You spent time with me today. I believe I made my feelings clear."

"Absolutely. Allow me to do the same." He seized her by the shoulders and planted a kiss on her mouth.

Choking, Mary shoved him back. "Stop that!"

"Why?" He looked sincerely confused, face puckering. "I thought we had an understanding."

Blood was pounding in her ears. "Not in the slightest. If you try that again, I will know you are no gentleman."

"But the kissing bough," he protested. "The new dress. The way you pursued me across the lawn."

Hot tears built behind her eyes. "None of that was done with the hope of enticing you to offer, sir. Now, please excuse me. I must see to my other guests."

He inclined his head, causing his shirt points to dig into his cheeks, just as Mr. Cowls appeared with his coat. Mary hurried back into the great hall.

All around her, people laughed, toasted the coming holiday, made plans for the twelve days of Christmas. The Yule log had been lit, and the scent of pine resin curled through the air. Normally she loved to sit in front of the log, bask in the light, the warmth, and dream of the year to come. But she couldn't dream and be pleasant, not now. She went to the refreshment table, yanked off the door of the gingerbread house, and took a big bite. At least the heady spices wiped away the taste of the kiss.

She'd never been kissed before, not on the mouth. She'd wanted her first true kiss to come from Julian. Now that was spoiled, and she didn't know whether to cry or shout. Her mother had wanted her to encourage Chester. She'd done the exact opposite, and still he'd thought her besotted. Oh, the ignominy of it. She took another bite.

"Your cook is talented," her cousin said, sidling up to her. "Perhaps I'll keep her on when I inherit."

Mary's free hand bunched. "Not now, Nigel. I am in no mood for your taunts."

He put his hand on his chest. "Taunts? You wound me, Cousin."

"Not yet, but give me a moment to find a knife."

He stepped back as if he weren't sure she was being sarcastic. "Now, now. I know it can hurt when the gentlemen take no notice of a lady as she is about to make her debut. But you need not worry. I doubt your mother will live to take you to London."

The gingerbread felt like a rock in her throat. "We will prove you wrong, sir."

"Perhaps." The word had never held more doubt. "But you have other options. I understand your guardian's sister, Lady Winhaven, is seeking a companion. She is not known for her patience or compassion, but at least she would give you a home."

She had a home, the home she'd been raised in, the home in which she'd celebrated every Christmas. She could not stop him from taking it one day, but she could prevent him from doing so as long as possible.

"Your concern would be touching," Mary told him, "if I didn't know you couldn't care less. Enjoy the party. If I have anything to say about the matter, it will be your last for a long time." She shoved the remainder of the gingerbread into her mouth and strode away from him.

Julian moved to meet her. "Mary? Is everything all right?"

She wanted to collapse against him, feel his arms around her, hear him say he would be at her side through whatever was coming. But he hadn't offered. He wasn't hers. The burden fell on her shoulders, and though she knew herself grown, she very much feared she would sink under it.

※

He had never seen her like this. He remembered Mary at the local assembly, smile teasing and steps light, her muslin gown floating about her ankles. He recalled Mary at church, face turned up in wonder at the stained-glass window depicting the birth of the Savior. Then there was Mary in challenge, eyes narrowed, head forward, as she raced her horse down the lane. Mary was strong, fearless.

At the moment, she was pale and trembling, eyes haunted, and he wanted to gather her close and promise to protect her always. Failing that, he wanted to find the fellow who had sapped the joy from her and pound him flat. All he could do was wait for her response.

She sucked in a breath as if trying to find calm in the middle of a storm. "Chester Godwin tried to kiss me, and my cousin threatened to pack me off as a companion, and I'd very much like to knock them both down."

So would he. Instead he touched her arm. "That's my girl."

She pulled away. "I'm not your girl. I'm not anyone's girl. I'm not a girl at all. I thought we'd settled that."

He could not deny her. He'd never been so aware of her as today. Her black hair was thick and rich; he could imagine it slipping through his fingers. Her skin would be warm and soft to the touch, and her lips . . .

"Quite settled," he said, cringing at the catch in his voice. Where was the calculated tone he'd cultivated? The charm that had endeared him to those far above his station at Eton?

She glanced up at him, blinking tears from her sable lashes. He felt as if she'd pierced his heart.

"I see," she said. "And you feel no call to elaborate?"

He managed to rally. "I could say nothing that would allow you to keep your good opinion of me."

She slumped. "So, you have only bad things to say of me now."

He felt ham handed and stutter tongued. "You mistake me."

"Then pray explain yourself." The request came out with a hint of desperation. He could not leave her so destitute. He took her hand and drew her into the farthest corner of the room, placing himself between her and the rest of her guests.

"I am in awe, Mary," he said, careful to keep his other hand at his side when all he wanted to do was touch her, hold her. "You are one of the most beautiful women I've ever seen. Your hair is dark as mystery, your eyes bright as the lilacs anointed with dew. I could pen poems about the curves of your figure, spin sonnets about the wonder of your smile. You are clever, compassionate. You are peerless, fearless. You will shortly be a power to be reckoned with. I find myself wanting to conquer some far off empire and lay the riches at your feet."

She was staring at him.

"But I'm no one," he continued, determined to make her understand. "I have no fame, no fortune to offer. You deserve a duke, a prince, not a would-be solicitor with years of toil ahead before he can make a name for himself. I have no business giving you expectations of a future together."

"I don't care."

He shook his head, certain he had misunderstood. "Pardon me?"

Mary raised her head. "I don't care. Fortune and fame mean nothing to me."

"They should," he insisted. "You need someone to protect you, from your cousin if nothing else. Your most logical choice is to marry."

"My thoughts exactly," she said, gazing up at him. "How can I encourage you to offer?"

Chapter Seven

SHE COULD BE no bolder or plainer. Mary waited for his answer, scarcely daring to breathe.

"Mary, I . . ." he started.

"Mr. Mayes," Nigel said, pushing in beside them. "Why do you persist in taking my cousin away from her duties? How many times must I protest?"

Julian's head came up, shoulders straightening, but Mary faced her cousin before Julian could speak. "Leave us alone, or I'll scream."

Nigel drew himself up. "Scream? I knew this man was troubling you. Come, Cousin. I will protect you. You have no need to throw yourself at this fellow."

Anger boiled up inside her. "Give me a moment, or I shall find something to throw—at you."

"The coal shuttle might be a good start," Julian suggested.

Nigel flushed. "Fine. I leave you to your ruin. You can expect no help from me in the future. But mark my words—you will rue the day you made light of Nigel Rose." He stormed off.

Julian shook his head. "He should have gone on the stage. He'd rival Kemble at Drury Lane for declamation."

If only she could believe her cousin was as good an actor as the famed tragedian. Nigel's threat hung in the air like smoke. He'd make her pay if he could, but she refused to give in to his bullying. She turned to Julian.

"Well, Mr. Mayes? I asked you a very important question."

"So you did." He took her hand and tucked it into his arm. "Give me a moment to speak to your mother, then walk me to the door."

He was leaving? Disappointment left her sagging. She'd misread him. Even after all those impassioned words, the praise of her looks and character, he didn't care, or at best he didn't care enough. Still, she had some pride. She nodded, and he led her over to her mother.

"Thank you for a lovely celebration," he said with a bow. "I want you to know that if you or Mary ever need anything, I am at your service."

Her mother gazed up into his face, then inclined her head, a smile making her face brighter than it had been for a long time. "Thank you, Julian. It's good to have friends."

With a nod, he started for the door.

Mary had to force her feet to keep pace. Until that moment, she'd never realized how much she'd believed in him. She'd laughed off other young men at the assembly rooms, chased away Chester Godwin, never intended to flirt with a single fellow if she went up to London. The only man for her was Julian Mayes.

And he was leaving her behind. Like Chester, he had outgrown her. And she had no idea how to stretch herself further to reach him.

As Mr. Cowls went to fetch Julian's coat, Julian turned to Mary. "Forgive me for not answering you immediately. A wise man once told me actions speak louder than words." He glanced up.

Mary followed his gaze and stilled. In truth, she had paid

little attention to where he led her, so dismal were her thoughts. Now the kissing bough hung right over their heads. Her gaze fell to his, and she licked her lips, trembling.

"Happy Christmas, Mary," he murmured, and he lowered his head and kissed her.

It was like breathing in Christmas. Warmth filled her, joy surrounded her, and she wrapped her arms around his neck and kissed him back, offering him all of her—her hopes, her dreams, her future. He was meant to be hers. She was meant to be his. How could she possibly let him leave?

༄༅

What a kiss. He'd toyed with poetry, but he knew he'd never find the words to do these feelings justice. She was all fire in his arms, all joy, and any doubts he'd had about his own capacity fled in the light. He drew back and peered into her dear face.

"I love you, Mary. I suspect I always have."

She pressed a hand over the sweet lips he had just kissed, eyes shining. "Oh, Julian. I love you too."

He wanted to shout, to sing, to dance madly about the room with her in his arms. Instead he shook his head. "I don't know if I'll ever be worthy of you."

"What nonsense!" she cried, hand falling. "You are all I want, all I need. You are perfection."

"No," he insisted. "I'm not. I'm vain and selfish and not entirely sure of my future. But I can do better if you give me a little while before making you my wife."

"But why must we wait to wed?" she begged, gaze searching his as if she could not get enough of him. "We have pledged our love. I'm sure Mother would allow us to marry."

He caught up her hands, held them against his chest. "I can't support you, not yet. Give me time to make my mark in London. I'm to start work at a solicitor's firm next week. Once

I've established myself, I can treat you as you deserve. I will work hard, rise higher. I will make myself a man you would be proud to claim as husband."

"I am happy with the man you are now," Mary protested.

"And I want more for you, my Mary, my beautiful Mary. Will you wait for me?"

She cast herself into his arms again, and it was some time before either spoke. If people passed them in the entry hall, coming in or going out, he was unaware of it. His entire world was Mary.

At length, she pulled back. "I'll wait. But Julian, I need help now. The physician will not speak to me about Mother's condition. I need to advise on her treatment. Perhaps, as my betrothed..."

He would do anything for her. "I might better serve you as your solicitor," he said, thinking aloud. "Is Dr. Parkins here today?"

She nodded. "He spoke to Mother earlier in the great hall."

Julian took her hand and steered her back into the room.

They located the physician easily enough, warming himself in the glow of the Yule log. Julian requested a moment of his time and took him aside.

"Miss Rose would like an update on her mother's condition," he informed the fellow.

Dr. Parkins's smile was as patronizing as his words. "I have assured Miss Rose that I am doing everything possible for her mother."

Small wonder Mary was at her wit's end. Julian kept his tone polite. "And what, exactly, are you treating her for?"

Parkins raised his chin. "I regret, Mr. Mayes, that I am not at liberty to discuss a patient's care with anyone but family."

Mary drew herself up, but Julian put a hand on her arm

to keep her from speaking. "I'm glad to hear that," he told the physician. "As Mary is her only surviving family, I'm sure you can share your findings with her."

He nodded across the room. "I send all my reports to the male head of the family, Mr. Nigel Rose."

Mary gasped. Julian released her to step closer, gaze narrowed on the physician.

"As Miss Rose's solicitor, and her friend, I can assure you your trust is misplaced. Mr. Rose has neither the care nor the income required to insert himself in this situation. If you cannot find the time to speak with Miss Rose directly, I will advise her to locate another physician, and I will suggest to the medical authorities in London that your ethics are questionable."

He stiffened. "Now, see here."

"No," Julian said. "You see here. Miss Rose has assumed the burden of caring for her mother. The least you can do as a physician, sworn by oath to do no harm, is to confide in her."

He glanced from Mary to Julian. "Very well. You've made your point. Be at my office the day after Boxing Day, Miss Rose, and I will go over everything with you."

Mary's eyes brightened, but she pressed her lips together as if holding back a squeal of triumph and inclined her head in agreement. Julian took her hand and led her back to the entry hall.

There was still no sign of Mr. Cowls and Julian's greatcoat, but he couldn't regret the wait. Already his mind was full of plans. A townhouse in London, with room for a family. His Mary at his side, growing old together. Nothing had ever sounded finer.

"Thank you, Julian," she murmured. "I feel as if I can breathe again for the first time in a long time."

He pressed a kiss against the back of her hand. "If you need me, for any reason, you have only to send word."

Her smile blossomed. "I know I can rely on you." She glanced down the corridor. "Unlike our butler. I've never known Mr. Cowls to be so slow in responding."

"Here you are, Mr. Mayes," the butler said, stepping out from behind the stairs. "I seem to have misplaced your hat, but I'm sure I can locate it by tomorrow. Perhaps you'd be so good as to call then."

Julian grinned. "I'd be delighted."

Mary clung to his arm as she walked him the last few steps to the door. Her cousin and Dr. Parkins had been put in their places. That could not help but lift her spirits. But more importantly, she was going to marry her Julian. The wonder of it lifted her off her feet until she felt as if she were dancing on air like a snowflake.

He bent and kissed her again, a promise of kisses and joys to come. She could dream of a home together, a family, a future. Perhaps there would be sad times, but there would be joy, growth, love.

Still, whatever lay ahead, she knew she would always remember their Christmas kiss.

The End

Dear Reader,

I'm delighted to bring you an origin story, if you will. Mary did get her wish to become Meredith, though misfortunes separated her from her beloved Julian for a time. They continue their courtship in my Fortune's Brides series, where, with the help of a matchmaking cat, an older Mary comes to the aid of gentlewomen down on their luck. If you'd like more information about her adventures or my other stories, please visit me online at www.reginascott.com, where you can also sign up for a free alert to learn when the next book is out or on sale.

Happy Christmas!
Regina Scott

Regina Scott started writing novels in the third grade. Thankfully for literature as we know it, she didn't actually sell her first novel until she'd learned a bit more about writing. After numerous short stories and articles in magazines and trade journals, and a good kick in the backside from her husband, she got serious about writing. Since then, she's had published more than two dozen clean historical romances for adults and young adults. Her traditional romances have earned praised from reviewers and readers alike. Booklist calls her work "quietly compelling" and "impeccably written." Huntress Reviews says, "Regina Scott delivers," and "I will always buy a book with Regina Scott's name on it."

Regina Scott is the author of the Everard Legacy series (The Rogue's Reform, The Captain's Courtship, The Rake's Redemption, and The Heiress's Homecoming), the Master Matchmaker series (The Courting Campaign, The Wife

Campaign, and The Husband Campaign), and the Lady Emily Capers (Secrets and Sensibilities, Art and Artifice, and Ballrooms and Blackmail). In November 2014, she launched her Frontier Bachelors series with the publication of The Bride Ship.

She makes her home in the Puget Sound area of Washington State with her beloved husband and a hyperactive Irish terrier named Fergus.

Find Regina online at her website www.reginascott.com
Blog: www.nineteenteen.com
Facebook: www.facebook.com/authorreginascott
Goodreads: www.goodreads.com/reginascott

A Yuletide Match

Sarah M. Eden

Chapter One

Sussex, 1810

IF ADELAIDE NORTHROP ever found herself short of funds, she fully intended to ply her trade composing a very detailed and, at times, scathing accounting of the traveling inns of England. She had eaten, slept, waited, or cringed within the walls of nearly all of them. The one in which she sat at the moment would be evaluated as both harmless and forgettable, which was not a complaint.

She almost hoped the gentleman she was meeting in this inauspicious corner of the kingdom proved equally dull and innocuous. Vapid people weren't her preference, but finding a match for someone astoundingly boring would certainly be a challenge. After years of being the ton's most sought-after and successful matchmaker, she needed a more ambitious assignment now and then.

Her arrival in Sussex had occurred a few minutes ahead of their decided-upon meeting time, giving Adelaide time to review her new client's letter requesting her services. Her abilities were in enough demand that she could pick and choose which ventures she took up. This one had been surprisingly intriguing.

Mr. Porter Bartrum. Widower. Young father. Dunderhead, apparently.

"I do need a wife," his letter said, "but I don't know that I could choose one well. A poor choice would cause my son to suffer, and I certainly do not wish for that. I need your help, as I fear I might bungle this."

The gentleman had been married before, yet he thought himself unequal to the task of managing the thing again. That part had stuck in her mind, refusing to allow her to set aside his request. He doubted his ability to do what he'd already done.

"Well, then, Mr. Porter Bartrum, let us see if you and your heart can be sorted out."

◆◆◆

"And she's in the private dining room at this very moment?" Porter's best friend, Vance, eyed the door to the dining parlor with misgiving. "A matchmaker? Truly?"

Why was this so difficult for him to comprehend? "Yes. I need a wife. She is known for making matches even for the most difficult of people."

Vance eyed him dryly. "You are one of the *least* difficult people I know."

"Yes, but if she managed to succeed under such unpromising circumstances, she can certainly find me a wife." He cringed a little at the mercenary sound of that. "Rebecca has been gone for two years now. That's more than half Lewis's life. He needs a mother."

"And this lady will find him one during the course of a single house party?"

Vance was making Porter begin to doubt this plan, the only strategy in which he felt even the slightest degree of hope. He simply could not afford to second guess himself. He'd tried a few times to sort out this business on his own and had failed miserably. He needed help.

"She will at least begin her efforts during the house party. If she is as miraculous as I have heard, she might even manage the thing by Christmas."

A laugh, threaded through with curiosity, touched his friend's expression. "How do the unattached ladies at this party feel about her arriving to 'manage the thing'?"

This was the bit he needed Vance's help with. "I'd rather the ladies not know. The ladies *or* the gentlemen."

Vance shook his head. "A fool's hope, my friend. She is too well known. The ladies eager for any match will toss themselves into the fray. Those with other options will retreat."

He had thought of that complication. "I need you and Chloe to put it about that Mrs. Northrop is a family friend and is here in order to spend the holiday season with the two of you. She can be seeing to the business at hand with no one the wiser."

"You're daft, Porter. Utterly daft."

"What I am is desperate." He set his hand on the doorknob. "Will you help me?"

Vance shrugged and nodded. "I always do."

That was true. They'd been each other's greatest allies ever since their days at Harrow. Porter had seen Vance through the unexpected death of both his parents. Vance had been with Porter during the grueling days and weeks after Rebecca's death. They'd shared happy times as well, celebrated life's triumphs. If anyone could be counted on to help him pull the wool over the eyes of an entire house party, Vance could be.

He pushed open the door. No matter that his mental image of Mrs. Northrop was a bit hazy, having only descriptions of her work to build upon, he was surprised by what he saw. She was relatively young, likely less than ten years his senior. She dressed in the trappings of Society. He had, for reasons he couldn't fully explain, expected her to be more severe, more like a governess or bluestocking. As it was, she would have blended in at any Society gathering. It was a bit of a surprise, yes, but also a tremendous relief. If she looked the part of a guest at a house party, few would doubt she was precisely that.

Mrs. Northrop rose and eyed him assessingly, then turned that same analyzing gaze on Vance. "Which of you is Mr. Bartrum?"

"I a—" He cleared his throat against the thickness there. "I am."

She gave a single nod and faced him directly. "I am Mrs. Northrop. Please, be seated." She gestured to the empty chairs at the table where she had been sitting before turning to Vance. "And you are?"

"Vance Munson, Bartrum's friend."

She nodded that same crisp motion and indicated Vance join them at the table as well. There was nothing of the shrinking violet about her, that was for sure and certain. Porter was a gentleman grown with a son and an estate and a great many responsibilities he saw to with competence. Yet, standing in front of her, he felt like a school boy again.

"It is good of you—thank you for—" Laws, he couldn't get a single sentence out whole. "A pleasure to—to meet you."

"And you." She lowered herself onto her chair. He did the same. "Tell me what it is you wish for me to do."

Odd. "I sent—I wrote to you."

She held up a letter—*his*, if he didn't miss his mark. "I have read it thoroughly, I assure you. But I want to hear directly from you what it is you are in need of."

"A backbone," Vance muttered.

Porter shot him a look of warning but earned only a bitten-back smile for his efforts. Vance was reliable, but he could, at times, be a thorn. An amusing thorn, but a thorn nonetheless.

After a quick breath to regain his equilibrium, Porter answered Mrs. Northrop. "I am in need of a wife."

She raised a single eyebrow. "Was that a question, Mr. Bartrum? It certainly sounded like one."

This was not going at all as he had imagined. The famous matchmaker would declare him a lost cause and simply leave. He was nearly certain of it.

"I *do* need a wife." He spoke a little more firmly despite her continued evaluating gaze. "I was simply caught off guard that you didn't seem to know that. Er, I mean that you needed me to repeat it. *Wanted* me to repeat it."

"Hmm." He hadn't the first idea what that sound meant. "I understood from your letter, Mr. Bartrum, that you have a son."

"I do." Lud, that had sounded like a question as well. "His name is Lewis. He will be four years old next month." There. That sounded more authoritative.

"And will he be present for this house party?"

Porter nodded. Mrs. Northrop watched him, clearly expecting something more. But what? He had answered her question.

"I believe the lady wishes to know where the little ragamuffin is," Vance said out the side of his mouth.

"Ragamuffin?" Mrs. Northrop repeated the word as if she found great significance in it.

Porter's protective fatherly instinct rose to the surface on the instant. "Lewis is a fine boy. Mr. Munson thinks so as well. He simply likes nettling me."

"That and Lewis is an utter delinquent."

Far from shocked, Mrs. Northrop simply continued watching him with the same look of intent interest.

"He isn't," Porter insisted.

"He also isn't present," she pointed out.

"Vance's sister took him out to the privy. They'll be here shortly."

"Hmmm." Again, that unrevealing sound of pondering. What did she think of him?

A moment later, quick, light footsteps approached, accompanied by the swish of skirts. Porter rose, knowing it would be Chloe and Lewis. His little boy flew into the room like a terrier in hunting season. Before he could go far, Porter scooped him up, holding him tucked under his arm. It was the only position the child tolerated when he was determined to run. Held parallel to the ground, facing the floor, Lewis laughed and pumped his legs.

Porter loved his son, but the boy was exhausting.

"Mrs. Northrop, this is Miss Chloe Munson." Porter motioned with his head toward Chloe, his arms full. "Miss Munson, this is Mrs. Northrop."

Chloe dipped a quick curtsey even as a smile spread over her face. "Are you the famous Mrs. Northrop, maker of matches and worker of miracles?"

The matchmaker took the question in stride. She took *everything* in stride. "I see my reputation has preceded me." With a dip of her head, she acknowledged the introduction before returning her attention to him. "Which brings me to the next bit of business, Mr. Bartrum. Your letter indicated you wish my purpose here to be kept secret. I am quite curious how you mean to accomplish that."

He would have sat once more, but Lewis would never have endured it. The boy continued his aerial sprinting tucked close against Porter's side. "Mr. Vance and his sister have agreed to put forth that you are a friend of their family and have come as their guest. We cannot prevent people from recognizing you and recalling your usual undertaking, but I would far prefer they not know—that people not realize—" How was he to get through an entire house party filled with clandestine matchmaking if he couldn't even talk about it? "I would rather not be an object of pity, curiosity, or amusement."

At the moment, Chloe was watching him with obvious amusement. It didn't bother him. She was the cheeriest person he knew, and her laughter was never at his expense.

"I don't know about my brother," she said, "but I am perfectly willing to perpetrate a falsehood if it means watching how this potential disaster plays out."

Mrs. Northrop folded her hands on the tabletop. "Why do you anticipate disaster?"

"Because everyone knows who you are and will wonder at your purpose no matter what we say that purpose is. Because Mr. Bartrum is the worst liar I have ever encountered in all my life. And because our host, Mr. Ellsworth, has all the curiosity of a bloodhound with none of the qualms." Chloe's lips twitched. "This may very well be the most entertaining Christmas any of us has ever known."

"Hmmm."

Porter suspected he would soon be heartily sick of hearing that sound.

"I find myself thoroughly intrigued," Mrs. Northrop said. "I accept the assignment and look forward to helping you find your happiness, Mr. Bartrum."

He hadn't realized her acceptance was not a foregone conclusion. Vance rolled his eyes. Chloe grinned unabashedly. Lewis squirmed and laughed in his arms. Mrs. Northrop simply rose and offered a brief dip.

"I will gather my things and have them placed in your traveling carriage." With that, she left the room.

Chloe, he feared, might have been more correct than he'd suspected. His plans might prove to be an absolute disaster.

Chapter Two

CHLOE HAD REVELED in her brother's many recountings of his and Porter's misguided bits of mischief over the years. Watching Mrs. Northrop study Porter as they waited to be greeted by Mr. and Mrs. Ellsworth, Chloe suspected this Christmas season would provide years of entertaining stories.

A matchmaker. Porter had secured the services of a matchmaker. The very thought rose as a bubble of laughter in her throat. Porter far preferred quiet settings with his most intimate acquaintances. A matchmaker would have him running all over creation, tossing himself into every social whirl she could find. What had possessed him to pursue such misery?

The guests who had arrived just ahead of them slipped away, following a chambermaid up the grand front stairs, no doubt on their way to the rooms they would occupy for the length of the house party.

Their small group took their place in front of their hosts. Porter executed an awkward bow. Lewis slept against his chest, making even that small effort more difficult. Chloe adored the mischievous little boy, but he was unendingly rambunctious. Greetings would be less complicated with him slumbering. Porter clearly agreed, as he was excessively careful not to wake his son.

The Ellsworths seemed to accept the clumsy bow. They turned their attention to Vance and Chloe. Mrs. Ellsworth offered a curtsey, her high-piled white hair bouncing atop her head. Mr. Ellsworth's wide eyes studied them both.

"Well met. Well met." He watched them with all the eager interest of an excitable puppy. Chloe had taken his measure the first time she'd met him: curious, often tactless, surprisingly sweet. Mr. Ellsworth looked her over, his bushy brows pulling low. "You've grown older."

She copied his expression, evaluating him. "Aging seems to be a common ailment."

His grin blossomed on the instant. "Well delivered, Miss Munson."

"And well deserved, Mr. Ellsworth."

His wife swatted at him. "You really must begin thinking before simply saying whatever enters your mind."

"If he does that," Chloe said, "no one will recognize him."

Both the Ellsworths laughed. No matter Mr. Ellsworth's unhealthy fascination with anything that was none of his concern and Mrs. Ellsworth's inability to rein in that particular tendency of his, they were rather delightful people, provided one could hold one's own.

"And who is this?" Mr. Ellsworth turned his sights on Mrs. Northrop.

"Mrs. Adelaide Northrop," the matchmaker answered.

"Northrop?" He filled the two syllables with all the awe one would generally reserve for shocking news of great international import. "Are you Mrs. Northrop who engineered a match for Lord Carraway's girl, Turnbill's son, and"—his eyes grew wider still—"the one Society called the Princess Pompous?"

Chloe let her eyes dart to Porter, desperately holding back her deep desire to gloat. Not two seconds into this introduction and Mrs. Northrop had been discovered, just as Chloe had predicted.

"One and the same," Vance answered, "but, for the duration of this house party, she is simply Mrs. Northrop, friend of the Munson family. I believe you were informed we would have an additional guest."

Mr. Ellsworth turned to Chloe, a hound on a scent. "Has she come to find a match for you, Miss Munson?"

Had Chloe been even the least bit sensitive about the state of her matrimonial prospects or the fact that she had been declared decidedly on the shelf two Seasons ago, she might have been embarrassed. Instead, she laughed unabashedly.

"Good heavens, no. Though our dear Mrs. Northrop could likely manage it, I have no desire to employ her services."

That brought Vance's attention to her, mouth downturned. "Have you abandoned all hope, then?"

"Utterly." She dipped a curtsey to their host and hostess. "I would be very much obliged if we could be shown to our rooms. As Mr. Ellsworth ascertained so quickly, I am not so young as I once was."

Mrs. Ellsworth quickly assumed command of the situation. A maid was assigned the task of accompanying Chloe, Vance, and Mrs. Northrop up to the wing of guest chambers where they would be staying. Another maid was tasked with showing Porter and his sleeping bundle to the nursery.

The first leg of their respective journeys proved identical. Chloe climbed the stairs beside Porter.

"Thank you for playing along with this little ruse," he whispered. "If Ellsworth knew Mrs. Northrop was here on my request—" He shook his head.

"He suspects she is here on *mine*," Chloe said.

Porter winced. "I am sorry about that."

She waved it off. "I will endure, I assure you. But know that you are deeply indebted to me for this."

He rubbed his son's back. "You declared me deeply indebted several times today already. I hope you prove a merciful moneylender."

"Always."

At the upper landing, Porter was led in the opposite direction the rest of them were. The corridor wound a bit, the uneven floors speaking of piecemeal renovations over the years. Chloe rather enjoyed old houses like this one. They were not the grand, picturesque estates one was likely to read about in a travelogue, but they had charm and character.

Mrs. Northrop was placed in a bedchamber adjoining Chloe's. The connecting doors were open, affording her a full view of that woman's lodgings. Their maids slipped out after seeing to the unpacking of their clothing, leaving the two of them, strangers at best, in each other's exclusive company.

"It seems our claim to be very dear friends has been believed," Chloe said, standing in the doorway. "We will not be rid of each other all week, I daresay."

Mrs. Northrop motioned her inside. "Tell me a little about Bartrum."

Chloe made a sound of pondering. "He does not care for plum pudding. He cracked his ribs falling out of a tree when he was twelve years old. His son is running him ragged."

A bit of amusement entered Mrs. Northrop's eyes. That was a fine sign. Chloe tended to annoy people who did not possess at least some sense of the ridiculous. "You have known him a long time, it seems."

"Since he and my brother met at Harrow."

Mrs. Northrop indicated she should sit on the bed. "Is he as bashful as he appears?"

"He does not appear bashful to me," Chloe answered.

Far from surprised, Mrs. Northrop nodded her agreement. "Why is he so unsure of his ability to find himself a wife? He was married before."

"Yes, but he didn't 'find himself' Rebecca. His parents found her."

"And were they happy?"

That was a bit more personal than Chloe was entirely comfortable discussing. She didn't answer.

Mrs. Northrop sat beside her. "I am not asking out of a love of gossip or selfish curiosity. I wish only to ascertain what he needs in a potential wife."

"Did he give you no indication of his preferences?" Poor Porter was so frazzled so much of the time. It was a wonder he'd remembered to sign his name to the letter he'd sent the matchmaker.

"He wishes his son to have a mother."

That made sense.

"But that is the only specific item he had on his list. I cannot say I am satisfied with that answer."

Odd. "Why is that?"

"Because I suspect he needs far more. He simply doesn't realize it yet."

Chloe rose again, shrugging as if about to make a very casual observation. "Perhaps we could simply *tell* him what he needs and then you can provide it. That worked with the little charade you and I and my brother are enacting."

Mrs. Northrop didn't appear displeased with the show of humor, but neither did she seem the least put off the scent. "Is Mr. Bartrum a good man? Beneath the trappings of a gentleman, beneath the awkward bumbling through discussions of matches, beyond being attentive in his care of his son . . . is he a good person?"

Chloe stopped in the doorway, looking back at Mrs.

Northrop. "I can say with full confidence that he is, quite possibly, one the *best* people I have ever been privileged to know."

"Excepting your brother, I assume."

"No, actually." She leaned her shoulder against the doorframe. "Now, I don't mean to imply that my brother is anything other than a truly lovely and good-hearted person. But Porter is something different. He is thoroughly good, to his very soul. Even as a much younger man, at an age when many children are blissfully unaware of the needs around them, he was deeply compassionate and eager to lift burdens and contribute to the happiness in the world." She was not doing justice to the heart so few people truly got to see. But how did one explain such a thing? "You asked if his marriage was a happy one. It is something of an odd question because he makes a point of finding happiness in every situation, and he works hard to help others be happy as well. He and his late wife were not, perhaps, the most naturally suited to one another, but they were happy, in large part because he would not have stopped trying to make it so."

Mrs. Northrop tipped her head a bit to one side, brow pulled in thought. "In what way were they ill-suited?"

Chloe might have objected, except she, herself, had made the admission. Further, if Mrs. Northrop were to make a match for Porter that was not either a misery or yet another marriage in which he would spend his days exhausted by the effort to find some success in a poorly chosen arrangement, she needed this information.

"He was not what she wanted," Chloe said. "She thrived in Society and lived for the whirl of constant coming and going. He didn't mind participating but was happiest at home or in small gatherings. He was willing to do what she preferred but was seldom given the same consideration."

"Oh, dear." Mrs. Northrop spoke with neither pity nor amusement. Rather, she seemed to simply understand the difficulty of such a situation.

"The late Mrs. Bartrum wasn't an unfeeling person. But quiet evenings and tiny social circles was her idea of purgatory."

Mrs. Northrop nodded. "That is very nearly the definition of 'ill-suited.'"

"I do not for a moment think he needs or even wants to marry a lady who is a hermit," Chloe said. "But I do hope he can find someone who understands him and who considers his happiness important enough to not disregard it."

"He deserves to be happy?"

She smiled a little. "He deserves it more than anyone."

Adelaide sat in the quiet of her guest chamber after Chloe returned to hers, pondering. She'd been right to take on this assignment. There was far more to Porter Bartrum's predicament than met the eye.

He'd not been given the opportunity to choose his first wife, and so had no experience making such a monumental decision. She had no reason not to believe Chloe's recounting of Mr. Bartrum's first marriage. Any gentleman who had invested so much effort into creating happiness in such a mismatched arrangement had reason to be wary of another. His hands were quite full enough with his very energetic son. To find himself once more struggling with marriage must have been a discouraging prospect.

His worry, his inexperience, and his timidity in the company of strangers made it far too likely he would bungle the entire thing if left to undertake his own matchmaking.

Adelaide would need to be circumspect in her efforts, as

this was a more complicated endeavor than she'd anticipated. He wished for his interest in a match to remain a secret. His son would require much of his time during the house party. He didn't quite know what he wanted or needed. He had allowed very little time in which to find his future.

And, though she suspected neither of them realized as much, Chloe Munson was in love with him.

Chapter Three

PORTER HAD ACCEPTED his invitation to the Ellsworths' Christmas house party specifically because it would be enormous. If one were to find someone with whom he could build a life, it seemed best to have a great many options. Yet standing in the drawing room that night in such a crush of people, he began to doubt the intelligence of his decision. He far preferred quiet, intimate gatherings. Still, he could endure a little anxiety if it meant him and Lewis living a less lonely life.

He slipped to where Vance stood chatting amiably. Neither of the Munson siblings were the least bit shy, neither were they dictatorial in matters regarding *his* participation in Society. When Porter felt overwhelmed and ready to retreat from gatherings he needed to attend, they had buoyed him and helped him navigate the shoals. When he desperately required quiet and solitude, they neither laughed nor argued. What would he have done without them?

"Porter." Vance slapped a hand on his shoulder. "Might I make known to you Mrs. Cunningham, who lives in the neighborhood, and her niece Miss Cunningham, who resides with them."

He offered a bow.

"Mrs. Cunningham, Miss Cunningham, this is Mr. Bartrum of Essex."

Curtseys. Expressions of pleasure. All proceeded as it always did, except that Porter found himself assessing the young Miss Cunningham. She was likely only five years his junior. Her manners were fine without being fussy. That, of course, told him little about her as a person. Would she make a good wife? He felt daft jumping to that question so quickly. That was what came of attending a party with the sole purpose of finding a wife.

In short order, Vance introduced him to a Miss Garland. Not long after that, a Miss Fallon was made known to him. Mrs. Ellsworth herself introduced him to Mrs. Talbot, a young widow who lived in the area.

This party was a crush in large part because so many families of significance lived nearby. The Ellsworths' guest list combined with their many neighbors and the guests those neighbors had invited made for quite a crowd. It was both perfect and miserable.

The gentlemen took their time with the after-dinner port. Porter might have found it a welcome respite, but Mr. Ellsworth allowed no such quiet before the storm.

"I noticed Mr. Munson and Mr. Bartrum were quick to make the acquaintance of many of our eligible lady guests." Their host grinned almost gleefully. "Did any strike your fancy?"

"They are ladies not horseflesh," Porter said, a bit under his breath.

Vance raised an eyebrow, as if challenging Ellsworth to disagree.

After a quick sputter, Ellsworth spoke again. "I hadn't meant to imply they weren't quite lovely young ladies. My wife is always telling me to think a bit longer before flapping my gums."

A few of the other gentlemen laughed, raising their

glasses of port. Conversation continued along gossip-focused lines. Ellsworth didn't seem interested in anything else. Vance did an admirable job of turning the topic away from his and Porter's potential romantic interest in the guests, something their host returned to again and again.

By the time the group joined the ladies, Porter was desperate for escape. Habit took him to where Chloe stood. She was an easy person to be around. They'd known each other nearly all their lives. She'd never seemed bothered that he was easily discomposed in company. She laughed with him but never *at* him.

"Mr. Bartrum," Chloe said. Formalities were necessary in company. "Have you met Miss Garland?"

"I have had that pleasure." He spoke quietly, but at least the words had emerged whole. They also emerged alone. He could think of nothing else to say.

Where was Mrs. Northrop? Wasn't she supposed to be sorting all of this so he needn't be so overwhelmed by it? He would bungle the entire thing if left to his own.

The matchmaker sat a bit aside, watching. It was a different sort of watching than he'd seen before. She seemed to somehow be observing everything all at once. And he suspected she didn't miss a detail, little or great. There was some comfort in that—she was likely to discover things about the other guests that he might miss—but it was also unnerving. What did she see about *him*?

"Friends." Mr. Ellsworth's booming voice broke through the din of conversations. "My wife has wisely suggested we play games. There are too many of us for a single undertaking, but we thought we might offer a few options, and each person can join in whichever appeals to him or her."

Murmurs of agreement met his suggestion.

One side of the room, he declared, would be dedicated to

a game of Pass the Slipper. That sounded far too rowdy for Porter's taste. The other end of the room would be undertaking Yes and No. Porter liked that option better. The middle of the room was assigned The Minister's Cat.

As Porter was already in the middle of the room and didn't object to the game, he remained where he was. Chloe did as well.

The game began with Mrs. Talbot. "The minister's cat is an agile cat."

Mrs. Cunningham took up the challenge next. "The minister's cat is an agile and brown cat."

Agile. Brown.

Miss Cunningham was next. "The minister's cat is an agile, brown—" She stumbled a bit over the rest of the sentence, apparently struggling to think of an adjective beginning with the letter C.

The group smiled and teased, all good-naturedly, and Miss Cunningham accepted her elimination in stride. A good sign, that, being willing to endure a bit of nettling.

A guest Porter had not yet met took his turn. "The minister's cat is an agile, brown, courageous cat."

Agile. Brown. Courageous. He could remember those, nothing too odd or difficult.

It was Chloe's turn. "The minister's cat is an agile, brown, courageous, dead cat."

The group sputtered. Porter laughed. Chloe was endlessly amusing.

"How can the cat be agile *and* dead?" Mrs. Talbot asked.

"Clearly he wasn't as agile as rumor would have us believe." Chloe spoke as if perfectly serious. "Or his courage was actually foolhardiness."

More laughter met the bit of wit. Chloe lit up every room she was in. Why was she unmarried? Mrs. Northrop could likely find her a match, but Chloe had insisted earlier that day she had no interest in one. That was a shame.

Next to Porter, Vance took his turn. "The minister's cat is an agile, brown, courageous, dead"—Vance rolled his eyes at his sister's contribution—"elegant cat."

Porter took a breath and began. "The minister's cat is an agile, brown, courageous, dead, elegant, foolhardy cat."

More laughter erupted, most especially from Chloe.

"You cheated," she said with a broad grin. "I said that word not thirty seconds ago."

"And I thank you for it," he said.

The group accepted his ill-gotten word, and the game continued. Porter felt more at ease the longer they sat there going around the circle. He needn't talk often, and what he said was predetermined. He was not nearly so drained by the gathering as he had been.

Those in the middle of the drawing room came to know one another. Porter took note of Mrs. Talbot, the widow, and her quickness. She was sharp of mind and didn't struggle at all with the challenge of the game or the necessity to speak. That was likely a good thing. Rebecca had been the same way, and that strength in her had helped him shed some of his hermit-like tendencies. It had also, though, led to a great deal of frustration between them. They were simply so different in that respect.

Miss Cunningham proved quiet and sweet natured. She might be pleased with a life of comparative solitude. She might not grow irritated with him when he felt himself unequal to the task of going about Society.

Mrs. Northrop had joined the game of Yes and No. Porter hoped she was learning something about the guests on that end of the room. Her success in this field was well-known; he would trust that.

Chloe offered another hilariously ridiculous adjective, and the gentleman beside her laughed quite heartily. Another gentleman in the group complimented her effusively. Another smiled rather warmly.

She had a way of drawing people to her. He had always appreciated that about her. He felt less appreciation for her admirers in that moment, however. Perhaps because they were being so obvious in their attentions. He didn't care to see her the object of speculation or whisper. Some in Society could be viciously unkind, choosing to willfully misrepresent a lady's being gregarious as being overly forward. He didn't want that to happen to her.

"What do you know of Misters Twickenham and Barber?" he asked Vance.

"Not very much," Vance said. "Both are gentlemen. Twickenham attended Cambridge. I believe Barber's estate sits very near the Scottish border. Neither belongs to White's."

"Neither is particularly subtle about his interest in Chloe."

Vance laughed under his breath. "Noticed that, did you?"

"I believe the entire room noticed."

Vance shrugged. "If Mrs. Northrop noticed, Chloe'll truly be in the suds. No matter her protests, she'll likely find herself matched and married by year's end."

"Mrs. Northrop won't force Chloe into a match against her will," Porter insisted.

"You're certain of that?"

He would make certain of that.

Adelaide would have to remember the Ellsworths when needing to assist a client with expanding his or her circle of acquaintances quickly. This house party was the largest she had ever been to. It was also a great deal of fun.

Since she was to be seen as nothing more than a participant, she chose to join in the games. She never forgot, however, the reason she was actually there. Several of the unattached ladies present had potential to be a good match for Mr. Bartrum. A lady who would urge him to be a bit more social would be good. Yet, Adelaide was in complete agreement with Chloe: Mr. Bartrum also needed a lady who did not resent his quiet nature. He had shown himself to be quick-witted in the game he had joined. A gentleman in possession of a sharp mind would be terribly discontented with a wife who was a complete featherhead.

He needed someone who would love and care about his son and help him manage the child, whom Adelaide had heard from both Munson siblings was rather a handful. But he also needed someone who would love and care about *him*. He could not give his child the happy, warm home he clearly wanted if he and his bride shared no tender regard.

Adelaide had no doubt she could find such a paragon. Doing so before the house party was over might be more daunting.

Yet, watching Porter interact with Chloe, a potentially obvious bit of the unformed puzzle began to form in her mind. She knew Chloe's heart harbored a deep affection for her lifelong friend. Porter's feelings in that direction were not as simple to ascertain, but he was far more at ease with Chloe than anyone else. He smiled more. Laughed. He even spoke without stumbling over his words.

Adelaide did not yet know if there was love there. But one thing she was certain of: there was potential.

Chapter Four

CHLOE WAS NEARLY out of her mind with boredom. The ladies of the house party were content to sit about, chatting and working on their needlepoint. She didn't mind those pursuits in moderation, but this had been ongoing since breakfast. In another two hours the dinner dressing bell would ring. Did no one else desperately wish to do *something*?

Like manna from heaven, Porter stepped inside and moved directly to her. "I have a favor to ask." He spoke quietly but urgently.

"If it involves leaving this room, I accept."

A little smile tugged. "That was easier than I expected."

"What is it you need?"

"Lewis has seen that it is snowing and wishes to play in the snow. His nursemaids are convinced he'll dart and be all the way to Scotland in the blink of an eye and, therefore, have refused to indulge him." Porter sighed. "They are likely not entirely wrong. He behaves well for me, but I would be far more likely to meet with success if you were with us as well. He listens to you better than almost anyone."

"He's afraid of me."

His smile grew. "No, he's not."

Chloe rose. "We had best go collect the little demon and take him out into the snow."

"Little demon," he repeated with a shake of his head. "I wish I could say he didn't sometimes earn that description."

"Lewis is wonderful," she assured him. "He is simply *very* energetic." She met Mrs. Northrop's eye. They exchanged a nod, both acknowledging her departure. As she and Porter stepped into the corridor, Chloe took up a different topic. "Mrs. Northrop has been quite busy on your account. I have seen her deep in conversation with every eligible lady here today. You may very well be married by tomorrow afternoon."

Porter actually cringed. She had expected a roll of the eyes or a shake of the head—she was being silly, after all—but his discomfort was unexpected.

"Are you not happy about her doing what you brought her to do?" Chloe pressed.

"I am happy. Grateful." His brow pulled low. "I'm nervous, is all. We need someone, Lewis and I, but I know I'd never find anyone on my own. What if she can't find anyone either? What if everyone she tries to convince takes one look at me and refuses? What if—"

"Oh, pish." Chloe likely ought not to have laughed, but the poor soul was so far off the mark that he might as well have been shooting in the opposite direction. "'What if ladies run screaming in abject horror at the thought of me?' Have you truly evaluated the situation and come to that conclusion?"

The droop in his shoulders indicated he had.

"You are young and handsome, though Vance would tease me mercilessly if he heard me say as much. You are not in the poor house nor an inveterate gambler." She counted off the arguments on her fingers. "You are spoken highly of. You claim membership at White's, which, while not as important to ladies, will certainly give you some cachet with their fathers and brothers. You are gentlemanly and pleasant. And, most important of all, you are not a terrible dancer."

Porter had turned a bright shade of red. "The dancing is most important, is it?"

"Crucial."

"And I am not an agile, brown, courageous, dead cat. That must be a point in my favor."

They had reached the nursery wing. Chloe's laugh brought the scolding eyes of several nursemaids on her immediately. She clamped her hands over her mouth to stifle the noise, hoping she didn't awaken any of their charges.

She needn't have worried about her noisiness. In the next instant Lewis flew across the room and tossed himself against his father. "Can we play? Can we play now? It's snowing." He looked at her. "It's snowing."

"No," she said solemnly. "I am certain you are mistaken."

He popped his fists on his hips and pouted mightily at her. "It is too. I saw it."

"I believe you will have to show me," she said. "If I put on my coat and gloves, you and your father and I can go outside and see for ourselves."

Lewis looked up at Porter. "Can we? Can we show her?"

Porter scooped him up. "That is the plan."

Not ten minutes later, bundled against the cold, the three of them wandered down a meandering back path surrounded on either side by a vast expanse of lawn being slowly covered in a blanket of snow. Flakes floated down toward them and stuck to their coats and scarves.

"I told you," Lewis said, pulling his hand from his father's to reach out and catch the lazily falling snow.

"Are you certain this is snow?" Chloe caught a flake as well. "It is possible someone simply spilled sugar from a very high window."

Lewis eyed her narrowly. "Are you being silly at me?"

She bent low and tapped the tip of his nose. "Yes. I. Am."

His face split into an enormous grin. "I like when you're silly."

"That is a very good thing, my little Lewis, because I am *always* silly."

His eyes darted to his father, then back to her, then back to him again. "May we play chasing?"

It was by far Lewis's favorite game, though it was exhausting. The child could run for hours without growing tired of the endeavor. She had no such endurance. She suspected Porter didn't either.

"His nursemaids would likely appreciate us returning him with some energy spent," Porter said.

"Do you really think *we* will be dragging his sleeping frame back inside rather than the other way around? Because I suspect he can outrun us both."

"I more than suspect; I know."

She took in a quick breath of cold air. "I have an idea." She bent low and said to Lewis, "We should play hide and go seek."

He bounced up and down, nodding eagerly. "Please. Please. Please."

"Follow my lead, Lewis. I know how to convince your father."

Staying low on Lewis's level, she looked up at Porter, jutted out her lower lip and gave him her most pitiful look of begging. Lewis copied her expression.

Porter burst out laughing. He was not an unhappy or grumbly person, but he did not often laugh out loud. She wished he did, though. The sound of it was almost magical.

"I think we should play hide and go seek," Porter said.

"Perfect." Chloe stood straight once more and took hold of Lewis's hand. "I think your father should have to do the searching first."

"Very well. I will give you until the count of twenty." Porter closed his eyes and began to count aloud.

"I know the perfect place."

Chloe pulled Lewis gently toward a high shrubbery along the side of the path. A break in the bushes allowed them to step behind and to the other side. She had walked in this particular garden before and knew that a small statue sat up against the back side of the shrub, with cobblestones all around it that she and Lewis could stand on and avoid the mud of the snow-moistened ground.

They hunched down a bit to the side of the statue. Lewis tucked himself up against her, and she wrapped her arms firmly around his middle. He bounced and shook as they stood there, waiting for Porter to come looking. Lewis was only ever still when he was asleep. It was little wonder Porter so often looked entirely exhausted.

"Will Papa find us?" Lewis asked in an eager whisper.

"I hope he does eventually, otherwise we are going to get very cold."

He bounced even faster. "We are hiding good?"

"We are hiding the most good of anyone."

"Anyone ever?" Awe filled the question.

She pulled him in closer. "Ever and ever."

Very little time passed before she heard Porter's footsteps approach. Truth be told, she and Lewis were not very well hidden. She knew the little boy too well to think he had patience enough for a prolonged bout of hiding.

"He's coming. He's coming." Lewis's whisper grew louder with each word.

Porter appeared in front of them. He looked about, making quite a show of not seeing them there.

Chloe stood, giving Lewis a nudge. "Run, Lewis. Save yourself!"

He darted. Porter reached for him but missed by too large a degree for his effort to have been anything but for show. Chloe made to rush past as well, but he caught her about the middle.

"You're not getting away so easily."

"Save me, Lewis," she said with a grin.

Porter's laugh rumbled against her. "I suspect, Chloe, you are something of a mischievous influence on him."

"I certainly hope so."

She met his eye, as she'd done many times before. In that moment, however, something was different. She was oddly more aware of him: of the precise shade of his brown eyes, the tiniest asymmetry in his smile, the hint of sandalwood in the scent of his shaving soap. The warmth of his firm, steady embrace. Her lungs seemed to narrow even as her heart expanded almost painfully in her chest.

"We are fortunate indeed to have you in our lives." He spoke with a quiet earnestness that tugged ever harder at her heart.

She recognized the feelings for what they were. She simply didn't understand where they were coming from. She'd known Porter for ages and, though she had always truly and deeply liked him, she hadn't ever felt something deeper. Until now.

"Papa, do I need to save Chloe?" Lewis stood near, asking the question with his brow puckered.

"That all depends," Porter said. "If she wishes to stay and we want her to stay, then she doesn't need to be rescued."

She knew he was indulging his son's imagination, but his words raised a question in her already befuddled mind: what *did* she want?

"Can we hide now, Papa?" Lewis asked. "Chloe can look for us."

Porter's arms slipped away. Chloe missed the feel of them on the instant. This was so very unexpected.

She managed a smile and agreed to continue the game. But her mind was spinning. Porter Bartrum had only ever been a friend. If her view of him had changed and her feelings grown more tender but he was actively looking elsewhere for a wife, their once easy and congenial connection was about to become extremely awkward.

From the window of her bedchamber, Adelaide watched the game unfolding below. These three were already very much a family, though none of them seemed to realize it. There was love and tenderness between them all. How was it people were so often unaware of what was so obvious to everyone else?

This matchmaking assignment was proving to be a rather simple one. Nothing stood between the would-be couple other than their own lack of awareness. Chloe, she felt certain, was beginning to see the truth for herself. Adelaide would focus on helping Porter make the same discovery.

The answer would be obvious to both of them soon enough. They simply needed a bit of matchmaker magic. Fortunately, that was Adelaide's specialty.

Chapter Five

WHEN PORTER TUCKED Lewis in to bed, the boy spoke of nothing other than their time playing in the snow with Chloe. Not everyone had the patience or energy to keep up with him. Heaven knew Porter struggled at times to do so. Having Chloe at the house party was a blessing. That she and Vance visited often was even more heaven-sent. Lewis was comfortable with her, and she loved him enough to appreciate him when others too often found him only exhausting.

Mrs. Northrop ran Porter to ground the next afternoon. He'd seen her many times over the course of the house party but had interacted with her very little. He'd tried to believe she was working on finding him a match, that the fee he would "donate"—ladies not being in a position to directly accept payment for work they did—would not be wasted. Yet the very determined glint in her eyes made him instantly uneasy.

"I have made an arrangement," she said without preamble. "Mrs. Talbot is visiting with the ladies here at the party and has expressed her wish to not have to walk back to her home. I quite casually mentioned that you had planned to go for a drive today and, perhaps, could take her home. She was quite pleased at the prospect. She will be ready to leave shortly."

The legendary matchmaker was very direct, that was certain.

"I'm to—she expects that—?"

"She has no suspicion that I have arranged this for any reason other than to help her return home in comfort." Mrs. Northrop gave a quick nod. "She is a proper age for you. Her manners are impeccable. Her financial situation is such that she would not be pursuing a connection in order to secure her comfort. More to the point, I have heard her speak longingly of children. You did indicate your primary motivation is to provide your son with a mother figure."

Porter nodded. Mrs. Northrop had the unnerving ability to render him mute.

"Drive her home," Mrs. Northrop instructed. "Get to know her. When you return I will let you know what else I have arranged."

"There will be—there will be more?"

She eyed him as if he were making no sense. "Of course there will be. You wish for a wife, and we have ample options here but little time. We must press forward."

She wasn't wrong on that score.

He released a breath, then firmed his resolve. "I will see that the chaise is prepared."

He stood by the equipage a moment, convincing himself to proceed. When he'd first engaged Mrs. Northrop's services, he'd been determined, if not entirely enthusiastic. Where had his resolve fled?

"Lewis needs this," he reminded himself. Still, his feet dragged as he pulled himself inside.

Mrs. Talbot was tugging her gloves on. She smiled when she saw him. "Thank you, Mr. Bartrum, for your generosity. I had a significant walk ahead of me."

He dipped his head and motioned for her to precede him outside.

"Will Lewis be joining us?" she asked over her shoulder as he handed her up into the carriage.

"He will not be."

She looked genuinely disappointed. That seemed to him a good sign. With both of them situated, he flicked the reins and set the horse in motion.

"How old is Lewis?"

At least she had chosen an easy topic. "He is nearly four years old."

"A very active age, from what I understand." She sighed wistfully. "My marriage was not blessed with children, but I do adore them."

Promising. "He is quite active. Not everyone finds themselves equal to the task of keeping pace with him."

She did not appear concerned. "Does he enjoy being read to?"

"Sometimes."

"I am certain he enjoys games," she said.

"Thoroughly."

Her smile softened. "I have so wished for a child to play with and read to, to sit with and teach and watch grow."

This was precisely what he wanted to find, yet he felt no relief or enthusiasm. Indeed, he was growing more and more uneasy.

"Do you think Lewis would like to hear a story?" she asked.

That was not an easy thing to predict ahead of time. "Should he request one when you are nearby, I will be sure to inform you."

Mrs. Talbot nodded. "I would enjoy that greatly."

They continued down the lane toward Mrs. Talbot's home. She asked after Lewis's favorite pastimes and if he was looking forward to Christmas. She asked Porter if he enjoyed being a father.

Conversation flowed easily between them, not slowing

even as they pulled under the front portico of her home. She thanked him before being handed down by a footman. Porter set the chaise in motion once more. His mind was not easy.

Mrs. Talbot was well-mannered, good-natured, and clearly interested. Interested in *Lewis,* at least. Perhaps that was the source of his discouragement. She liked children, felt a pull toward his son, but seemed utterly indifferent to *him.*

"I don't particularly want someone in my life for my sake. Do I?" No one but the horse was nearby, so he didn't expect a reply. Still, the answer felt surprisingly crucial. "Do I?"

He was struck in that moment by the strength of his emotional response. He did want someone in his life. He was lonely and, other than the company of a three-year-old, alone. His heart quietly longed for someone to care about and care for him. Without warning, his previously simple search took on a new dimension.

He fully intended to retire to his bedchamber and attempt to sort all this out, but Mrs. Northrop was waiting for him in the entryway.

"Mr. Bartrum, excellent timing. I am having a lovely visit with Mrs. and Miss Cunningham and intend for you to join us." She took the steps, looking back once to motion him to follow her. "Miss Cunningham is young, but not infantile. She is pleasant company and of a good family. I believe she is a fine candidate."

He really couldn't refuse. This was what he'd asked her to do. He followed her all the way to the sitting room where the lady in question, and her mother, were seated.

"Mr. Bartrum means to join us." Mrs. Northrop gave the impression of this having been a happy coincidence.

He sat on the edge of a sofa, facing the Cunninghams.

"I understand you reside in Essex," Miss Cunningham said. "I have visited there often. It is lovely."

"I have always thought so."

Mrs. Northrop spoke with Mrs. Cunningham, leaving Porter solely responsible for conversing with Miss Cunningham. He didn't necessarily object, but conversations weren't a strong suit of his.

"I was grateful to see the snow has stopped." She did not seem to need him to lead the conversation.

He was happy enough to follow her lead, as he had done with Mrs. Talbot. "It does simplify travel. But my son will be disappointed. He thoroughly enjoys playing in the snow."

That seemed to surprise her. "He must be soaked and muddy by the time he returns to the nursery."

"Well, yes. But he's also very pleased to have become soaked and muddy."

"The nursemaids are likely a bit disgruntled, but I am certain they are accustomed to such things." She didn't speak unkindly nor with disapproval, but her response was a little disinterested in Lewis's concerns. "Do you go to London for the Season?"

"I do."

Her face lit. "I just adore Town when Society is there en masse. So many diversions, so many friends and acquaintances to call on." She smiled much the same way Mrs. Talbot had when speaking of reading and playing with children. "I confess I am not one to run myself ragged attempting to attend *every* event, but the ones I enjoy, I *thoroughly* enjoy."

He could relate to that. "As do I."

"You simply must call on us when you are in Town next Season. We would very much like to continue our acquaintance." A great deal of *I* lay in her use of *we*. It was flattering, especially after Mrs. Talbot's lack of interest. And yet . . .

"I do hope you will dance with me should we find ourselves at the same ball." It was a touch forward of her but not shockingly so. She was certainly not shy about letting her interest show.

"I confess I do not attend as many balls as some gentlemen. Being out so late night after night would make it difficult to be awake for my mornings with Lewis."

Her brow pulled. "You spend every morning with him?"

"Nearly. He takes great joy in our time together. As do I."

How was it possible she found that surprising? Mrs. Talbot had shown little interest in him. Miss Cunningham showed little interest in Lewis. For the first time since undertaking this apparently hare-brained scheme, he began to suspect he'd underestimated the complexity of it. He'd told Mrs. Northrop with such confidence what his wishes were for a wife only to realize now that what he'd told her was wrong.

He excused himself and, after a quick bow, slipped from the room.

A mother for Lewis, he'd said with finality. But he needed so much more. Someone who loved his son, yes, but also someone who loved *him* and whom he could love in return. Someone he felt at ease with rather than on edge. Someone who brought both him and his son joy and who would be made happier herself by having them in her life. Someone like—

He stopped in the middle of the corridor. His lungs suddenly turned to stone. His pulse echoed through his head as his mind seized the unexpected and undeniable truth.

Someone like Chloe.

Adelaide continued her conversation with the Cunninghams even as she indulged in a moment of inward triumph. Her arrangements that day would do the trick, she had no doubt. Both ladies she'd thrust upon Mr. Bartrum were perfectly acceptable and fine people. But neither offered the entirety of what he truly needed.

She had seen in his face the moment he'd realized that for himself. He knew what he *didn't* want. Now, to help him see with clarity what he did.

Chapter Six

CHLOE HAD MANAGED to maintain her equilibrium despite her realization of the change her feelings had, at some point without her taking note of it, undergone where Porter Bartrum was concerned. He was actively seeking a wife, and she had no reason to believe she was anywhere on his list of possible choices.

She was not yet certain what she meant to do. Ought she to attempt to find a way onto that list? Ought she to speak with Mrs. Northrop? If Porter did not share her growing tenderness, admitting to her own would simply interject awkwardness into what had always been an easy and comfortable friendship. She didn't want to lose that. Yet, once he was married and her heart was broken, she would lose it anyway.

"Miss Munson."

Chloe had all but forgotten that she'd left open the door connecting her room with Mrs. Northrop's. The matchmaker stood in the threshold.

"I understand from your brother that you are very accomplished on the pianoforte."

She couldn't help a laugh. "My brother is a troublemaker."

Mrs. Northrop hadn't smiled very often during the first few days of their acquaintance. She did so more easily now. "Was he gammoning me, then?"

"No, but he knows I don't particularly care to play for others, and telling you I have that talent meant I would likely be asked to do so." She narrowed her gaze theatrically on Mrs. Northrop. "Is that what you've sauntered in here to do? Force me to perform for strangers?"

Mrs. Northrop nodded solemnly. "I will require it under penalty of torture."

"What if I consider the task itself to be torture?"

"Then I would remind you that Mr. Ellsworth expressed his wish for a musical evening, and he is not one to be put off a scent easily."

Oh, what an apt description. "And he does know that I play."

Mrs. Northrop offered an empathetic look. "You had best accept your fate."

She managed to reconcile herself by the time the evening's entertainment began. Mr. Ellsworth did, indeed, insist upon a musicale. Chloe kept a bit to the back of the room, hoping to at least not be selected to play first. As luck, or perhaps misfortune, would have it, Porter stood there as well. Never before had she been uncomfortable around him. But too much was yet unknown.

"Are you hiding back here so you won't be forced to play?" How well Porter knew her.

"If my brother knew how to keep his jaw locked, I'd not have to slip into dim corners during musical evenings."

Porter's gaze shifted to where Vance sat. "He is the one who betrayed you, then?"

"Who else?"

He looked at her once more. "Did he happen to tattle to Mrs. Northrop?"

How had he guessed that? "He did."

"Hmm." Porter's eyes shifted to Mrs. Talbot, who had only just sat on the stool at the pianoforte.

"Are you upset with Mrs. Northrop?" His tone certainly hinted at displeasure.

But he shook his head. "I'm merely piecing together a bit of a puzzle."

"Involving her?"

He nodded. "And you."

Her heart clenched. What was he trying to sort out where she was concerned?

His mouth turned in thought, his brow pulling low.

"Is this puzzle something unsettling?" Asking seemed the best approach.

He seemed to suddenly realize he'd given that impression. He smiled softly, setting off a fluttering in her middle. "Mrs. Northrop earlier today had a long conversation with a certain gentleman who expressed a wish for someone to play the pianoforte tonight during the musical evening."

"Where does Vance come into this?"

Porter grew noticeably uncomfortable.

She shook her head, fighting down a grin. "You don't get to weasel out of this as easily as that. You may have sorted the puzzle, but I have not."

With a noticeable lightening of his expression, Porter leaned closer. Heavens, the tantalizing scent of his shaving soap only added to the flutter she felt. "I suspect Mrs. Northrop is undertaking a bit of matchmaking."

"For me?" In her shock, she forgot to keep her voice lowered. Several people in the music room looked back at her.

Porter laughed silently. "Oh, pish." He mimicked well the inflection she'd used when uttering that exact phrase only a couple of days earlier. "You are not a terrible dancer, and that is really all that matters. I am certain Mrs. Northrop is aware of that."

"And that is why she is choosing to show me to advantage to this as-yet-unnamed gentleman?"

Porter had no opportunity to answer. Mr. Ellsworth's booming voice prevented any conversation anywhere in the room.

"Indulge us, Miss Munson," he said. "We wish for another song on the pianoforte."

"Mrs. Talbot played wonderfully," she said. "Do allow her to continue doing so."

"Nonsense," the young widow said. "There is time enough for everyone to play."

Drat that Mrs. Talbot. And drat Mrs. Northrop. And drat Vance.

"I don't think you'll be given the opportunity to escape," Porter said. "You would do well to get it over with."

He wasn't wrong. Chloe steeled her resolve and moved to the instrument. She sat, placing her fingers over the keys. It wasn't that she was ashamed of her playing or particularly bashful about it. She simply didn't enjoy performing.

Her eyes met Porter's, who yet stood at the back of the room. He offered a tiny nod and a smile of encouragement. It helped more than he likely knew.

She chose a simple song, one that would not last long but also wasn't likely to disappoint. How tempting it was to continually glance at Porter and receive the encouragement he offered. She feared if she did so too often, the entire room would see her heart hanging in her eyes.

As her selection came to a close, she looked up once more, just in time to see Mrs. Northrop exchange glances with Mr. Twickenham. The puzzle Porter had not entirely divulged became clear: Mr. Twickenham was the gentleman, Mrs. Northrop was, indeed, matchmaking, and Vance, she suspected, was part of the effort.

Mr. Twickenham was a good enough sort, but she had no interest in a match with him. Indeed, until she'd realized the state of her heart, she'd had no interest in a match with anyone.

There was only one thing for it. She would watch Porter over the next day or two, whilst doing her best to avoid Mrs. Northrop's choice for her. If she saw any indication that her dear friend felt something more for her than the casual connection they'd always had, she would somehow find the courage to interfere with the matchmaker he'd hired and attempt to be matchmaker herself.

Before Adelaide had undertaken her current line of work, she had been quite quick to dismiss as foolish people who did not figuratively rip their hearts out by confessing their love when they had no reason to believe doing so would end in utter humiliation, pain, suffering, and the loss of friends and loved ones.

Why do they not simply have a conversation? she'd so often said to herself. *If they would just lay bare their souls, all would be mended.*

She now recognized her arrogance for what it was. How readily one insists that a risk ought to be undertaken when that person has nothing on the line. How quickly people were to criticize others' vulnerabilities from a place of utter security.

Watching Miss Munson and Mr. Porter that evening, her heart ached for them. They were so very close to their happiness, so near to toppling the wall of uncertainty between them and that future. If only one of them would inch closer to that place of vulnerability, Adelaide felt certain they could close the remainder of that gap.

She would simply have to create an opportunity for them to do so.

Chapter Seven

PORTER HAD WRESTLED with his unexpected insight for two long days. Days in which Mrs. Northrop arranged for him to spend time with ladies he had no interest in. Vance teased him mercilessly about his distraction, and Lewis complained at length that Chloe hadn't spent enough time with him. And in the midst of it all, Twickenham had grown a little nauseating in his attentions to her, beginning with his puppy-eyed gazes the night of the musicale.

Christmas Eve arrived without the usual cheer. His mind was heavy, and his heart was worried. The guests would be gathering the traditional greenery, divided in small teams.

Mrs. Northrop pulled him aside. "I know who I would like to see you teamed with. She comes from a good family."

He knew where this was headed. "I am planning to ask Miss Munson. Lewis is joining me, and they enjoy each other's company. We all enjoy one another's company."

She tipped her head a bit. "Miss Munson? I thought I heard Mr. Twickenham say he intended to ask her."

Twickenham? The man was as irritating as a rash. Porter looked over the gathered people and found Chloe. She stood with Vance—not Mr. Twickenham. He crossed to her, forgetting in his haste to bid farewell to Mrs. Northrop.

"Have you a partner for the greenery gathering?" He

asked the question without the slightest pause for a greeting. What was the matter with him today?

"I do," she said.

His heart dropped.

"Lewis asked me this morning," she said with a smile filled to the brim with mischief.

He felt an answering smile tug at his lips. He looked to Vance. "Will you be joining us as well?"

He shook his head. "Mr. Caster has invited me to join his wife and daughter, and I fully intend to accept."

Relief swept over Porter. He offered Chloe his arm. She accepted. How was it he had never noticed before how pleasant it was to assume this very commonplace arrangement with her? Did she take pleasure in it as well? How he hoped she did.

The children arrived from the nursery in the next moment. Searching for Lewis proved unnecessary. He darted to them, throwing himself at Porter's legs.

"Let's go, Papa. Let's go."

Chloe simply laughed, neither distressed by Lewis's enthusiasm nor displeased with Porter's presence.

They were given a small sled to pull behind them as they traipsed through the snow in search of pine boughs and holly and all the other traditional Christmas greenery.

Lewis sat on the sled, eagerly taking in the scenery. Chloe was sure to remind him to hold still enough to be safe, though she walked with seeming contentment at Porter's side. If not for Lewis so nearby, he might have made an attempt to discover if her feelings went at all beyond friendship, if there was any hope of something more.

Porter removed a few low-hanging pine branches with the little saw he'd been provided. Chloe helped Lewis pile them on the sled. He climbed atop the bows, and Porter pulled the sled to the next tree. Again and again they undertook the task. All the while Chloe kept Lewis calmly engaged without stifling him. Her wit and humor repeatedly pulled laughter from Porter.

They were never lonely when she was with them. Somehow he hadn't ever seen that or recognized it.

"Do you think your papa can reach that?" Chloe was pointing up into the branches of a tree.

Lewis, standing beside her, looked up as well. "The green clump?"

She nodded. "Yes. It is the most important of the yuletide plants."

Lewis bounced. "It is?"

"It is," she confirmed.

Porter, curious, moved closer and looked up as well. Ah. "Mistletoe."

"And we found it!" Lewis spun about in a circle.

"We certainly did," Chloe said. "And do you know the tradition of mistletoe?"

Lewis shook his head.

"Two people who stand under the mistletoe at the same time are supposed to exchange a kiss."

"Oh." Lewis was not yet old enough to find the prospect displeasing. "Do they have to? Will they get in trouble if they don't?"

"No," she said with an empathetic smile.

"But they can give a kiss because of the missing toe if they want?"

She shot Porter a look of wide-eyed amusement and mouthed, "Missing toe?"

He managed to stifle his laugh.

Chloe turned back to Lewis. "They can if they wish."

Lewis took her hand and tugged her downward. She

hunched low in front of him. The boy stretched on his toes and gave her a sweet, little kiss.

Chloe pulled him into a hug. "Oh, I do love you, Lewis."

Lewis looked past her to Porter. "Your turn, Papa!"

"My—" He choked against the words. "My turn?"

"You are under the missing toe. You are supposed to kiss her, but you won't get in trouble if you don't want to." Lewis looked at Chloe, who stood facing Porter. "Did I tell him right?"

"Yes, you did." She spoke to Lewis but watched *him*.

He leaned his saw against the trunk of the tree and took a single, tentative step toward her.

"Lewis did say you don't have to." She spoke quietly, not looking away from him.

"I know." He reached out and took her hand. "You don't have to either."

"I know." But she didn't move, didn't pull away.

Porter's heart pounded as he closed the gap between them. He took a breath, trying to calm his nerves, but it helped very little. She set her free hand on his chest. His pulse leaped on the instant.

He wrapped his other arm around her waist. She bent her neck, looking up at him. He brushed his lips over hers, light and gentle. Her hand slipped from his chest to his neck, her fingers feathering along his chin.

He kissed her again, more fully, more deeply. She slipped her hand from his and wrapped her arms around his neck. She returned his kiss with all the fervor with which he offered it.

"Do I need to rescue you, Chloe?" Lewis asked.

Chloe laughed, and their kiss broke. He didn't release her. She didn't move away.

"*Does* he need to rescue you?" Porter asked.

"I understand rescue is only necessary if the one being

kept doesn't wish to be or the one doing the keeping no longer wishes to keep her."

Porter nodded. "I've heard that as well." He, himself, had said that the day they'd played in the snow.

Her hands shifted, resting at the front of his coat, her fingers fussing with his buttons. "No, Lewis. You don't need to rescue me."

All the nervousness he'd felt melted away. He was no longer uncertain, no longer worried about the future.

"Are we keeping Chloe, Papa?"

"If she'll keep us," he whispered.

She pressed a quick kiss to his lips. "That would be the finest Christmas present I have ever received.

"We agreed to this amount." Mr. Bartrum had been trying for a solid ten minutes to convince Adelaide to accept the monetary consideration they'd previously agreed upon.

She assumed her most determined expression and posture. "I applaud your integrity, Mr. Bartrum, but please believe me when I say that being part of this party and enjoying the hospitality of our hosts for a week has been ample compensation for an assignment which required I merely nudge two people enough for them to see the truth right in front of them."

Miss Munson slipped her arm through Mr. Bartrum's. "You knew?"

Of course she had. "I did."

"How quickly did you sort it?" Miss Munson asked.

With a smile she wasn't entirely certain she kept free of amused pity, she said, "The very first day."

Miss Munson laughed heartily. Mr. Bartrum watched his darling with unabashed tenderness. This soon-to-be family would be a thoroughly happy one.

"Why did you insist upon thrusting lady after lady upon Porter if you weren't attempting to make a match?" Miss Munson asked with a smile.

"And attempt to impress Mr. Twickenham with Chloe's musical abilities?" Mr. Bartrum added.

"Sometimes the best way to help people finally see what they already have is to show them what they could have but don't want."

"Chloe! Chloe!"

Miss Munson turned toward the open front door of Ellsworth Manor. Lewis was bounding across the entrance hall toward the threshold. Chloe hurried to him, catching him up in her arms.

Mr. Bartrum watched the scene, though he spoke to Adelaide. "You could have simply told me that I was in love with her since you sorted it so quickly. That would have saved us all a great deal of time."

She shook her head. "The heart does not work that way. It cannot be told what to feel; it simply must make that discovery on its own."

"My heart has given me the greatest Christmas gift imaginable," he said.

Adelaide was not an overly sentimental person, but his sincere gratitude for the happiness he had found touched her. "This has been a fruitful Christmas house party for me as well," she told him. "I have secured a new assignment thanks to my presence at this gathering."

"You have? That is a fine thing." Mr. Bartrum was a good-hearted person, precisely the kind she found pleasure in securing a future for.

"It is, indeed. And I depart immediately. So I will bid you farewell and wish you every happiness."

Mr. Bartrum shook her hand and expressed his gratitude once more.

Miss Munson had just returned to where they stood, Lewis bouncing excitedly in her arms. "Are you leaving us?"

Adelaide nodded. "I don't suspect you need my intervention any longer."

Even with a wriggly child in her arms, Miss Munson managed to hug her. "Thank you again and again for everything."

"It is my pleasure."

"Are you ready, Mrs. Northrop?" her newest client asked through the lowered window of the traveling carriage.

The usual new-assignment excitement bubbled inside. "I am always ready."

On that declaration, she climbed into the Cunninghams' carriage, eager to help another deserving soul find her happiness.

The number of matches she had facilitated numbered in the dozens, all of them loving and promising and hopeful. A life spent in such a noble pursuit was a life worth living. And she meant to live it fully.

Sarah M. Eden is the author of multiple historical romances, including the two-time Whitney Award Winner *Longing for Home* and Whitney Award finalists *Seeking Persephone* and *Courting Miss Lancaster*. Combining her obsession with history and affinity for tender love stories, Sarah loves crafting witty characters and heartfelt romances. She has thrice served as the Master of Ceremonies for the LDStorymakers Writers Conference and acted as the Writer in Residence at the Northwest Writers Retreat.

Sarah is represented by Pam Victorio at D4EO Literary Agency.

Visit Sarah online:
Twitter: @SarahMEden
Facebook: Author Sarah M. Eden
Website: SarahMEden.com

The Forbidden Duke

Jen Geigle Johnson

Chapter One

The new Duke of Salsbury hardly noticed the guests as he took each hand, welcoming them into his London townhome. Christmas boughs lined the entry where he stood. The smells of his favorite Christmas punch should have warmed him, brought back memories of childhood. He supposed he said all the niceties and guests responded in kind, but in truth, his mind was elsewhere. The Asters had come to his ball. All morning his mother festered and worried as to why they would accept the invitation. It was a curiosity for certain, but not one to exert oneself over. Though, he admitted, news of their arrival did tighten his throat in a familiar sorrow. The formal mourning for his father's untimely death finished last month. He didn't think his mother would ever be finished mourning . . . or urging him on to all sorts of pursuits she felt vital to his well-being.

She nudged him. "Lady Fenningway has arrived." His mother insisted he do his duty by dancing with this new debutante. His father had set up an alliance with her family before he passed, a powerful meeting of two ducal houses. He hoped Stephen would court and marry the woman. Her family hoped the same. Unfortunately, Stephen did not share the general enthusiasm for the idea of marriage to the big-toothed, awkward twelve-year-old he had met years ago.

He did, however, have a strong sense of duty. The music for the first set began, the three-step of the waltz. He turned in the direction of his mother's demanding finger just as the footman finished announcing an auburn-haired beauty. A daring lilt lifted her chin. Her eyes sparkled, and a half grin warmed her face. Her dress draped down around a slender figure, her arms rested gracefully at her sides. His smile grew. Perhaps a union with her house would not be as tedious as he at first envisioned. Had they not met as children? Surely he would recall such a face. Did his father not allude to mediocre looks but a sharp wit? He couldn't remember, and he had considered all talk of marriage most decidedly not urgent, so, regretfully, he had only listened with half an ear. But this woman could never be described as mediocre. She attracted him and many young men around her, immediately.

He approached the lady, her creamy skin in beautiful contrast with the red tint in her thick, dark hair. He bowed over her hand, placed it on his arm, and led her to the floor.

They began the waltz without yet speaking. She fit remarkably well in his arms, just the right height, not exactly eye level, but he imagined he could rest his chin on her head in an embrace. He stepped closer, his body tingling with a new awareness. His hands were aware of every shift of her fingers in his, of the rise and fall of her breath under his palm at her back. Suddenly the very air around them created a sensation on his skin.

She cleared her throat.

When he met her eyes, he was surprised to see a raised eyebrow and an aura of expectation.

He had been so caught up in these new sensations, perhaps he had assumed she was equally taken away. "You look lovely tonight."

She smiled. "Thank you." Her smile lit her face. A soft

pink colored her cheeks. The prospect of courting and marrying this woman became more enticing to him the longer she danced in his arms.

Strange she didn't say more.

He tried again. "I'm happy you could come."

"Thank you. My grandma arranged it for me. It's a lovely ball. I'm quite taken with the décor."

Her grandmother. He thought they had sent the invitations to her father. He nodded absentmindedly. Something about this lady's eyes, a spark of intelligence, intrigued him. Certain she could talk of much more than ballroom décor, he asked, "Have you been to any of the operas lately?"

"Oh yes. I go to every one I can." Her eyes sparkled up at him. "Do you also enjoy the opera?"

"I'm pleased to hear it. I, too, enjoy the opera. Of course we shall attend together. And the museum? Art? What are your other interests?" Perhaps their courtship would be less tedious than he thought, were he to court her. The more he thought on a life with this beauty in his arms, the faster his heart picked up.

But her face did not look as pleased as he would hope. Her eyebrows lowered, and a cloud of confusion darkened her eyes.

As they twirled through the room, he nearly stumbled at the sight of his mother's deep scowl. He glanced back, and the pinched disapproval of his uncle's face surprised him. All around them, covered whispering mouths clustered together, and wide eyes tracked his movement.

On the other side of the room, others held an abnormally strong interest in him and Lady Fenningway. He would expect to create a bit of a stir to declare his interest by dancing the first set with the lady, but the reactions in the room were not positive, and his mother's face was most disturbing of all. Was he not doing her bidding?

The lady in his arms tilted her head, seeming puzzled.

He cleared his throat. "We've created quite a stir."

"I imagine we would." She titled her head to the side as if it were obvious.

He frowned. "Why is that?"

"We haven't been introduced, for one—"

"Haven't been introduced? Of course we have, admittedly as children. Or rather, who did you suspect that I was?" Could she not remember? They had actually met. Years had gone by, naturally, but that didn't signify. They had agreed to the first set this evening.

"I'm sure we haven't. I would remember."

He raised his eyebrows, and she blushed prettily. She looked so charming, perhaps he could overlook her absentmindedness.

She waited, again expecting something from him. When he continued in silence, unsure what she would have him say, she huffed. "Well, I'm Lady Catherine . . ." She paused.

He sucked in a breath. "Lady Catherine? Are you certain?" How could she be Lady Catherine?

"Yes, quite. And you are . . . ?"

He stammered. Hadn't his mother pointed to this very woman? He looked for his mother. Her frown, still present, created deeper lines on her face. A mealy, pasty woman stood at her side, eyes red and swollen. He turned his attention back to the woman in his arms. "So you are not Lady Fenningway?"

She laughed. "No, I'm most decidedly *not* Lady Fenningway." She indicated the mealy, pasty woman.

His affront grew. "But they announced you as Lady Fenningway. If you are not her, then why are we dancing?" He couldn't have anyone pretending to be his intended if she were in fact going to become his intended. Great disappointment increased his irritability past the bounds of politeness. His new hope that the word *intended* would forever describe this new beauty in his arms was dashed unfairly in a matter of seconds.

"You ask why we are dancing?" She scoffed, her breath coming faster. "Because you placed my hand upon your arm without a word and dragged me out on the dance floor."

"What! I did nothing of the kind. We had it all arranged. I merely came to collect you for our dance."

"If I had agreed to dance with you, that would make perfect sense."

They continued their waltz, the obvious surprise of many in the room beginning to settle unnaturally in his stomach.

She cleared her throat. "And you still haven't told me who you are."

"Confound it, you don't know. I'm the eldest Harrington, Duke of Salsbury."

She gasped. "You're a Harrington? Salsbury himself?" She paled and stopped dancing, pulling away.

"Well, we can finish the dance." His arms longed for her, the sudden distance between them chilling him.

Another couple whirled by them. Not expecting anyone to stop, they nearly ran into the duke.

"Here now, let's move off the floor in a respectable manner."

Her face had whitened, and she made a great effort to swallow. "Don't come near me again." She whirled around and ran from the room.

He didn't move for several moments, couples dancing past him, as he watched her retreating form. Confound the woman. His arms ached to hold her. And he puzzled. What had gotten into her? He had never experienced such a look of fear and abhorrence from a woman. He was left with a decided discomfort and yearning. He was torn between retreating to his study and running after her, pleading her return.

Chapter Two

CONFOUND IT ALL. A veritable army of people greeted him off the floor with frowns and accusatory stares. His mother's lip trembled. It seemed the goodwill of the Christmas season beginning tomorrow was no match for whatever caused this discontent.

He made his way to Lady Fenningway. Her eyes still red-rimmed and swollen, she stared at her slippers. "I do apologize for neglecting our dance. Perhaps we could finish it out . . ."

The small voice that responded lacked life, vibrancy. Perhaps it was unfair to compare her to the bright and interesting Lady Catherine. Who could appear favorably when next to her? But he hoped Lady Fenningway would prove to be an interesting conversationalist.

Alas, he had never had a more tedious dance, even a waltz. "And what are your other interests?"

"Needlepoint." Her small voice wavered. She spouted off the typical list. Nothing uniquely intriguing caught his attention. He sought Lady Catherine's rather remarkable tresses. She had disappeared from the room. Staring at the top of Lady Fenningway's dull and lifeless hair, listening to her silence, he found himself dreading any future moment with the woman. But to make up for his mistake and to please his mother, he secured the supper set.

In between sets, his mother pulled him aside. "How could you?"

"Mother, I'm fixing the problem. Lady Fenningway will be fine. I cannot understand everyone's deep shock at such a thing."

"Can you not? You can't understand why I would be hurt, torn apart even, by your dancing with an Aster?"

His mouth dropped open. "An Aster?"

She eyed him and nodded. "Of course you would not know." With a pat on his arm, she led him farther back into a corner. "Though we have worked to avoid such a thing all these years, you have just been introduced to the eldest Aster daughter."

Of all the most wretched circumstances in which to find himself. The one woman with any spark of interest to her would turn out to be an Aster. "How could I know, then, if I had not been introduced?" He saw no reason for his mother to be so accusatory. Naturally, now he knew who she was, there would be no repeat sets. Though he sorely wished that were not the case.

"You've been away. She walks with a different set. I should have known you would not know her, as distracted as you always are at any social function." Her exasperated face made him smile.

"I am not so very distracted."

She raised an eyebrow. "Oh no? And could you name even five of the ladies in this room?"

His eyes flicked with disinterest to the people milling about the room. "No, why would I need to be able to do that?" He had never been intrigued by a single one—until today.

She laughed. "I do wish you would pay better attention. You created quite a stir."

"People need to concern themselves with their own lives and leave mine well alone."

His mother shook her head. "And that they will never do. It's quite all right. We shall weather the curious and biting tongues."

Regret shuddered through him as he saw his mother lift her stoic chin. Of course she would bear the brunt of the wagging of even sympathetic tongues, as surely the talk would force her to relive her own husband's death multiple times throughout the night.

"I apologize, Mother. If you wish, you could find your way upstairs with a headache."

"And give them more reason to cackle behind our backs? No. I will stand with strength until the last of them leaves these doors."

"You are an angel, most undoubtedly sent from heaven." He placed her hand on his arm and led them in a walk around the room. "Now come, Mother, the decorations. I have been admiring them all evening in an effort to avoid human interaction."

She laughed, and his heart was comforted at the sound.

"Lovely. I don't know how you acquired the greenery here in London, but it does you credit."

"Thank you, son. We have our ways, you know."

"Ah yes, women and their ways."

Three approached, and his mother greeted them. He made his bows.

The first, a woman slightly older than the dowager, said, "Oh my dear, how are you holding up? People are sure to talk, the shock of it all." Her eyes flicked to him, standing at her side. "Forgive me, your grace. But that dance was nothing if not the most shocking thing we are likely to see this season. The books are going to be filled at Whites with all the wagers."

The lady at her side added, "A Salsbury and an Aster on the dance floor. I never thought I'd see the day." She whipped out her fan and began furiously puffing the ringlets under her cap out around her face.

He kept his face impassive, but inwardly his irritation brewed. Could they not let the old rivalry go? Not just his ridiculous family, but the rest of the ton as well. There is nothing they loved more than scandal. If he could just talk to the new Aster duke, young as he was, surely they could come to an agreement and move on from the decades-long ill feelings.

The concern in his mother's eyes told him it wasn't likely, but he refused to think that he and future generations would be controlled by this deeply held prejudice.

Chapter Three

LADY CATHERINE REFUSED to acknowledge all the scowls and looks of shocked surprise. She must leave before her uncle—

A firm hand gripped her upper arm with vicelike talons. "What do you mean, dancing with Salsbury? Have you lost your mind?" Her uncle's voice raged in its whisper tone.

"I didn't know it was him. Please. Let me go." His overbearing attempts to control her behavior were growing more alarming of late.

He shook her. "What do you mean, you didn't know?"

"Unhand me." She stood taller, eyeing her arm with great disdain. "How dare you grasp at me as though I were one of your maids?" She tore her arm out of his hands, trying to ignore the sharp sting and lingering sensation of bruising.

He released her as if he had been scorched. Then he bowed. "My apologies." Over his shoulder, he added. "Your father would be most displeased."

Didn't he think she knew that? Was she herself not already *most displeased*? How could such a thing have happened? Who could confuse her with that sickly creature, Lady Fenningway? And why had she allowed herself to be led onto the floor by a stranger?

She shuddered. Because she had thought him handsome. The most handsome man of her acquaintance. The feel of her hand in his had sent gooseflesh up her arm and, she admitted, she was curious. When had a ball started in such an intriguing manner? Swept out onto the floor by a tall and handsome gentleman. *A man unknown to her.* The thought of it thrilled her even now. With every curiosity they'd discussed, she became more intrigued.

She fisted her hands. Until she had learned he belonged to that most evil of all families, the Salsburys. Curse their wretched name. The hurt in her mother's eyes whenever their names were mentioned sank a knife deeper into Catherine's own pain. *Your father would be most displeased.* Her uncle used comments like that to control her. She could not know how displeased, for she would never see him again, only hope for a thought or two, a wisp of familiarity at his graveside.

Almost to the front door, she told the footman to summon her carriage. She couldn't stay here another moment, not when she had allowed hands sullied in her family's blood to cradle her gently, to entice and excite her as they had. Bile rose in her throat. Curse her wretched attraction. A part of her longed for him still.

She stepped up into her carriage, the maid's pale face startling her.

"Hannah!" Catherine halted in her entrance. "What are you doing here?" She couldn't fathom how her maid had come to be in the carriage so quickly.

"I summoned her." Her uncle's slippery voice slid over her like the icy wind on the moors. He stepped in to join them, sat in the opposite corner, and rapped on the ceiling for the carriage to start moving.

Catherine fell to her bench, nerves shaking and prodding, stealing her breath. "Uncle."

His icy eyes narrowed. "You were wise to leave when you did." His tone soothed.

She preferred the complimentary, colluding uncle to the harsh disciplinary one of moments ago.

He sat back, brushing off his jacket front. "Pity, though, that you couldn't be introduced to His Grace." He grimaced. "His *other* Grace."

She nodded. "I know." Her voice sounded small even to her own ears. The family sought an alliance with the Lennard family. The Duke of Halcor's son had recently been widowed, leaving him with two children. She supposed him a decent enough man. He had treated his wife well. His father was ailing and would soon be passing his title on to his son. Her family wished the alignment of their two ducal houses to solidify their power in England. Her stomach tightened again in nervous energy. They told her of a great amount of debt, unpaid, and recklessness in her father. If she didn't marry well soon, it might be too late for her to marry into a ducal house at all.

She bit back a groan. And now Salsbury sought Lady Fenningway, of the other ducal estate, with marriage potential. Such a combination of power would rival their own. She kept the new knowledge from her uncle.

One week after her fateful meeting with the Duke of Salsbury, she had seen him close on ten times. He passed by her at Vauxhall. He exited the tearoom as she entered. He even passed in front of the dressmaker yesterday after her fitting. She huffed out in frustration as she prepared for her day. And each time, he was more handsome than the last. He never acknowledged her again, but she saw it in his eyes: he wanted to. His gaze followed her where she went, and she drank in its delicious forbidden cloak as it shimmered over her skin. She shivered with the goose bumps that trailed up her arms. All night she couldn't get thoughts of him out of her mind.

She had breakfast in her room, dressed early, and hurried out of the house. She didn't admit it, but she knew where her walk in the park would take her. For decades her family had lived on one side of the park, directly opposite from the Salsburys' London townhome across a large field of green and several copses of trees. A part of her feared running into him, and the other part longed for an encounter even if they didn't speak. She wanted to see him again, to see if she was still affected by him.

As young children, they had come across each other at the park, their nursemaids giving the other a wide space. But she hadn't seen him for many years and had learned since that he went to Cambridge and was rarely in town. His tall, commanding bearing, strong jawline, and thick, dark hair made him just the kind of man she hoped to know better. His eyes, the interest he had shown in her, his plans for the opera, and a hint at great wit intrigued her all the more. She had already left a note for her mother that she wanted to attend the opera this week. She cringed at her own duplicitous nature. How could she be so captivated by a man from that family? A Salsbury. For years she had heard the stories. The Duke of Salsbury, this man's father, had cheated their family. The Salsburys wanted them ruined, poor and destitute, or so everyone said.

The butler opened up the door for her, the brisk air interrupting her thoughts. "Perhaps I shall grab a scarf."

"I'll ring for warmer attire, my lady."

"Thank you, Moorsby."

Soon she was bundled in woolens, and the air had less of an edge. She rushed out the door, a maid in tow. She wandered the paths and circled the area between their homes until her cheeks were a bright cherry red from the cold. And no Salsbury. How strange to spend the entirety of one's life actively avoiding a family to then, after the course of one evening, seek them out.

No, she couldn't be seeking them out. How could she betray her mother, her own deceased father, knowing Salsburys had been the cause of his death? And yet her heart betrayed her, betrayed them all, with this new beating rhythm spurred on by Salsbury's memory, by the thoughts of dancing in his arms. She shivered, and not from the cold.

She was about to turn back, to return to a morning of callers and tedium, when laughter carried over from a small copse of trees. A girl perhaps a few years younger than Catherine jumped out from behind a tree. "Here I am!" Then she turned and ran to the next tree and hid behind it. Catherine smiled, the girl's laughter contagious. Catherine stepped closer, her new intrigue making her forget the cold. Then she stopped just outside the thickest area of trees because the door to the Salsbury townhome slammed shut and Salsbury himself ran out, pulling on his jacket as he came. "Penelope!"

The girl giggled and fell back behind the nearest tree. She held a finger to her mouth. "Shhhhh."

More intrigued than ever, Catherine stepped out of the trees so Salsbury could see her and waved him over. Her heart pounded at the sight of him approaching. She feared and welcomed his reaction to her.

His eyes widened, but he lengthened his stride in her direction. As he approached, the girl, Penelope, jumped out again, "Here I am!"

"Oh!" Salsbury hid behind the tree to his right, then jumped out as she had, "I see you!" He moved back behind it, peering out at her from the other side.

The girl erupted in a chorus of giggles.

And Catherine found the whole situation charming.

He jumped out again, sending Penelope squealing and running behind the next tree.

Catherine laughed before she could stop herself.

Penelope suddenly looked nervous. She looked to find Salsbury—but he was still behind a tree—then back to Catherine, who smiled the warmest expression she could muster with stiff and cold lips. "Hello."

Penelope twisted her hands together and started rocking from foot to foot.

"No, it's all right. I'm a friend." She stepped closer, wanting nothing more than to hug away this girl's worries.

She peeked up at Catherine and stilled her rocking. "Friend?"

Catherine nodded. "Yes. Friend."

She seemed so much younger than she appeared. Catherine wondered if something wasn't totally right in her head. But she felt drawn to her, drawn to her laughter and her delight in something so simple.

Salsbury jumped out from behind his tree, startling Catherine and making the girl jump up and down. "You caught me!"

She ran to him. "Look! Friend." She pointed back at Catherine who smiled. "Yes, friend." She nodded and waved at her.

Full of curiosity, Catherine waited. Her heart warmed to see the silly smile and hug Salsbury gave the girl. But when he turned to face Catherine, his stern face made her take a step back.

He nodded at her and put his arm around the girl's shoulders. "Come, Penelope, it's time to get back inside."

"Wait! Friend!" She pointed at Catherine.

Unsure what to do, Catherine walked toward them. "It's awfully cold. I think we should all get inside. Before you go,

I'd love to meet you, though." She approached slowly, more for Salsbury's benefit than Penelope's. He seemed skittish, like he was about to bolt. And his protective stance, partially shielding the girl gave Catherine the message: *I don't trust you.*

But she felt drawn to this girl. And she couldn't control her yearning for Salsbury. An hour wandering about the park was proof of that. Something about the situation felt important. Her feet crunched through leaves as she moved closer. Then flakes began to fall all around her. She held up her hands, a huge smile on her face. "Oh look! Snow." She caught one on her glove and held it up. "Look, see how pretty?" She held it out.

The girl looked up at Salsbury, who had not taken his eyes off Catherine. Something in them softened, and he nodded.

Penelope approached and peered over the top of Catherine's outstretched hand to examine the melting white prism. "Oh!" Penelope held up her own hand to catch one but did not have the patience for a flake to land. She waved her gloves around as if to scoop up the flakes all at once. Catherine reached out and placed a hand on her arm. "Wait. Be still."

Penelope widened her eyes and nodded. They both watched with wonder as a flake swirled through the air and landed on the back of Penelope's glove. She breathed in her excitement and held her glove still while whispering to Salsbury. "Look! Stephen, look."

His face now gentle, his eyes kind, he smiled at Catherine, and she warmed down to her toes.

"Look! You've caught another!" Penelope pointed to her glove. Catherine looked away and compared flakes with Penelope. Every time she returned her gaze to Salsbury's, he was watching her with a delicious intensity, and she wanted nothing more than to sit for hours basking in his interest. Their new flakes melted, so they reached for the heavens to catch another.

"I've got one!" Salsbury surprised her again. "And it is by far the prettiest."

"What, no. Mine's the prettiest." Penelope stepped closer to him, and they compared the two until they melted.

When the flakes fell faster and the wind picked up, Catherine's maid cleared her throat. Catherine knew she must get back. She curtsied to Penelope and Salsbury and said, "It was my pleasure spending time with you. I'm Lady Catherine Aster."

Salsbury nodded. "Pleased to make your acquaintance, officially." The corner of his lip twitched as if he might smile again. He turned to the girl at his side, then studied Catherine's face for a moment. She held her breath, feeling as though something large weighed in the balance. He stepped closer, asking her to do the same. His voice was low, and its secretive rumble rolled through her in a thrilling wave. Then he said, "And this is Penelope. My sister."

Catherine puffed out her breath. *Sister.* No one told her the Salsburys had a sister. She stepped forward and held the girl's hand in her own. "I'm so pleased to meet you."

She nodded. "Me too. You are a friend."

Catherine thought her smile might break her face, so sweet and special it felt to be accepted by such a person. She nodded. "Yes. We are friends." She curtsied again and then turned to leave.

"We come here in the mornings. Sometimes." Salsbury's voice held hope, a catch at the end that melted Catherine's heart.

"Then so do I." She smiled at Penelope. "I'll see you soon."

The girl jumped up and clapped, and Catherine laughed

with her. Her eyes met Salsbury's, and the intensity held her captive. Then he nodded, and she hurried after her maid, warmed from her toes to the top of her head. She loosened her scarf and tried to control her breathing. "That was wonderful!"

"Yes, my lady." Hannah's voice sounded less than enthused, but a small smile lifted the corner of her lip, and Catherine knew she was secretly pleased. Catherine didn't care if she wasn't. This maid was loyal to her over her uncle.

Catherine had never spent a more delightful morning. And Salsbury had invited her back. She squealed and skipped her next step. Already she counted the moments until she could see him again. She couldn't tell if her heart pounded with the risk and secrecy of the meeting, knowing her uncle would strictly forbid her, if she was this affected by his shattering good looks, or if she was charmed by his sister. No matter the reason, no matter the risk, tomorrow couldn't come soon enough.

Chapter Four

STEPHEN LIFTED HIS chin while the valet tied his cravat. They would be attending the opera with Lady Fenningway and her mother. He ground his teeth and lowered his chin without thinking. The cravat immediately squeezed against his throat. He corrected.

Sleep had evaded him all through the night. So many conflicting emotions had paraded about in his mind, he didn't know which to grasp and which to discard. He shook his head, and his valet paused, eyes opened in question. When Stephen didn't say anything, he continued.

He didn't want anything to do with Lady Fenningway. He wanted Lady Catherine.

But they could never entertain even the barest slip of hope to be together. His family was so hurt by hers, her relations so ruthless and cunning. He couldn't even be sure her presence in his life was not part of some scheme to bring further pain and suffering to his family. But his rebellious heart cared nothing for all the reasons an alliance with her would be impossible, and his ardent attraction filled him to the point he could think of nothing else. He had never found a creature more fascinating, more captivating of all his senses than he found her.

Yet tonight he would accompany the extraordinarily *not* captivating Lady Fenningway to the opera.

He met his mother on their front stoop. He lifted her hand, aiding her into the carriage. She sniffed. He was still not forgiven for dancing with an Aster. Though he tried to explain *she* had pointed her out.

After only but a moment of blessed silence, his mother began. "Remember we are to make up for that awful debacle you created at last week's ball."

"Mother, I hardly think we need to continue to make up for it. I feel our early morning call and this lovely evening at the opera will put us on the firm footing where we need to be."

Another sniff made him inwardly wince. "You obviously have not grasped the gravity of what you have done. Not just to Lady Fenningway by snubbing her but by doing such a hurtful thing in such a scandalous manner."

"I thought we had talked through this. Dancing with another member of the peerage is hardly scandalous." He refused to be pulled into the bitter grudge his mother insisted on carrying. His heart softened when he saw her lips quiver. It was her husband, after all, who had died. Not a day went by that Stephen didn't miss him. But he died precisely because he gripped, white-knuckled, to an age-old grudge against the Aster family. If they would all let it fall away like a thin piece of silk in the wind, the younger generations, like himself, could move on in the world.

He knew words to that effect were useless with his mother. "I hope to enjoy the opera," he said. "Perhaps Lady Fenningway shares my affinity?"

His mother looked away. "Perhaps."

"I do hope to enjoy my wife, find things in common. I would not seek solely a marriage of convenience. There has to be some semblance of potential there, Mother."

She stared out the window, sighed, and then turned to face him. "I am listening, son, but the practicalities of life do not always lend themselves to the fancies of youth. Sometimes we just do our duty."

He cringed. His duty. Memories of his father's kind eyes, his determination, his work to build their estate, to influence the House of Lords. The man spent a lifetime dedicated to England and to his estate and family. A Fenningway alliance had seemed so important to him before he passed. And until Stephen met Lady Catherine Aster, he had planned to carry forward all his father's dying wishes and to push forward his causes. Though he had not felt overly enamored with the idea, he could not dishonor the memory of his father by ignoring such a strong wish.

He began to talk himself into the idea once again so much so that by the time the Fenningways joined them in the carriage, he was able to talk pleasantly and even flirt with her a small amount.

She responded with dropped eyes and the barest smile, but perhaps she was shy and would soon overcome those tendencies when she knew him better.

His mother carried most of the conversation after a few more attempts on his part to draw out Lady Fenningway. He sat back, somewhat relieved to let the women discuss their own pleasantries.

Only when they arrived at the front of the building did his heart rattle inside him with the expectation that perhaps Lady Catherine would be present. And if she were, how would they react to each other in a public setting? Did they continue to act as though they had never been introduced? Surely he must acknowledge her. Of a truth, he desired to engage her in conversation, encourage the sparkle to lighten her eyes. But he knew such a thing as congenial conversation would cause a disruption similar to what their dance had.

He grimaced, thinking of it. They entered the front doors

of the newly rebuilt Covent Garden, and he already searched the crowd for Lady Catherine. The small hand on his forearm weighed nothing at all. Lady Fenningway must work to touch him as little as possible with her gloved hand. He led her up the stairs. "I'm so looking forward to this evening. Thank you for accompanying me."

Her lips curled in a small smile. "I as well, thank you."

And that was to be their conversation. Would she initiate any? "Do you have an opera you most like? What are some that you have seen?"

"Oh, well..."

Her mother answered. "She saw *Messrs.* Last year. That was quite good, was it not?"

"I did enjoy it, yes." And then silence followed. So discussing the opera would not be their lot, but nothing could prevent him from enjoying a good opera even if no one would converse about the performance.

They made their way to his box. Candles lit the darkened hallways surrounding the box entrances. He held the curtain back for them all to enter, his mother first, then hers, and then as Lady Fenningway turned to enter, Lady Catherine came around the corner outside their boxes.

She faltered on the arm of Lord Channing. Jealousy scratched at his insides. They walked toward him, Channing totally unaware that her eyes had grown wide and a small smile lit her face.

His mother called from inside.

His eyes held Lady Catherine's a moment longer, and then he let the curtain fall back behind him. He had never experienced anything like the pull he felt to be with her. The curtain between them may as well have been thin translucent silk for the waves of enticement. He yearned to succumb. But he could not. The fabric was a sheet of rock for all the opportunity they would ever have. But, he smiled to himself, there was always tomorrow morning in the park.

As soon as intermission began, he rushed Lady Fenningway out of their box and into the hallway, turning in the direction Lady Catherine had gone with Channing. He clenched his fist. *Channing.* He was a good sort of chap, the kind that might make a decent match for her. He rounded a corner, Lady Fenningway's small legs hurrying to keep up, her small, short breaths becoming more obvious at his side. He turned to her to make some small apology, and then ran right into a soft lavender dress, a lady's feathers tickling his nose. "Pardon me." Lady Catherine's brilliant eyes smiled up at him. His heart thrilled with excitement. He reached to steady her. And his hands lingered, wanting nothing more than to whisk her away in private somewhere. She gripped his arms longer than necessary. Everywhere she touched tingled with awareness.

Channing approached, and his eyes widened in concern as he looked from one to the other.

Her face turned up to Stephen, a faint pink to her cheeks. "How clumsy of me."

"No, it was I, certainly. I was in a bit of a hurry."

"As was I."

Channing wiped his brow. "You most certainly were. I couldn't keep up. The moment the intermission began, she was out in the hall." His eyebrow rose, again eyeing the two of them.

"I'm thirsty." She shrugged.

Stephen turned. "This is Lady Fenningway."

She curtsied. Channing introduced Lady Catherine, and they all continued together to the lemonade. Stephen's arm brushed Lady Catherine's as the crowds pushed them closer together. He let his hand linger, and his fingers lingered over hers. She stared ahead, but the next time their hands brushed, she ran a few fingers across his palm.

Energy surged up his arm, his breath coming faster.

They approached the lemonade, and Lord Aster, her uncle, joined them. Lady Catherine stiffened beside him. Stephen turned to the detestable Lord Aster and nodded. "Aster."

He nodded in return, a barely perceptible lowering of his chin.

Lady Catherine looked from one to the other, fear in her eyes. Stephen couldn't understand that fear. Lord Aster raised his lemonade. "I hear congratulations are in order, and I applaud myself for standing here among all the happy couples."

Lady Catherine's face drained of all color. Stephen almost reached for her to catch a swoon, but Channing beat him to it. His arm wrapped around her waist, and the look of tenderness on his face disturbed Stephen in such a way that he considered shoving the man aside to stand in his place.

Lord Aster continued to talk, and Stephen paid closer attention. "And so I am pleased to announce the engagement of my niece, Lady Catherine Aster, to Lord Channing, son of the Duke of Halcor."

"What? Uncle, no." Lady Catherine would not meet Stephen's eyes. "We have not come to an agreement . . ." She allowed her voice to trail off as she looked at all the people around them.

Then Lord Aster raised his glass in Stephen's direction. "And this might be only slightly more premature than my first announcement. I hear congratulations will soon be in order for the two of you as well."

Stephen stood taller. "You forget yourself, Aster."

"Not any more than any Salsburys have in the past."

"Uncle." Lady Catherine's face was stricken. Stephen

wondered at the intense emotions tightening up around her eyes.

"Aster. You have made the ladies uncomfortable and clearly overstepped. No such agreements have been made, at least in our case." He searched Lady Catherine's face, hoping she might declare the same. But she just shrugged and stared at the floor.

Lord Aster's laugh chilled the area around Stephen. "Glad I could be the bearer of such welcome news." He downed his lemonade. "I believe they are calling us in after intermission."

Chapter Five

CATHERINE COULD BARELY wait to find her mother. How could Uncle start announcing courtships? Nothing had been decided. She felt as embarrassed for Channing as she did herself and then horrified at what Salsbury might think. She threw her things at Moorsby, picked up her feet, and ran to her mother's room. Knocking, she entered without waiting for a response. "Mother."

She sat in bed, the candles still lit at her side, a book in her hand. The peace on her face gave Catherine pause. Since the loss of Catherine's father, peace was a precious treasure for her mother. She walked more slowly, reconsidering what she could say.

Her mother patted the bed at her side, and Catherine climbed up to sit beside her. "What are you reading?"

"Our family journals." Her smile lit her face.

Curious, Catherine moved closer. "Really? What are you learning?"

She sighed, a great glow of happiness so foreign to her usual pinched face. "The story of my grandparents. They loved each other very much." Her smile was wistful. "And then I've been reading my letters from your father."

Grandparents. Perhaps they would have answers as to what happened with the Salsburys.

"Tell me the stories. Of our grandparents." She loved to hear them, all the fun family anecdotes passed down over the years, from the times before the Salsburys ruined their family memories.

Her mother patted her hand. "Another day. Now I want to read you some letters."

She read, "Dear Julianne." Her voice smiled while she read, and Catherine leaned her head back against the wall, listening. "You are my sun, my moon, and my stars all in one. Please ease my suffering and say you'll be mine before that weak-minded Salsbury even asks for your hand."

Catherine gasped. "Salsbury?" She widened her eyes.

Her mother nodded. "Yes, they both vied for my hand. And I flirted with the two of them, equally enamored. I suppose I loved them both, for different reasons." She sighed.

Catherine was left reeling. "Father and Salsbury both wanted to marry you?"

"They did. They courted me, both often visiting at the same time, competing to stay longer than the other." She giggled. "I received more flowers that month than I ever had."

Catherine could see nothing funny at all in the situation. "One was bound to be hurt when the other won your heart." She thought of the older Salsbury and for the first time felt a bit of pity for him. "Once Father convinced you he was the one..."

She sighed and shook her head. "It was Salsbury who convinced me."

"What?" Catherine didn't know what to say. "You preferred him to Father?"

"I did at last. But even after I explained that to both men, it was Aster who came for me. He said Salsbury had given up his suit." She read the paper again, folding it up and placing it in her box. "He never came calling any more after that. He dropped out of my life, leaving room for only Aster."

Catherine couldn't believe what she was hearing. "And Salsbury never forgave Father?"

"I don't imagine he did."

"Is that why they have done so many awful things to us all these years?"

"I fear it is they who have great reason to hate us."

"What?" Catherine was astounded at the thought. "But Uncle is always vilifying..."

"I know. He has his reasons too, I'd imagine." A great sadness filled her eyes, and Catherine regretted asking so many questions. "I'm sorry, Mother. Let's talk of something else."

"You must know the truth. Sometime I will tell you all." She leaned her head closer to Catherine. "Let me read you more."

"I met the Duke of Salsbury."

Her mother's hands stilled. "He is the image of his father." Her small voice held a lilt of yearning, and Catherine wondered how much and for how long she had preferred the previous Salsbury.

"Why must we hate them so?"

Her mother shifted between journals and pulled out an old and worn book, the leather scratched, the pages yellow. "Someday I will tell you. Is he ... a good man?" Her eyes searched Catherine's face.

"I think so."

She nodded, then waved her hand as if the discussion were over. She ran a hand up and down the old journal, as though it were precious to her.

Though Catherine waited, her mother would not speak more of it.

Chapter Six

FOUR DAYS PASSED before Stephen could again go to the park with Penelope. They always went early in the morning with the hopes of avoiding most everyone of high society. The existence of a Salsbury sister was known by only a few; the knowledge that she had some challenges and behaved in such a juvenile manner even at the age of nineteen was known by almost no one outside their family. He had never personally spoken of it to anyone but Lady Catherine. He shocked himself as the words came out of his mouth. But though that moment carried with it certain risks, he could not regret it. Even though she was an Aster.

They guarded the potential in their family line to birth such children as Penelope with a careful eye. If you looked at the family journals, it was obvious that every other generation claimed someone of questionable age and behavior. In the early years, unthinkable things happened to these relations. Sent off to live in solitude as wards was the most merciful thing he had read.

As he and Penelope made their way across the street to the expansive park, he shivered to think of what someone would do with Penelope in such a time. Even now, the gossip and tongue of the ton could be ruthless.

His eyes searched the snow-covered ground for Lady

Catherine. He had little hope she would come, especially since it had taken him so many days to return. If she held him in any kind of regard, what had she thought, all those days when he and Penelope had not come outside?

"Snow!" Penelope laughed as she reached down to grab a handful. She threw it up in the air, the soft powder falling all around her, lighting on her eyelashes.

"You will get all wet."

"Not wet. It's too cold." She reached down again and grabbed a handful as if to throw it above her head again but instead threw it in his face.

He coughed in surprise. Loud, musical laughter called out to them from across a small expanse of green between two trees. Lady Catherine ran to approach them. "Good throw, Penelope." When she stood at their front, her cheeks rosy, her eyes alight with energy, he had to resist a strong urge to swing her around in his arms in welcome. "Hello, Your Grace." She curtsied, her suddenly shy smile warming him.

"*Your Grace*, she says." He shook his head. "The woman who will agree to a dance with a stranger insists on calling me *Your Grace*."

"What would you like me to call you?"

A wicked idea nudged him. His interactions with Lady Catherine were already so clandestine, he longed to hear his name from her lips. "I'd love you to call me Stephen."

She gasped. "Surely not."

He tilted his head. "But as we don't know each other as well as I would like, would Salsbury do?"

She cringed.

"Salsbury carries with it a certain hesitance, does it not, given our ridiculous family situation?" He didn't have another suggestion, and he longed to hear his name on her lips.

She stepped closer, her expression pensive. "I wanted to

share something with you—something I learned—and to ask you a question."

He gestured to a bench. "Shall we sit?"

"No! No sit." Penelope put her hands on her hips. He had almost forgotten she was there.

Lady Catherine stepped toward her. "Oh Penelope! We are talking quite a bit, are we not?" She stooped to gather her own bit of snow. "Too much talk when we could be doing this!" She threw it up in the air above Stephen, and it fell all around him.

Penelope laughed and grabbed more.

"Oh no. You two. That's hardly fair."

"Fair. No fair, Stephen." Penelope threw snow over her shoulder at him as she ran away. He barreled after her until he heard the sought-after squeal of her laughter.

Lady Catherine's face lit with happiness.

He stopped, caught by it, the magic of her carefree joy filling him as a good snow at Christmastide would. He held out his hand. She took it, their gloved fingers interlocking. "Will you be in London over Christmastide?"

She nodded. "We will. Mother does not wish to travel."

He nodded. "Mine neither."

They paused a moment. Stephen assumed both in respect for the mourning of their mothers. Then he said, "I'm sorry for your mother's sorrow."

Her eyes misted. "And I yours. These past two years have been sad ones for both our houses, I would imagine."

He nodded.

Penelope began lifting piles of snow onto the bench. He turned to Catherine. "What did you want to tell me?"

She burned bright red, and he found her even lovelier.

"I . . . well . . . I came upon my mother reading old letters and journals." She stepped nearer to him, and as her big eyes widened further, he fought the desire to wrap his arms around her. "She said that your father desired her hand, that they were to marry at first."

His eyebrows raised. "Were they?" He had not heard. "I shall dig up what I can to find out what happened there."

"Would you? I cannot get any more information out of my mother. And I . . . I'm interested."

He lifted her chin. "As am I."

The air between them crackled, pulling them together. She leaned in. "When will I see you again?" Her face showed a touch of pain, and he considered the torture of the past four days.

"Perhaps I shall come call?"

Her face blanched. "You mustn't."

He shook his head. "This feud is not mine. I share no animosity for your family that others seem to cling to."

"My uncle."

"Is he always at home?"

"Whether he is or isn't doesn't signify. He rules the household. My brother, the duke, he is too young and hesitant to cross our father's brother."

"Then meet me here? Or at the opera?"

"We just went. And so many attend. People we may not wish to see." She looked down.

He remembered their uncomfortable conversation with her uncle. "Are you to be married?"

"No!" She cleared her throat. "Nothing has been decided, nothing discussed openly, except by my uncle the other night."

He felt an undeserved relief. He couldn't ask for her hand, not without alienating his family, not without bringing more Aster wrath and threats on them all. And yet he was happy things were still undecided between her and Channing.

"And Lady Fenningway?" Her small voice warmed him.

"I cannot abide the woman." He held up his hand. "I apologize for my abrupt manner. But we have nothing in common."

"But there are expectations." She looked away, her hand still in his.

"There are, yes. For you as well, I'd imagine." The hopelessness of their situation settled around him again, dropping the corners of his mouth. "And yet, I long to see you. I have made no promises. Shall we meet here again, as often as we are able?"

She nodded. "And, perhaps, the museum?"

His heart picked up. "Capital idea! Tomorrow?"

She grinned. "If I can manage it. I'll be there during the afternoon, after tea."

"Perhaps we shall come to an epiphany while admiring the great creative genius of our time."

"Perhaps." Her eyes, her countenance, her shoulders all seemed to droop for a moment, then she squeezed his hand and stepped away. "Penelope. What are we doing here?" She moved to help her collect snow for the pile she had gathered on the bench.

He watched the two of them, marveling at Lady Catherine's large and sweet heart, wondering how fate had smiled on him in such a way as to enable him to know her.

But the more he spent time with her, the more he watched her with Penelope, the more he wanted her in his life. As yet, he could find no easy way to court her, and the longer he waited, the more they each became entrenched in other entanglements. Perhaps the solution lay in the source of their family's age-old hatred for each other. The fact that his father had courted her mother, however unsuccessfully, gave him hope. He determined to discover those secrets that very night.

Chapter Seven

THE PACKET OF letters weighed his pocket as he and Lady Catherine moved through the museum together. Her maid followed behind. How could he tell her what he discovered? It had shattered him on behalf of his father, crushed him on behalf of his mother. Did his mother know the history? How could she have put on such a happy front all these years, knowing her husband loved another?

Lady Catherine kept glancing in his direction. Likely she sensed something in his quiet mood. Remarkable how connected they were, how connected he felt to her.

They moved to sit in a quiet room against the far wall. A large sculpture took up the space in the middle of the room and shielded them from many who would be walking by. He pulled the packet of letters out of his pocket.

Lady Catherine's eyes widened.

"I have made some discoveries."

Her eyes held concern along with the open curiosity that filled her face. "What? Tell me what you have learned."

"It is a sordid tale. Of sorts." He cleared his throat. "And a romantic one."

He enjoyed the sparkle in her eye even though it was clouded by hesitation, by the expectation of bad news.

"So, it turns out, my father did indeed love your mother."

Her eyes widened, and a delicious awkwardness settled between them, the kind created by two who had yet to disclose any sort of feelings for the other, feelings he suspected existed in her and he knew ran powerfully through him.

He rested a knuckle at the side of her face, allowing the moment to linger. "He writes of his feelings, pages and pages. The man was a terrible poet." He grimaced, and Lady Catherine laughed.

"Tell me. What happened between them?"

He looked out over the room. "My father and your mother arranged to meet. He was to come for her and ask for her hand. She waited for him at the back swing. I have a letter from her as well."

"From my mother?" she reached forward. "May I see it?"

"Of course." He handed her a well-worn piece of parchment, the fold lines rubbed bare, the words still visible, the handwriting fading.

My dear Jorge.

You never came. I risk much in writing you, but I must know if your feelings are still engaged. You seemed so distant at the musicale the other evening. It was as if we had not spent the past summers admitting what we have. I love you still, Jorge. If you are to continue with the plans we discussed, please ease my mind as to your feelings. I am left with a great deal of uncertainty regarding your many promises. Mother is pressuring me to make a decision. I am ever yours.

Amelia

"What?" Her hands shook. "What could this mean?"

"I have discovered the rest of the tale through my father's words in this old journal." He reached for her hand. The trembling made him wish to pull her into his arms. "It seems that on the very day they were to meet, the day my father would approach Amelia's father to ask for her hand, my father received a visit from a caller."

She squeezed his hand, a troubled expression crossing her face.

He regretted what he was about to say to her. "It seems His Grace Lord Aster had similar designs on your mother."

She grimaced. Then nodded.

"When my father was unmoved by his petition to allow him the opportunity to court her as well, for Salsbury to hold off on his proposal, Lord Aster turned angry and with many threats demanded that my father step aside. All of which my father ignored until your father mentioned Agatha."

"Agatha?" Her voice shook, and she cleared her throat.

He nodded. "My father's aunt. She is very much like Penelope. Every other generation, someone special is born into our family line."

Her eyes widened.

"And the knowledge is kept secret, especially for that particular generation, as they were certain to give birth to someone who might behave . . . might be . . ."

She moved her hand to his forearm. "It's all right. I understand."

"History was unkind to some of the past Salsburys, and there have been many who viewed these siblings as an embarrassment, a scandal, even. What family would want to unite with our bloodline, knowing a member might need Bedlam or worse?"

"No, Penelope would never need Bedlam." Her face pinched in pain.

Stephen warmed toward her even more. Her appreciation for Penelope showed a gentle and caring heart. "She would not, that is true, but for many generations, the treatment of the Salsburys with her condition has been suspicious and often unkind. Until my father. He wished for Agatha to live with him, to be a part of the family. His father and mother supported the idea, but as was wont to happen, knowledge of her existence and condition leaked out, and Aster became aware."

Lady Catherine dipped her head. "I don't know if I want to hear the rest."

Great sympathy filled him. "I don't have to continue." He waited.

She was silent. At length she said, "I fear I know what you are about to say. Keeping it from me does not make it untrue, though I wish it were. I need to know."

He wished to know what thoughts ran through her head. His sorrow grew. How dreadful to be the one to discover any bit of unpleasantness about another's family and especially to be the one to deliver the blow. He continued. "My father's journals claim that Aster threatened to reveal the family secret, to tell your mother what she would have to bear as a mother to a child like Agatha, like Penelope. He promised to shout it to the ton in the most negative terms if my father didn't immediately back away and withdraw his attentions."

Stephen's anger for Aster simmered just under the surface. When he had read the account last night, he punched the wall, anger coursing through him at the injustice dealt his father. But soon a sense of logic entered. His father had been happy in his marriage, with his family. And his mother had happily accepted the existence of Agatha and had loved, did love, Penelope with the fiery love of any mother. He received a great amount of peace in the happy turn for his father, for his family. But he didn't think his father had ever fully recovered from the loss of his first love.

"My father threatened yours so he could pursue my mother." She shook her head. "And all this time I thought the Salsburys were to blame."

He bristled. He couldn't help it. "For what?"

Her eyes flew to his.

His voice sounded sharper than he intended. "What could we have possibly done to you that hasn't been done ten times already to us at the Aster hand?"

She withdrew her hand. "Come now, we can't believe only the words of one journal, one person, to give a complete account. The Salsbury and Aster dislike began generations before our fathers." She stood.

He stood to join her. "But you can't possibly think the Salsburys have treated the Asters wrongly, even knowing the great extortion . . ."

"I'll think whatever I like. I'm surprised you would not even consider the possibility that Salsburys were to blame. No family is without fault." She choked on her words. "Perhaps it is time we leave." She walked in the direction of the exit.

Hurt she would doubt the word of his father in his own journal, he wanted to lash out as much as he wished she would stay. "Just like an Aster."

She stopped, turning to face him again. "What?"

"Feeding anger, creating discord." Perhaps there was more in her of her uncle than he had originally realized.

She began to walk away again and wiped at her eyes. "I'll ask for a hack to be called." She hurried from him.

His anger dissipated at the signs of her distress. He chased after, regretting his callousness. "No, wait. I'll see you home."

She didn't look at him, just nodded.

Their ride home with the maid present was oppressively silent. Every time he looked at her, she was angled firmly from him, her eyes focused downward. He thought of her almost engagement to Channing, of his duty to court Lady Fenningway, and of all the discord between their families. A wave of hopelessness filled him. From their first moments, dancing, he discovered a fascination with Lady Catherine that had not lessened over time. He could not imagine happiness with any other, knowing how strongly and with so little provocation his heart hammered for her.

"Lady Catherine, please."

She stiffened and then turned to him; the red-rimmed, hollow eyes struck him.

"It doesn't have to be this way."

She shrugged. "I don't know how else it could be. It's best to discover this unpleasantness now, before . . ." She didn't finish.

Perhaps she meant before her heart was engaged. He knew his already had been. But perhaps hers wasn't. They had hardly spent any time together.

And if he was talking sense, what did he know about her, really? She was an Aster. That enough gave him reason for distrust. He hadn't admitted it to her, but the anger for her father lingered. What a snake. So much like her uncle. Her brother seemed more malleable, less intractable, but what did he know about them? And how could he consider opening up a closer association with that family? How could he do that to Penelope, knowing what danger she would be in if Asters were to learn of her existence? He saw no reason to believe her uncle would be any nobler than her father had been.

He shook his head at the irony. He sat in the same position with a difficult choice that his father had before him, except he had avoided the attachment of an almost engagement. He should be grateful for an early warning to dissuade him from further risk and hurt, even potential disaster.

But Lady Catherine's stiff posture when she left his carriage tore at his insides.

Her last words, "Give my love to Penelope," nearly broke his resolve to let her go.

Watching the door close behind her, he suspected if they ever saw each other again, it would be with pretended disinterest. And he prayed his heart could endure the pain that thought created inside him. He rapped on the roof. It was time he started moving forward with his own duty: Lady Fenningway, or if not her, someone he thought would be a good fit for his ducal estate.

Chapter Eight

CATHERINE'S UNCLE STOOD at the top of the stairs when she entered. He didn't nod or greet her, just watched with his awful, narrowed eyes as she made her way past him down the hallway and entered her bedroom. She paced, uncomfortable with the hold her uncle had on them all. How could she live with her family name, knowing what she did? It was time to talk to her mother.

She exited through the servants' panel and made her way down the narrow, drafty hallway to her mother's room. She slid the panel aside to an angry uncle, bearing down on her mother.

"Leave her alone, Uncle." She wanted this man gone from their lives.

They turned to her, a moment of shock on his face, great lines of pain on her mother's. She said, "She deserves to know, Ethan."

"So she can run and tell all the family secrets to her new lover?" He turned on her. "How could you spend time with them? Have you no sense of loyalty, of family honor?"

"I know of no reason not to spend time with the Salsburys. Unless you are addressing the fact that my own father blackmailed the former duke into staying silent in his pursuit of my mother?"

She regretted her harsh delivery as soon as she heard her mother's gasp. "You know this?"

Catherine rushed to her mother, bearing her weight until she sat in the chair by the fire. "Yes, Mother, and you know it too, don't you?"

She whispered her response. "I suspected." She clung to Catherine. "Do you think me a coward?"

Confused, Catherine shook her head, "No, of course not, Mother."

Then she turned to her uncle. His face disgusted her. "What is it I must know?"

"You don't know what you ask. The burden is best borne by those of us who can bear it. Your job is to marry Channing and lead a happy life with a good family. Is that too much to ask?" For a moment, his eyes pleaded, and she saw the years of care he had given to the Aster name, saw that he believed himself to be doing the right thing by her and her family. But a crazed glimmer gave her pause, and she admitted to herself what years of suspicion and distrust had been trying to teach her. This uncle, Lord Aster, had his best interests in mind, truly disguised even to himself as watching over her family.

"Share your burdens, Uncle. It is my right to know. And my brother's as well."

He scoffed. "Your brother wouldn't know how to sully his hands with this. You either. Your mother is barely holding on to her small part. You all sit here enjoying the spoils of the Aster fortune while moving forward on the shadows and work of our dirty hands."

Her mother whimpered beside her, and she wrapped an arm over her shoulders. What could possibly be so dreadful? What dark secrets did the Aster family name keep? She waited. Her uncle stared her down.

He twitched.

Her mother was the one who at last spoke. "We live on blood money. We've preyed for years from the lives of the very Salsburys who we profess to hate."

Catherine sucked in her breath, looking to her uncle.

He laughed, a mirthless sound. It sent gooseflesh up her arms and down her neck. "Blood money. No one has died. Don't sound so maudlin."

"No one has died?" Her mother's face blanched. "Were you not the second? Did you not carry our lifeless Frederick back to us while the Salsbury father was returned to his home?"

"That was their idiotic manner in which to deal with the situation." He turned to Catherine. "The truth, Catherine, is that the Salsburys and the Asters have competed for years over the same piece of land in Jamaica, a sugar plantation."

"We own a plantation?"

That same laugh chilled her. "That's the question, now, isn't it? Who owns it? A bit of gambling gone wrong years ago between the late great Aster and the late great Salsbury. One says they won the bit of land; the other says they did not."

"Can we not share it?" Incredulous, she could not believe such a heated hatred could last over something so simple.

"Not when the Salsburys refuse the use of slaves."

Horrified, she shuddered. "Slaves?"

"Yes, how does that feel, knowing your gowns were purchased with slave money?"

Of a truth, she wished to shed the very garment she wore. "And the fathers, they dueled? To the death?"

"Over a matter of sale. They at last agreed on a sale of the property, but Salsbury, he demanded we free the slaves. They came to blows, your mother was mentioned, and then a challenge was issued. They met at dawn like the idiots they both were."

Her mother's breaths shook with each intake.

"And we keep pestering and hurting and tormenting the Salsburys over this matter of slaves?" She couldn't see anything at all amiss in the Salsbury behavior.

"Oh ho, their past is not the dove white you think it is. Is it?"

Her mother refused to look up.

Catherine stepped between them. "Whatever it is, I see no call for us to threaten Agatha the way Father did."

Uncle at last looked shaken. Perhaps he had a bit of a heart after all. "I had no choice. Your father, he would stop at nothing to have your mother. It was the kindest solution."

She fell back to her seat. Hearing of this side of her father hurt her more than she had admitted even to herself. "And now, must we continue to hurt them, to tear at their happiness? What of Penelope? Must we attack her now too? Let it go, Uncle. The plantation—"

Her uncle's eyes turned calculating when she mentioned Penelope, and she immediately regretted her words.

He said, "If we give away the slaves, we lose everything. Your father"—he ran a hand over his mostly bald head—"he gambled away our fortune."

"Then let it go." She shook her head.

His face reddened further. "So naïve. The Salsburys are doing everything they can to destroy our estate."

She turned away.

"Besides, it's not your decision. And if it were, the Aster name would be in ruin."

"As if it isn't already?"

Her mother and uncle refused to look at her.

He turned from them. "There, Mildred. She knows." He left the room, and a heavy chillness followed him. But in its place was a desolate hole, one she didn't know how to fill. And the truth of what she realized with her Salsbury sunk deeper. No matter how kind his eyes, hope for them together had fizzled into nothing.

But perhaps she could help her brother negotiate a better agreement about this plantation; perhaps she could do something to protect Penelope. With that in mind, she hugged her mother, rocking, making plans in her mind for how to fix what she could and how to live with what she couldn't fix. One thing for certain, she determined to make sure Penelope was out of reach of harmful speculation. They couldn't ship her off somewhere. That was too lonely, too cruel. She closed her eyes. Perhaps instead of shunning her, they could do the opposite, throw her into society, accept and admire her in front of the ton. She considered her idea and prayed she would be brave enough that Salsbury would see what she was trying to do and forgive her.

Chapter Nine

MANY OF THE top families, certainly all of the dukes still in London, attended one of the larger balls of the holidays together. Salsbury sat near Catherine, the sweet torture twisting her insides, happy fluttering competing with balls of dread. At one point in her life she would never have recognized the new duke of Salsbury but by family resemblance, and now that he was vital to her happiness but out of reach, he was everywhere.

She learned he had spent much of his time before his father's death at school at Cambridge, and her parents had gone to great lengths to avoid his family when he was in town. Consequently, she hadn't met him. They were polite enough now, but neither said more than was required. How could she approach him, knowing what her family had done to his, knowing how their fathers had behaved? The very knowledge of Aster behavior shamed her. She wouldn't know how to bring it up or discuss it even if she thought it would help. She was embarrassed of her reaction to Salsbury's earlier conversation, embarrassed she could not just apologize on behalf of her family. Did it matter what the Salsburys had done? What mattered to her was what her own father had done.

Her uncle and her mother both attended the party. Her brother was expected to arrive. It seemed a family reunion of sorts—all family members were in attendance as well as all the families of the dukes and earls who were in London during Christmastide. Surprisingly, many lingered in town this year. The yule log burned in the fireplace. They had played charades, sipped punch, and enjoyed readings of Shakespeare. Until that evening, she had nearly forgotten the holiday was upon them.

Everyone was talking about the upcoming Twelfth Night and Epiphany that a great friend of the prince regent, one Lord Timton Smithson, would host. All the dukes and their families and the royal dukes and their families were invited. A Duke's Christmas, he was calling it. They were to come to Carlton House and celebrate with His Highness.

Dinner seemed desolate but quiet. Catherine avoided conversation even with Lord Channing, who sat at her side. Salsbury seemed to be doing the same with Lady Fenningway also seated at his side. Then a ruffling disturbance fluttered at one end of the room. Conversation stopped in a wave as it approached her. She craned her neck to see what was causing such a shift in attention. Then her heart went into her throat. She stood quickly, her chair tipping over behind her. Penelope wandered into the room, Catherine's uncle not far behind. She played with the feathers on the ladies' turbans as she passed. Whispers sounded in a great rush of rain as soon as she passed.

"Friend!" Penelope shouted when she saw Catherine. She ran to her. "Uncle said you would be here."

Salsbury rushed to Penelope, his face tightened, his eyes stony. He wrapped his arm around his sister's shoulders. "Come, sweet. Let's go see what Cook has in the kitchen."

But Penelope stiffened. "No! I want to see my friend."

Catherine hurried to her side. "I'm here. Hello, Penelope. Let's find Cook like Salsbury said."

"Salsbury? Who's Salsbury?" She giggled.

"Stephen." She corrected and savored the name on her lips. They started to move away, Salsbury's calm and patient exterior belying the fast rhythm beating on his neck.

Uncle's sneering voice called from behind them. "Behold the Salsbury sister."

A few ladies sucked in their breath.

"Oh yes, he keeps her hidden away. Embarrassed, are you, Salsbury?"

Stephen stiffened beside her, but to his credit he kept a steady stream of conversation with Penelope.

Catherine whispered to Stephen, "I'm so sorry." She showed his sister a bracelet. "Look, Penelope. So pretty."

When Catherine caught his eye, Salsbury glared, furious. She shrunk, swallowing, and would have stepped away into the nearest hallway were it not for Penelope clinging to her arm.

They made their way out into the hall, and a carriage was called. Forward-thinking servants had it ready much more quickly than she thought possible. Catherine waited awkwardly, talking with Penelope until they moved to leave. "Can I help you into the carriage, my friend?" She grabbed hold of Penelope's arm.

Salsbury barred her way, wrapping his arm across his sister's shoulder. "You've done enough already. Leave. Us. Alone." They entered with only a half-hearted calling out for "friend," from Penelope to wrench in Catherine's heart. And then the carriage departed.

Catherine could not face the guests for the rest of dinner. She called for her carriage as well, not caring what her uncle managed for his ride home. She didn't know if she could face anyone ever again.

Any sliver of hope she harbored that perhaps she and the

duke could overcome the difficulties between them shriveled up with his glare. He hated her. And, as guilt tore at her, she realized he had good reason. She had behaved as every other Aster had to his family by carelessly sharing the name and existence of a sister, setting Penelope up for mockery and disdain to the very man who would deliver such cruelty. Salsbury was rightfully furious.

The more she thought on the evening, the more agitated she became. Pacing in her room, Catherine could scream at the audacity of her uncle. She would pen a letter to her brother straightaway, right after she sent off this one to Stephen. Was Gregory not the duke? Could they not cast Lord Aster from their immediate lives, ask him to go stay at another Aster holding?

Her uncle's words about their financial state concerned her. Could they be out of money? Had her father and his before him lost everything? She couldn't believe it. And she suspected her uncle preyed on her perceived naïveté and lied to her.

She would speak to the steward right after she paid a visit to Penelope Salsbury.

She had many things to coordinate before Twelfth Night at Carlton House. But she was determined to make one thing right, if that's all she ever did as an Aster.

Chapter Ten

STEPHEN HAD NEVER felt more betrayed. He watched as Penelope drew pictures. She was surprisingly adept with her charcoals, and the activity calmed her when she might otherwise be excitable.

Asters were of the devil. He should have listened to his mother and the decades of Salsburys behind him. After grilling the staff, he learned that, although no one knew for certain, apparently while Penelope was outside in her gardens, Lord Aster lured her away with the promise he would take her to Lady Catherine. What a wretched trick.

He watched his sister, but Penelope did not seem worse for having visited a ball. In fact, she quite enjoyed it and was drawing a girl in a pretty gown right now.

"I want to dance." She waved her hand in the air with a flourish.

"Shall we?" He stood, and she jumped up.

"Yes! Oh yes."

She had been taught to dance, and she was quite good at a few of the reels and line dances, and she could adequately perform the waltz. Really, what harm could there be in bringing her out in society? She loved it so much.

The reaction of others. He reminded himself how cruel people could be. But if handled appropriately, with great care, with the ducal name behind her, Penelope could have a positive social experience. The only event left of the holidays was a great Twelfth Night dinner at Carlton House, hosted by that eccentric, Lord Smithson. He shook his head. They needed something smaller.

A servant stood at the entrance to the family sitting room.

"Enter."

The maid curtsied and delivered a note into his hands. "They said it was important, from the house of Aster."

His eyes narrowed, but he thanked the maid and then tore it open.

Stephen, it is just I. Please know I had nothing to do with Penelope's visit to the ball this evening. I would never betray her in such a manner. I suspect Uncle heard me let slip her name once when I decried everything that had transpired with the Agatha situation. Her name and yours are safe with me, though I cannot guarantee the same from my detestable uncle. He seems bound and determined for Salsbury misery, and for that, I much belatedly apologize on behalf of all the rest of the Asters who wish you every peace and happiness.

Yours,

Catherine

If we are going to do something so scandalous as send notes, I feel we have now earned the right to use first names. I hope you don't mind.

Chapter Eleven

THE PRINCE REGENT had outdone himself on behalf of his friend. Catherine had never seen so much greenery or mistletoe. Already, upon entering the hallways leading to the great dining room, she had seen five quite scandalous kisses under boughs of mistletoe. She shook her head. The ladies at Almack's would be shocked. A few would likely be in attendance.

Penelope only laughed at the exorbitant displays of affection. She walked with such beautiful decorum, Catherine could only smile. But her insides quaked at what Stephen would do when he saw them arrive. But no matter, she would make amends for the awful manner in which the Asters had treated the Salsbury family. She would introduce Penelope in society in such a way they would have to love her or be thought less of. She swallowed. At least, that was the hope. Luckily the prince was in agreement. He said the feud between two of his ducal families was a nuisance. He said he would do whatever it took to get the blasted Asters and Salsburys to agree on something.

Catherine wrapped an arm across Penelope's shoulder. "You look lovely."

Penelope held her head up higher. "Thank you."

Catherine smiled. "You know, here, they must all call you *Lady Penelope.*"

They stood at the entrance to the dining hall. Fires raged in both hearths. The room felt warm and cozy. She knew all ducal families to be invited as well as others of Prinny's set, the wilder bunch from the looks of them. She looked away from a man who pulled a finely dressed lady onto his lap. Giggling, she rose quickly, but Catherine knew the night would progress in a similar manner. She took a deep, fortifying breath, telling herself over and over this was a good idea. She gave their names to the footman.

Stephen searched the room for Lady Catherine. He couldn't resist her no matter what her family had done, no matter how angry he had felt. Once he had decided that he would try to bring Penelope out in society more, he could hardly fault Catherine for Penelope's presence the other night. Her letter showed true intentions in her heart. He was much relieved to receive it, yearning as he had to see her again.

A pang of guilt nudged him. He understood his father's angst, his desire to at last drive the Asters to the ground. That was one reason for the alliance with the Fenningways.

Once his father had learned that the Aster estate was suffering, he knew the power the Salsburys had over them with their joint ownership of the plantation. Stephen knew that with just a few more years and a hold-out of sale on the property, the Asters would be no more. They would have to sell the estate piece by piece. What's more, his father had been buying up the Aster debt in secret. And it was now in Stephen's power to complete the plan his father set in place years ago.

And he would have, without qualms, had he not met Lady Catherine.

The master of ceremonies called out, "Lady Catherine Aster and Lady Penelope Salsbury."

He almost ran into the couple in front of him, who stopped still at the announcement and stared at the ladies as they entered the room. Everyone around him had turned their attention to the entrance. His sister and Lady Catherine stood at the head of the room, grinning to each other as though they were pleased to suddenly be the center of attention.

He moved toward them. They probably were pleased. He shook his head. Yesterday, this brazen act by Lady Catherine would have infuriated him, but now he just admired her bravery.

He arrived in time to hear Catherine say, "Look, Penelope. Smile at all our new friends."

Penelope did and nodded her head in the most regal way.

"Well done. You look like the duke's daughter you are."

She giggled. "This is fun."

Catherine squeezed her hand. "Let's find our table, shall we?"

"Stephen!" Penelope called out. Those nearest heard and raised eyebrows, but nothing more. Everyone could expect much more shocking behavior from others as the night progressed.

Penelope closed the distance between them. "Catherine has brought me to the prince's house. We are here for the dinner."

Salsbury bowed over her hand. "You look lovely, Penelope."

She curtsied. "Thank you." Then she giggled again in her hands and whispered, "This is fun!"

He turned to Catherine, eyes full of questions.

"She wanted to come."

He grunted. "And you had nothing to do with it?" He could not let her get away with so brazen an act without his permission.

"Well, I might have had a few things to do with it."

"She helped me do my hair." Penelope turned so that they might see it.

"You hair is beautiful, and that's the truth." He offered his elbows so that they each might take one. Then, for Lady Catherine's ears only, he said, "This is risky. I can't know what you were thinking. A smaller dinner might have been better."

"So you aren't furious?"

"I might be furious." He teased.

She faltered. "I wanted to do this for you. To make up for my awful family."

Then his face broke into a smile, and he winked. "I'm actually quite pleased with the situation." He enjoyed the sudden relief that played across her features.

"You are?" Her eyes showed such a large amount of hope, he almost pulled her to his chest.

"I thought of something similar just last night." He approach their chairs. "Looks to me that we are not sitting together." He turned to his sister. "But you will be by Lady Catherine." She smiled so large that he grinned. He held out her chair and then Catherine's in turn. "I'm just up the table." He pointed and looked meaningfully at Catherine until she blushed and looked away.

Catherine introduced Penelope to everyone near them. They looked curiously on at her overexuberance but otherwise seemed to accept her presence. Stephen assumed many had heard of her entrance with Lord Aster the other evening. Stephen sat farther back in his chair, let his shoulders relax, and ate a few bites of food. Perhaps this would all work out better than he hoped.

After a delicious dinner, servants served slices of the cake, the yearly cake of Twelfth Night. And Lord Smithson announced a game. "The pea and the bean are hiding in someone's slice of cake, and one belongs with the other. We all know that. A waltz for the lucky couple, and I will join you."

Excited murmurs filled the room as people picked at their cake, looking for a hidden treasure.

Stephen kept his eye on Penelope, counting the seconds until someone else had the small legume in their cake, someone besides his sister.

Then the lady next to her shouted. "She's got it! She's found the pea."

Everyone clapped, and Lady Catherine stood.

Stephen let out all the air in his chest and sat back in relief.

Lord Smithson gestured that she come forward.

"Wait here," she told Penelope.

Lord Smithson rubbed his hands together with a huge smile. "Now, who will join Lady Catherine?"

A long, weighty silence filled the room, and when no one shouted out, a wild feeling of possibility energized Stephen. He dug into his cake, mashing through it with his fork until it looked more like a great nondescript pile. And then his fork hit something solid.

"I have the bean." He shouted, happier about this turn of circumstances than any other.

His mother gasped nearby, and Catherine's uncle likely fumed wherever he sat. But Stephen had never been happier but for one thing. Penelope. He could not leave her to sit alone.

Lord Smithson called out. "Come now, we haven't got all night. I promise, Salsbury, Lady Catherine is quite lovely up close."

A low rumble of laughter rolled through the room.

"While he is making his way *slowly* up to the front, I would like to announce my choice of a dance partner this evening. May I introduce Lady Penelope Salsbury."

Penelope stood as though she had won the grandest prize of all, clapping and squealing and running to the front.

Lord Smithson continued, "This exquisite beauty has the heart of a child. And she will always be welcome in any of the homes that I would care to visit." His gaze traveled across the room, and then he smiled at Penelope. "Would you like to dance, my lady?"

She giggled in her hands and then widened her eyes. She glanced at Catherine and then stood taller and executed a low and graceful curtsy. "I would be delighted."

The room responded with pleased chuckles, and a huge wave of relief filled Salsbury. Penelope would be accepted. For now.

"What a ridiculous show of sentimentality." Lord Aster's voice scratched through him like a horsehair brush. "Lady Catherine is already spoken for." The hairs on the back of Stephen's neck stood on end as a rush of anger rolled through him. Salsbury had had enough.

Lord Aster continued in his nasally voice. "Now is as good as time as any, I suppose, to announce our happy news. She is engaged to be married—"

Stephen stepped forward. "I don't know how that could be when she told me herself she was not spoken for. I am thinking of asking for her hand myself."

Lady Catherine gasped and held a hand to her mouth, tears welling in her eyes. Stephen hoped that boded well for him and not the opposite.

Lord Smithson placed a hand on Stephen's shoulder. "I have it on the best authority, she would be pleased with that arrangement."

Then she blushed a brilliant shade of red.

"But her guardian—"

"He supports the suit completely. Now come, man, you

are dampening the joy of the evening more the longer you stand there making noise with your mouth." He clapped his hands, and the music began.

Lord Smithson led a very proper-looking Penelope out onto a cleared area of the floor.

Stephen pulled Catherine close to him, wrapping his arm around her back. "We've created quite a stir."

"We would, wouldn't we?"

"But we've been introduced." He raised an eyebrow. "I'm certain of it this time."

She nodded. "I'll give you that." She waited, and he could tell she expected more from him.

He chuckled.

Then she huffed out a breath. "You mentioned something to the room..."

Then he let his face break into the grin he had been hiding. "To think, this all began with your dance with a stranger. Just think if I hadn't made the best mistake of my life." He raised her hand to his lips. "You've made me the happiest of men. Thank you for protecting Penelope as you have. She is now safe from censure." Penelope's giggle carried over to them. "And happy as I've ever seen her."

"It was the least I could do. I wish to repair some of the damage done to your family by mine." She looked down. "I don't know how you can abide being near me."

He waited until she looked back up into his face. "My dear Catherine. What I cannot abide is being apart from you."

She sucked in a breath and widened her eyes.

He loved that he could create such a reaction. "I meant what I announced to your odious uncle. I wish to try and win your hand, to court... and marry you." He cleared his throat, suddenly unsure. "If you'll have me." A moment of insecurity filled him. She would have to deal with unpleasantness, a possibly large amount of difficulty. They would both be faced with family obstacles. But he would never be happy if they didn't try. "I love you, Catherine. I can't live without you by my side. Please, marry me?"

Her mouth twitched, and she closed her eyes. His heart sank. He couldn't tell if her response was positive. He waited, trying to decipher her expression, leading them gently in the waltz. She waited so long, he began to worry. But when she opened her eyes, their brilliant depths were filled with joy. She said, "Yes, I would love to marry you. Come call at my house, sit in my parlor, and disturb all and sundry. Stephen. I love you too."

He thrilled to hear it, and with the racing of his heart, he pulled her up against him, her lovely laugh filling the air around them. Then he kissed her. He pressed his lips to hers with all the intensity he dared with the whole party looking on. And when he and Catherine pulled apart, everyone cheered.

They stepped apart, and she curtsied and he bowed, which brought more laughs. Then Prinny called out, "They're engaged!"

As the dinner party was nearing a close, a fuming Lord Aster asked to speak with them both. "I absolutely refuse this union. You do not have my permission."

Lady Catherine stared at the man who used to rule her life. "I don't need your permission, Uncle."

Stephen squeezed her hand. "But we would like his blessing, would we not?"

She couldn't imagine why she'd care, but something in Stephen's eyes gave her pause, so she stayed silent.

He reached into an inside pocket and pulled out a stack

of papers. "I have here several reasons why you might want to consider our union a happy alternative."

Her uncle's eyes narrowed. "Alternative?"

He started reading each slip of paper. "Lord Atwater over a matter of two thousand pounds."

Lord Aster's face paled.

"What is this, Uncle?"

"Lord Smelling, fifty pounds. Lord Tellington, one hundred pounds." Stephen shuffled through the stack. "Some in here are quite significant, some small, but rest assured, Lord Aster, I own them all."

Lord Aster stood taller and fisted his hands. "You bought up our debts." Then he sneered. "Seems fitting. You should have to lose so much to get the wife you desire, the Salsbury way, is it not? To lose out." His smug and calculating manner made Catherine's shoulders tighten in anger. How could he be so brazen when the future of the Aster estate rested in Stephen's hands?

She stepped nearer to Stephen. "Why don't we assume all the Aster assets and combine them into our own Salsbury estate?"

"We could." Stephen tapped the pile in his hand and then placed it back into his inside pocket. "Though who would the Salsburys be if we didn't have our rivals the Asters to contend with? At the very least, I do feel there is one Aster we could all do without." He pulled a different paper out of his pocket. "I have proof of your nefarious and illegal dealings in the matter of the Jamaica plantation and with regards to several of your other dealings of late. I don't plan to press charges if I don't have to see your face too often."

Her uncle fumed. The tips of his ears were almost purple. But he remained silent for several moments. And then, through clenched teeth, he said. "And just where would you like me to go?"

"Don't you have a holding in Wales somewhere? Perhaps you could spend the remainder of your days managing that property. I will have a steward come check in with you to keep things on the up and up, of course."

Her uncle nodded his head and turned from them. His stiff gait spoke of his great restraint as he made his way through the crowded room. When he had turned the corner and was out of sight, Catherine let her shoulders relax. "Oh Stephen, you were wonderful! How did you accomplish such a thing?"

His face clouded with guilt. "It was my father. I'm afraid he has been planning for that moment, the demise of the Aster estate, for many decades."

Her heart pinched, but she could feel only gratitude, thankful for this magnanimous man in her life. "Will you simply acquire all the properties?" She could only feel pleased that she and her husband would be managing her family's situation.

He stared out across the room, then he turned to her with a new light in his eyes. "I think your brother deserves a chance to make his mark and our two families to make things right between us."

"What?"

His eyes had travelled up above her and watched something across the room.

Her heart skipped as her brother made his way to them and held out his hand. Watching the Aster duke and the Salsbury duke shake hands, she held a hand at her heart, hardly believing such a thing was possible. Then those nearby began clapping their hands, joined by others as the news spread until the room was filled with applause, Penelope's loudest of all.

An award-winning author, including the GOLD in Foreword INDIES Book of the Year Awards, **Jen Geigle Johnson** discovered her passion for England while kayaking on the Thames near London as a young teenager. She still finds the great old manors and castles in England fascinating and loves to share bits of history that might otherwise be forgotten. Whether set in Regency England, the French Revolution, or Colonial America, her romance novels are much like life is supposed to be: full of brave heroes, strong heroines, and stirring adventures.

Follow her at JenGeigleJohnson.com
Twitter:@authorjen
Instagram: @authorlyjen

Mistletoe at Willowsmeade

ANNETTE LYON

Chapter One

"Do you think we'll have snow for Christmas?" Suzanne asked, looking up from her book in the nursery.

"No, silly. There are no storm clouds in the sky," her brother Thomas said. "The chances of snow by tomorrow are awfully small." Clearly, as a boy of eleven, in his first year of boarding school, he knew much more of the world than a girl of a mere eight years.

"I know all of that," Suzanne declared in her most exasperated voice, tossing her walnut-colored braid over one shoulder. "But one may still wonder and wish. *You* don't know everything, including the future."

She had him on that point, at least. For the moment, Thomas appeared debated into silence. Not even he, nearly a man—or so he thought, apparently—could argue that he knew the future.

From the window seat, Eleanor Hadfield, governess of the Brunson family, smiled to herself. She'd spent the last fifteen minutes in quiet reading, an activity the children were supposed to have been engaged in as well. On most days, her charges consisted of the three young Brunson girls, but now their two elder brothers were home from school for the holidays. Suzanne's question made Eleanor gaze out the window and wonder about snow on Christmas Day as well.

November and the first half of December had certainly seen several cold snaps, but no real snow yet.

Thomas appeared before the window seat, apparently done with his reading of *A Pilgrim's Progress*, if he'd ever begun it, which was rather doubtful. He peered past Eleanor, searching the landscape.

"Looking for something?" she asked, leaning to the side to accommodate his unmannerly usurpation of the space.

"For *someone*, actually," he said, straightening. Thomas clasped his hands behind his back in the manner he'd surely seen from both his father and grandfather. "I'm eager to see the men returning with the Yule log."

Five-year-old Kate's head popped up from her primer. "The Yule log is coming today?" She dropped the primer to the table and shook her chubby little fists excitedly. "Does that mean it's almost time to eat the plum pudding? We've been waiting ever so long." This last statement was spoken with the tone of a weary eighty-year-old.

Oh, how Eleanor loved these sweet children. They embraced the world and everything in it, and firmly believed that a child was every bit as important as an adult. Society rarely gave children much notice and certainly gave no stock to what they said or did. But Eleanor nurtured in them the belief that they did matter, that they could seek after *and* find the things they dreamed of.

The rest of the world seemed determined to crush children's souls and dreams, to stop them from dreaming, and instead make them wake up to reality. But Eleanor refused to be complicit in teaching such worldly lessons. Better to arm a child with happiness and dreams rather than drag them into a sad "reality" at a young age.

"The Yule log," Eleanor began, "is brought into the house and lit on Christmas Eve—"

"I know!" Suzanne said. "That is also why the maids have been decorating the house with greenery, isn't it?"

"It is indeed," Eleanor said. "That's another sign of Christmas Eve." She pointed a finger toward Suzanne. "But you shouldn't have interrupted, my dear."

The girl looked properly admonished as she nodded, folding her hands in her lap and crossing her ankles like a proper young lady all in the same motion. Thomas gave her a haughty look, as if pleased to hear his sister admonished by the governess. The sight sent Eleanor's mouth twitching with a laugh she had to work at holding back. She remembered what it felt like to be laughed at by adults, and she would not do that to her charges.

She savored every day of their learning and discovery and development because at two and thirty, Eleanor knew quite well that the fates would not be sending her own children to be borne and reared. Becoming a mother would require a husband, and women who'd been given the designation of an old maid a decade hence didn't find husbands.

She didn't pine or worry over the simple facts. She had a life much easier than many unmarried women her age. She had much to be grateful for. Therefore, each day, she chose to thoroughly enjoy her position as governess and to teach them the things she would wish her own children would learn, if she'd ever had any.

"Tomorrow, we will indeed eat the plum pudding as part of the Christmas feast," she said, finally answering Kate's original question.

Gazing out the window, Thomas sighed.

"Something weighing on your mind?" Eleanor asked.

"Not exactly." He shrugged and sighed again. "I just wonder how many more years it will be before I can go along to fetch the Yule log."

"It's hard to be seen as too young," Eleanor said, rising and placing an arm about his shoulders. *In my case, I'm seen as too old,* she thought. But again, she'd made peace with the reality. She wanted to help Thomas make peace with being too young, a struggle for her because he wouldn't remain too young. All too soon, he'd be fully grown.

"Father won't let me go on the fox hunt either."

"He will soon, I'm sure of it."

"I hope you're right." Thomas sat on the window seat and stared out the window again.

She patted his shoulder and crossed the room to Suzanne and Kate as the door opened to reveal the eldest of the Brunson children, Andrew.

"It's here!" he announced.

At once, Eleanor and the children, including three-year-old Emma, looked to the window.

"You won't see them out there," Andrew said, sauntering into the room as if he felt that he, like his younger brother, had long-since outgrown the nursery. "They've brought the log into the ballroom, and they're about to light it. I've been sent to fetch the children."

He turned about and left with the air of one having completed a mission in a foreign land. Eleanor chuckled at the thought; he'd spent many a day in this very nursery, and not all that long ago either.

She clapped and announced the need to tidy the nursery before they could go down to participate in the festivities. As she put a few books back on their shelf, she thought of Andrew's superior manner. If he needed to be taken down a peg or two, she could certainly remind him that he had not yet been deemed old enough for the fox hunt this year either. But she'd wait to have that discussion with him in private.

She recalled all too well the feeling of being called to task before her elders, usually at the hand of the late Mr. Brunson, the uncle who'd taken her in when she was orphaned. He gave her a roof over her head, yes, but he'd never treated her as anything but an interloper. Fortunately, his son, the current Mr. Brunson, did not take after his father, which was precisely why Eleanor agreed to return to Willowsmeade as governess.

Most of the year, the boys were at school, but when they came home for holidays, their mother tended to come down with various ailments of a nervous nature, often complaining of the noise and chaos.

At such times, Eleanor cared for the boys as well as the girls. It was the least she could do for their father, who, though Eleanor thought of and referred to him as Mr. Brunson now, had as her cousin once been almost a brother, who, when she'd come to live here after her parents died of cholera, both teased and fiercely protected her as if she were his sister. When she'd been but eight—the same as Suzanne now—he was known to her simply as Henry.

In truth, she still had days when hearing "Mr. Brunson" recalled to her mind the severe, selfish man who'd reluctantly taken in his orphaned niece. He'd treated her harshly, as if she were the one who'd lost a fortune rather than her father, who'd speculated his wealth away. She had to remind herself that now, the name referred to the father of these children, her dear cousin Henry, who'd offered her a position at Willowsmeade when she refused to be taken in on charity.

After her one failed Season, the elder Mr. Brunson had—reluctantly—paid for some schooling that enabled her to find employment. He'd done so entirely thanks to Henry, who'd argued in the only manner his father cared about: that without an education, Eleanor would be a drain on his household. Not so if she could support herself. A modest education for her would be a sound investment for Willowsmeade.

Thank the stars for Henry's interference. He'd secured for her the education that had allowed her to live in some comfort as a governess in two other households, until Henry brought her back after his father's death. If not for Henry, she might have ended up on the streets, starving, sick . . . perhaps dead.

She had dreams of her own—to be independent, to live on her own one day—and she saved every penny she could to that end. Henry insisted that so long as he breathed, she would have a home at Willowsmeade, that she could live in the dowager cottage on the estate if she so chose. Perhaps she would move into the cottage years hence, when she'd grown too old to manage rambunctious children—perhaps after being governess to Andrew's children—but for now, she would earn her keep through honest work.

At last Eleanor declared the nursery tidy enough for them to venture down to the ballroom, but she insisted they line up first and listen to her reminders about behaving properly in the company of adults. When she had their promise of good behavior, she led the way through the door and along the corridor. Little Emma lagged behind, so Eleanor scooped her up and carried the girl on her hip.

Thomas didn't trail behind as he'd done several years ago, when she first joined the household. Instead, he walked nearly abreast to Eleanor—one more sign, she supposed, that he viewed himself as her equal.

Or my superior, she thought realistically. *Despite the fact that I am old enough to be his mother.*

"I can hardly wait for the plum pudding tomorrow," he said. "Why does it have to be at the *end* of the Christmas feast?"

"I had no idea you were so partial to plum pudding," Eleanor said as she smoothed back a bit of Emma's hair from her face.

"Oh, it's not the pudding itself I'm partial to," Thomas said.

Eleanor could sense he was deliberately leading the conversation, but where to, she did not know, and she hadn't any idea whether the destination was a trap he was hoping to horrify her with or something entirely innocent. "If it's not the plum pudding you anticipate, what is it, then?"

The boy's step came up short right before they descended the staircase. Eleanor turned to him, curious yet dreading what he was about to say. "I cannot wait until it's brought into the room *on fire.*" He nearly whispered the final two words, but he said them leaning close, his eyes wide with excitement.

Of course the boy's favorite part of Christmastide was a flaming dessert. She should have guessed. He grinned and raised his brows, waiting for her response.

"I can see why you would find that thrilling," she said, striving for the same tone she'd use when discussing a matter of grave importance. Biting back chuckles around the boys was becoming harder and harder. At this rate, she'd be laughing outright well before they returned to school.

Thomas nodded, wearing a silly grin, which contained a few gaps as well as too-large teeth that weren't fully grown in. "I'm going to ask Papa if Julian can light it this year. I'm sure he'd drench it with more brandy than Papa does, so the flame would be bigger—maybe higher than my head!"

With that, Thomas trotted ahead down the stairs, leaving Eleanor and the girls standing atop the first step, staring after him.

Julian.

The name rang in her mind over and over like the bells on a church, only it didn't stop at twelve times. She'd heard his name spoken only now and again, and not at all of late. Whether Henry spoke of Julian often when she wasn't in his company, she didn't know. As for herself, Eleanor never mentioned him and hadn't since he left Willowsmeade for war and she left for her one Season in London.

There had been a time when she'd thought Julian Stephens would always be part of her life. He'd been part of her heart from the day she'd crossed the threshold at Willowsmeade as a young girl. Just as Henry had been her playmate, so had Julian, the gardener's son, even though he was two years older than Henry.

Julian used to say that she was above his station, and that when he returned from the navy, she'd be a duchess or some such. He was wrong. The few times she'd heard Henry—rather, Mr. Brunson—talking of Julian had told her that he'd risen through the naval ranks quickly and even had his own ship. He was Captain Stephens now, while she was still an orphan with no dowry and a father who'd squandered their name. The one thing she'd had that could attract a man—her youth—was long-since lost.

Perhaps Thomas is mistaken, and Julian is not coming for the holiday. Somehow, her feet regained the capacity of movement, and she led the girls down the stairs. She took each step slowly in hopes of not making her heart race any faster than it already was.

The only Christmas guests she'd heard mention of were the Edgleys, who'd arrived in time for Advent, more than a fortnight ago. Guests did not generally arrive as late as Christmas Eve. Surely Mr. Brunson would have mentioned the possibility to the servants, and if she'd missed the announcement, it wouldn't have been for long, as the older servants who'd known Julian since boyhood would have been abuzz with the news.

Eleanor took a deep breath, easing her racing pulse. She had no reason to think that the boy who'd once said he'd return to her after he'd made something of himself was actually here.

That is, she had no reason to think so until they approached the ballroom door, and laughter poured into the corridor.

Including the one laugh Eleanor Hadfield would never, ever forget.

Julian had come to Willowsmeade.

Chapter Two

"It's been far too long, old chap," Henry said to Julian as they lugged the massive Yule log into place with help from a couple of male servants. With a few more pushes and pulls, the log was positioned just so in the massive ballroom fireplace.

Julian wiped his gloves against each other to get off any remaining soil, lichen, and twig pieces. "Too bad my arrival wasn't one hour later," he told Henry. "I could have avoided the physical labor."

"We both know your otherwise plain visage is enhanced by physical exertion." Henry gave a pretended sad shake of his head. He came over and placed a sympathetic hand on Julian's shoulder. Henry's mouth twitched, a clear tell that he was on the verge of laughter. "If you are to ever woo a woman to be your wife and end your miserable bachelorhood, you'll need all the aid the world can provide. This bit of labor brought a handsome flush to your cheeks, for which you may thank me later."

The two laughed and slapped each other on the back. When they pulled apart, Julian shook his head, still grinning. "It's good to be back, though it's strange to think of *you* as the master of the house."

Henry laughed from his belly at that. "Am I not brooding

and suspicious? I can certainly work on those qualities, though I never aspired to take after my father."

"I was thinking more of the pranks you used to play and blame me for," Julian said.

"But I still got the whippings, if you recall," Henry countered. "Somehow, he trusted the gardener's son more than his own flesh and blood."

Something Julian would always be grateful to the grumpy old man for. Without the former Mr. Brunson's approval of Julian, the two boys would never have interacted, let alone been like brothers, and he wouldn't have had a career in the navy either.

"You must visit sooner next time," Henry said. His voice held a note of something more serious, almost melancholy, as if he'd truly missed his friend.

Julian's heart was touched, and a bit of emotion suddenly stuck in his throat. With the servants who'd helped with the log still nearby and plenty of others dressing the ballroom and the rest of the house in the customary Christmas Eve greenery, he wished to keep his private emotions out of public scrutiny. He cleared his throat and turned back to the fireplace, preparing to ask about the remaining piece of last year's log, with which this year's would be kindled.

Before he could get a word out, however, several pairs of footsteps sounded in the corridor as a group entered the room. Julian and Henry turned in unison, the latter with an expectant expression.

Several of the Brunson children ran in—Julian never could remember how many Henry had now, let alone their names—calling "Papa! Papa!" and "The Yule log!"

Henry bent his knees and held out his arms, only to be half bowled over by his children a moment later as they swarmed him, throwing their arms about him—neck, arms, torso. There seemed to be childlike arms just about everywhere.

"Happy Christmas, children," Henry said after regaining his balance. He hugged each child, tousled the hair of the two boys, and turned toward the big, dried-out tree trunk. Henry gestured toward the log. "Isn't it beautiful?"

"Breathtaking," Julian murmured quietly. But he hadn't turned to the fireplace, and the object of his admiration wasn't the log. He yet faced the ballroom door.

There he saw a woman with one more child on her hip. A ladder stood beside her, and Julian couldn't help but notice that on it, a servant worked to hang a bough of mistletoe to a chandelier. Right above her head.

Julian stared at her with disbelieving eyes, for the moment seemed like a dream. Was it possible that Eleanor stood before him?

I did not know she had a child. She probably has several. And a husband, of course.

Blast Henry for not mentioning that Eleanor would be visiting this Christmastide. If Julian listed things he did not want, the very first on the list would be spending Christmas with Eleanor and her husband, seeing the life he might have had.

How many children did she have? What happiness and hardship had she experienced? Whom did she marry? *Do I know the man?*

Julian found himself wanting in equal measures to look about the place to learn the identity of her husband and to never look away from the dreamlike vision before him. He settled on gazing on her form for as long as his imagination deigned to offer him the sight or until she spoke and proved herself flesh and bone after all.

Behind him, Julian was vaguely aware of a voice. "You

remember Andrew and Thomas, of course, but I don't think you've ever met my daughters . . ." The voice trailed off and then said, "Julian. Julian?"

He was pulled out of his reverie—somewhat. He didn't tear his gaze from Eleanor or stop thinking about how she stood below the beribboned bough of mistletoe, which, newly hung as it was, bore many pearly berries. He'd have to keep an eye on the little shrub; with each kiss stolen beneath it, a berry would be plucked, and when the white pearls were gone, no more kisses could be exacted from those standing beneath it.

"Julian, my dear man, what is the matter?"

He inhaled suddenly, as if waking up from smelling salts, and glanced Henry's direction. "Pardon?"

His confusion amused Henry, who looked to the doorway and the object of Julian's distraction. The latter steeled himself for a good-natured ribbing about old flames not quite dying out, perhaps connecting the comment to the Yule log. Or Henry might say something about how a naval captain should have the ability to concentrate on a simple conversation and not be distracted by anyone who did or did not enter the room. But Henry did none of those things.

"Eleanor!" he said, spreading his arms wide as he had for his children. "We have a surprise guest for Christmastide, as you see. I invited my old friend months ago, but he didn't know whether he could come until two nights hence, and here he is."

Eleanor stood at a distance of perhaps two dozen paces, thus seeing and interpreting her expression and manner posed a challenge. Julian did detect one thing for certain: she looked awfully pale. Was she ill?

Don't run to her side to find out. You'll look a fool.

"Come, Eleanor. Surely you remember Julian Stephens," Henry said, as if he genuinely believed she might not remember Julian.

Could she have forgotten me? Is it arrogant of me to think not?

The little girl in Eleanor's arms wriggled to get free, and Eleanor obliged, setting the child on the floor. The girl ran, laughing and squealing as only a free-spirited young one could. She stopped short of Henry, wrapped her arms about his leg, then settled in place with a thumb in her mouth. Eyeing Julian, she pointed at him, sort of, with her thumb-sucking hand. "Papa, who's that?" she asked around her thumb.

For the briefest of moments, Julian felt shock and panic at the thought that this child's parents were Henry and Eleanor. But no, that couldn't be; word of Henry's being widowed would have reached him even at sea, wouldn't it?

"This, my dear Emma, is Uncle Julian," Henry said. "He grew up at Willowsmeade as I did."

At that moment, Eleanor reached them. Her gaze flitted between Henry and Julian, as if she didn't know where to look. He could relate to the feeling. There was so much he wanted to know, so much he wanted to say to her. He wanted to wander the gardens with her on a long, meandering walk as they told each other all about the years they'd been apart.

He could tell her why he never had settled down, how it had never been because of the navy, though he was happy enough to let others assume as much. Unlike many sailors, Julian didn't feel bound to the sea or his ship. He'd served what felt like a lifetime, and he was ready to spend the years to come on dry land. But only if he had the companionship of someone he loved and admired, someone he could feel completely at ease with. Someone like . . .

Forget finding someone like *her*, he thought. *I've always wanted it to* be *her.*

He had the means with which to begin a life with a good

woman, assuming he ever found one who was both Eleanor's equal *and* who would have him. He wasn't entirely certain the two weren't opposing, incompatible concepts altogether.

"Eleanor, it is so good to see you again after all of these years," Julian said with a bow.

She is a member of the Brunson family, while I am nobody, the son of a gardener.

He continued, "Rather, I suppose I should properly call you Mrs. . . ." His voice trailed off as he waited for her to provide the requisite information.

"Hadfield," she said, extending her hand. "Still *Miss* Hadfield."

The beauty and total surprise of her reply sucked his breath away. He'd seen battle and death and suffering. He knew firsthand that life, quite simply, was not fair. The absolute last thing he'd expected was to find Eleanor unmarried. And never married, by the sound of it. Perhaps . . .

No. Stop that line of thinking, he ordered himself. *I'll never be a landed gentleman, never have a title, never have the money and status that a true lady such as she is should have. She deserves to have everything.*

When, after a few seconds, he didn't answer, Eleanor tilted her head in question and glanced at Henry. "Don't tell me you two have been playing Snapdragon."

He didn't blame her for thinking he might have partaken of spirits already; he wasn't known for having a tongue twisted into a knot, so she was trying to make sense of his silence. Julian found the ability to loosen his tongue and managed, "I'm quite well, thank you. And I have *not* been drinking. It's a bit early in the day yet for that, at least for a captain used to being an example of maintaining order for his men."

"That's right—you're a captain now," Eleanor said. "*Captain* Stephens. That sounds rather prestigious."

He cringed. "Don't call me Captain, I beg you. That is not who I am at Willowsmeade, not in the presence of those who've known me my whole life." He chuckled. "I can't imagine that you, who saw me unsuccessfully attempt to saddle a cow, would be able to call me Captain with a straight face."

A little voice behind them piped up—one of the boys. "Uncle Julian? Did you truly try to saddle a cow?"

Henry gave Julian a look with one raised eyebrow. "Don't give them any ideas. They're mischievous enough as it is."

"Oh, it was a dreadful thing I did," Julian said, "and a dangerous one, as well." He put on a look of utter innocence as he faced the children. "I could tell you the full story, but it would give you frightening dreams at night."

"Really?" the middle girl asked, as if she craved a terrifying story.

"Most certainly." Julian gave a serious nod. "Don't ever go into the stables unattended, and *never* touch a cow."

"We won't," the middle girl and her older sister said in unison.

Henry sent the girls off to find their mother so the entire family would be present for the lighting of the log. After they scampered out, the adults stood in silence for a moment. Julian finally broke it. "Miss Hadfield—"

"Absolutely not," Eleanor interrupted with a shake of her head. "If I'm not to call you Captain Stephens, then you mustn't call me Miss Hadfield." She held out her hand as if waiting to shake to seal a bargain.

He looked at it a moment, wanting to kiss the top of her hand rather than shake it.

Henry elbowed him. "After the stories I've heard from the nursery, you'd better agree to her proposition, or tonight *you'll* be the one with frightening dreams."

Eleanor gave him a look, then rolled her eyes with a laugh. "You've heard no such thing."

"Oh," Julian said, light dawning in his mind. "You're the governess." He felt as if he were putting together a very large and complex puzzle, one tiny piece at a time, and this was the latest he'd uncovered.

"As you see," Eleanor said with a dip of a curtsy. "I've been planning to teach the children about plants. Perhaps during your stay, you could show us about the hothouse and tell us about the plants growing there? That is, assuming you remember those things after all these years."

"I'd be happy to help," Julian said. He hoped she would understand from his tone and eyes that he meant so much more than that. Teaching the children with her at their side would not quite be like taking a turn about the gardens with her alone, but it would be better than nothing. Eleanor was seeking out his help, or perhaps his company. That was a good sign. At least, he chose to see it as such. "Being the son of a gardener means working in the gardens so much that those things are emblazoned in one's memory for life."

Standing this close to her, he noted a few evident signs of the decade they'd spent apart—a handful of lines about her eyes and forehead, more clearly defined cheekbones and jawline. For the most part, however, she looked very much as she had. The lighthearted girl had merely been replaced by a mature woman. How did he appear to her? He was four years beyond his thirtieth birthday and had a hint of gray above his ears. Would she find him dreadfully old?

The boys, likely tired of waiting for their mother's arrival, chased one another in an intricate game of tag that came close to toppling more than one servant and did, in fact, tear a wreath of holly off one wall. Henry called to them in an abrupt tone only a father could muster.

After the boys settled down, Henry leaned in to Julian and spoke quietly. "Keeping the two of them happily and safely occupied until they return to school may well take the steady hand of a man such as yourself."

Julian looked at Henry in surprise.

His friend turned his back to Eleanor and whispered, "If you're looking for reasons to spend time with her, I can provide several more."

Feeling oddly as if Henry could read his mind, Julian stepped away slightly, as if a little distance would prevent his thoughts and emotions from being exposed to his friend. Julian now found himself close enough to Eleanor to smell her hair. It still had the scent of lavender and vanilla. She looked at him expectantly, but his mind had been wiped clean like a slate. He didn't know if she'd spoken, and if so, what answer she expected. He merely smiled, which seemed to be the appropriate response, as she spoke next.

"Today, Thomas asked when he'd get to have the plum pudding, not because he likes to eat it, but because he likes to see it afire."

Her wide eyes made his heart soften all the more. Oh, how he'd missed those eyes. He fought the urge to run his thumb across her jaw, to cradle her head in his hands, and kiss her as he had the day they'd said goodbye in the gardens so long ago.

He shoved thoughts of kisses out of his mind and returned to the subject at hand—flaming plum pudding. Julian leaned in close to her and, when he spoke, was gratified that she didn't draw away even a quarter of an inch. "I always like the plum pudding too, but not because of the flames."

She turned her head and looked up at him. Had she taken a step closer? He wasn't sure, but she certainly felt nearer, and if she drew any closer, she'd be able to hear his heart thrumming against his chest. "Why did you like the plum pudding, if not for the flame? I don't recall that you ever found it particularly delicious."

"Remember how the whole family would gather in the kitchen with the servants on Stir-up Sunday when the pudding was first made?" he asked.

"And each person got to stir it with the special wooden spoon used only for the plum pudding. I always closed my eyes when I got to stir and make my wish."

"As did I."

What kinds of things had she wished for? He'd always wished for Eleanor to be his wife when they grew up.

After the stirring, Mr. Brunson had done the honors of dropping several trinkets into the batter, which would be cooked into the pudding. The finder of each had a certain fortune predicted for the following year: a silver coin for wealth, a small wishbone for luck, an anchor representing safe harbor, and a ring indicating marriage.

The Christmas before he enlisted, Julian found the ring in his serving of pudding. He never did tell anyone, and the family assumed it had been lost in the kitchen somewhere or accidentally swallowed.

"Too bad I missed Stir-up Sunday this year," Julian said as he slipped his hand into his coat pocket and touched the tin ring he always carried on his person.

Chapter Three

THE NEXT DAY during the Christmas service at the chapel, Eleanor found herself in a circumstance of simultaneous pleasure and disappointment. The rambunctious children had been successfully washed and dressed in pressed clothing early enough, by some miracle of the season, that even with a fifteen-minute walk to the chapel, they arrived with several minutes to spare. Most of the adults had gone ahead, riding in a carriage, but Eleanor stayed behind to escort the children.

When she shepherded them into the second of the family pews like so many sheep, she was pleasantly surprised to have her attention drawn from the children to the handsome Julian. He stood farther down the aisle, speaking with Mr. and Mrs. Brunson. The boys giggled, drawing Eleanor's attention back to the children. She gave them her best scolding look, perfected over the decade she'd been a governess.

The boys promptly stopped elbowing and poking each other and sat on the bench with straight backs and forced smiles they'd put on in an attempt to show their innocence. She kept her stern expression on for a few more moments, though doing so took effort, as the boys' sudden pious behavior was so clearly for her benefit.

Little Kate toddled in last, but when Eleanor stepped into the pew, she felt Julian's presence behind her. She glanced up and felt her middle do a little flip. Perhaps she'd get to sit beside him during the service. She couldn't guarantee she'd be able to do her duties as governess, as her attentions would be entirely diverted by the naval captain beside her. The prospect of being physically close to him again after so long filled a tiny corner of her heart with excitement, a corner she'd thought had died long ago.

"Captain Stephens!" Thomas said, in what the boy likely believed was a whisper, but surely carried ten feet or more. "Can we sit by you?" No doubt the boys hoped to hear stories of sea battles, which would not happen under a church roof.

"Please, Captain?" Andrew echoed. "*May* we?" he added, correcting his brother's grammar.

Eleanor turned to the boys with her strict governess's expression back in place, only this time with her eyes even wider. The boys' eyes widened to match hers, and their mouths clamped shut as they folded their arms and faced forward like good boys.

"Impressive," Julian said. He leaned in and spoke quietly, so only she could hear. "You're able to make them behave without saying a single word. It's like magic."

The compliment sent a ripple of gooseflesh along Eleanor's arms. Silly that such a simple statement would affect her so. "I've had practice," she said with a smile.

"Would my sitting with the boys help them remain quiet throughout the service? Or would it only encourage them to be noisy in the one place they oughtn't?"

His question made her heart drop slightly. She shouldn't have gotten excited over the prospect of sitting beside him. Yes, they would have sat in silence, but she would have reveled in having him within whispering distance for a solid hour or more, even if they whispered nothing. Merely being near him again would have felt like a Christmas wish come true.

Though she hadn't made any wish on this year's Stir-up Sunday.

She used to. But on the last Sunday of November, while she'd encouraged the girls to close their eyes and made their own wishes on their turns stirring the pudding, Eleanor didn't do the same. She'd lived through enough Christmases to know that silent pleas made on Stir-up Sunday were only childhood fancies. She'd made plenty of such silent requests over the years, and they hadn't come true. She knew better than to put stock in such things.

"Sitting with the boys would likely help," she admitted. "They'll want to impress you with their maturity, no doubt."

"Then I'll sit with them." Julian nodded in lieu of a bow, then entered the pew and worked his way to the far side of the bench, where the boys demanded—though to their credit, quietly—that he sit between them. He draped his long arms around both boys, who, under Julian's strong influence, appeared as immovable as stone.

"Good men," Julian told the boys, who sat up even straighter at his praise.

Little Kate reached up to Eleanor with both arms. "May I?" she asked, then clarified, "Sit in your lap?"

"Of course, dear." Eleanor slipped into the pew and sat on the polished wood, where she settled Kate onto her lap. "Now it's time to be very good and very quiet as the minister speaks to us."

Kate cupped her hands about her mouth and whispered, "About Jesus?"

"About the night he was born, yes. It's time to be very still." Eleanor pressed a finger to her own lips.

Kate mimicked the gesture with a single pudgy index finger and nodded with sober eyes.

"Good girl," Eleanor whispered into the child's ear just as

the minister climbed the steps to the pulpit and the congregation went quiet.

Oh, that I could hold my own child thus, Eleanor thought with a bittersweet ache.

Such had not been her fate, alas, but if she wasn't to have her own children, at least she had the fortune to work closely with those born of someone else—a far preferable choice to many other types of employment older single women had to rely on.

For the entire service, Eleanor tried to pay attention, but the presence of one Captain Julian Stephens a few feet away succeeded in creating a distraction beyond her ability to overcome. Halfway through, she allowed her thoughts to take flights of fancy along the lines of what she'd once imagined of her life with Julian, back when they were still young, before the world had schooled them in realities.

That was before he'd made a respectable name for himself, rising well above the humble station she'd forever be compelled to remain in. Most days, she accepted her lot and enjoyed educating the Brunson girls in everything they needed to know, from literature to French and Latin to etiquette and even some arithmetic.

The latter wasn't often seen as necessary for girls to learn, but Eleanor knew that many a lady served an important function in running her household and found far more success doing so if she understood how to count basic figures and manage money. Generally, Eleanor felt content enough, knowing that she performed an important work in raising little girls who would one day be women in need of the very skills they were learning from her.

Moments of discontent crept in, of course, but they were rare and quashed without much more than an intentional shift of thought or attention.

But not today. Not with Julian so near, not with so many hopes she'd once dreamed returning to the fore unbidden, many of which had been forgotten. They now showed themselves with greater clarity, as if a bright ray of sun lit them up and removed all shadows—shadows Eleanor had placed them in deliberately, to protect her heart.

At long last, the service ended, and the two Brunson pews emptied. Eleanor led the way with the girls, followed by Julian and the boys, then their parents and the Edgleys. The family servants who were working over the holiday descended the stairs from the gallery.

As Eleanor walked outside into the wet day, she wished she and the children had been able to take the other carriage instead of walking, no matter that they were so near the house. Rain had come down during the service, making the road little more than a winding ribbon of slippery mud. She took Kate's hand on one side and Emma's on the other and proceeded to pick her way through the worst of the mud, which ran along the road before the chapel.

When they reached the lesser-traveled road leading to the house, the way proved far less treacherous. And after preventing two falls from Kate and one from Emma on the muddier road, they emerged on the other side of a particularly bad area onto mostly wet gravel with the occasional divot and small puddle for the remainder of the way.

The boys had somehow convinced Julian to walk with them instead of taking the carriage back, and soon Eleanor discovered that the road was plenty wide for several adults. When Kate released her hand and skipped ahead with Emma toward home, Julian stepped to Eleanor's side and walked with her.

"I hope Henry sends a buggy to fetch the goose," Julian said suddenly.

For the slightest moment, Eleanor didn't know what he meant—having him so near made thinking difficult. "Oh, Cook is on her way to fetch the goose." 'Twas a rare kitchen, even at a fine estate, that possessed an oven large enough to fit a large goose for the Christmas feast. Some years, the family had other fowl, which didn't necessitate a trip to buy a fully-cooked goose on Christmas Day.

Eleanor tried to find something to say in response but found her tongue firmly attached to the bottom of her mouth. A strange tension spread between her and Julian, and she didn't know how to break through it. Then again, ten years was plenty of time to build a barrier. Removing such a barrier couldn't be done in a matter of hours.

And if such a barrier and its accompanying tension were successfully removed, what would conversation be like then? Eleanor the Spinster would still be speaking with Captain Stephens. He wouldn't see the young woman she'd once been. Perhaps breaking down the awkward barrier would not be worth the effort after all.

They walked along for a few moments in silence before hearing rapid footsteps behind them. Henry appeared, pink-cheeked and smiling widely.

Julian looked at him, puzzled. "Where's Mrs. Brunson?" he asked Henry.

"She's gone with Cook to fetch the goose."

"Ah." Julian said, and they continued walking. The girls had all but disappeared into the distance, and the boys were close on their heels. That left the three adults who'd once been young friends.

Why did growing up have to introduce complexities? A grown woman simply wasn't a girl anymore. Societal rules were different about how men—even those she'd known all her life—spoke to and interacted with her. Add to that the fact that she was considerably lower in station than either of these two men, and it was no wonder she felt an awkward unease.

How, precisely, did one navigate uncharted waters such as these?

"Miss Hadfield, I'm glad you stayed through the holiday," Henry said.

"You are?" she said, aware of her voice quaking. She swallowed to prevent it from cracking again.

This was her fifth year as governess at Willowsmeade, and not once had she ever left for the holiday. Why would she, when her only living relations were her cousins? She supposed she could request to not work during the Christmas holiday, but in that case, her presence at Willowsmeade would complicate matters. Was she then family or servant? Best to simply continue on as governess through the holiday season as if nothing had changed.

And nothing ever had. Not until this Christmas. Julian's return changed everything.

"I'm very glad you're here," Henry continued, "because I'm concerned about our dear friend Julian." He thumped a hand on Julian's shoulder. "You see, Miss Hadfield, I'm in need of your assistance."

Eleanor and Julian exchanged befuddled glances. "You are?" she asked.

"Indeed, I am. You see, I've long said that Julian must find a good wife. I suspect he's finally ready to abandon naval life, and the proper time has come for him to find a suitable lady."

"I may need some time to lose my sea legs," Julian said with a smile. A bit of color crept up his neck, though Eleanor wasn't entirely sure what to make of it.

"Your sea legs will be gone soon enough," Henry said, batting his hand as if the idea were a fly. "The difficult part is in finding the right lady."

Henry leaned forward to look around Julian at Eleanor, who prayed he didn't note her own pinked cheeks. A similar color continued to rise on Julian's neck, though likely for different reasons. He probably did not enjoy being the subject of such a conversation.

For her part, Eleanor's cheeks felt so hot that they were surely nearing crimson. Thinking of Julian with another woman as his wife set her heart racing and her throat tightening. She daren't look up at Julian again to see if he approved of the idea, but he didn't voice any protest, which was answer enough to her silent question.

And why wouldn't Julian want a wife? He should want one, and she should be glad to see him happily married. *Should.* Instead, the idea felt like a brick in her middle.

Henry continued, clearly unaware of the awkwardness he'd created, "I need all the help I can get to marry off my sorry bachelor friend, and you, dear Miss Hadfield, are just the person to help."

Eleanor wanted to say that seeking out and finding Julian a wife was the very last thing she was suited to do. Any Mrs. Stephens had to be worthy of him, which eliminated most women out of hand, including Eleanor herself. If her father hadn't squandered his estate, lost her dowry, and died penniless, and she were several years younger, then things might have turned out differently. But they hadn't.

"I'm considering hosting a ball," Henry went on, "with the specific object of finding Julian a wife."

"Please," Julian began, "there's no need—"

"I insist." Henry clapped his hand on Julian's shoulder. "You deserve the happiness of a wife and children. If you're done exploring the world by ship, I can lead you to happiness on terra firma."

"Can you, now?" Julian replied dryly. He clearly didn't

believe Henry could do any such thing, no matter how pure his intent. "We are very different men, you and I."

"Why does a difference in character have any bearing whatsoever on your finding a suitable match?" Henry demanded. "Especially when I'm enlisting the help of the one other person who knew you as a boy and therefore knows your temperament as well as I do." They reached the drive leading up to the house. Henry stopped and turned to look at them. "So, what say you?"

Was he directing the question at her or Julian? She had no memory of walking the last several minutes, only of the hideous conversation. She must have traversed those yards under her own power, one foot after the other, all without conscious thought, her mind entirely preoccupied by Henry's intent on finding a wife for Julian—and his insistence that she have a role in the venture.

"Hmm?" Henry murmured, brows raised. He clearly expected an answer. "Can I rely on you to help me find the perfect wife for Julian at a ball?"

"I'm standing not two feet from you," Julian said. "I can hear every word, Henry."

The corner of Henry's mouth quirked with amusement. "I should hope so. You aren't so old that you need a listening horn, but you *are* a pathetic old bachelor, and you'll remain one unless those of us who care about you take action to prevent you from growing old and miserable all alone."

"You're daft." Julian walked down the drive alone.

Henry folded his arms and watched their friend's retreat. He raised his voice to Julian, calling down the drive. "Only the slightest of differences exists between *daft* and *genius.*"

In response, Julian waved Henry off and kept walking without another look back.

"He'll come around," Henry said to Eleanor.

"Will he, though?" she said, speaking without thinking.

"He will, if *he's* not the one who's daft." Henry laughed at his own joke, clapped twice, and rubbed his hands together with anticipation. "I daresay this will be rather enjoyable. Come, Miss Hadfield. We have a ball to plan."

"But what about my duties with the children?" This was the biggest and most obvious argument against giving her aid to Henry's mission.

"They won't fall behind in their studies. It'll be just a few days, is all. If you'd taken the holiday season off, we'd have managed, wouldn't we?"

"I suppose so."

Eleanor looked down the drive after Julian, who was quickly growing smaller in the distance. She wanted to take his arm, walk with him, talk with him. Be with him. But not with Henry as witness. Not after being asked to help Julian find a wife. And he'd seemed more amused by the venture than opposed to it.

The one kiss they'd shared a decade hence, when he'd said goodbye on these very grounds, had lost its meaning. He no longer loved her. Naturally, he didn't. They were barely more than children then. They'd both had life experience and lessons in the interim that had changed them. He was no more the man he'd been than she was the same girl. She could not begrudge him from growing in a different direction, away from her.

In somewhat of a daze, she headed inside with Henry, knowing that on Christmas, of all days, there would be precious little time to do any sort of thing like planning a ball at which Julian was to meet his future spouse.

Inside, as Eleanor took off her pelisse and hat, she dearly hoped Henry would abandon his plans. How long would Julian be at Willowsmeade? Through Twelfth Night? She could hardly bear the thought of him leaving, yet part of her hoped he'd depart soon so she didn't have to plan her future misery.

Chapter Four

THE CHRISTMAS MEAL was divine. After so many years spending the holiday in various ports or even aboard ship, Julian had nearly forgotten how lovely a true feast cooked by someone with a full kitchen and weeks to make it could truly be. The black butter alone—made of apples into a delicious spread—almost made him weep with pleasure.

The only flaw was that, though Eleanor had been seated on his left, the Edgleys' daughter on his right latched on to every chance for conversation with him, scarcely taking a breath, it seemed, and certainly not pausing to eat. He had a suspicion that Henry had deliberately seated Miss Edgley beside him, and if the girl's prattling was any indication, she was quite keen on the arrangement.

The few times someone else addressed Miss Edgley or a footman served her, Julian turned on the instant to Eleanor, but not once through the meal did she give him any notice or want to converse with him. At the very least, he wished to exchange looks of exasperation about the young Miss Edgley's chatter, but he did not even find that in Eleanor. She quietly ate her meal, eyes fixed on her plate, almost as if she wished she could escape the room altogether.

Escape his presence altogether? Why was her manner so

clearly uncomfortable near him? He thought back to Henry's ridiculous proposal as they'd walked home from the morning service—and how quiet Eleanor had been even then. The fiery spirit he'd once known would have piped up in protest at what a silly notion such a ball would be.

But not if she is eager to find me another to wife.

Julian had to swallow a knot in his throat at that. He tried to cover the emotion by sipping his wine at the same time. Miss Edgley continued to prattle about something—dresses or the millinery in town or some such. He could not have said for certain what her subject matter had shifted to, even if he'd been faced with walking the plank unless he gave the correct answer. He could not have recalled so much as the color of her gown, because his attention was entirely diverted by the governess seated on the other side of him. Even so, he did his best to be a gentleman, for he would not offend Henry's guests for the world.

After the feast, the men enjoyed their port while the women retired to the drawing room. Julian held his glass of expensive drink but had no stomach for it. As he watched the door close behind the women, he thought 'twas truly a pity that men and women separated after supper. He had no desire to talk about Parliament, or the navy, or international trade, or the prime minister, or anything else, unless such a conversation were with Eleanor.

What *did* she think of the current Parliament? He had no doubt that she had an opinion, and that opinion had been of her own creation through careful study and thoughtful consideration of the matters after thoroughly reading about them on her own. As a young woman, she'd eagerly read every newspaper and leaflet she could find, and he had no reason to think her curiosity about the world—or her tendency toward strong opinions—had changed.

Henry and Mr. Edgley sat across the room, discussing women they should be sure to invite to the upcoming ball, which apparently would be held for certain, Julian's feelings on the matter being irrelevant. They added women to the list based on things like keen eyes, delicate features, and glossy hair. Having Mr. Edgley present felt uncomfortable at best, as the man added comments about how his daughter would make a good match.

None of the comments from any of the men ventured into anything about the women's minds or hearts. He appreciated a pretty face as much as any man, but pretty faces did not endure, and a keen mind was far more attractive anyway. Eleanor had both.

Julian sipped his port and tried to ignore the discussion over whether Miss Merchant or Miss Pilcher had the more pleasing laugh. He'd hoped Christmas Day would end with some kind of other diversion—a game of whist, if nothing else. Did Henry's household indulge in entertainment the likes of Snapdragon? The elder Mr. Brunson had been deeply spiritual and wouldn't have approved, of course. If he hadn't allowed a mistletoe bough, he most certainly would not have approved of raisins soaked in rum, floating in a sea of more rum, then set afire.

Julian prided himself on being quite adept at the game of Snapdragon: he could snatch several raisins in a row without getting burned. But perhaps that was the sailor in him, and proper folks like those at Willowsmeade didn't lower themselves to such amusements. Then again, a mistletoe *had* been hung above the doorway into the ballroom. What other changes had Henry brought to Willowsmeade after his father's death?

Perhaps I should propose a game of Snapdragon to test his reaction. Julian swirled his port around and around.

Watching it spin, he tried to imagine Eleanor playing Snapdragon. He'd seen some women play it, including several ladies, and they always squealed and yelped like panicked birds.

He felt quite confident that Eleanor was incapable of either squealing or yelping. Such an act of silliness wasn't in her mettle. Though he hadn't spent more than a few minutes in her presence in ten years, he knew if she were to play, she'd walk right to the burning bowl, perhaps walk around it to analyze the locations of the raisins and determine the best angle at which to snatch one, and then, in one swift movement, she'd stick her hand into the bowl and pluck out a raisin. She'd place it victoriously in her mouth, no worse for the wear and without so much as a singe on her lace cuff.

And if she were singed, she'd calmly pat the spot to be sure it was extinguished, and then carry on as if nothing untoward had happened, as indeed, to her, nothing had. She would not squeal or yell over singed lace. That was the old Eleanor. He didn't seem to know the current one. Would that he could test the theory, but amusements of that nature were not to be, as the entire household retired at a maddeningly proper hour. The men would be up early for the annual fox hunt, and the women would be up equally early to prepare the boxes for the Brunsons' tenants for Boxing Day.

Julian hardly slept that night. For the first time in memory, he had no desire whatsoever to go on any hunt. And, for the first time in five years, he was home from the sea during Christmastide. Last time, the hunt had been a welcome distraction, something to do to keep him from thinking about how Eleanor, who had always been a fixture of Willowsmeade to him, wasn't there.

He hadn't visited since, and in the intervening years, as holidays came and went, he'd thought of the fox hunt with fondness. Standing on the helm of his ship as the weather grew cooler, he'd looked forward to one day participating in the annual hunt one day. Each year, something kept him away. Usually, the navy kept him away, but one year it was the death of his father and his burial at their family lot several days' journey away. The year after that, he didn't want to return right after Mr. Brunson's death, during the mourning period.

But now he had returned. Eleanor had too, and he didn't want to leave even for an hour. He couldn't wait for daylight and a chance to see Eleanor again. He wanted to spend some proper time with her. Yes, even if that meant a day in the noisy and unruly nursery with Andrew and Thomas and three energetic little girls.

When morning dawned, gray and damp, Julian dragged himself out of bed and got dressed for the hunt. He'd likely be glad he went, or so he told himself, much as a parent tried to coax a child. If he stayed behind, Henry would be liable to call a physician or otherwise cause trouble, and Julian didn't want to draw such attention to himself.

As he headed toward the stables, he caught a glimpse of Eleanor carrying an armload of something and walking toward the main house. He waved and called to her. She glanced his way but didn't return his greeting with so much as a nod. A moment later, she'd slipped inside and out of sight.

He sighed, disappointment creeping into his soul. She didn't seem to care a fig for him any longer. Seeing her again, even fleetingly, turned out to be enough to torment Julian. His yearning to be with her expanded with each step he took through the gravel, his boots making a rhythmic beat as he went. He felt pulled toward the house, to find Eleanor—likely in the kitchen, preparing boxes, he presumed—but forced himself to keep going to the stables, where the men were to meet in but a few minutes. Every step that brought him farther from the house, from Eleanor, proved painful, like a dull knife blade slowly reopening a barely healed wound.

At least she wasn't visiting, so he could feel some assurance that any time in the near future that he would be at Willowsmeade, she would be too. Whether she'd want to spend time with him and whether seeing her regularly would bring only pain or eventually be a pleasant experience, he did not know.

The hunt itself seemed to last an eternity. He was cold and wet and tired, and he didn't care about spotting foxes or bringing back any quarry. The hours felt like days, and the day itself the single longest of his life. This was not the dream he'd envisioned last Christmastide while on his ship.

When they turned their horses about to head back, Julian breathed a sigh of relief. But then Henry pulled his horse abreast of Julian's and insisted on talking. Up to that point, the day's subject matter had been mostly about hunting and horses, but the look in Henry's eyes set Julian's teeth on edge. This interchange would *not* be about horses. He hoped it would not be about the silly aim of finding him a wife at a ball like some children's tale.

"I don't suppose you can guess what I've had Miss Hadfield—" Henry cut himself off. "I suppose I should call her Eleanor when speaking with you, but she's been our governess for so long that I'm in the habit now of referring to her that way. What was I saying?"

"Something about Eleanor."

"Ah. Yes." Henry laughed, as if he knew that whatever he was going to say wasn't something that Julian wanted to hear. "I'd wager you can't guess what I've had her working on today."

"I'd assume she's tending to the children, unless she is seeing to the traditional Boxing Day activities with Mrs. Brunson," Julian countered. "Am I wrong?"

"Oh, well yes, she's done some of both, I imagine, but there's something else, too. Something very specific I asked her to do." Henry laughed again in the way he used to when he'd laid a mischievous prank that had yet to be discovered by the victim.

Julian felt quite certain he knew what Henry had requested of Eleanor, but he wasn't about to mention the ball. His stomach went sour just thinking about it. "What task did you ask of her, then?"

"What, no guesses? You disappoint me." Henry grinned expectantly, but Julian would not be drawn in. He merely grinned back silently, mirroring Henry's expression and waiting for his friend to continue. At last, he did. "After our conversation on the road with her yesterday, I thought you'd surely guess."

The sourness spread beyond Julian's stomach. Julian tightened his grip on the reins but didn't allow himself to reveal any other outward sign of displeasure. Henry was treading on places Julian did not wish anyone to be, but if he admitted as much, whether in a gesture, tone, or something else, Henry would be spurred on by the reaction like a horse under the hand of snapping crop. Fortunately, military life had taught Julian how to keep a neutral posture and facial expression.

"You will have to enlighten me," he said, then silently tried to find a way to make sure the ball wouldn't happen at all. Usually, a dance over Christmastide could be enjoyable, something to anticipate, and more so knowing Eleanor would be in attendance. But any enthusiasm he might have felt was dampened by Henry's dastardly plan of a bridal ball.

Henry drew his horse a bit closer to Julian's, so close their stirrups almost touched, and he leaned in. "If she has managed to do as I requested, and I have no reason to think Miss Had—rather, Eleanor—hasn't, as she is so entirely capable, then the ballroom will be fully decorated with greenery and gold paper, ready for a ball to be held in two days' time." Henry laughed in an almost victorious manner.

"T-Two days?" Julian said, and hated how his voice nearly squeaked.

"Two." Henry looked rather pleased with himself. "A ball for *you.*"

Julian felt as if Henry had poured a pitcher of freezing ocean water over his head. "I hoped you weren't in earnest."

"I most certainly was—and am." Henry stroked the neck of his mare, patted it, then faced forward as he went on. "You really must find a wife, and I'm going to see to it. I'm that good of a friend, Julian. My father saw to it that you had some education and a chance at a military career. My duty is to see to it that you are wed."

"I assure you, that is quite unnecess—"

But Henry was having none of it, and he continued as if Julian hadn't said a word, "Getting you to return to Willowsmeade for any length of time is a feat, so this is my first true opportunity to find you a wife—something that should have happened a long time ago. And now that the opportunity is here, I am not about to let it slip away. If I have any say in the matter—and I believe I do—you, my dear man, will be engaged by Twelfth Night."

Julian was shaking his head miserably. He'd rather be in a brig with rats than endure a holiday ball thrown entirely for the purpose of finding him a wife. The thought of being ogled and fawned over by women he had no interest in made him want to flee to the sea after all.

He already loved a woman, and she wouldn't be one of the ladies there vying for his affections. Alas, Eleanor didn't appear to return his feelings. Perhaps she'd found contentment in her life as governess, knowing she had a home at Willowsmeade even when she grew too old to work.

Eleanor always had been strong and independent—qualities that made her an equal when the three of them were young, as she could climb trees and run as fast as Julian or Henry ever could, even in a dress.

He'd never suspected that her strength and independence would mean she'd end up a spinster with no interest in spending time with him. He came from humble beginnings but had made something of himself—a captain in the navy. Yet she was a member of the Brunson family, and as such, perhaps not even Henry would view the son-of-a-gardener-turned-captain as good enough for his cousin. He had changed his social standing, but not his blood.

Perhaps a predictable life of comfort at Willowsmeade was preferable to a potentially risky, laborious life with him as he tried to make his way in life with a new profession—one he'd yet to choose.

Yet a sliver of something inside him whispered that she'd always wanted to be a wife and mother. Like the whisper of a breeze, the idea floated about him, hinting that her wish mightn't have changed, that the possibility existed of Eleanor wanting to marry after all, even to someone born of a lower station.

I could make her happy, he thought. *I'm sure of it—if I could but convince her.*

"I've had Eleanor and Mrs. Brunson working on the guest list and decorations all day, with specific instructions to invite every eligible woman within two leagues who Eleanor believes would make a good match with you."

Henry laughed again, dug his heels into his horse's flanks, and galloped off, as if he had given the final word on the matter. As if Julian himself had no say in whether to remain a bachelor or wed. As if he had no say over whom he could marry.

The tiny flicker of hope he'd felt on seeing Eleanor again and finding her unbound in matrimony was snuffed right out. How could he hope for the things in his heart—a life with the only woman he'd ever loved—when she was, at that very moment, planning an event for which she would determine the best women for him to choose a wife from?

I want to choose her, he thought miserably. *But I won't ask her to bind herself to me if she wishes to remain free. She must, if she finds the search for my future wife an easy task.*

But *did* she find the task easy? He'd spent the day assuming as much because she hadn't rejected the notion of the ball when Henry first suggested it.

I cannot know anything for certain without asking her.

He would not be able to dance even once at the ball unless he heard the truth from Eleanor's own mouth—did she or did she not yet care for him? Were they merely childhood mates reunited in friendship? Or did the kiss they shared when they said farewell still hold them together like a silky thread?

Julian rode on, determined to reach the house as soon as he could, seek Eleanor out, and determine where her heart lay. He'd never have a moment's peace until he did. He daren't think about what the next step would be if he learned her love for him had cooled.

One task at a time, he thought. *I'll regroup and determine my next course if needed. Until then, onward.*

Chapter Five

ALAS, ELEANOR FOUND it of no use to insist to Henry that she had no relevant experience in planning a ball or that the children needed her. He rebuffed any attempt she made at evading the assignment by stating that the best possible qualification was knowing Julian as well as she did, and that the children would be cared for by other members of the staff—and, before she could mention the girls' lessons, he added that his daughters might as well have a holiday recess from lessons, like their brothers.

Thus, Eleanor found herself working with a few members of the serving staff on decorating the ballroom. The group allotted to her was rather small, considering the scope of their job, but many servants had yet to return from their own well-earned holidays, so she had to make do with only two men and three women. Mrs. Brunson was overseeing the food, and tomorrow afternoon, the two of them were to finalize the guest list, with special attention to the young women most likely to make a good match. The thought of that meeting—and the list she would be required to review—made her stomach turn.

To avoid feeling queasy, she threw her energies into decorating, and while the ballroom looked splendid, Eleanor failed to find enjoyment in the fruits of her labors. She would have much preferred guiding Kate through the next section of her reading primer or helping Suzanne improve her elocution with the latest William Blake poem she was memorizing. Eleanor would have even preferred taking the boys to the hothouse to show them how the gardener grew vegetables for the household in the winter, even if such an outing meant the boys running wild among the plants and returning to the house covered in soil. She could picture the dismay on the face of Mr. Wells, who had replaced Julian's father as gardener, if she were to take the boys to the hothouse.

Naturally, thoughts of Mr. Wells led to thoughts of the man he'd replaced, which inevitably led to thoughts of Julian.

Clutching a silver candlestick that was only half polished, Eleanor cleared her throat, hoping the sound would be enough to halt the direction her thoughts were taking. She looked up and surveyed the room, hoping to clear her mind further.

Hours of decorating had yielded walls festooned with greenery, ribbons, and gold paper; Yule candles; and wreaths dotted with colorful Christmas roses. The latter didn't look a thing like regular roses, and when Eleanor questioned their name, Betsy, one of the younger servants, explained in a whisper. Apparently, Christmas roses held some mystic or pagan history, which explained why the house didn't have them about during any of Eleanor's Christmases as a child; the elder Mr. Brunson wouldn't have allowed so much as a whiff of paganism to cross his threshold.

Yet the story Betsy related about the flowers, told that morning over making the wreaths, had seemed plenty religious to Eleanor. According to Betsy, legend said that on the first Christmas, when a poor girl had no gift for the Christ child, she wept in distress. Her tears landed upon the white snow, and in each spot a tear fell, a colorful flower sprang to life—Christmas roses.

Such a story would likely have satisfied even the late Mr. Brunson, had he heard it, Eleanor felt quite certain, unless he considered it a falsehood. She had to admit that was likely; he hadn't allowed novels or poetry in the house because they weren't strictly truthful.

As a girl, Eleanor had read a few pieces of poetry and even a novel before coming to Willowsmeade. After arriving here, she'd listened, rapt, to the governess, Miss Monson, tell fairy tales, which touched Eleanor's heart and awoke an understanding in her of new fantastic worlds. Reading fairy tales to the children was the crime that got Miss Monson dismissed. One morning, she simply was not in the nursery. When young Eleanor learned why, she marched angrily to Mr. Brunson's library and told him that Miss Monson's stories had more truth than anything in the Bible. She'd been whipped and sent to her room without food for the entire day, and then only bread and water for a week.

As a grown woman, Eleanor still believed she'd had a valid argument. Truth comes in many forms. Even Jesus told fictional stories to teach in a way nothing else could.

Dear Henry had definitely not trodden the same path as his father, and he continued to add more and more changes to the household. Christmas roses were one of the more recent evidences, as was the mistletoe bough.

Unexpectedly, an image flashed into her mind of being kissed by Julian beneath the bough. She stared at the beribboned mistletoe and could see the two of them under the bough, kissing as they had in the gardens the day he'd left for naval training. Only in this waking dream, he wasn't saying goodbye. He kissed her again and again, periodically stopping only long enough to remove a white berry from the mistletoe.

Her eyes burning, she tried to estimate how many kisses the white berries would justify.

Twenty? That would not be enough.

Not that she would ever be kissed by Julian again. Of all people, Henry should have suspected that she yet loved Julian, and Henry would be the only person to know whether Julian returned her feelings. Yet Henry suggested this foolish, wife-finding ball, which could mean, quite simply, he knew Julian did not have such feelings.

She tried to banish him from her mind, even with the knowledge that her effort was in vain. She could not keep him from her mind and heart so long as he remained at Willowsmeade.

What if he never leaves? At the thought, she gripped the silver candlestick harder and stared at the intricate floral design. Her stomach sank at the idea of a future wherein Julian would always be near but never hers—a future that was entirely probable.

He had retired from the navy and could now settle anywhere he wished. Living at Willowsmeade, or at least living in the same county, would be reasonable, expected, even. He would marry, and she would be forced to bear a life of seeing him regularly, having to forevermore wear a false mask before him. Even before Henry and Mrs. Brunson. She had to ignore her love for Julian—no, more than that, she had to stamp it out, extinguish it like a candle thrown into the snow.

No, she'd never have a moment's peace unless she left Willowsmeade. Eleanor dabbed the cloth in the polish and returned to her task with vigor as she thought through new plans. If asked, Henry would give her an impeccable letter of recommendation. She could find a position in another household far away. Once there, she would direct all her energies toward a new set of children to love and train up. And as she had once before, she'd deliberately forget Julian Stephens.

Her eyes burned again, this time at the pain that leaving Julian would cause, though the pain of staying would be far worse. She would also be leaving the Brunson children behind. Little Emma had never known another governess. Kate had been so young when Eleanor arrived that she didn't remember another. Departure would be heartbreaking, but staying near Julian would be *heartrending*. In a word, it would be impossible.

Every breath she took while Julian remained at Willowsmeade was already painful. Foolish to have thought that her memories of Julian and her feelings for him had been entombed and scarred over.

Footsteps with a heavy tread entered the ballroom and echoed throughout the mostly empty space, likely a male servant bringing in a small table or another armful of greenery. The servants seemed to know the plans for the room and what needed to be completed, so unless someone addressed her specifically, she needn't turn. Good thing, too, as her vision grew blurry with unshed tears. She turned her back to the entrance, unwilling for fellow servants to see her emotional.

The candlestick was quite polished, but she continued the work with zeal, willing the room to empty before she went to the next task. With every second, sadness washed over her again and again, like the waves breaking against the shore. If only they would ebb and remain so. If she could but direct her thoughts toward something happy, away from the reality of her future in a strange place with strange people... away from Julian and the children.

She became more aware of the footsteps when they grew

louder and then stopped directly behind her. Eleanor held her breath as she waited for the person to ask their question about decorations. She would be able to feign a cheerful tone for a three- or four-word sentence.

Instead of a voice speaking, a warm hand rested on her shoulder with a familiar weight.

"What is it?" Julian asked behind her. His touch and words came so unexpectedly that she turned to him without thinking.

And as she did so, the tears that had threatened before now spilled over. She pressed a hand to her mouth, trying to look pleasant and somewhat indifferent. Julian clearly did not believe her act, as he stepped closer and fully encircled her in his arms. The gesture only made her love him more, which made her that much more miserable—if she could only *stop* loving him, rather than feeling her love increase by the minute . . .

Despite herself, she relaxed into his embrace, allowing herself this one brief moment of having him to herself. She cried thus for a minute or two, mostly sniffling—somehow, she reined in the threatening sobs—then evened her breathing and dried her tears. Only then did she lift her head from his silky shirt but didn't look up, not yet. She noted several tear spots left on Julian's cravat and smiled sheepishly as she wiped them, though that didn't fix them, of course.

Julian's hand came up and pinned hers to his chest. "Eleanor, what is it?" he asked again, oh-so-gently.

His touch sent fire up her arm. If she didn't take care, she would collapse in a heap, for her knees wouldn't hold her up much longer. She lifted her chin and looked at him, took a deep breath, and tried to speak. "It's—it's nothing," she said as she stepped backward, away from his embrace.

He tilted his head forward and raised his brows, clearly unbelieving and wanting to know the truth.

Such a good man. And he knows me too well, even after all these years.

She gestured about the room. "Preparing for a large event can be daunting. I'm rather fatigued."

He surveyed the room and then worked his jaw as if highly displeased. "I wanted to discuss the ball with you."

Did he not approve of her efforts? Julian had never been a dandy. She couldn't imagine him caring two shillings about ribbons or anything else about the ball.

"What about it did you wish to discuss?" She turned her head to examine the room, partly to look at the place as he might see it and partly to avoid his deep, piercing eyes.

"Let's take a turn." He put his hands behind his back and began to walk, indicating that she should follow. His relaxed tone set her at ease as they slowly traced the perimeter of the room together. Still, she didn't speak, waiting for him to broach the subject and whatever grievance he wished to air about the ball

"The fact of the matter is . . ." Julian's voice trailed off before he finally said, "I don't want the ball to happen at all."

"You—you don't?" Eleanor asked in surprise. He hadn't seemed against the idea when Henry proposed it, not really. "You do enjoy dancing, if I recall. At least, you used to."

"I do." He took a couple of steps and then sighed heavily. "But I'm not particularly keen on being expected to find a . . . a *match* in a single evening."

Eleanor couldn't help but notice how he forced out the word *match*, as if the very idea of marriage was utterly distasteful to him. Perhaps he had no interest in women and would never marry. If that was the case, Eleanor could remain at Willowsmeade, and the two of them could continue to be friends.

Yet I will never stop loving him. Friendship with Julian will never make me content.

She found her eyes welling up again, so she looked away and blinked, pretending to inspect some of the fireplace and Yule log as they continued to walk, so slowly. At this rate, a full circuit would take a quarter of an hour. The two of them had what felt like a cavernous room all to themselves. Where *were* the other servants? Shouldn't someone have returned from an errand by now?

Eleanor finally found her voice. "I confess I'm surprised to hear you have no wish to find . . . a match." She used the same word, as she couldn't bear to say *wife*.

"A match formed in another manner would be more to my liking." Julian kept walking forward, chin up, lips pressed together—all of which Eleanor noted from a sidelong look, not wanting to give away her curiosity by turning to look at him.

"Oh?" Her throat dried right up, so she swallowed to moisten it. "You are *not* opposed to matrimony, then?"

Julian shook his head and chuckled, but when he answered, something husky had entered his voice. "Rather to the contrary."

Her middle fluttered and warmed. What were his true feelings and thoughts? How would this conversation end? She hadn't predicted his words so far, and she couldn't imagine what he would say next.

But he did oppose the ball. Why? Because he had a certain lady already in mind? If so, likely one he'd met on his many sea voyages—perhaps a Spanish maid or a French mademoiselle.

I should have suspected as much.

His purpose speaking with her now was in her capacity as a friend who would listen. Henry and Mrs. Brunson most certainly would not.

She lowered her eyes to her hands, which she clasped to

mask their trembling. She'd buried her emotions for Julian so long that she'd believed them dead. Apparently, they'd only slept, and they'd awakened stronger than ever.

"If you'd like," Eleanor ventured, "I could extend an invitation to any particular young lady you have in mind." She forced herself to take a breath. "If Henry knew you have already found a lady, he'd be quite content to invite her, or perhaps cancel the ball altog—"

"Eleanor."

Her name was all he needed to say; her speech stopped mid-word, and her feet stilled. He stepped in front of her and took her hands—her cold, trembling hands—in his and drew her near. The warm look in his eyes was almost more than she could bear. She wanted to bury her head in his chest once more, if only to feel that nearness one more time. If only to keep herself from seeing him wax poetic as he proclaimed his love for another woman. A burning temptation told her to embrace him quickly to stop him from talking and then flee the room.

Resisting the impulse, she instead looked into his dear face, tightened her fingers around his, and steeled herself for whatever he said next.

Julian didn't speak right away. He glanced up and around them, then stepped backward, holding her hands as he went, leading her. He wore a smile she could make neither heads nor tails of. He almost looked like the mischievous boy who'd slipped a toad into Henry's bed years hence.

A few more steps backward and a final upward glance and then Julian stopped and planted his feet before her. He smiled and quirked an eyebrow before looking up once more, this time *very* slowly, as if telling her that she should follow his gaze.

Comprehension dawned on her like the sun at noonday.

Right above them hung the mistletoe. She suddenly had difficulty breathing. She hadn't noticed where he was leading her, because her emotions had been in such a muddle that she hadn't noticed much of anything.

Am I asleep and dreaming?

He drew nearer and nearer still, until Eleanor could feel the warmth of his breath on the curl on her temple. "Plenty of berries on it yet," he said, his voice low but filled with meaning.

Heat flared in her chest and spread throughout her body, setting her heart beating as fast as a galloping horse. Clearly, this was no dream. She stood still, half afraid that any movement or sound would shatter this beautiful moment, half disbelieving that he had any intention of kissing her. Or that if he did, he'd kiss her hand or her forehead as a friend.

She could *not* hope for more, because hopes of fancy brought brokenheartedness when they were dashed. Eleanor Hadfield could not hope for anything at all, until the moment Captain Julian Stephens lowered his face to hers and gently—hesitantly—pressed his lips to hers.

Chapter Six

As Julian kissed her, he prayed Eleanor wouldn't pull away or—worse—merely tolerate his touch like a statue. To his joy, she returned his kiss. The realization draped him with warmth from crown to toe. This kiss outranked their first from so long ago, like a captain outranked the lowliest cabin boy. This kiss burned brighter and hotter, eclipsing their first like the brightness of the sun eclipsed a weak candle.

It ended with both of them breathing shakily, unsure of what to say or do next. Julian wanted to yell with a cry of triumph, but one's voice carrying over the vast waters of the ocean was quite a different thing from attempting the same within the echoing walls of one's childhood home.

He leaned closer to Eleanor's ear and whispered, "Shall we take a turn about the gardens?"

"Yes . . . please," she said, then slipped an arm through his.

He placed his hand over hers, and together they left the ballroom and walked through the house until they reached a door leading to the gardens. After what felt like far too long, they found themselves alone along the manicured garden paths, colder than the last time, but not yet covered with snow. Their steps crunched gravel beneath their feet in what was otherwise a burning silence between them that waited to be broken.

As a gentleman, speaking first was his duty. But what to say? Eleanor had returned his kiss, but he could not assume that such a moment would necessarily mean she cared for him in the way he loved her or that she would ever want to leave her home at Willowsmeade, along with the life she'd created here with Henry's family. No matter how eagerly she'd welcomed his kiss, it mightn't have meant what he wished it to. If she yet loved him, why hadn't she shown it before?

"You've done well for yourself," Julian said, then mentally berated himself for sounding stiff and formal.

"I suppose I have," Eleanor said in an even tone that left him at a loss to interpret her meaning.

"Are you . . . happy at Willowsmeade?" he ventured.

She glanced over warily, then looked away. "I am, yes. The Brunsons have been most generous, and I adore the children. The life of a governess isn't one of permanence, so I've come to accept that my duties include saying goodbye to children when a certain time comes. That is the hardest part, I admit."

"You aren't anticipating parting from the Brunson children anytime soon, are you?" Julian worried he'd overstepped his bounds. "I, er, apologize for my presumption. I assumed your position here *was* of a permanent nature. Is it not?"

"This is the understanding with Mr. Brunson . . ."

"But?" Julian offered. When she didn't answer, he stopped walking and faced her, taking her hands in his as he had in the ballroom.

She didn't look up and instead studied their clasped hands. Oh, how he wanted her to lift her face and meet his eyes.

"Eleanor."

"Mm?" Her gaze remained on their hands.

He stroked the back of one hand with his thumb. Such smooth, soft skin. "You have a home at Willowsmeade for as long as you wish. Henry has told me so. You needn't work as a governess any longer. You needn't say goodbye to Henry's children."

She nodded, making ringlets bob at the sides of her face. Her stubborn Brunson pride, inherited from her mother, kept from accepting supposed charity by not working for her keep, even though she could take her place as a family member at any time.

Eleanor swallowed hard as she listened, then said, "I am unsure what you expect me to say." She seemed on the verge of adding a *Mr. Stephens* or *Captain Stephens*, and he was most grateful she left them off.

He tried again. "You have your future assured if you stay here. I know you have no need to seek a suitable match of your own. But . . ."

Her fingers grew cold, her grip stiffening. Before she could refuse him, he hurried to say his piece. "I'm only the son of a gardener, but I've raised my station to a naval captain. I am not and never will be a wealthy, landed gentleman. My life, and that of my wife-to-be, will not be as secure as Henry's. Any woman who takes my hand in marriage will face a somewhat uncertain future. Odds of a comfortable existence are good, but not a grand life, not one such as Willowsmeade can provide." Following this speech, which to his ears came from him in halting, awkward phrases, he paused and waited for her to reply. Surely she'd understand his intent.

He watched her fanned lashes blink once, twice, before she spoke. "Any woman should find herself fortunate to marry you."

"Do you mean that in earnest?" Julian waited with bated breath.

"Of course, Captain St—"

He quickly pressed a finger to her lips to stop the name. "Please, don't call me that."

She closed her eyes and then slowly reached up and took his finger from her lips. She finally looked at him in a manner he could only describe as wary. "What would you have me say?" Her voice wobbled.

Julian curled his fingers about hers and narrowed the distance between them even more. "Say whether you love me still as you said in this very garden when we parted so long ago." He pressed a kiss to her palm. "If your feelings have changed over the many years, please say so, and *I* will be the one to depart. You needn't leave the children or your home. Say the word, and I will stay away, never to speak of this again. But you must know that my feelings have not changed except to grow stronger. I love you, Eleanor, as much as ever."

"You do?" Her eyes closed tightly, and a tear fell, streaking down her right cheek. But the tear was followed by her lips slowly curling into a smile. Her eyes opened, and she gazed up at him, aglow with happiness.

He cupped her face in his hand and ran his thumb along her jawline. "I do," he said insistently. "*More* than ever."

Eleanor leaned in as he stroked her chin. "And I you. Always."

Their second kiss of the day was better than the first. Julian felt as if he could fly, defeat Napoleon single-handedly, vanquish any enemy, all because Eleanor loved him still.

The kiss ended with several small ones, and then he rested his forehead against hers. He closed his eyes and breathed, then quietly, so as not to shatter the moment, said, "Would you do me the honor of becoming my wife?"

"With all my heart." Eleanor squeezed his hands, and he squeezed back, hoping to convey his joy through his touch. He opened his lips to speak, but a single word escaped her lips first, one that would have dashed his dreams, had it not been in the playful tone he knew from a lifetime of loving her: "However..."

The tone, as well as the fact that she'd just declared her reciprocal love, set at ease any worries Julian might have had. For that moment, they were not an aged bachelor and spinster, but people in love, with stars in their eyes, and perhaps a penchant for entering into mischief together, such as the time they put syrup in Henry's boots.

"However what?" he asked, gazing into her eyes, certain he'd never tire of the sight.

"We'll have to inform Henry that the dreadful ball is not necessary."

Julian clucked his tongue. "Tragic, that." He smiled, and the two of them broke into laughter. He drew her hand through the crook of his elbow and led her along the garden path back toward the house. "However..."

Upon hearing his repetition of her protest, she leveled a playful gaze at him from the corner of her eye. "However?"

"Before we inform Henry of our recent understanding, I believe we—that is to say, you and I—should return to the ballroom posthaste."

"May I ask to what end? Do you plan to remove the decorations prior to having an audience with Henry?"

"No, nothing like that." He paused in his step and gave her a knowing smile. "Our errand is much more practical—and necessary. You see, we must ensure the mistletoe is rendered useless." He spoke in such a serious tone that a light chuckle escaped Eleanor, a sound that bore witness of the young spirit still within her.

She leaned in, pressed onto her toes, and kissed his cheek. Then she spoke, tickling his ear with her words. "That, my dear Julian, is a most excellent idea."

Annette Lyon is a *USA Today* bestselling author, a four-time recipient of Utah's Best of State medal for fiction, a Whitney Award winner, and a five-time publication award winner from the League of Utah Writers. She's the author of more than a dozen novels, even more novellas, and several nonfiction books. When she's not writing, knitting, or eating chocolate, she can be found mothering and avoiding housework. Annette is a member of the Women's Fiction Writers Association and is represented by Heather Karpas at ICM Partners.

Find Annette online:
Blog: http://blog.AnnetteLyon.com
Twitter: @AnnetteLyon
Facebook: http://Facebook.com/AnnetteLyon
Instagram: @annette.lyon
Pinterest: http://Pinterest.com/AnnetteLyon
Newsletter: http://bit.ly/1n3I87y

Follow the River Home

KRISTA LYNNE JENSEN

Chapter One

MR. FORBES SAT across from Arabelle in the drawing room of Hybrigge House, studying the paintings above the fireplace, running his hand along the carved arm of the settee, and patting the upholstery as if assessing the value of a racehorse he wasn't quite impressed with. He'd been here two hours already, and Arabelle wondered if she should ask him to dine with them. Out of hospitality, not desire.

He set his tea down and crossed his long legs. A grin stretched across his handsome face. "I was surprised to find you indoors today, Miss Hyatt."

"I assure you, I had every intention to be out of doors." Her mother coughed. "But when I learned you were coming I canceled my morning walk to the river. All that dreadful fresh air and dirt and rush of water. What is that compared to your company, Mr. Forbes?"

"Knowing how you feel about nature, I will take that as a compliment, though I've never compared myself to the 'rush of water.' Or dirt."

Arabelle stifled a laugh. "Do you not like the out of doors?"

"Not in December."

"I suppose I learned to love the winterscape from my brother. George was always rambling about on some adventure with me in tow."

Indeed, the chill of December had descended upon their valley. Christmas was coming. She and Mama had put away the black dresses of mourning for George and his wife, Jane, both lost to consumption a year ago. George had just enough time to contact their father's cousin's estate, as Hybrigge was entailed to that distant family. Mr. Hewitt Forbes's family.

And now he was here. Courting Arabelle.

His brow lowered in concern. "I am sorry for your loss, Miss Hyatt."

"Thank you, sir."

He immediately brightened. "But what of London in winter? You've had a season, correct?"

Arabelle composed her near-gape at the turnabout of subject. "That is correct, sir. Two years ago."

"Did you enjoy it?" He waited, his dark eyes alight.

"Some of it."

"Only some?"

"I do not care much for London, sir."

He narrowed his gaze. "Not enough dirt, I suppose."

She smiled.

"And no offers?" he asked.

Mama had the decency to answer for her. "My daughter was very young at the time. Barely sixteen. But she was seldom in want of friends or dance partners."

His gaze darted back to Arabelle, his eyebrows twitching upward. "I have no trouble imagining that, ma'am."

Arabelle shivered. The truth was, she'd spent much of her time in London with George and Jane. No offers had even been hinted at. Well, except one. And that was hardly real. Yet even now, she felt her cheeks grow warm at the memory of one silly paragraph in one silly letter. It hadn't even been her letter. It had been sent to George.

"That color becomes you, Miss Hyatt. You should wear it more often."

Arabelle glanced at her brown wool day dress.

Mama leaned forward. "I believe he means the color in your cheeks, darling."

Arabelle chided herself for giving Mr. Forbes the impression her blush was for him. She straightened, perturbed. She was meant to accept Mr. Forbes's suit. She was meant to accept—should he ask—his proposal of marriage. She and Mama had discussed it and agreed. This was the best course. Because it was the only course to keeping Hybrigge House, and their way of life, and providing the best chance for little—

Clark appeared at the doors. "Mum, the babe is awake and asking rather loudly for Miss."

Arabelle could have kissed Clark. She stood, Mr. Forbes just after. "I'll be right up."

Clark nodded and disappeared again.

She turned to Mr. Forbes. "Would you care to accompany us for a walk, Mr. Forbes? I think I'll be taking one after all."

He looked outside at the gray morning, his mouth drawn tight. "Hm. Rain threatens."

"Doesn't it always?" Arabelle answered cheerfully. "We are in England, you know."

He chuckled and turned to Mama. "Mrs. Hyatt, your daughter is a delight. Nevertheless, business calls me away."

Mama stood. "Do call on us again soon."

"I look forward to it." He bowed elegantly over Arabelle's hand and bid farewell.

When she heard the front door shut, she hurried toward the stairs.

"Arabelle."

She turned. "Yes, Mama?" The drop of her mother's shoulders pricked Arabelle's guilt. "I'm sorry, Mama. I was too candid with Mr. Forbes."

"Too candid? Honesty is not a vice. Using your helpless niece to cut a visit short is beneath you."

"He was here for *two hours*. It's not as if I paid Clark to come in just then. And say what you will about your granddaughter, but that child is not helpless. Have you seen her order Edith about? She'll have her as a lady's maid before her third birthday. You and I will be fastening up each other's gowns."

At that, Mama smiled. "She is much like George."

"He was ever the boss."

Mama's eyes glistened. They both turned to the sound of a wailing child who clearly wanted more attention than the spare staff could give.

Arabelle moved to go, but Mama caught her hand.

"Promise me you'll take care with Mr. Forbes. Despite his pomposity, I believe him a good man."

"He doesn't show any interest in Eleanor. He talks above her, not to her."

"As most men would. It will not matter. She will be loved."

"It would matter to George and Jane."

After a long pause, Mama sighed. "Arabelle, please. We have no other option."

She squeezed Mama's hand. "I promise." But while Arabelle agreed Mr. Forbes appeared to be a good man, she battled the question of whether Mr. Forbes was a good man *for her*.

༺❀༻

"I do not understand, Linny." Arabelle watched her niece bend down and pick up a stick with her mittened hands. "How could anyone not be enamored with you?"

Eleanor dropped the muddy stick in Arabelle's lap. "Fro." They sat at a favorite gravelly bar on a calm, shallow stretch of river just before the water turned frothy and wild again.

"Yes, I'll throw it for you," Arabelle said. "Watch." She drew her arm back and gave the stick a launch into the drifting water. "Watch it now, Linny. See it go?"

Eleanor's eyes danced. "Atch."

The stick drifted through the slower water, then bounced and spun as it hit the drop-off at the end of the bar and was sucked under where branches and larger drifts of wood gathered in the erratic current.

Eleanor lifted her hands. "Ere go?"

"*Wh*ere go. Watch." Arabelle stood and took her niece's hand, hurrying to the end of the bar. She scanned the water, then pointed. "Look there. See it?" The stick bobbed and bucked its way downstream, reminding Arabelle much of her own life and how little control she had over it.

"Abibelle find?"

"Yes, dear, Abibelle find. Should we throw another?"

Eleanor clapped mutedly with her mittens and took a few running steps.

"No, no, hold my hand this close to the water."

The little girl giggled and darted away, but Arabelle anticipated the move and grabbed Eleanor's hand more securely. "I forget. Somebody says stay here and you dash in the opposite direction. Mama says you're like George. There's a lot of Abibelle in you too. Poor darling."

Her gaze wandered to the wooded bank, the twiggy bushes with clinging winterberries not yet picked clean by the birds that stayed, and the high, silver clouds above. She took a deep, clear breath.

Perhaps that was her problem with Mr. Forbes. It was simply that someone was telling her to stay put, and she grappled with that innate sense to run in the opposite direction.

"Really, Arabelle," she said, straightening her shoulders. "Time to grow up."

"Time a row up," came the echo from below. Eleanor blinked up at her.

Arabelle grinned. "Not you, little Linny." She crouched down and met her blue eyes. "What shall we do next?"

Eleanor bent down and picked up a rock. She placed it in Arabelle's glove.

"Fro."

Arabelle gathered the girl into her arms. "I'm giving you an entire basket of sticks and rocks for Christmas. I don't care what Mama will say."

❧

Isaac Linfield stared at the open fields of Hybrigge. The house remained obscured by woods. A rare bit of winter sun beamed down over the small valley sided by gentle hills and split by a river seldom wider than a rod. On one side of the lane, bramble canes mounded down the riverbank. On the other, three large oak trees stood guard, hosting clumps of mistletoe he'd helped gather during Christmases past.

He gazed into the bare branches at the clinging stuff believed to bring luck to all who kissed beneath it and remembered some of those too-brief kisses. He might have smiled, but the memories were bitter now.

He urged his horse forward. He'd made most of the trip by coach, but he would finish on horseback. His valet and trunk would arrive that evening, as planned.

He couldn't explain the need to arrive at Hybrigge House astride a horse of his own instead of rolling up in a carriage, except that he'd always equated the maneuverability and speed of a horse with freedom and independence, two things he longed to feel right now.

As he sat waxing poetic, he'd absently begun kneading his leg just above his knee. He frowned at the mild throbbing pain setting in since he'd paused. Wouldn't be the first time he'd pushed himself too hard. Sometimes it was the only thing that made him feel a fraction of his old self.

He crossed the old arched stone bridge, and the house came into view, a sturdy edifice of lime-washed rock with two rows of tall windows—six below and seven above, centered over an arched front entry—flanked by two chimneys. Some might consider Hybrigge small in the way of country estates. But to Isaac it was a friend's home, and it had come into difficult times.

He passed the front doors, painted the blue he remembered, and rode around the carriage house to the stables. A stableman met him, but Isaac only required a hand down, then he gave the man orders to announce his arrival. Isaac led the horse to one of the stalls where he could brush the animal down and tend to water and feed. He told himself he wasn't avoiding his duty, merely working up to it. Slowly. With his stomach knotted in nerves.

But before reaching the stall, he stopped altogether. Before him in the dusty afternoon light stood a woman, her forehead pressed to that of a winter-coated white mare, her eyes closed, her lips moving as hushed words left her mouth. Wisps of hair nearly as pale as the horse's had escaped the knot at the back of her neck, and her bonnet hung loosely by ribbons in her fingers.

Denial that he knew her warred with certain recognition erupting inside him. Without another hint of who she was, one name bloomed in his mind.

"Abby."

She turned quickly at the hushed sound he'd made, her blue eyes wide with shock.

He shouldn't have startled her.

She stepped back from the horse, her brows knit together.

He froze as if his movement would scare away a rabbit, his heart pounding under her scrutiny, and he realized with a drop of his gut . . . that the fear was all his.

"Who are you?" she asked.

◆

The stranger opened his mouth to speak again, but he halted. He removed his hat, inviting the light to better illuminate his face. Only a handful of people had ever called her Abby. Coarse, sandy hair brushed his temples, and he squinted as his mind worked.

She swallowed. "Isaac?"

His gaze met hers directly.

"Isaac, is that you?" She stepped toward him, emotions rising up like a wild wind.

He stepped back unsteadily, as if he'd stumbled in a hole, and her gaze went to his foot and what might have caused the misstep. But instead of a tall riding boot beneath his great coat, she found a wooden leg and a short leather boot attached with buckles at each side.

Bringing her gaze up quickly, it caught on something else. The hand that held his horse's reins was not a hand, but a narrow loop of iron, bent inward to form a hook.

She stared too long, she knew, and when she brought her eyes up, they were wet. "You've returned from Spain," she whispered.

He searched her gaze without emotion, then gave a brief nod.

"You didn't die."

"Your mother didn't receive my letter?" he asked, his voice tight.

She shook her head.

Concern creased the corners of his eyes. "Then you're not expecting me at all."

Again, she shook her head, unable to take her eyes off him.

"Forgive me for imposing," he said.

"You didn't die," she repeated.

The statement finally seemed to register with him. "No. I did not."

Before she could think to stop herself, she launched herself into him, wrapping her arms about his waist. Images flooded her mind of George and Isaac on a sunny bank playing swords with sticks, laughing in tall grass, and swinging her between the two of them. "I think we shall forgive you, then."

It wasn't until she realized that Isaac Linfield was not returning her embrace and had—in fact—become as stone that propriety seized her, and she let go with a jolt. She turned to Snowbird and stroked the horse's nose to hide her mortification.

"Miss Hyatt?" he asked, his tone cautious.

She glanced his way again. "You needn't worry about arriving before your letter. Mama will rejoice in seeing you. But do you know—I mean to say—did you hear that George, and his wife—"

"Yes. It's why I've come."

She stared at him. "You know?"

"Yes. I'm very sorry for your loss. I came as soon as I could."

"It is your loss, too," she offered.

"Yes," he replied.

After a moment she blinked, glancing around. "Seth can take your horse."

"I sent him away to let your mother know I'm here." He donned his hat and pulled his horse closer. "This stallion's new to me, and I wanted time with him."

The brown stallion wore a white stripe down his nose and a mane black as ink. "Did you get him at Tattersall's?" she asked.

"No. A breeder friend of mine. He's a thoroughbred cross, meant for the army."

"So you saved him," she said.

"You might say that."

"He's beautiful. What's his name?"

"He doesn't have one yet."

She nearly offered to help him name the horse, but after throwing herself at him she didn't want to appear too forward.

"Is she yours?" His question pulled her out of the awkward silence.

"Who?"

He motioned to her right.

"Oh. This is Snowbird. She was Jane's. She left her to me."

He nodded, apparently having nothing to say to that. What did one say to that? *How nice.* Or, *How good of her.* Or, *What a shame.*

"I'm sure she is in the best hands," he said.

His words drew a small smile from her.

"I'll just use this stall, then, shall I?" He was already leading the horse past her, his limp apparent now.

"Of course. I should probably go help Mama. She really will be thrilled."

"I hope so."

"And Isaa—Mr. Linfield?"

He turned to her. "Yes?"

She tried to read the emotion in his gray eyes. "Your visit couldn't have come at a better time."

He studied her a moment, his brow furrowed, then dismissed her with a nod.

Chapter Two

AFTER AN EMOTIONAL welcome from Mama, Isaac had retired to a guest room with a tray of food and orders to eat and rest. Now he and Mama conversed at the fire as Arabelle worked quietly in a corner embroidering a shawl. At least, she made herself pretend to embroider a shawl.

"I received a letter from George seven months ago," Isaac told Mama. "I'm certain the only reason it found me was because I had been injured and conveyed to a hospital. Even so, I was too weak—too incapacitated to return home."

"Of course," Mama said. "No one would expect you to drop your service, wounded or not, to return here because of this. Nor to make the journey while still in danger from your wounds. Certainly, George didn't?"

"No. He simply wanted me to have the news from him." Isaac glanced at Arabelle, and she ducked her head back to her needle.

"We are filled with gratitude that you are alive, sir," Mama said.

"Yes. I don't know how or why. There were times when ... well, I survived when others did not. And when it was deemed I couldn't return to battle, I was released and sent home."

"What an ordeal. And you've been to your family. I'm sure they were overjoyed to see you."

"And I them. But the words in George's letter never left me. I wrote to you and—forgive me for not waiting for your reply—I left them to come here."

"Your mother must've been very reluctant to let you go."

"Indeed. But she also knew I could not rest until I spoke to you myself."

Mama reached for Isaac's hand and bowed her head over it, her shoulders shaking with sorrow. "Bless you, dear boy."

Isaac's expression softened toward his best friend's mother, then he lifted his gaze and found Arabelle watching. In that moment of firelight and candle glow, Arabelle remembered a Christmastime evening when guests filled the house and she watched the party from behind the window seat curtains. Isaac had spied her across the room as he talked to a group of pretty girls, and just when she thought he would expose her, he'd placed a finger to his lips and winked.

"Miss Hyatt?"

She blinked, and the memory faded. "Yes?"

"Will you join us at the fire?" Isaac nodded discreetly toward Mama, who dabbed at her eyes.

"I was just feeling a draft at this window." Arabelle stood and approached. She sat next to Mama and eased the woman toward her shoulder. "There, there, Mama. You are much warmer than that shawl I shall never finish."

"You shall finish it," Mama sniffled. "And it will be lovely." She straightened, still close to Arabelle's side and clinging to Isaac's hand. "Now, how long will you stay? As long as you like, I hope. I shall write to your mother. It's been too long since we exchanged letters. She'll want to know that you are well. Gracious, are you well?"

A smile teased at the corner of his mouth, another reminder of the boy he used to be. "Well enough after my rest, thank you."

"You must be hungry again. That tray of food was barely tea. Cook has made roast chicken and creamed potatoes. A simple dinner, but always one of my favorites."

"One of mine as well, ma'am."

Mama smiled. "Then you shall join us."

"As you wish."

"I promise you a more lavish meal tomorrow when Mr. Forbes dines with us. Now that you're here, I shall make the most of it. And I daresay you'll find Mr. Forbes an interesting enough fellow and quite agreeable, am I right, Arabelle?"

Arabelle opened her mouth, but no words for nor against Mama's prediction came out. Truthfully, she'd forgotten about Mr. Forbes and that he would be coming to dinner the next day. In the end, it didn't matter, because Clark came in and all three heads turned.

"Yes, Clark, what is it?" Mama asked.

He looked at Arabelle. "Miss, a word?"

Arabelle rose and approached. "What is it?" she asked in hushed tones. "Is something wrong?"

"The babe, Miss. It's Thursday and somehow she knows it."

Arabelle closed her eyes. "I dine with her on Mondays and Thursdays. With Mr. Linfield's arrival, I'd forgotten. Has her dinner already been sent up?"

"Yes. She noticed it was too small and asked where 'Abibelle's' was." His brows rose expectantly. "Edith sent me to fetch you."

Arabelle glanced back at Mama, who watched with interest. Isaac only gazed at the fire.

She turned back to Clark. "Tell Edith I'll be right up. And ask Cook to send up a little something more."

"Yes, Miss."

Isaac rose as she returned to the fire.

"I apologize," Arabelle said, "but I've forgotten a previous engagement and shall be late for dinner."

"A previous engagement?" Mama asked.

"It's Thursday."

Mama smiled. "Ah. Yes, you shan't miss that." She looked up at Isaac. "When George wrote to you, did he mention that he and Jane had a daughter?"

"He did. To be honest, the child has weighed heavily on my mind, but I'd not presumed to ask yet." He turned to Arabelle. "Is everything well with her since your brother's passing?"

His concern intrigued her. "She is very well, thank you. Would you . . . would you like to meet her?"

༄

To say that Isaac was conscious of the young woman walking next to him as he limped up the stairs was a grand understatement. She graciously matched his snail's pace, though he imagined her darting up this flight like a bird.

He shook his head. "I'm afraid our days of racing to the nursery are done."

She paused. "I cannot decide if you are serious. I remember how you would tease, but do you tease about this, sir?"

He released a half-aggravated laugh. "If I can't tease about this, then what do I do, Miss Hyatt? Bellow? Moan? Perhaps it's just a façade, but teasing helps."

"In that case," she said, "I would have to balance on one leg, and perhaps borrow George's cane for leverage." She glanced sidelong at him.

"Ah," he said, taking the opening she'd allowed him. "Tie one hand behind your back. Then I might have a sporting chance."

Her eyes danced. "Of course, we'd have to put you in a gown, to really even things up."

He broke into a laugh. "You might have me there."

She smiled as they continued up the staircase. She'd grown up rather prettily. When she'd followed George and Isaac around the estate, she'd been a waif of a thing. Six years separated them, just enough for her to keep up, but not close enough for them to be thrilled about it. To her credit, she was a good sport and kept their secret escapades. And she'd had them laughing more often than he'd give any six-, eight-, ten-year-old girl credit for.

"Will you tell me about it?" she asked quietly. "How it happened. Someday?"

He frowned, the lightness gone. He'd given her permission to address his injuries. He should have known she'd ask further. "I'll not promise you that. It's difficult."

"I understand," she said, though he knew she could not.

He changed the subject. "Tell me about Eleanor."

"She is thoughtful for one so small. Perhaps it's because relationships mean so much to her. She was only a year and a half old when she lost her parents. People dismiss the effect that has on an infant. But believe me, we watched her mourn just as we did. She knew." Her gaze narrowed as if in contemplation, and she paused on the stair. "She is a person. As much of us as George was."

He wondered at her ardent tone. "I do not doubt it. Loss comes in all forms, to all ages. It affects each differently. But I've learned that it is not what happens to us, but rather what we do afterward that determines our course. She has your example to learn from."

She lifted her chin, studying him. "Sometimes I believe I'm the one learning from her. Is that childish of me?"

He studied her. The last time he'd seen her she was

fourteen, with ringlets on either side of her face and wide eyes watching him say goodbye before he took his commission. He'd bowed over her hand and told her something silly to watch her break into a smile, because he couldn't have borne leaving her in tears.

"In all my years of knowing you as a child, Miss Hyatt, you were never childish."

Again, she smiled, the action lighting something inside him he'd not felt in a long time.

Again, he reminded himself of his duty here.

They made the first landing and walked down the hallway to the narrower staircase leading to the nursery. He sighed inwardly. If he ever built a house, it would have scandalously few staircases.

"Are you all right, Mr. Linfield?"

He nodded. "Still recovering from the ride, that's all."

"I should have thought better and brought Eleanor down."

He gestured for her to lead up the narrow flight. She moved gracefully, and he caught himself appreciating his perspective for more than one reason. He'd known she would have grown. It seemed a lifetime had gone by since he left England. But when he'd pictured Abby here, he'd somehow removed the "woman" part of the experience, and now reality mocked him. Isaac shook his head to clear his thoughts and focused on his steps.

"What sort of fellow is Mr. Forbes?" he asked, more to keep himself on task than anything.

She halted on the stairs, then quickly resumed. "He's a good man. He is . . . sure of himself."

"Fortunate. George mentioned he was to inherit. What are his intentions for Hybrigge House?"

She'd reached the nursery door and turned to face him,

her eyes over-bright. "The best intentions, I'm sure. He's paid the structure more attention than the inhabitants inside it."

He frowned, puzzled by her response.

At that moment, the maid opened the door. "Miss. Sir." She addressed Arabelle. "All is ready for you. If you need me further, only ring."

They entered the room Isaac knew well. Before the familiar surroundings and scent could settle with him, his gaze was drawn to a little girl in folds of sprigged muslin, with pink cheeks and white curls atop her head. Arabelle stepped toward her, hand extended. The little girl took it, her gaze glued on Isaac, then to his leg.

"Eleanor, meet our friend, Mr. Linfield. He's come a long way to see us." She smiled up at Isaac. "Mr. Linfield, this is Miss Eleanor Hyatt."

"Of course it is." Isaac bowed. "Hello, Miss Eleanor."

"Show him your curtsy, darling."

The tiny figure held her dress out with one hand and dipped, wobbling. "Hello."

Isaac couldn't help smiling. "May I join you for your dinner?" He motioned to a small, waiting table.

She followed his gaze and nodded. Then she let go of Arabelle's hand, crouched, and as Arabelle gasped, touched his wooden leg.

He put his hand up to silence Arabelle's protest, his face warming with the awkwardness of the moment.

"You leg hurt?" the child asked. She waited for Isaac's answer to her simple question, her finger tapping softly on one of the buckles holding his boot on.

He cleared his throat. "Yes, I am hurt." He flashed her a trying smile. "But I'm getting better."

Eleanor frowned, but nodded. "Better. Hurt aw gone."

"That's right." He wished he could believe as she did. Pain was part of him now.

Without another word, Eleanor stood and reached for his false hand—he'd changed out his riding hook for the less off-putting carved hand. He quickly reached across with his good hand and allowed her to lead him to the table set with bread and butter alongside miniature crocks of chicken and potatoes and an apple tart the size of a tea saucer. He pulled out a chair for her, then for Arabelle, whom he caught watching him perplexedly, then seated himself in the tiny space.

"It hasn't changed much," Isaac said, looking around. "It's smaller than I remember."

Arabelle smiled. "We were smaller. Though you and George seemed like giants to me. Even when you were twelve. May I?" she asked, holding his dish near the crocks. She didn't wait for his answer. "Usually it's just Eleanor and I. Edith has so much to do that I manage without her."

"Yet another example of how I've disrupted your routine."

She set down his plate in front of him and dished Eleanor her food. "Not at all. Things can get a bit monotonous here. Hybrigge hasn't been as it was. Here you are, Linny. Use your spoon, now." She lifted her gaze. "A visit from an old friend is a balm, even when unexpected. Perhaps especially then."

He found himself without words, because she was unexpected, and if he could describe the effect her presence had on his nerves, it would be something like a balm.

It was her kinship to George, he told himself. The familiarity of better days.

"Eleanor," she said once they'd each been dished up a plate. "Tell Mr. Linfield about our walk yesterday."

The little girl's blue eyes lit up. "Fro rocks." She giggled.

"Throw rocks?" he asked, intrigued.

She nodded. "And tick. In da water."

"In the river?" He eyed Arabelle, who watched them both, amused. He continued with Eleanor. "Did you throw it with all your might?"

She nodded with fervor and put a piece of chicken in her mouth.

"I do most of the throwing," Arabelle said. "But one day she'll be skipping rocks across the water better than her father."

"Well," he said with a chuckle, "that shouldn't be too hard. Many perfect skipping rocks lie at the bottom of that river by George's hand. Alas, they never met their full potential."

"He taught me," she exclaimed with a laugh.

He shook his head. "He did not."

"He did. I remember his hand around mine, moving me through the motions and then letting me try, over and over until I did it."

He pushed a potato around his plate. "That was me." Peering up at her, he caught her stare. She busied herself with a piece of chicken. Aware he might have stolen what she believed to be a warm memory of her brother, he amended himself. "George was right there cheering you on, of course."

She nodded, and quickly helped Eleanor with a sip of water. "Of course. I just presumed."

"Naturally. While I could best him in skipping stones—which requires some finesse, as you know—George always had the stronger arm. He could clear the river and then some, every time."

"I do remember that."

"He would save the best skipping stones he found for you."

She paused, her fork halfway between her plate and mouth. Her light blue eyes became glassy. "Thank you, Mr. Linfield."

He nodded, biting back the urge to ask her to call him Isaac.

They resumed eating.

"And thank you," she said. "For teaching me to skip rocks."

He smiled. "It was my pleasure. You possessed finesse."

"Kip rocks," the little girl said, both hands flat on the table, looking between the both of them. "Kip rocks."

"Now we've done it," Arabelle said, grinning. "She'll not rest until we've made her the best rock-skipper in all of England."

Isaac leaned forward. "I believe those particular seeds of destiny were planted the moment you became her aunt."

She beamed at him, as though his words were the greatest compliment he might have paid her.

Chapter Three

ARABELLE PACED HER bedroom floor as Edith pushed two gowns at her. She paused, realizing Edith was speaking. "I'm sorry, what was that?"

"Miss, you must dress for dinner. Mr. Forbes will be here at any moment."

"Is Mr. Linfield down yet?"

"I do not know, as I'm up here with *you*." Edith lifted a brow.

Arabelle took one of the gowns. "No need to get cheeky."

"Beg your pardon, Miss. The red is right pretty on you." She helped pull it over Arabelle's head. "I dare say both gentlemen will have a hard time focusing on their meal tonight."

"Both gentlemen?"

"Yes. Mr. Linfield may not be here courting, nor may he have all his limbs, but he's both his eyes—and he's an old acquaintance who knew you before you bloomed, not that you were ever plain, mind you. Only a bit wild. And here you are, no more a child, a lovely woman born from the fires of trial, for sure."

"Edith, I didn't know you were a poet," she teased, attempting to cover her blush.

"To be sure. Now sit while I make something of those tresses."

Arabelle sighed and sat. "He's changed so much. Do you remember how full of life he was?"

Edith nodded, beginning a crown braid. "Yes, Miss. I'll venture to say he still is. Just as you and the missus still are. Life fills us, whether it's the kind we want or the kind we don't."

Arabelle had no response to that except to stare unfocused at the glass before her, thinking on Edith's words, and on Isaac, and on losing a leg. And a brother.

༺༻

Downstairs, Arabelle approached the drawing room doors with a twisting stomach and hands clasped. Her state of nerves weren't on Mr. Linfield's behalf, as he seemed confident despite his injuries. It wasn't on Mr. Forbes's behalf, as she hadn't felt this way over his previous visits. And yet her insides felt as though she were about to step up to a pianoforte and play for a hundred people, and Arabelle knew not one note of that instrument.

"Good evening, Miss," Clark said as he opened the doors for her.

She nodded absently. Just as she crossed the threshold into the room, her slipper caught and she stumbled, only slightly. All sound ceased, and she lifted her gaze to find Mr. Forbes and Isaac having just risen to their feet, their expressions startled.

"Forgive me," she managed to say. "I can't imagine what I did to the carpet to offend it so."

Mr. Forbes broke out into a genial laugh, but Isaac only stared.

She blushed under his gaze.

"No person or thing could be offended by your presence, Miss Hyatt," Mr. Forbes said with a grin and bow.

She curtsied. "Then you don't know me very well, Mr. Forbes."

He laughed harder, and Isaac seemed to remember himself and bowed as well.

She curtsied and lifted her gaze to him with difficulty. "Mr. Linfield."

"Miss Hyatt. You look lovely."

The pull in her stomach mysteriously tightened. She'd only left him an hour ago in the library, where he'd been going over business with George's steward. She'd pretended to read. "You sound surprised."

He gazed at her steadily. "I suppose I shouldn't be."

She had nothing clever to say to that but observed the room growing warmer. She took a deep breath and looked about her. "Where is Mama?"

Mr. Forbes offered her his arm, leading her to the settee nearest the fire. Arabelle wished for a fan.

"Addressing a question from your cook, I believe." He took the chair next to her, leaving Isaac leaning against the fireplace.

"I'll assume you two have been properly introduced," she said. "What were you discussing before I entered so gracefully?"

"I was getting to know the war hero, here," said Mr. Forbes, gesturing to Isaac.

"The war hero?" She looked at Isaac expectantly, but he frowned at the fire.

"Yes," said Mr. Forbes. "Of course, when I read about the battles at Badajos in the papers, I had no idea I would one day be standing with Major Isaac Linfield in your drawing room. Another unexpectedly pleasant event arising from very difficult circumstances—making your acquaintance being the first, Miss Hyatt. It's rather exciting."

"Major?" she asked, with still no response from Isaac except a clenching of his good hand resting on the mantel.

"Indeed. Saved his commanding officer's life, and his company as well. Can't imagine. I've often asked myself how it would've been, to not have had to stay home to manage the family assets, but to have instead gone off to war in name of crown and country." His expression drew uncharacteristically grave. "At such a cost. Such a cost." He glanced toward Isaac's leg and shook his head. Then blinked away. "Good man," he said. "I'm honored to be in the same room with you. And the fact that you were George Hyatt's good friend raises him in my eyes."

Arabelle frowned. "Did George need raising in your eyes, Mr. Forbes?" Movement from Isaac drew her attention. Indeed, he watched her, amusement in his expression. But she returned her attention to Mr. Forbes.

"I didn't know your brother," he said. "Therefore, the more I learn of him, the more my opinion of him may rise, or sink. One learns a great deal about a man by the friends he keeps, and their loyalty. The fact that he has your loyalty, my dear Miss Hyatt, is another testament of his good character. A man could be content having such loyalty and the capacity with which to keep it."

My dear Miss Hyatt.

Arabelle had stiffened at the term of endearment, the easy way it had rolled off his tongue. She knew it was coming. With every visit, Mr. Forbes had become more forward, more familiar. No one had ever called her *my dear Miss Hyatt* before. She thought it would feel less . . . confining.

"And in what way would you keep it, Mr. Forbes?" she asked.

"I beg your pardon?" he asked.

"Such loyalty. You mentioned desiring the capacity to keep it." She smiled.

"Ah. Well." He tilted his head in thought. "To earn it, of course. In acquiring property and the means to provide comfort, hospitality, amusements. I do have friends." He chuckled. "I hope I've earned their loyalty to some extent." Then his brow rose. "Perhaps not to the same extent as that of a war hero's friends." He beamed at Isaac.

"You would be surprised, Mr. Forbes," Isaac said, "at how few loyalties remain when a soldier, hero or no, returns home with fewer parts of himself than he left with."

The expression on Mr. Forbes's face fell with the gravity of Isaac's words. To his credit, he did not try to save the moment with some glib remark. Arabelle's heart sank for both men. Mr. Forbes was ignorant in his remarks and had been set down. But Isaac . . . he had opened up about his injuries to the point of joking about them with her. But how far did the consequences of war go for him?

The rush of air caused by her mother's swift entrance into the stifling drawing room startled Arabelle.

"Gentlemen, forgive me," Mama said. "Nothing to worry about. I've been neglectful of this holiday season and have determined to do something about it. Don't you look lovely, Arabelle?" Arabelle stood to greet her and took her outstretched hands. "I'm sure you've been a splendid hostess in my absence. Ah, here is Clark. I trust you gentlemen have been getting to know each other. What wonderful company. Shall we go to the dining room?"

❧❧

Isaac sipped his port, observing Mr. Forbes, who perused the art on the dining room walls. After his own brilliant display in the drawing room, Isaac attempted to make amends to both Arabelle and Forbes by being the most sparkling dinner guest he was capable of being.

Which meant he smiled, took part in conversation when appropriate, and complimented Mrs. Hyatt on the meal, all while maneuvering around his plate with one hand. He'd become fairly deft at cutting meat as long as his knife was sharp and the weight of all eyes weren't upon him.

Gratefully, the subject of his service hadn't come up again.

He'd also struggled to keep his gaze off Abby. Arabelle. Miss Hyatt. Her form in that vivid red gown left no mistaking that she was indeed a woman. And her eyes, how pale blue they'd become when he'd cut Forbes down. He'd wanted to go to her and tell her something silly so they'd warm in his direction again.

He rolled his eyes and glanced toward the windows, thoughtful of the assignment George had given him. He leaned back in his chair and absently rubbed his knee. "Tell me, Forbes..."

"Yes, Major?" Forbes turned from the still life he'd been examining closely and dusted off his fingers.

"What are your intentions toward Miss Hyatt?"

"Ah." He wagged a finger at Isaac, picking up his port. "The older brother's best friend feels obligated to take his place in these matters. I thought I saw this coming."

"Did you?"

"What else could your arrival mean?"

"Hm. What else, indeed?"

Forbes took to pacing. More of a strut in front of the fireplace. "I assure you my intentions are genuine. I'll ask for Miss Hyatt's hand on Christmas Eve Day. It will be the best gift I could offer both her and Mrs. Hyatt, you see. A rescue from their sad predicament."

"And Eleanor, of course."

Forbes paused. "What was that?"

"Eleanor. George's child? She is part of this rescue as well?" Eleanor had been brought in during the dessert course dressed in finery and been allowed to take a sweet back up to the nursery with her. Forbes had barely acknowledged the girl over his pudding.

"Ah, yes, of course. Poor child. She'll have the best nanny Forbes money can buy. Miss Hyatt is far too attached to her. What can one expect, though, under such circumstances? However, to be not only an orphan, but an overly coddled orphan . . . I fear that in Miss Hyatt's inexpert care, the child would continue to go wild."

So, he thought, *Eleanor was to be "the orphan."*

Beneath Isaac's calm, an inexplicable rage grew. "Would not your own children be in Miss Hyatt's inexpert care?"

The man chuckled. "Certainly not. She is practically a child herself." He faced Isaac, his hands clasped behind his back. "I see what you're doing. A test of sorts, eh? How shall I convince you next? Though I speak of Miss Hyatt's lack of experience, I assure you she has captured my heart. I had no idea what I might find in her when I came to examine Hybrigge and consider my options—"

"And their options. It is still within your power to bestow Hybrigge House into their care without connecting yourself to Miss Hyatt. You would own the property; they would live here and manage it. The income would be yours."

"Oh, I don't intend for anyone under my guardianship to live here or manage it."

Isaac frowned. "I don't understand you, sir."

"The estate isn't profitable enough to keep. I intend to sell it."

"What was that about buying property to attain one's loyalties?"

"Well," Forbes huffed, "it depends on the property."

"This estate means the world to Miss Hyatt. If she knew you were selling it, she would see you in a very different light."

The man leaned forward. "Then I know I can trust you to keep that to yourself until after the banns are read. When Miss Hyatt realizes what luxury I am offering her in exchange for this *estate*, she'll come to see me in a very different light, indeed." He rolled back on his heels and grinned.

"The hero," Isaac murmured.

Forbes pointed conspiratorially, then finished his port.

The men entered the drawing room to rejoin the women, and Isaac halted.

"Well, this is splendid," Forbes exclaimed, striding into the room aglow with candles.

"I know it's not Christmas Eve yet, but I could not help myself," Mrs. Hyatt said in return. "We missed Christmas last year, and I felt like putting things up a few days early. It's only the drawing room."

"It's wonderful, Mama," Arabelle said. "George would be pleased."

Garlands of ivy and rosemary draped the mantel and hung above the windows. At least two dozen cut-glass candlesticks graced every flat surface available, holding tall pillars lit for the evening. The pungent scent of rosemary and candle wax filled the room. And in its center stood Arabelle, with Forbes bowing over her hand.

Isaac frowned and limped into the room, taking a seat near the fire. His knee ached and the heat would do it—and perhaps his agitated state of mind—some good.

"Do you like it, Mr. Linfield?" Arabelle asked, walking to him on Forbes's arm.

He nodded at the fire. "I do. It reminds me of those Christmases I spent here as a boy. Not the parties and the dances, but the quiet evenings in between. We'd play chess or commerce."

"Or sometimes spillikins."

He glanced up at her and smiled. "Yes." His conversation with Forbes had exhausted him, and he hoped it didn't show. He struggled to imagine Arabelle and Mrs. Hyatt anywhere but Hybrigge House for Christmas. But perhaps it would be good to be somewhere less saturated with memories.

Arabelle took the seat across from him, the candle and firelight illuminating her skin and hair. "Shall we play something now? For old time's sake?"

He shook off his melancholy as best he could. "What would you have us play?" He pursed his lips. "We can hardly climb trees and pretend at pirates."

Mrs. Hyatt gasped, but Arabelle's grin encouraged him, and he leaned toward her. "Or shall we play Bow Street Runners and track the cat across the vale?"

Arabelle laughed, a fresh, genuine sound, and he paid Mr. Forbes's huff no mind, watching her eyes dance.

"Shall you give away all our secrets, Mr. Linfield?" she asked.

"Indeed not. I've no wish to betray your brother and my friend. He's resting well knowing his mother never knew who let the chickens into the ballroom for races."

Arabelle's eyes grew wide. "The chickens," she exclaimed.

"Oh my," Mrs. Hyatt said, "the chickens." And then a giggle burst from her as well. "We thought a door was left open."

"Oh, a door was left open, ma'am. During our speedy escape when we heard Mr. Hyatt coming." He smiled at the memory. "I'm certain no three children moved faster."

"I suppose," Forbes said, "that small children, left to their own devices, can get into all sorts of mischief."

"Small children, yes. But George and I were sixteen, and Arabelle had just turned eleven."

"No doubt she was led by your poor examples."

Isaac turned his gaze to Arabelle, who had drawn her mouth closed in a pretty bow. He lifted a brow.

"Actually, Mr. Forbes," she said, a blush in her cheeks. "The chicken races were my idea. I'd believed they were as bored as we were on that rainy day. We each chose the chicken we thought the fastest, and, well . . ."

"And, uh, whose chicken won?" Forbes asked.

Arabelle sighed. "We never found out."

"We did, however, learn who the fastest of the three of us was." Isaac grinned at Arabelle, who fought to cover her pride with propriety.

He'd had his game.

He turned back to Forbes. "Do you have a favorite entertainment, sir?"

"Love the hunt. But I think you mean the indoor variety. Occasional games of cards or dice, I suppose. I am known to be an asset to my whist partner."

"Is that so?"

Arabelle stepped in then, utterly composed. "Shall we play whist, then, Mr. Forbes? I find a clever partner most stimulating. Mama, shall you partner with Mr. Linfield?"

Mrs. Hyatt nodded as Forbes bowed curtly.

Isaac took Mrs. Hyatt's arm and led her to the whist table.

"Thank you," she said quietly, "for bringing laughter to my son's memory."

"And thank you, ma'am, for leaving us *to our own devices* enough that such laughter is part of his memory."

A look of worry passed over her expression. She pulled him back a moment.

"Have I upset you, ma'am?" he asked.

She shook her head, and her gaze went to Arabelle on Forbes's arm. "Do you think," she asked, her voice barely a whisper, "that I gave Arabelle too much freedom as a child? After her father passed away, I—"

"Ma'am."

She turned round eyes on him.

"Arabelle has grown into an exceptional woman, and any man worth his salt will see that."

She squeezed his arm and nodded. "Thank you."

"Happy Christmas, Mrs. Hyatt."

"I think it might be."

He led her to the table, and they took their seats.

"I warn you, Linfield," Forbes said, "I give no exception to my opponents, even war heroes."

Isaac steadied his breath and nodded. "I expect no less from my challengers." Then he took it upon himself to beat Forbes soundly at whist for the remainder of the evening.

Chapter Four

ARABELLE FOUND ISAAC in the hall, pulling on a glove with his teeth, then adjusting it slightly with the hooked hand he'd worn when he'd first arrived. All the curiosity she had about him rose again—not only the circumstances of his injuries, but how it would be to go through the dailies of life with not only one leg, but one hand. She'd found herself making the attempt to undress, tie a boot, or open a letter with only one limb.

She lifted her gaze quickly as he turned her direction.

"Abb—Miss Hyatt. Forgive me. Good morning to you." He placed his hooked hand behind his back.

She smiled at the slip of her name, grateful she was not the only one dancing along the lines of their childhood familiarity. "I'm not sure I can forgive you for the thrashing you and Mama gave us last night." She grinned, and he returned it. "I didn't see you at breakfast."

"No," he said. "I rose early. I'm taking my horse out for a run before this weather turns."

"It is a beautiful morning. Have you named him yet?"

"I haven't."

She shook her head. "He shall begin to wonder his purpose, sir."

"Perhaps you can help me."

A thrill leaped inside her. "Well, that would require some time with him. I can't just spout off names like I'm dealing whist."

"Walk with me to the stables, then."

"I'll do one better and take Snowbird for a ride." She stopped, remembering herself. "But that was forward and thoughtless. You mean to make the most of your time. I'd have to change into my riding habit and convince someone to chaperone."

"Things were much simpler when we were younger, were they not?"

Her face flushed. There he stood with one leg and a hook while she complained of having to change clothes.

"Was it very hard to learn how to ride again?" she asked before she could think not to.

His brow arched. "Yes. Quite."

"Did it hurt terribly?"

His eyes seemed to intensify and dim at the same time. "Yes. Fear was also a factor."

"But you learned."

He hinted at a smile. "I learned."

She nodded and clasped her hands together, wondering at his bravery.

"Why don't you change," he asked, "and I'll talk to your mother about a chaperone?"

"Really? What of the weather?"

"Maybe it will inspire a name for my horse. Downpour. Or Drizzle."

"Those are awful."

"Which is why I need your help." He smiled, and she found herself rushing upstairs to change out of her morning dress.

Atop Snowbird, Arabelle allowed her gaze a sort of

routine: follow the thin, high clouds toward any break of blue sky, drop to the horizon at the west end of the valley, then over to Isaac's horse in contemplation of a name, and then to Isaac, if she could do so surreptitiously. If she was caught, she would offer one of several names she had in mind. If she wasn't caught, she would study him, searching for glimpses of the boy she knew so many years ago.

"On to tree names?" she asked when his gaze met hers. "He is a lovely deep brown, but I suppose Walnut is out of the question. Perhaps Chestnut? He is not red enough for Mahogany."

"Walnut is out of the question. Everyone names their horse Chestnut. And Mahogany is a bit of a mouthful, don't you think?"

"Something simpler, then. He seems steady and is very strong. What about Oak?"

"Hm. He's certainly the coloring for it."

She watched him consider. He sat handsomely in his beaver hat and high-collared coat. His sandy hair had always been neither blond nor brown, but the color of the pebbles along the river's wider places. While George had always been more particular about his hair, Isaac had not, and it still worked for him.

"What are you thinking of, Miss Hyatt?"

She blinked. "Oh. Um. I was thinking of your hair."

He pulled his horse to a stop. "My—hair?"

She stopped as well. With a quick glance back at Edith, whom she'd persuaded to bundle up and act as chaperone for their ride, and who was keeping a good distance behind them, Arabelle mustered the words to finish her thought. "I remember your mother often wondering aloud how you'd managed to escape the hairbrush again. The mussed look is quite in style." She smiled. "Who would have known that your disdain for a hairbrush would make you the height of fashion?"

The corner of his mouth lifted, and he dropped his gaze to his horse. "And to think I took extra care with my coiffure this morning." He threw her a good-natured glare.

She laughed. "It is good to have you home, Mr. Linfield. It is healing, in a way."

He urged his horse forward, and she followed the motion.

"Your mother said something similar last night. I admit I didn't know what my presence would bring here."

"We have many happy memories with you and George. I can scarcely think of an unhappy one—oof, maybe dance lessons."

He chuckled. "Dance lessons. Yes, not our favorite way to pass time. Though . . ." he paused as they ducked beneath some low-hanging boughs.

She waited for him to finish as they righted themselves, but he didn't. "Though what?" she asked.

"Though . . . had I known how few years I'd have to dance, I would have welcomed every quadrille."

Arabelle's heart tightened for him as she chastened herself for bringing up dancing. "That was thoughtless of me. I—"

"Don't, Miss Hyatt. Don't apologize for remembering better times with me. As you said, it has been good to be here. Healing, in a way."

His smile eased her chagrin. "I'm glad to hear it."

They rode on a little longer and reached the place on the river where it was best to play pirates. Her father had built a small platform around one of the trees leaning over the water. Though he'd meant it as a fishing spot, the boys and Arabelle had quickly adapted it to their own games.

She sensed Isaac remembering similar images, ghosts of children barely recognizable as themselves.

"You were in his last thoughts, you know," she said. "You were like a brother to him."

"I felt the same."

"He expressed his worry—we'd not heard from you in so long. He hoped that you were healthy and alive."

"An excellent combination."

"To be sure."

He frowned at the water. "I fell short by half."

She frowned as well. "By half? Are you unwell, Mr. Linfield?"

"Surely you jest."

"Indeed not. The term *unwell* denotes physical or mental illness. You show signs of neither."

"The term *healthy* denotes a state of being whole. A term you can't possibly use in reference to me."

She turned to him. "If I were to lose my arm tomorrow, would you think me unwhole?"

He looked away. "No."

"And neither do I."

He met her gaze directly, his expression stern. "But you would believe it of yourself, Miss Hyatt. You would be reminded of it, haunted by your dreams, waking to reach for something only to come up empty-handed with a hand that no longer exists." His voice deepened as if pained. "You'd battle constantly between a desire for who you were and who you must now become. Wondering who would consider going down that path with you when all others have fled."

Arabelle steadied herself, taken aback by the emotion their conversation had stirred. "Forgive me," she said, swallowing the lump in her throat. "I cannot pretend to understand."

"No. You cannot. Pretending is for the past." He turned his horse as if to ride on.

"Who fled?" she called after him.

He turned again, and she knew he'd heard her. Even in

his silence she could guess. Colleagues. Women. So-called friends.

"George would have never," she said.

"I know that."

"Neither would I," she said.

His expression softened. "Because of George."

"No. Because of you." Her heart beat inexplicably fast awaiting his response.

His mouth remained closed, his jaw clenched. His horse sidestepped, and Isaac corrected him using hushed tones, brushing his hand along the horse's withers. "What other names have you for my horse?" He lifted his gaze.

She looked at him—trying to ignore the deflating sensation in her stomach his change of subject brought—then to the place where they'd played. She took a cool, deep breath and released it slowly. "River," she said.

He studied her with that unreadable expression, then watched the steady, constant water moving through the winter landscape. At last he turned his attention to his horse, rubbing its ears, speaking in low murmurs. "River," he said softly. After a moment he sat tall in his saddle. "Thank you, Miss Hyatt. River it is."

Satisfaction bloomed in her center, tempered by his reserve. She drew Snowbird up alongside him. "I'm glad you like it. It suits him."

"I believe it does."

"He now has purpose."

"A gift, indeed."

She studied him for as long as he let her. "You've grown up, Mr. Linfield."

His head dropped, and he half laughed. Then he lifted it as if it carried all the weight of the world. "As have you, Miss Hyatt."

His gray eyes locked with hers. For how long, she knew not, but her pulse pounded again as her fingers entwined firmly in Snowbird's mane.

"Isaac—" she whispered.

"Don't, Miss Hyatt," he said quietly. "There is nothing for it. I'm here to see you're taken care of as George would have. Nothing more."

She nodded because her words stuck painfully in her throat, and her eyes stung.

His expression softened with what was likely pity. "Shall we return to the house?" he asked.

She shook her head and found her tongue. "I want to run."

With a nod from him, she turned Snowbird in the direction of the meadows, determined to run and run until these unwelcome emotions shook free. Then she would find Eleanor and spend all afternoon with her, stealing sweets from the kitchen and readying for Christmas Eve.

※

Isaac paced in front of George's desk in the library, looking between the two letters in his hand, warring between how the two were connected and what he was supposed to do about it. Sighing heavily as he took the chair, he read the older letter for the hundredth time.

Dear Isaac,

I hope you are well. I know that is a severe generalization, but it's the truth. I myself am not well. To be short (and forgive me for being so) I've been hit by the consumption and will likely be gone from this world even as you read this. I wish I could write that I'm at peace with this turn of my life, but three things prevent me from accepting my demise with grace. First, my dearest Jane is dying by my side. To bear this horrid disease on one's own is awful, but I could bear it. To see my Jane so wracked in pain and fading undoes me. Which brings me to the second thing. We have a child, our daughter Eleanor, who is but a year. She is safe, as she was taken from us at the first sign of illness and is with my mother. I believe, though, that the separation of child from mother has weakened Jane's will. Dear Isaac, the love for a child is something I never fathomed, could have never predicted. To know she is with Mama and Abby is a comfort. But our hearts break. To miss her Christmas is one thing; to miss her life—Third, Hybrigge is entailed to a cousin, one Mr. Hewitt Forbes. I've never met Mr. F, and have little idea of his intentions toward my family. I have written, asking him to break the entailment, but he refused with a note saying he'd visit the estate and make his decision then. Hybrigge is large enough to be profitable while small enough to avoid the heavier taxes, with loyal, fourth-generation tenants, so I see why he'd want to have a look. But I have no assurances of my family's future. A is of age. Do not think I haven't considered the possibilities there, as Mr. F is wealthy and unattached. E is but a baby and will be at this man's mercy. I have hired a solicitor to learn what he can of the Forbes family and Mr. F's character. I've given him your father's name with his permission. Isaac, if there is any possibility, might you write to my mother? Words of comfort go a long way when from a trusted friend. I understand you are at war and can likely do little. But I beg you, think of my family as yours. There is nothing better I can do for them. I wish I had happier tidings for you. To be hopeful is a battle. A much quieter one than those you've experienced, I'm sure. My thoughts often drift to our adventures on the river with little

A in our pockets. Be good to her, Isaac. Tell E tales of her wild father. Until I see you next, brother.
 Your friend,
 George Hyatt

Isaac pushed his hand through his hair. The other letter, short and to the point, stated that Mr. Hewitt Forbes had sold three of the family's holdings in the last two years. No motive was given. Hybrigge House would be the fourth. It could be that this was a business strategy, that the profits could be going into other investments, or to help pay—or avoid—the ever-increasing taxes the war had brought on. But something tugged at Isaac's gut. Something told him to keep digging, especially now that Mr. Forbes intended to make Abby his bride.

He shook his head. Today on their ride he'd come too close to revealing feelings he'd been denying for a week. Or perhaps longer than that.

Now Abby had named his horse, forever tying herself to the creature and Isaac to that moment. It had been a selfish thing of him to ask, perhaps some underlying desire to have that connection with her before he left. How quickly it had turned on him, already torturing him.

But the horse's name was River, and it would have no other.

He picked up the quill and wrote a letter to the solicitor, then another to his father. And he tried to blot out his thoughts of the moment he'd nearly reached out to Abby—to touch her flushed cheek—with his hook of a hand.

Chapter Five

"Our luminary walk is a Christmas Eve tradition, Mr. Forbes. We missed it last year. You must come." Arabelle smiled and tilted her head in a way she knew won her many arguments.

"How can I refuse, Miss Hyatt? Only it's so cold for the infant. It's for her sake I worry."

Arabelle allowed herself to be touched by his concern for Eleanor, since it was the first he had shown. Perhaps he was warming to her niece. "I assure you, she is not bothered by the chill and will be bundled well. Her hand will be in mine the entire time."

He smiled and leaned closer. "Oh, that I were that hand."

Arabelle flushed at the nearness of him and the reference from Shakespeare's tragic love story.

"A hand, a hand, my kingdom for a hand."

Arabelle turned, her eyes wide.

Isaac joined them in the drawing room. "What? I thought we were playing a game. Famous Shakespearean hand quotes. An odd game, I must own."

Arabelle shook her head at the man who had avoided her the last two days. "The quote is, 'A horse, a *horse*, my kingdom for a *horse*.'"

"Ah," Isaac said. "That's it. What shall we play next? Famous Shakespearean leg quotes? Let's see." He pretended to think hard. "I know. 'God hath given you one leg'"—he gave his good leg a pat—"'and you make yourself another.'" He pushed his wooden leg forward.

Arabelle scoffed. "Sir, the correct word is *face*. God hath given you a *face*."

"And a good job he did of the thing, so as to distract from the leg, don't you think?"

She giggled, unable to help herself.

"This is quite silly," she heard Mr. Forbes say.

"Oh!" she said. "I have one. 'A good leg will fall, a straight back will stoop. A black beard will turn white, a curled pate will grow bald—'"

"Ghastly," Mr. Forbes murmured.

She continued, having captured Isaac's full attention. "'—a fair face will wither, a full eye will wax hollow. But a good heart is the sun and moon . . . for it shines bright and never changes, but keeps its course truly.'"

Isaac remained silent, his gaze fixed on her.

"I've made you speechless, Mr. Linfield."

He blinked out of his stupor. "Indeed, Miss Hyatt. You didn't misquote Shakespeare once."

"I have it now," Mr. Forbes said. He cleared his throat. "'The fault, dear Brutus, is not in our *legs*, but in ourselves, that we are underlings.'" He looked between them both. "Is that how it works? That was Julius Caesar. I said *legs* instead of *stars*. Why are you both staring at me? Did I win?"

Arabelle glanced at Isaac, who turned to a servant just delivering a letter. He paid the post and slid the note into his waistcoat pocket.

"Here," Mr. Forbes said. "It's a bit rude to get a person caught up in a game, then leave him at the crux of the thing."

Arabelle smiled. "Indeed. Forgive us, Mr. Forbes. Your use of Julius Caesar was quite clever." She glanced again at Isaac. "Don't you think, Mr. Linfield?"

"Brilliant," he said. "I take it upon myself to declare him the winner. Ah, here is the loveliest lady now."

Arabelle followed his gaze to find Edith ushering in Eleanor in a pink wool overcoat and bonnet with cream worsted mittens hanging by their tethers.

"My darling," Arabelle said, walking to Eleanor. "Look how charming you are. Are you ready for our Christmas walk?" She crouched down and kissed the child's fingers as Mama walked in.

"The luminaries are lit," Mama exclaimed. "We walk just as dusk settles. Shall we? Mr. Linfield, will you lead us out? George always did after Mr. Hyatt passed."

"I would be honored, ma'am." He used a cane with his good hand, then Mama took the elbow of his opposite arm.

"You'll let me know if you are uncomfortable," Mama said quietly.

"Of course not, ma'am."

"Oh." Mama shook her head. "You were always such a tease."

"Thank you, ma'am."

Arabelle puzzled at herself as she pushed Eleanor's mittens on and stood with their hands linked. Though she'd liked Isaac's playful mood just now, she could not completely enjoy it. He'd not broached any conversation with her since their morning ride when she'd all but thrown herself at him like a heroine in a novel. He'd remained calm and detached. Yet she wouldn't have entertained certain ideas if she hadn't felt something on his part. Something.

"My arm, my dear Miss Hyatt?" Mr. Forbes said, his smile genuine and steady.

Indeed, Mr. Forbes was here, and all intentions were to be aimed at that gentleman. Isaac was her brother's best friend, looking out for her family's settled future. Nothing more.

She took his arm. "Thank you, Mr. Forbes." She looked down at Eleanor. "Are you ready, little one?"

Eleanor nodded. "Eddy, little one."

Arabelle grinned and looked up at Mr. Forbes.

He smiled. "Charming." Then he nodded in the direction Mama and Isaac had gone, and they followed.

They soon caught up to their leads, and Eleanor ran ahead to take her grandmother's hand. She happily pointed out the luminaries along the garden path, under trees, and leading out toward the river walk. Isaac walked tall even with his limp, his silhouette momentarily reminding Arabelle of following behind the two boys even when they'd made it clear she wasn't to follow them.

Her brow furrowed at the idea.

Pulling Arabelle from her thoughts, Mr. Forbes tugged her to a standstill in front of the Grecian birdbath—a heavy marble bowl supported by a chubby cherub Eleanor called "Beebee Tuck," which Arabelle suspected translated as "baby stuck."

"Did you need something, Mr. Forbes?"

"I believe I do." He knelt down, or nearly did, then thought better of it as he eyed the damp dirt of the garden path. He stood tall again, but lifted Eleanor's hand and kissed her glove quite firmly. "My dear Arabelle—that's an unusual name, is it not?"

Arabelle blinked, caught with a sense of foreboding. "Is it? My family has called me Abby on occasion."

He cleared his throat. "My dear Arabelle, I do find myself in need. In need of you."

"Oh."

"I admit I had no notion of what might come of this visit, but I find myself twice blessed. One, with this quaint cottage—"

"Cottage?"

"—and a country cousin I am delighted to find far more refined and enlivening than I'd expected."

She swallowed. "What was it you expected?"

"It doesn't matter. My dear Arabelle"—he kissed her glove once more and then gripped her hand to his chest—"would you allow me to rescue you and your family by taking you as my wife?"

Arabelle blinked at him, her heartbeat thumping in her ears. Her mother's words returned to her full strength. *This is essential. The only way. Eleanor's future.*

She envisioned Isaac's boyish grin, then his stormy gray eyes, and his words came. *There is nothing for it.*

"Yes," she heard herself say. "Yes, Mr. Forbes, I will be your wife."

She heard a small gasp. Mama had stopped ahead with Eleanor, who tugged on Mama's hand to keep moving. Mama beamed and nodded before allowing Eleanor to pull her toward the river walk.

Then Arabelle saw Isaac beyond Mama, leaning on his cane, looking worn. He gave her a smile, then turned away.

"Arabelle."

"Hm?" She returned her focus to their rescuer.

"You've made me happy indeed. I hope I have made you the same."

Arabelle looked beyond him to the house, to the stone bridge, the woods, the sound of the river underlining it all. "Yes. Thank you, sir."

He pulled her a fraction closer. "Hewitt," he said. The scent of his cologne—smelling strongly of bay leaves—tickled her nose.

"Hewitt." She tried to recall what Isaac smelled like. Cool and warm at the same time. Like saddle and river and linen. Like dance lessons and hearth, tea and—

She turned her head away just as Mr. Forbes—Hewitt—attempted a kiss on her mouth. He pressed cold lips to her cheek instead, then pulled away with a grin.

"You are demure. As you should be." He pulled her hand through the crook of his arm. "I am both pleased and left wanting."

Gratefully, he began to walk again, because Arabelle was too dazed to move of her own accord.

She had just agreed to marry a man she barely knew, whose temperament she could scarcely determine, who seemed barely more pleased with her accompanying assets than herself, and whose cologne made her want to sneeze.

And yet the look of relief on Mama's face, the sight of Eleanor toddling along a path she knew well ... Arabelle tightened her grip on Mr. Fo—Hewitt's arm and threw a rather shaky prayer of gratitude heavenward.

Mrs. Hewitt Forbes.

It would take some getting used to.

The luminaries dotted the river walk to the sand bar where Arabelle always took Eleanor to "fro." As Hewitt led her down the path to the crushed rock, she found that Isaac had stayed on the grassy bank above, watching Mama and Eleanor. Mama turned at her approach, joy in her countenance.

"Congratulations, my daughter. And to you, Mr. Forbes. Oh, what an auspicious beginning to our Christmas season. We shall add extra festivities and make sure to invite plenty of guests for a dinner, and perhaps a ball! We shall need more ivy for the hall and ballroom, and a kissing bough! Oh, what shall I serve? Goose or boar's head? And Arabelle shall have a new gown, of course, Mr. Forbes."

Hewitt smiled. "Of course. I'll leave the two of you to

planning." He left them, strolling farther down the small shore.

"Fro rock," Eleanor said with one mittened hand clinging to Mama's skirt and the other rooting around fruitlessly on the ground for a rock. "Kip rock."

"Oh, Arabelle, he is so handsome. We are saved!"

"Shh, Mama," Arabelle whispered. "Yes. I am happy for that. But do you think it right to make our Christmas so elaborate? We have not the savings, and I refuse to touch our allowances just in case—"

"In case what? Did you not hear him, my darling? He is marrying you and rescuing your family. What else could quiet your worries?"

"I . . . I'm not sure." At that moment, Arabelle glanced around. "Where is Eleanor?"

"Eleanor!" Isaac cried from above. He pointed, and Arabelle followed his direction.

"Fro tick," Eleanor was calling, toddling to the far end of the sand bar. "Atch. Atch tick."

"Oh heavens," Arabelle muttered. "The drop." She rushed forward. "Eleanor, stop!"

The little girl giggled and darted ahead.

So did Arabelle. "Mr. Forbes!" He stood not far from the end of the bank and turned toward her. Alarmed, he took a step forward.

"Miss Hyatt. You're running."

"Yes," she called, pointing. "Eleanor—stop her!" Eleanor was already splashing in water past her ankles, the cold not yet registering as a warning to the little girl.

"Atch tick foat." She pushed her little legs through the water where calm met the rush of the drop.

"Oh please," Arabelle murmured. "Stop her!" she cried. Eleanor stumbled forward, her clothes heavy now with wet.

Then Mr. Forbes, in all his handsome haberdashery, pointed to his tall leather boots with a shrug. "They're Hessians," he said and stood still.

In the shock caused by his statement, Arabelle halted, then heard the cry of a babe who finally realized what danger she was in. Arabelle launched herself forward to the water just as Eleanor's eyes grew huge with fright and the rushing current pushed her stumbling toward the drop. One more step, and the babe would go under.

But not if Arabelle could help it. She splashed through the icy water, her skirts sticking to her legs and tangling her boots. She threw herself forward, wrapping her arms around Eleanor. She savored the feel of that little girl's body next to hers for but a moment before a whirling thrust of current pushed her from behind, knocking her forward as her feet tangled in debris. They would go under.

Hard splashing sounded from behind, and a strong arm wrapped around Arabelle's middle, pulling hard against the current.

"Have you got her?"

Arabelle turned, finding Isaac at her ear.

"Get your feet underneath you, or we're all going in."

She nodded, stunned, and scrambled to get her feet on firmer ground.

"Hang on, we're going to fall backward into the shallows," he said.

Her grip on Eleanor tightened, and as he heaved backward, so did she. As promised, they landed on their backs in the frigid but calm water, Arabelle wrapped in Isaac's arms and Eleanor crying on top of them.

"Are you all right?" Isaac asked, his hand stroking her face, her hair. "Is she all right?"

At the second question, Arabelle tore her gaze from Isaac

and sat up, checking Eleanor over. "She's just frightened. And cold."

"We must get you both back to the house. You're shivering all over. Come on." He gave her enough nudge so she could stumble upward and out of the water with Eleanor, where her mother was stripping off her own cloak.

"That was brave of you, my darling," she said as she took Eleanor from her, wrapping up the babe. "And Mr. Linfield—Isaac—thank you."

"Here you are, my good man," Mr. Forbes was saying to Isaac, handing him the end of his cane to pull him out of the water. Isaac took it and pulled himself up, hobbling on one leg. A buckle had come loose, and the boot hung crooked.

"Mama," Arabelle said through chattering teeth. "Get Eleanor to the house."

"What about you?" she asked.

"Go," Isaac said, coming up behind. "I'll get Miss Hyatt back. Hurry."

Mama nodded and rushed on with poor Eleanor wailing away.

"Ahem. Don't you think *I* should be escorting Arabelle back to the house?"

Arabelle turned to Mr. Forbes, a different kind of chill firing in her veins. "*You* will not be escorting me back to the house, or down the aisle, or anywhere, Mr. Forbes. You call yourself a rescuer? That little girl did not survive the deaths of her parents only to drown because somebody couldn't stand to get their feet wet. Any man who puts his *boots* before a child's life is not worth any house, any land, any space to call home. My father and my brother are dead. We are at your mercy, sir. But I will not marry you."

Breathing came with difficulty, both from fear and cold. But Arabelle stood firm.

Mr. Forbes straightened, his gaze darting between her and Isaac like a trapped fox. Finally, he spoke.

"Here." He gave Isaac his dry cloak. "Too late, I know, but it's something."

Isaac took the cloak and wrapped it around Arabelle's shoulders. She shuddered again but felt steadier. Without another word, she and Isaac began the ascent back up to the river walk, her arm looped tightly through his as he leaned heavily on his cane and focused on keeping his false foot under him.

"C-can you fix it?" she asked.

"My valet has the tools needed, and spare buckles," he answered through clenched teeth.

"Are you in pain?" she asked.

He hesitated replying. "Yes-s."

A minute of quiet passed as they made their way back along the luminary path.

She took a steadying breath, but her teeth still chattered. "You c-came for us."

"Of course I did. As soon as I saw the danger. That idiot just stood there. I only wish I could have been . . ."

"Faster? Stronger? More gracef-ful?" She laughed. "Doesn't matter. You acted. That's what counts. That's what saved her."

"Your actions saved her as well. You were always fast on your feet."

"Running is un-n-ladylike."

"You were every bit a lady back there." After a few more steps he paused to catch his breath, wincing.

"What can I do?" she asked.

He shook his head and leaned against a low garden wall. "Just give me a moment." She shivered and pulled Mr. Forbes's coat tighter, ignoring the smell of bay leaves.

"What will I do, Mr. Linfield?" she asked, catching a glimpse of Mr. Forbes walking to the stables, his head low. "I've ruined Christmas. And more."

"Abby," he said. "Look at me."

She met his gaze, the only sure thing about his stature at the moment.

"You did what George would have had you do."

There it was again, in his gaze. As if the mention of George tied them more closely to each other. "What of you?" she asked. "What would you have had me do?"

"The same." He averted his eyes and stood once more. "I'll not rest until this is figured out." As he wobbled on the first step, she once again took his arm under the guise of being cold. He seemed to straighten because of it.

"Promise me you'll take *some* rest, sir."

He smiled.

They said nothing more as they drew near the house. Several servants, including Edith and Isaac's valet, met them outside and made a fuss.

"Has a bath been drawn for Eleanor?" Arabelle asked.

"Yes, Miss." Edith said. "And another is being drawn for you, and then Mr. Linfield. The fires in your rooms are blazing. Are you in need of being carried, Miss?"

"No, thank you," she said as someone threw a blanket around her. "I can get inside on my own two feet."

"Easy for you to say," Isaac quipped. "I seem to require a sedan chair."

A laugh bubbled up from somewhere inside her. "Someone get a farrier for Mr. Linfield. He's thrown a shoe."

His unfettered laughter warmed her more than any blanket would.

Chapter Six

AFTER ARABELLE'S BATH, Edith brushed her hair by the heat of the fire until it shone, then twisted it up in a simple chignon with a pearl comb. Arabelle dressed in a soft blue velvet gown and was left to rest by the fire before growing fidgety and heading downstairs.

The door to Isaac's room opened just as she passed, and Isaac's valet exited.

"Pardon me, Miss Hyatt." He bowed before the partially open door.

"Is Mr. Linfield downstairs?"

"He is just coming out, Miss." With another bow, he left toward the servant's staircase.

Arabelle stared at the open door, barely breathing as she waited for Isaac to appear. But he did not. With a glance up and down the hall, she pushed the door open and stepped into the room.

Isaac stood with his back to her, his sleeve rolled up as he harnessed his wooden hand to his bare forearm. The sight of the stump shocked her into a stupor.

"Close the door, will you, James? I've had to redo this."

Shaking herself into some lucidity, she closed the door. Not knowing if she should speak, but not wanting to deceive him, she timidly cleared her throat.

He turned at the sound, jerking his sleeve down to his wrist. "What are you doing here?" He shot a glance to the closed door. "Where is James?"

She lifted her chin, ignoring the anger in his voice. "He said you would be right out."

"He was correct. You shouldn't be in here."

"Why?"

"Because of basic propriety, for starters, Miss Hyatt. And out of respect for my privacy."

She felt her cheeks warm and lowered her head, overcome with remorse. "Of course. I'm sorry. I only wished to— I'll go." She turned, and as she did, her elbow brushed against the low-boy, knocking a bottle and hairbrush to the ground.

"Oh no," she said, diving for the items as he did.

The resounding crack at her forehead was followed by Isaac's grunt. They both rocked backward, landing on the floor.

"Oof," said Isaac, peering at her as he rubbed his temple. "Are you all right?"

She nodded, wanting to be swallowed into the carpet. "That's twice today you've fallen on my account."

"Yes," he said, picking up the unharmed bottle. "Fewer lives were at stake this time, though."

"And we're not soaked through."

He shook his head, laughing silently, then rubbed his hand over his face. "I find myself at a complete loss."

"Because I'm a country girl with horrible manners?"

"No. Because I should offer you assistance to your feet, but I can't get to my own."

"Oh," she exclaimed, and rose on all fours. She crawled to his cane and handed it to him.

He took it in silence, then got his footing and hoisted himself up. He set the cologne down, then offered her his hand.

After he pulled her up, he let go quickly and stepped away, buttoning up his sleeve at his wrist. For the first time since she entered, she got a good look at him. He appeared to have bathed, brushed his wet hair, and shaved. "You look well," she said quietly. "You smell of oranges and clove soap."

"Better than river water?"

"On some occasions," she said, trying to clear her head.

The corner of his mouth lifted.

"Are you angry?" she asked.

"Only a little," he said. "Does your head hurt?"

"Not much."

He returned to straightening his sleeve. "You smell of lemon and flowers."

"It's called Lily of the Valley. Jane took me to Floris on Jermyn Street during my season and helped me choose." It had been one of the highlights of her stay.

"You two were close?" he asked, pulling on his jacket.

"Yes. She didn't judge my wildness and had a way of making me want to be a lady. And you would have loved her sense of humor. I suppose being married to George required one." She smiled.

But he frowned. "I'm sorry I didn't have the opportunity to meet her. George wrote of her, of course. He was enraptured from the moment they met."

"Indeed. They were wonderful together. And Eleanor won't know either of them."

"Yes, she will. We'll tell her all we know." He straightened the brush and bottle and moved to the door.

"We?" she asked.

He stopped in his movement. "You'll tell her. I'll share what I can when I'm here."

"Here?" She shook her head. "Mr. Linfield, we have lost Hybrigge." Emotions welled up in her eyes, and she blinked them back. "*I* have lost us Hybrigge. Where is it you think you'll find us?"

He glanced at the door and stepped toward her. "Listen here. You didn't lose Hybrigge. Nobody in this house would ever accuse you of that. You were perfectly right in your estimations of Forbes out there on the river today. He showed his colors and you—" He gently chucked her chin. "You stood up for your niece's entire future like you were her mother. Nobody will fault you for that."

"Mr. Forbes will," she whispered. "Her entire future is now in peril."

"Abby," he said, "do not cry. I cannot stand to have you cry." He drew closer. "You'll get through this. You all will."

She drew in a deep breath, determined to make him proud. "I suppose I must believe you, musn't I?"

He gazed at her. "Yes."

"What more can be done?" she asked.

He dropped his head, his shoulders rounding as he thought. Their heads were so very close together that if she leaned forward, her nose might have nuzzled his hair.

He lifted his head suddenly, and she drew back inches. "I'll talk to Forbes again," he said. "See if he'll reconsider breaking the entailment or allow you and your family to reside here." He frowned. "I don't understand why he wants to sell the place."

"Sell?" Panic widened her eyes. "Why would he sell Hybrigge?"

"I don't know." He held her shoulder. "You must not give up hope. You are still young and beautiful, and you may have another season again. Perhaps I can find a sponsor for you. Hewitt Forbes is not your only chance at a future, Abby."

"And who would offer for me . . . *and* Eleanor?"

He dropped his head again.

"You think me beautiful?" she added.

He looked at her once more, his expression unreadable. She swallowed, aware of how very near he was. "Two years ago, before my first season, you wrote George a letter. You wrote and said . . . you wrote—" Her courage was failing her, but the interest in his eyes encouraged her. "You told George to keep an eye on me, to keep me close, that it was a good thing you were away at war, because if you were home you would be fighting all the other men for my first dances, and even my last."

His gaze narrowed. "He read that to you?"

"It amused him."

He swallowed. "It was a silly thing to write."

"Yes, it was. I never forgot how silly it was, and that you were the one who wrote it."

His gaze over her deepened. The space between them seemed to shrink, though neither moved. The thought of that space disappearing entirely gave rise to feelings she'd only read about in books, and her heart beat with a rhythm new to her.

"Abby," he whispered, his hand moving from her shoulder to her cheek.

"Yes?" she replied, welcoming the shiver his touch brought.

Then he stepped away, dropping his hand.

She recovered her breathing and persisted. "You said that had you known your future, you would have danced every quadrille. Had you imagined some of those dances with me?"

He turned completely away from her. "Don't do this, Abby."

"Do what? Am I ridiculous? Is there not something between us? Or are you tired of me following at your feet, as if I were ten years old and you cannot get away fast enough?"

He turned sharply. "My feet? Abby, I am half. You have seen for yourself only a fraction of my inadequacy—"

"I have seen nothing of your inadequacy—only that you will do everything you can for those you care about—those you might love—"

"Miss Hyatt," he shouted.

The entire house seemed to still in Arabelle's ears, and tears blurred her vision. She would not cry.

He collected himself and his shoulders slumped. "I ought never raise my voice to a lady, or a friend," he murmured. "And yet I have. I shall leave in the morning and conduct my business in town."

"But tomorrow is Christmas Day, sir," she said, fighting humiliation.

"Then I shall leave the next."

She nodded, unable to manage anything more.

He went to the door and opened it, looking both ways. He then motioned to her, and she willed her feet to move quickly past him and turned, standing modestly outside his door.

She fought to catch his eye, unwilling to leave things as they were. She knew he sensed it.

"Abby," he said, his voice almost sad. "I cannot offer you anything."

She swallowed back her tears. "Cannot, or will not?"

He continued to avert his gaze, his jaw clenched.

"You know," she said, "a friend recently told me that it is not what happens to us, but what we do afterward that determines our course. I wonder if he truly believes that, or if they were just words."

His response came a moment of silence later. "I shall see you downstairs, Miss Hyatt."

She made herself curtsy, then continued down to the

library to sit at George's desk and gather herself before going to Mama and assuring her that she was well and that everything was going to be all right.

It would be the biggest pretend of her life.

※

Mama dabbed at tears, but drew herself taller in her chair. "Perhaps I should write to Mr. Forbes."

"To what end, Mama? Surely you don't hope that he will renew his offer?"

"No," she said, glancing at Eleanor, who played with blocks on the drawing room rug. "No, I saw for myself how little he thought of either of you there on the bank—oh if I only hadn't have let go of Eleanor's hand—no, we would have no idea of his true nature, then, would we?" She sighed. "This is so very vexing. I am vexed. But I will not be now. It is Christmas Eve, and this little one," she nodded to Eleanor, "is beginning to give me that look of concern that one so young should not have."

Arabelle smiled and went to Eleanor, plopping down to help build a tower before the child knocked it down with glee.

Eleanor's hand reached toward the ceiling. "Tall tower. High, Abibelle."

"Yes, I'll build it very tall."

"I do have some interesting and happy news," Mama said, glancing at the doors. She lowered her voice. "It is about Mr. Linfield."

Arabelle's tower toppled.

"I crash it. Not you crash it."

"Mr. Linfield?" Arabelle also glanced toward the doors. He'd not yet come down as promised. Quickly she began to build another tower. "What do you know?"

"I've had a letter from his mother. Naturally, I'd expressed our gratitude for his presence, my concern for his future, and a wish that we could do something for him in return for his kindness. His mother hoped to ease my concern."

Arabelle stopped building. "And has she?"

Mama nodded. "Mr. Forbes revealed that Mr. Linfield—Major Linfield—had saved his commander's life and was a war hero, but there is more."

"Tall, Abibelle."

Arabelle resumed building. "Oh?"

"Yes. It turns out that his colonel, Sir Dorset Upton, is a childless widower, with no entailment—brilliant man—who felt so indebted to the major for saving his life with loss of his own limbs that he has granted the major a substantial living and made him bailiff over his lands until his return from war. Major Linfield is to be under the tutelage of Sir Upton's steward once he leaves Hybrigge. Isn't that wonderful?"

Arabelle stared, a knot turning in her chest. "Wonderful."

"It's unusual, of course, for a gentleman to be given a working position—"

"He is a younger son," Arabelle said, still dazed. "Isaac has worked his whole life on his father's farm."

"Yes. It's quite perfect."

Arabelle stared out the window, her breathing stalled.

The door opened, and her tower toppled once more.

"I crash it, Abibelle, not you crash it."

"You build the tower, Linny. Then you can crash it."

"Happy Christmas, ladies," Isaac said.

"Happy Christmas, Major," Mama said, and rose to curtsy.

Arabelle had pulled her legs beneath her to rise when Isaac was there, his hand extended to help her up.

"I seem to be constantly finding you aground, Miss Hyatt."

"Yes," she said, equally flustered and determined to

appear serene. She took his hand and stood, smoothing her gown. "Life has been funny that way. The currents change, and you find yourself run into the rocks wondering how in the world you thought you could float in the first place."

He gave her a perplexed look and lifted her hand, bowing over it and placing a kiss there. "You were meant to fly, I believe, Miss Hyatt."

She remembered herself and curtsied. "And what of you, Major?"

His brow rose at her address, and he let go of her hand.

"I hear congratulations are in order. Mama has just told me of the circumstances awarded you by Colonel Upton." She kept pushing the words out. "A bailiff with your own living. How wonderful for you. Your own set of wings."

He looked to Mama and back at Arabelle. "Thank you. It's new. I'm still uncertain of it all."

"Uncertain, or just modest?" Mama asked with a smile.

He turned to her. "Humbled, ma'am. Forgive my surprise. I've not yet accepted."

"Your mother wrote to me."

"Ah." He glanced at Arabelle. "That accounts for it."

"Why would you not accept the living?" Arabelle asked.

"I'm sure the major has his reasons, and they are none of our business."

Isaac lifted his hand. "It's a reasonable question." He turned to Arabelle, whose heart pounded against her chest in a bothersome manner. "The living comes with stipulations I'm not sure I could live up to," he said, meeting her gaze. "It will take some consideration."

"Mister? Play. Play blocks. Build tower high."

He looked down at Eleanor and a half-built stack of blocks. "Yes, I see. How very high."

"*I* see," Arabelle said, and he looked up at her. "Some

things take consideration, while others need almost no thought at all."

"Abby," he said as she brushed past him.

"Mama, forgive me, I am tired after all."

"But we have yet to light the Yule log," Mama said, half bewildered as Arabelle exited the room. "Arabelle, wait."

She turned, surprised to find Isaac stopped not far behind her. "What is it, Mama?" she asked.

Mama pointed upward. "The kissing bough. Mistletoe." Her brow rose. "It's for luck."

Then, to Arabelle's horror, Mama looked to Isaac. "You must admit, Major, we could use all the luck we can get."

He shifted nervously. "Yes, ma'am."

"Well," she said. "Get to it."

"Det to it," Eleanor piped up, then toppled her tower with a crash.

He looked to Arabelle. "With your permission?"

She must've nodded, because he stepped closer, his cane in one hand, his gaze on the ground.

He reached her, thankfully blocking Mama from her sight.

"Why are you doing this?" she whispered.

"Tradition," he whispered back, setting his cane against the wall.

"Not this. I mean, yes this. You were very clear upstairs, and I thought I understood, but now I learn that you have some means, some purpose before you and you didn't tell me, and—"

"Abby."

"What?"

In the instant he caressed her face, her eyes closed, then his lips were upon hers, a brief touch, and then again, softer and less brief, and when she pressed back he met her, matching her desire, surpassing it.

Until he released her, stepping back, blinking.

She regained her breath as he reached for his cane.

"Why did you do that?" she whispered.

"Tradition," he said, sounding strained. "For luck."

"A peck on the cheek would have sufficed."

"You need more luck than that, I think."

"Bravo, Major," Mama called from her chair.

"Bavo, mister," Eleanor parroted.

"Now both of you get back in here," Mama said, "and I'll hear no more talk of retiring early. We need to celebrate while we have something to celebrate. Oh, how dreadful that sounded."

"No more blocks." Eleanor toppled her tower and walked to Arabelle. "Tories."

"You'd like a story?" Arabelle asked, welcoming the distraction since she'd been ordered to stay. Eleanor took her hand, and then Isaac's, and led them both to the window seat. Arabelle took a deep breath, to no avail. Her pulse still raced, and the nearness of him muddled her brain.

The next hour was spent reading stories and playing games with Eleanor, avoiding eye contact with Isaac while her thoughts kept returning to that kiss. Finally, with Eleanor asleep on Isaac's arm and Mama snoring softly across the room, Arabelle found an excuse to leave.

She reached for Eleanor. "I'll take her upstairs," she said, hushed.

"Miss Hyatt—"

"So which is it?" she asked. "Abby, or Miss Hyatt? You seem to use either depending upon your need."

"I beg your pardon?" he whispered, glancing at Eleanor.

"Abby, touch," she said. "Abby, save your life. Abby, kiss. But then, Miss Hyatt, do not think it. Miss Hyatt, there is nothing for it. Miss Hyatt, I have nothing to offer you."

He blinked at her.

"Nothing to offer me," she continued. "Nothing."

"Miss Hyatt, please, you don't—"

"Understand? I think I do. I think when you said you had nothing to offer me, what you meant was that you are afraid." She hoisted Eleanor against her shoulder, pressing a tear to the little girl's pinafore. "But think nothing of it. It was a silly thing to hope for. A young girl's dream. You are very much like Mr. Forbes, you know?"

Alarm crossed his expression.

"You would put your boots before a life, sir."

She turned and left the drawing room, and this time, he didn't follow.

Chapter Seven

Dear Isaac,

We have discovered that Mr. F is steeped in gambling debts, and this is the reason he has sold his lesser properties and likely the reason he would sell Hybrigge. He is desperate. A marriage connection with his family at this time would not be wise, and I am relieved for Miss H.

However, the family is still in peril. I shall look into it further, see if we can secure them a cottage somewhere and find Miss H a sponsor. Unless you can come up with something better? It is good you are there. Give them our warmest regards and hope for their situation. Happy Christmas. Write your mother.

Yours,
Father

ISAAC PACED SEVERAL minutes with his father's letter clutched in his hand. His leg throbbed, but he'd learned to ignore it. Abby crossed his thoughts so often anyhow, and he could not ignore her.

Why had he kissed her? She was absolutely right. He had used her with no intention of following through with anything more. He hadn't meant to, but that didn't change the fact that he had. And she was so . . . perceptive. Nothing got past her, and she spoke her truth like an arrow shot from a bow. He knew that about her. For thirteen years he'd known that about her. Loved that about her—

He stopped, standing tall. He studied his carved hand. "You are a coward, Isaac Linfield. And she called you on it."

After a moment of contemplation, he moved to his desk to a small pile of letters, plucking one off the top and smoothing it out.

Major Linfield,

I write to let you know that all is ready. The papers have been drawn, and I have written my steward. The duty of Bailiff of Merigrove and all other holdings will be a temporary position, as I have named you my sole heir. There will be much to learn, but you have proven your ability as a soldier and a man. Upon my return, God willing, we shall make a good team of it. You shall fill the rooms of Merigrove, Furton, and Upton Hall with wife and family—for you must take a wife—and I shall rejoice in the sounds of it. There is much life ahead, Major. I intend to live it well. Join me.

My steward awaits your consent. I don't really need it, you know.

Col. Sir D. Upton

Isaac closed his eyes. He wouldn't change one action in saving the colonel. He was too good a leader, too good a person to be lost in this infernal war.

The living Colonel Upton offered had been one thing. The stirrings of purpose, of independence, of what good, honest work meant had invigorated Isaac, and he appreciated the colonel's offer. What else could he do? Burden his parents and his brothers? Not that they would ever make him feel as such. But his father's farmlands were smaller than Hybrigge's.

And he had this offer before him. Not only a living, but an inheritance.

It was too much.

You shall fill the rooms of Merigrove, Furton, and Upton Hall with wife and family . . .

The image of Abby closing her blue eyes at his touch, her nose upturned, her pink lips barely parted, and the scent of her perfume pulling him closer . . . kissing her once had been easy. For luck. Kissing her again ended him. Pulling away from her had been like losing . . . well, a limb.

Yet how could he ask her to accept him, as he was? See him, really see him, as he was? He'd no intention of ever marrying after his stint in hospital. His friends had left, feeling uncomfortable that he was not who he used to be. Any girls he'd hoped to return to before his injuries had long turned their attentions elsewhere. Except for one. Abby had been both a friend, and, he'd come to realize, a hope.

He looked down at his boots. He was half.

And a coward.

You put your boots before a life, sir.

What kind of life could he give her? *Any help, George?*

Isaac sat at the desk, pushing his hand through his hair, looking between the two letters.

Then he sat bolt upright. Almost too hastily, he dipped the quill in ink and began to write.

Christmas Day passed quietly. After church—and to Mrs. Hyatt's dismay—Abby had presented Eleanor with a small fisherman's creel filled with sticks and twigs of all sizes and an assortment of smooth rocks—some round for throwing and some flat for skipping. Eleanor had hopped and sorted and tried to "fro rock" in the drawing room, but she had been thwarted in the attempt and promised a walk if she behaved.

After the walk and much "frowing," the family and their guest retired to the drawing room and blazing fire. Eleanor toddled to Isaac and patted his wooden leg. "Leg aw better?" she asked.

"Somewhat," he said, running his hand over her curly head.

She yawned, then leaned down and rested her cheek against the wood. "Ah luh loo," she said, then kissed his leg.

"Ah luh loo?" he asked, then looked to Abby for interpretation.

She lowered her gaze, her fingers working her embroidery. "She said, 'I love you,' Major."

The words struck him, and he allowed the child to crawl onto his lap, where she curled up and fell asleep in front of the fire. "Sleep, little Linny," he said. "All will be well." But he watched the fire fretfully, glancing Abby's way as often as he'd permit himself.

༺☙☙༻

Isaac had been gone to town three days. "Really, Mama," Arabelle said, tearing out a row of stitches that she could not get even. "I see no reason why Mr. Linfield couldn't conduct his business from Hybrigge House."

"You know very well why he had to leave, Arabelle."

Arabelle frowned at the seam in her hands. "I do not," she said around the needle gripped in her lips.

"Because, my darling, it was no longer proper for him to stay here."

"And why is that?" she asked, removing the needle to thread it.

"Because you are in love with him."

Arabelle froze, no longer seeing her embroidery. "I don't know what you mean, Mama." But her beating heart argued that she knew exactly what Mama meant.

Clark entered then with a tray. "A letter for you, mum."

"Thank you, Clark."

Arabelle watched, only half interested, as Mama unfolded the letter. How had Mama deciphered her feelings for Isaac, and what did it mean that he left? Mama had implied that he knew of Arabelle's feelings. She hadn't played the shrinking violet, had she? But then he left. Because it was no longer proper. And because he didn't return her feelings. And she'd equaled him to the horrible Mr. Forbes. Who held their whole future in his clammy grip.

Arabelle tossed her stitching aside and stood, walking about the room, vaguely aware of her mother reading her letter.

"Oh heavens," Mama said, her hand to her chest.

Arabelle stopped immediately. "What is it?"

Mama lifted her gaze to Arabelle. "Oh. It is nothing. Major Linfield will be here within the hour, and we must change. Have Edith help you first. I must speak with Cook." With that, Mama stood and left the room.

Upstairs, Edith pulled the laces on the back of Arabelle's coral muslin gown. "I wonder why Mama is acting so strangely about Mr. Linfield coming to dine," Arabelle mused aloud. "He stayed with us for ten days."

"Have you not heard, Miss? Mr. Linfield has bought Hybrigge for himself."

Arabelle dropped the matching slippers she held. "He what?"

"He intends to make Hybrigge his home."

"And what of us?"

Edith paused. "I do not know, Miss."

Arabelle frowned, then she spun, searching the floor.

"What are you looking for, Miss?"

"My riding boots."

"But you're dressing for dinner."

"Right now I'm dressing for my horse. Tell Seth I need her ready. No, don't bother with my riding gown. Just the coat will do. Ah, my boots." She sat down to pull them on but felt Edith's stare. "Edith. Seth. Now."

"Oh. Yes, Miss. Sorry, Miss." And with a quick bob, she was gone.

Seth had Snowbird ready when Arabelle arrived. He helped her mount and without so much as a nod of thanks, she urged Snowbird into a gallop. They'd just crested the bridge when she spotted a horse and rider stopped in the distance under the old oak trees. She urged Snowbird into a run, a burning in her core and spreading outward. She recognized his horse first, then his posture. He saw her and dismounted, no easy feat, she was certain. He was still steadying himself when she pulled her horse up and dismounted herself.

She crossed the remaining distance at a brisk pace. "You bought Hybrigge? How could you? When you knew. You knew how much it means to Mama and I!"

He removed his hat. "Miss Hyatt."

"I don't understand. After everything!" She reached him, the exertion from her march, or her anger, obvious in her erratic breathing. "You bought it from that awful man."

"Miss Hyatt—"

"Don't you 'Miss Hyatt' me. After I confided in you—trusted—"

"Abby."

"What?"

He wrapped his arms about her and pulled her close, then

kissed her quite thoroughly. As her anger eased in his arms, he pulled away enough to gaze into her eyes.

"How—" she stammered, quite breathless. "Why—"

He glanced upward, then back down at her. "Mistletoe."

Her gaze went to the clumps in the oaks, and she swallowed. "Oh."

"But that's not why."

"Oh?"

He shook his head. "I bought Hybrigge with a portion of my living from Sir Upton. I bought it for you."

She blinked. "Why? I thought—"

"I love you, Abby."

She could only watch him and allow the burning in her core to change into something softer, yet just as fiery.

He ran his finger along her cheek. "Be my wife. Live here with me. We'll raise Eleanor as our own. Take slow winter walks. Run Snowbird and River. Say you'll take me—as I am. Make me the happiest man there ever was."

She nodded, tears in her eyes. "Yes."

"Yes?"

She grinned. "Yes, Isaac. To all of it."

"'All of it.' Interesting choice of words."

"What do you mean?"

"I'll tell you everything, my love." He kissed her again, whispering against her temple. "My dearest Abby."

Nearly every one of **Krista Lynne Jensen's** elementary school teachers noted on her report card that she was a "daydreamer". It was not a compliment. So, when Krista grew up, she put those daydreams down on paper for others to enjoy.

Krista has lived in lush Oregon and rugged Wyoming, but Washington is her beloved home state. She likes to choose familiar settings for her stories, and she is grateful to have such inspirational places to choose from. She is a mother of six, gramma of three, a gardener and cook, loves to travel, and lives to make the best of what she's been given.

Krista writes inspirational romance, and fantasy. She is the author of OF GRACE AND CHOCOLATE (2012 Whitney Award Finalist), THE ORCHARD (2013 Whiney Award Finalist), FALLING FOR YOU (2014), and KISSES IN THE RAIN (2015 Whitney Award Finalist) with Covenant Communications. She has novellas in Love Unexpected: With All My Heart (2014), Christmas Grace (2017), and Timeless Romance Anthologies: Love Letters (2014) and Yuletide Regency (2018) with Mirror Press.

Visit her blog at: kristalynnejensen.blogspot.com

The New Earl

HEATHER B. MOORE

Chapter One

CELIA THOMPSON READ the horrible words of the letter in her hands. Her fingers shook, her breath stilled, and her heart skipped. She reread the date to be sure she didn't have it wrong. Tomorrow's date was written in a bold, sure script. There was no doubt.

Her father's second cousin would be arriving on the morrow to take possession of his inheritance, which happened to be the estate Celia had lived on her entire twenty-three years. If the death of her parents years ago wasn't terrible enough, followed by the death of her bullheaded brother in a battle in the colonies three months before, someone might as well drive the final nail into her own coffin.

Celia was an orphan. She was without her beloved brother, Bart. And she was about to be displaced.

Her eyes filled with angry tears when she reread the final line of the letter.

Lady Celia is, of course, welcome to reside at Banfield Estate as long as she wishes.

Oh, wonderful.

Celia eyed the fire in the parlor hearth. She was tempted to crumple up the words of the odious Mr. Aaron Thompson, second cousin to her father. Aaron Thompson happened to be an accountant by trade, and only upon the death of her brother had he become a member of the nobility. She supposed she'd have to call him *Lord Banfield* now that he would be earl.

The first tear fell. Her *father* had been Lord Banfield and her *brother* should still be Lord Banfield—they were the men whom she loved so much and who could never be replaced. Not by anyone. Celia knew nothing about Aaron Thompson. She'd never met him, and she wished she'd never have to lay eyes upon him.

The second tear fell. There was no time to pack and leave. He'd be here *tomorrow*. Besides, where would she go while she waited for her aunt Marianne to return from her third honeymoon? She'd offered to bring Celia to her home after Bart's death, but at the time Celia had wanted to stay in her own home. Aunt Marianne was quite . . . eccentric. And she was always having parties, or taking extravagant shopping trips, or asking Celia to fetch things for her as if Celia were a lady's maid.

Celia had no time or patience to fetch and carry. She had her own life to live. In fact, she had been in the middle of writing one of her romances (unpublished and written under a *nom de plume*, of course) when the life-changing letter had arrived. To be fair, Celia had known that the estate would be entailed to someone.

This shouldn't have been a surprise. What simple accountant wouldn't want to take possession of his vast inheritance right away?

But couldn't he at least have waited until after Christmas? Banfield Estate was wonderful during the season. It was tradition to host a holiday dinner at the manor, and Celia had been presiding since her parents' death. Because of her brother's death, there would be no dinner, but Celia still planned to create and deliver the gift baskets. She would have to stay on through the season to make sure they were done right.

Celia crossed to the hearth, standing mere inches from the warmth, but she couldn't feel it one bit. The ceaseless December rain outside matched her mood. She really had two choices: live here as a charity case, or move in with Aunt Marianne. Yes, there were perhaps other choices for a lady of her station. She could marry, but if no one had offered for her in the past five years, they certainly wouldn't now. Her dowry was decent, but she'd already passed her prime.

Besides, her hair was the color of red cardinal, and if that wasn't off-putting enough, so many freckles speckled her face that powder did little good. A final option would be to take on the job of a governess. At the very thought, Celia could practically see her parents turning over in their graves.

Yet Celia had already written to Aunt Marianne that she planned on joining her after Christmas. The plans were all set.

Celia rubbed her cold, ink-stained hands. It seemed she was destined to live out her life as a burden to someone unless she could get published. Then she could have her own income, take a cottage by the sea, and write for the remainder of her days.

"Lady Celia?"

She turned to see the housekeeper, Mrs. March. The woman looked as nervous as a cat. Perhaps Celia had let her mood affect the entire household. "What is it?"

"There's ... uhm ... a carriage coming up the lane," Mrs. March said, her eyes wide. "Mr. Garner thinks it's the new Lord Banfield. Come a day early."

Chapter Two

"ALMOST THERE, STANLEY," Aaron Thompson said, patting the old dog who sat by him in the carriage seat—a rented carriage for now, though Aaron knew he'd surely have use of multiple carriages soon. The dog continued to shiver even though Aaron had draped two blankets over the poor thing. Yes, Stanley was old, and yes, Aaron was taking his pet to Banfield Estate.

The news of the death of Bartholomew Thompson, Earl of Banfield, had been shocking. First, the man was not yet thirty, and second, it meant that Aaron had apparently inherited an earldom. If his parents were still alive, he could imagine that his father would laugh with mirth and his mother would weep with joy. But neither of his parents was alive, and his sister had married several years ago and had established a home of her own.

Stanley lifted his scruffy head and whimpered.

"Getting hungry, boy?" Aaron asked. He wasn't exactly sure what type of dog Stanley was. He'd been a ball of fur and energy when Aaron had first spotted him outside his London office. The young pup had been friendly, but also hungry. Aaron had started feeding him, and after a week or so, he'd brought the pup home.

Aaron hadn't planned on setting off today, but someone

in his office had mentioned that it was cold enough to snow overnight. It would be impossible to travel for the next few days if it snowed. So Aaron had gathered up his things, set off for home, finished packing, and hired a carriage.

The carriage slowed, and Aaron looked out the window, past the driving rain to the three-story mansion looming at the end of the lane. He'd seen a drawing once of Banfield Estate, but had never seen it in person. And seeing it now made this transition all the more real. Aaron was a man of business, yes, and could balance any ledger set before him, but how was he going to manage farms and tenants and . . . Lady Celia?

He wished his mother were still alive because she would have known how to advise him on managing a young girl. He guessed her to be close to her coming out. Who would handle those sorts of matters? As distasteful as it sounded, Aaron would have to appeal to one of Lady Celia's female relatives.

Aaron certainly wasn't going to take up the Banfield residence in London and escort the young lady between balls. Although he knew the expectations of his new station in life would require vast changes to his activities, the thought of stepping into a ballroom made his stomach roil. But he was only focusing on one step at a time. And the next step was to get in out of the rain and find Stanley a proper meal.

The carriage came to a stop, and a moment later, the door was opened by the hired driver—a service that Aaron wasn't used to and wondered if he ever would be.

The driver then proceeded to unload and carry Aaron's single trunk to the front of the house and up the wide stone steps. As if on cue, the front door opened, and there stood a gray-haired man in a dark suit—clearly the butler.

"Come on, Stanley," Aaron said, ushering the dog out of the carriage.

The dog moved slowly. He was probably stiff just as Aaron was from the long, jolting ride. But the rain encouraged the dog to move a bit faster, and by the time they reached the front door, Aaron was only spotted with drops.

"Welcome, sir," the man at the door said. "I'm Mr. Garner, butler here at Banfield."

Aaron held out his hand to shake the butler's, and although the man looked surprised, he shook Aaron's hand.

"And this is Mrs. March, our housekeeper."

Aaron focused next on a middle-aged woman whose hair was about the same mottled gray as Stanley's fur. "Nice to meet you, Mrs. March."

She curtseyed. *Heavens.* He'd never been curtseyed to before.

He reached to pick up the trunk at the front door, but Mr. Garner stepped forward. "I will take that for you, Lord Banfield."

Lord Banfield. That was his new title, Aaron knew, but it was strange to hear someone actually say it.

Mr. Garner reached into his jacket pocket and pulled out some money to tip the driver of the carriage.

"I was about to do that," Aaron protested, but his words died out when Mr. Garner flashed him an incredulous look.

So Aaron stopped talking and let Mr. Garner handle whatever it was that butlers did.

"Lord Banfield," Mr. Garner said. "Did you come alone or is your valet bringing the rest of your luggage?"

Aaron blinked. "This is all my luggage, and I do not have a valet."

Mr. Garner exchanged glances with the housekeeper. She stepped forward. "We can procure one right away. An earl needs a valet."

Although she didn't speak any criticisms, he caught her

quick perusal of his attire and the slight tightening of her mouth.

He cleared his throat. "Thank you. I would appreciate your help in finding a valet." He'd never had use for a valet, but he knew running an earldom would have different expectations from the life of a mere accountant. "Might I ask if there's something I can feed Stanley?"

Her thin brows lifted. "Stanley." Then her gaze lowered to the dog on the floor. "Oh, the dog."

"He's a friendly thing, but getting on in years," Aaron said. "His old bones don't like the cold."

For the first time since Aaron's arrival, Mrs. March's face softened into an almost-smile. "I understand." She bent and patted Stanley's head. "Follow me, dog. I've got some scraps and a nice fire in the kitchen."

"Uh, Mrs. March?" Aaron said. "Once he's fed, can you bring him to the . . . library?" He looked past her, not sure about the layout of the house. Surely there was a library in a place this massive. And Aaron would definitely feel right at home in a room full of books.

But when he again looked at Mrs. March, he found that she was staring at him, her eyes rounded.

"What's the matter?" he asked, wondering what sort of blunder he'd made.

"The dog had better stay out of the main rooms. Lady Celia would not want—" She cut herself off.

Aaron blinked. "Does Lady Celia not like dogs?"

"I don't rightly know," Mrs. March said, her tone lowering. "She is quite fastidious though. I'm not sure she'd approve of a dog in the library."

Aaron wasn't sure he'd heard right. How much power did a young girl have over a seasoned housekeeper?

"Is she allergic to dogs?"

Mrs. March's brow furrowed. "Not that I know of. I've seen her pet the neighbor's dog before."

"Very well, then," Aaron said. "Bring Stanley into the library when he's had something to eat."

Mrs. March's face pinked, and she again curtseyed. "As you wish, my lord."

After he watched Mrs. March head for what must be the kitchen area, Aaron looked about. Mr. Garner had disappeared upstairs someplace, presumably to whichever bedroom Aaron was meant to occupy.

Aaron walked through the great hall. Doors on the right led to a parlor, its fire quite cheery. He continued, passing another room—a music room by the looks of it—then he arrived at a very respectable library.

In fact, it was the nicest library he'd ever been in. He walked into the room and spun slowly around, taking it all in. Bookcases rose to the ceiling, and Aaron knew that he could never read so many books in his entire lifetime, even if he started this very moment.

Then a movement at the door caught his attention. A woman stood in the shadow of the doorframe, her russet dress nearly blending in with the woodwork. But nothing else of her blended in. For one thing, her hair was the brightest red he'd ever seen, and second, her eyes were a startling blue. The look on her face, though, was beyond description.

If he was not mistaken, this woman wished him anywhere but here.

Chapter Three

HE'S NOT OLD. His shoulders aren't stooped. There isn't a strand of gray hair on his head. He's not gone too fat. And he doesn't have those bushy side whiskers so many men prefer.

Celia needed to stop staring because the man standing in the middle of the library was none other than Mr. Aaron Thompson, now the Earl of Banfield. She estimated him to be close to thirty, maybe a year or two older than her brother. His hair was a gold-brown, and his eyes a shade darker.

Although she'd never laid eyes on the man, she had not expected him to be so young . . . and tall . . . and, well, handsome. Celia didn't do well around handsome men or beautiful women. It only made her more aware of her flaming hair and imperfect complexion.

But if Celia was being rude by staring at the new Lord Banfield, he was being equally rude by staring right back.

"Lady Celia, I presume?" His low voice held a note of surprise in it.

The sound of his voice brought her back to her senses. She dipped into a brief curtsey, not taking her eyes off him. He wasn't exactly imposing, no, not in his second-rate suit and the scruff of evening whiskers upon his jaw. But the directness of his gaze and the tenor of his voice told her that he was a man of intelligence.

"Welcome, L-Lord Banfield," she said, hating the tremor that had entered her voice. She'd already raged and cried and mourned, then raged some more. Unless her brother miraculously came back from the dead, the man in front of her was the new earl.

And now he was coming toward her. Did he mean to take her hand? Kiss her cheek? With wide eyes, she watched him approach. But when he stopped in front of her, he didn't make any such advance.

"We are cousins, aren't we?" he said. "Perhaps you might call me Aaron. I am not quite used to . . . the title."

"I suppose not," she said. "But I do not think it proper to call you by your Christian name." Her pulse moved up a notch as his gaze skittered over her person. He looked at her hair, her face, her neck, her shoulders, and lower.

His eyes snapped back to her face. "What is your age?"

She swallowed. He had few manners, this new earl. "I am three-and-twenty." Feeling bold, she said, "How old are you?"

The edges of his mouth softened, and the brown of his eyes flashed with amusement. Briefly. Then it was gone. "One-and-thirty."

"I—I thought you'd be closer to my father's age." It was her turn to scrutinize him. His eyebrows were at least two shades darker than his hair, and the length of his eyelashes would make any woman envious.

"My parents had me in their later years," he explained. "I thought you were a young girl."

"No, I am quite on the shelf, as you can see." She lifted a shoulder.

Again, his eyes roamed over her, and she realized this man needed lessons in manner and deportment. He'd need to learn to keep his curiosities more subdued. Granted, she was curious about him. He reminded her of a new colt who was learning to stand on his feet for the first time. She was finding it hard to continue the hatred she'd built up in her mind and heart.

"Excuse me if I am too blunt," he said. "I am told it's one of my downfalls. But you are hardly on the shelf, Lady Celia."

His tone had softened when he spoke her name.

Celia opened her mouth to respond before she realized she had no idea what to say to the round-about compliment. More likely, he hadn't meant it as a compliment at all, but was merely being "blunt."

Then he stepped back as if he'd just remembered something.

And at that moment, Mrs. March came into the library, leading a dog.

Celia stared at the scruffy creature that looked fresh from the streets of London—and perhaps it was.

"Hello, Stanley." Lord Banfield bent and scratched the dog behind his ears. "Are you happy now?"

Lord Banfield's entire demeanor had transformed, and Celia had a flash of understanding of how he might have looked or acted as a young boy. The dog thumped his tail at the attention.

But the dog was a dirty thing and likely had fleas at the very least. "You brought a dog all the way to Banfield Estate? Does he hunt?" Clearly the dog was some sort of mongrel and probably wouldn't know what a bird was.

Lord Banfield looked up, wry amusement on his face. "He doesn't hunt that I know of. I rescued him as a pup from the streets."

Celia considered this. She didn't want to think of positive attributes this man might have; it was much more satisfactory to think of his negative qualities—chief among them that he was in the line of succession after her father. This man's future children would inherit the estate next. Celia would permanently lose her home.

"We can ask the stable boy to prepare a place for your dog," Celia said, resigning herself to the fact that Banfield Estate now had a pet.

"Oh, that won't be necessary." He straightened and brushed his hands. Bits of fur floated down as a result.

Celia tried to hide her shudder. It wasn't that she was opposed to pets on principle. If they kept to the outdoors.

"Stanley will be sleeping in my room," he said.

Celia's mouth fell open.

Lord Banfield didn't seem to notice her horror at his announcement. Celia wanted to argue with him, but with Mrs. March in the room, Celia didn't dare defy the new master of the house.

Lord Banfield's gaze went to Mrs. March. "Perhaps I can use an old blanket for Stanley's bed? If you'll but direct me, I can get things set up. The old dog's used to taking more than one nap a day."

Mrs. March smiled at the man, then quickly schooled her features when she noticed Celia looking at her.

"Lord Banfield," Celia spoke up. "You might reconsider where you house your dog. Dog hair is difficult to manage, and what if he barks at night?"

Lord Banfield met her gaze, his brown eyes focused solely on her, as if he could read her thoughts. "Stanley doesn't bark at night."

Celia looked to Mrs. March for help, but the woman refused to make eye contact.

Why couldn't Aunt Marianne be home now? Instead, Celia would have to live in this house with a new master, an old dog, and a traitorous housekeeper.

"When is the dinner hour?" Lord Banfield asked, effectively changing the subject.

Celia exhaled. *Fine.* They'd return to polite conversation. "Eight o'clock," she told him.

"Very well," he said. "I will see you then."

Celia blinked. Had she been dismissed? Apparently so because he next asked Mrs. March to show him to his quarters. Celia watched as the two of them left the library, the scruffy dog following.

Who named a dog *Stanley* anyway?

Alone again, at least until dinner, Celia decided it would be the perfect time to work on her newest novel. With it raining outside, none of the staff would wonder why she was keeping to her room. As she started up the steps, Mrs. March was coming down them.

"Lady Celia," Mrs. March said, pausing when they reached each other. "I would like to ask Kate if she's available to come and serve as your companion." She glanced up the staircase. "I did not know that Lord Banfield was so close to your age."

"Neither did I," Celia murmured. Mrs. March was right, although Celia would miss her relative freedom. As the vicar's daughter, Kate had been Celia's childhood friend, despite their age difference. But station had eventually created a distance between them.

Kate was nearly eighteen now, and most likely would marry within the coming year. Kate had a head full of blonde curls and a quick smile. She'd come to the house when Celia needed to get ready for an event, of which there had been very few lately due to her brother's absence, and now his death.

"We don't want gossip in the village," Mrs. March continued.

"Of course not." Celia nodded. "Yes, please send for Kate. If she arrives before dinner tonight, she can join us."

Mrs. March agreed and continued down the stairs.

Once in her room, Celia located the locked box she kept in the wardrobe. Inside were her manuscript pages, which she kept hidden away from the world.

She sat at her vanity table and unstopped the inkwell, then dipped her quill inside the ink. She'd reached the part of the novel where it was time for the hero to kiss the heroine against a beautiful backdrop of a sunset in India. The only problem was that Celia had never been kissed before, so she couldn't write with experience. So Celia would have to guess, especially since this kiss was an illicit kiss. One that took place before any sort of marriage proposal.

Since it was raining outside, she decided that the hero and heroine would also kiss in the rain. A very light summer rain in India, which she assumed would be warm. None of this cold winter rain.

Frederick looked deep into Lady Miriam's eyes and only saw love. Love for him. He was sure of it. Ever so slowly, he drew her into his arms. She gasped at his boldness, but didn't move out of his embrace. So Frederick kissed her. Lady Miriam wrapped her arms about his neck and kissed him back. That was when Frederick knew all was right with the world.

There. That would do. She reread the lines a few times, made one adjustment, then set the quill down. The rain was coming down in earnest now, and Celia wondered if Kate would be able to make it to the house tonight. Surely the mud puddles were growing.

Someone knocked at her door, and Celia called out, "Yes?"

Mrs. March spoke through the door. "Lord Banfield requests your presence in the library before dinner is served. Do you need help dressing?"

Celia looked at the clock and realized it was much later

than she thought. When it was only her in the house, she didn't bother changing for dinner.

"Yes, just a moment." Celia put away the manuscript pages, locked the box, and set it in the wardrobe. Then she went to open the door to Mrs. March.

Chapter Four

MRS. MARCH HAD informed Aaron that they'd have a guest for dinner tonight, and Aaron could only agree. He knew enough about the elite to realize that they were big supporters of propriety. Kate Jones, the vicar's daughter, would serve as companion to Lady Celia until she left Banfield Estate. Which was apparently in a few weeks' time, he'd been informed by Mrs. March. For Lady Celia intended to stay through Christmas, then travel to her aunt's home.

Aaron supposed he should feel guilty because he knew it was his inheritance, and his subsequent occupation of said inheritance, that was the reason for Lady Celia's departure. Granted, the young woman had suffered much and the changes to her life were unfortunate. So Aaron would do his best to be kind and agreeable, apart from insisting that Stanley remain in the house.

Even so, Aaron requested that Lady Celia join him in the library so he could propose his idea to her before the evening was filled with another guest and resulting conversations.

Stanley perked up where he was sitting on the floor at Aaron's feet. "Is she coming, old boy?"

Before Stanley could reply, the door to the library opened and in walked Lady Celia.

Her eyes were even more blue than he remembered, contrasting with the black gown she wore. Lady Celia's hair had been artfully arranged atop her head and revealed the creamy expanse of her neck and sloping shoulders. Aaron knew he shouldn't be noticing so many physical details about Lady Celia, but he could truthfully say that her coloring was the most unusual he'd ever encountered.

Yes, he'd seen red-haired women before, but Lady Celia was like a red posy on a bright summer day.

"What is the meaning of this?" she asked, closing the door behind her as if she didn't want anyone to hear their conversation.

Something niggled in the back of his mind. If a companion had to be sent for, wasn't it suspect to be alone in the library with Lady Celia? Should she have left the door open?

Aaron rose to his feet. "Thank you for coming."

"This is very unusual." She folded her arms.

"Please, have a seat." Aaron gestured to one of the wingback chairs. "Mrs. March said that you'd be leaving after Christmas, and I'd like to discuss the arrangements before your friend Kate Jones arrives."

Lady Celia hesitated, and Aaron wouldn't have been entirely surprised if she refused. Finally she sat, looking down as she smoothed her dress over her lap.

When she looked up again, he saw that her eyes were wet. *Blast.* She was upset.

"I am sorry," he said, not sure what exactly he was apologizing for. His existence?

Her mouth opened, then shut. She looked toward one of the bookcases. "You don't need to apologize for anything. I mean, my brother's death wasn't your fault."

Ah. She was mourning her brother. "I am sorry just the same," he said in a quiet voice. "I wish I had known your brother and your father. It's strange coming into the home of someone I didn't know."

She remained silent.

"I don't know what their daily routines were, their likes, dislikes." He moved to the chair across from her and sat down.

She glanced at him, then quickly away.

"I'd love to know the history of your family, Lady Celia," he said. "I'd love to hear about your brother. This is a fine estate that I'm sure you're proud of. I can tell you love this home, and I don't want you to feel like I'm running you out."

He leaned forward in his chair when she didn't respond. "This is still your home, Lady Celia. You're welcome to stay here as long as you wish, until your own marriage or some other interest takes you away."

A tear fell down her cheek, and Aaron's first instinct was to reach out and blot the tear. Instead, he fished for a handkerchief, located one in the pocket of his vest, and handed it over.

For a moment, she didn't react. Then she took the handkerchief and dabbed it at her face. When she next looked at him, she said in a trembling voice, "I'm sorry too."

He waited for her to continue.

"I wished some terrible stuff upon you." She twisted the handkerchief in her hands. It was just as well since he wasn't expecting it back. "I guess it's fortunate that I'm not a gypsy fortune teller, because none of it came true."

Aaron leaned back in his chair, wondering if he should be amused or slightly terrified. "What sort of stuff did you wish?"

She lifted one of her delicate shoulders, keeping her gaze on that twisting handkerchief. "Carriage accident. Sudden heart attack. An accidental fall down the stairs. A rabid dog bite. The usual."

Aaron laughed. "The *usual?*"

She looked up at him, surprise on her face. "Well,

unusual would be things like drowning in your own soup or choking to death on the library dust." She didn't even crack a smile.

Aaron chuckled. "I suppose that would be unusual since there's not a speck of dust in here. I checked."

That earned him the smallest of smiles from Lady Celia, which in turn made something in his chest soften and warm.

"Aside from the death wishes, I am sincere in my desire to learn more about Banfield and to see it through your eyes."

Lady Celia nodded, and Aaron took that as a positive step.

"Tomorrow morning we'll start right after we break our fast," Celia said, her voice more confident now. "If that's all right with you?"

Her blue eyes connected with his, and Aaron thought of how her future husband would have trouble denying any of her requests. "Very well, I shall look forward to it. And I assume Miss Kate will accompany us?"

The faintest pink stained Lady Celia's cheeks. "Yes." She rose to her feet, the handkerchief still clutched in her hands. Aaron rose as well. She made no move to give the handkerchief back, and he made no move to retrieve it. "As to your offer of staying here past Christmas, until my marriage or some other event, I can assure you that I'll never marry. So I will stick to my original plan of residing with Aunt Marianne. I cannot feel settled about living on your charity."

Aaron opened his mouth to refute her answer as well as question her about why she was so convinced she would not marry, when a knock sounded at the door.

"Come in," Aaron said, for what other choice did he have?

Mrs. March opened the door. "Dinner is ready, my lord." She looked over at Lady Celia. "My lady."

Chapter Five

WHY DID THE new Lord Banfield have to be so pleasant? So generous? And handsome. If it weren't for his grumpy dog, the man would be perfect. Even Kate had noticed Lord Banfield's exceptional looks and manner. In fact, she was practically flirting with the man. Celia couldn't entirely blame her friend because Celia also felt the rush of heat whenever Lord Banfield turned his warm brown eyes upon her. And the kind words he'd said to her in the library played over and over in her mind.

Kate was spending a great deal of time talking about her upbringing at the vicarage, and truthfully, Celia was feeling a bit envious as Kate talked about her multiple siblings and constant activity. She also took the opportunity to toss her blonde curls from time to time.

Celia tried not to be envious of her friend. After all, when had the daughter of an earl ever wished to step down a station? Still, Celia envied Kate's youth and outlook on life, not to mention the fact that Lord Banfield seemed completely enamored of the conversation. Was he . . . *interested* in Kate? No, Celia decided. Yet stranger things had happened. Earls had married well beneath them before. It would create a scandal, yes, but Lord Banfield had no hovering parents or relatives marking his every move and decision.

Like her, Lord Banfield was quite on his own in this world.

Celia was no longer hungry, and even when dessert of her favorite chocolate custard was brought in, she turned it down. Yes, she'd invited Kate here, but Celia hadn't meant for the woman to be so amiable toward Lord Banfield.

With dinner finished, the three of them went into the parlor. Stanley lifted his head from his umpteenth nap of the day as he lay before the hearth. Did the dog do nothing else but sleep?

Celia passed by the dog to sit in one of the armchairs, and the dog emitted a low growl.

"Stanley," Lord Banfield warned. Then he proceeded to pour himself a brandy as if his growling dog was nothing out of the ordinary.

"Won't you play for us?" Kate asked Celia.

Lord Banfield took a sip of his brandy and looked over at her. It was about time he paid her some attention. "Do you play the pianoforte, Lady Celia?" he asked.

His eyes had a completely innocent look in them.

"Passably," she said. "Do you play, Lord Banfield?"

One of his dark eyebrows lifted. "I do, in fact. It's been quite a while since I've had the pleasure though."

Kate clapped her hands. "Oh, you must play for us then."

Lord Banfield kept his gaze on Celia. "Only if the lady of the house agrees."

Celia was no longer the lady of the house, and Lord Banfield knew it. But the way he kept his gaze on her made Celia feel like she'd just eaten the richest dessert. "We'd love you to refresh your talents tonight."

One side of his mouth lifted into a smile, and Celia could well imagine the sound of his laughter. But he didn't laugh. He took a final sip of the brandy, then set down the glass. He bowed to Celia, then to Kate, which made her giggle. He crossed to the pianoforte and took his place at the bench.

Celia noticed the seams of his coat had started to wear. He was similar in size to her brother, and there was no reason that he couldn't wear Bart's clothing until Lord Banfield could have his own wardrobe made up. Would she be betraying her brother if she made the offer?

Lord Banfield played a short song that Celia didn't recognize. It was lively and playful, and when he finished she and Kate clapped.

"That was wonderful," Kate said. "You are very talented."

Lord Banfield laughed. "That was my warm-up song. It seems I still remember how to play." He turned back to the pianoforte and picked out a melody with only his right hand.

Celia wondered if Lord Banfield had been a willing student of music or if his parents had insisted upon it. Whatever the case was, she soon forgot her questions when he played the first notes of a Haydn concerto.

Celia exhaled. The concerto had been her brother's favorite, and he'd asked her to play it for him almost every night. Tears pricked her eyes as the melody continued, slow and methodical, each note bringing back memories of her brother. How he used to lounge across the settee with his eyes closed, and how as soon as she finished, he'd ask her to play it again.

Celia was well familiar with the song that she'd long ago memorized, yet listening to another person play made it feel different. Her chest felt like it had expanded, and her heart hurt. Hurt with the memories, hurt with how much she missed Bart. Hurt with how she had to live on without any of her family members.

The tears were impossible to stop now, and even if she'd had a dozen handkerchiefs, she couldn't have soaked them up.

She hiccupped a silent apology, then she rushed out of the room. She didn't have a destination in mind, but she ended up in the cool, silent library. Celia pressed her back against the wall next to the door, trying to breathe. The notes of the concerto drifted through the house, still reaching Celia's place of hiding.

The notes faded, then stopped, and Celia closed her eyes. *Please don't come find me. Just stay away.* She didn't know what was wrong with her. She hadn't felt such intense grief since the early days after her brother's death. She supposed having the new Lord Banfield arrive had made everything all the more permanent, and she now had to face changes in her life.

Conversation echoed down the hall—a man and a woman's—Kate and Lord Banfield. Then footsteps, going up the stairs. Good, they'd look for her upstairs and hopefully give up soon. After all, she was a grown woman of twenty-three and didn't have to be continually supervised.

"Lady Celia?" someone whispered.

Without opening her eyes, she knew it was *him*.

She'd tell him that she was tired and had a headache. Then she'd make her escape to her bedroom for the night. Tomorrow she'd once again be composed and would fulfill her promise of showing Lord Banfield the estate and telling him about her family history—

"Lady Celia?" His voice was low, soft.

He was standing right in front of her. She couldn't open her eyes since she didn't want him to offer her another handkerchief. He'd run out soon enough.

"Are you all right?" he asked, and she felt him watching her, waiting.

She kept her eyes closed, trying to steady her breath, so that when she explained, her words would be calm. "That concerto was my brother's favorite song."

Lord Banfield didn't respond for a moment, and when he did it was unexpected. "My mother taught me to play. She said that music uplifts the heart and comforts the soul."

Celia nodded, even though her eyes were still closed.

"Your brother had good taste in music."

Celia nodded again as another round of tears started. Before she could swipe them away, Lord Banfield pressed a handkerchief against her cheeks, soaking up the tears for her.

She opened her eyes, but he didn't move away, didn't apologize for taking such liberties. In the dimness of the library, he continued to dab at her cheeks. He was so close, and he smelled of after-dinner brandy and musk.

She couldn't exactly explain how it happened—if he stepped closer or if she leaned into him—but he pulled her into his arms. All she knew was that he was holding her. And even though she estimated he was a similar build to her brother, being in his arms was nothing like embracing her brother. Lord Banfield's chest was warm, solid, breathing, and she felt the slow thud of his heartbeat against her own body. She slid her arms about his waist, and his arms tightened around her.

For the first time in a very long time, Celia didn't feel alone.

She didn't know how long they embraced, but eventually her tears dried, and the ache in her chest lessened. And even after he released her, and she stepped away, she still felt his embrace.

Chapter Six

Aaron watched as the shadows from night clouds racing past the moon played across the ceiling. He'd been staring at the shifting patterns for what felt like hours. It was certainly well after midnight, and except for Stanley's snores coming from his bed near the window, the sounds of the house had fallen into silence some time ago. The dog seemed to have settled into the household quite well, and Aaron had seen Mr. Garner giving the old dog treats.

Yet Aaron had not expected to be confronted with so many emotions upon his arrival at Banfield. He especially hadn't expected to find Lady Celia a woman of twenty-three, and to be so... fiercely stubborn and independent, yet in need of comfort at the same time. And he could not forget how she'd held onto him in the library that evening. How her hair smelled like lilacs in the summer, and how the silky-smooth hair brushed against his cheek and neck. He should not be noticing these things about a grieving woman.

But he could not get the image of her red hair, her bright blue eyes, and the slope of her neck out of his mind. He closed his eyes and tried to let himself drift into a world of dreaming, but all he saw was Lady Celia and the paleness of her skin beneath a sprinkle of freckles.

Aaron sighed. Giving up on sleep, he sat up in bed and threw off the covers. Stanley lifted his head, and Aaron told the dog to go back to sleep. There was plenty of work to do, and Aaron might as well start on it. Perhaps after an hour or two of poring over ledgers, he'd be tired enough to sleep.

He pulled on a dressing robe and left his bedroom. Mrs. March had told him that he occupied the master room, and Celia's quarters were at the other end of the house, past the large staircase. As he approached the staircase, he spotted a square patch of light down the opposite hallway.

Aaron paused, wondering where the light came from. There were no windows in the hallway, of course, and no candles burning on a side table. Then he realized that the light was coming from beneath a closed door. Without venturing any further, Aaron guessed that it was Lady Celia's room.

Could she not sleep either? Was she still too distressed over the song he'd played after dinner? Or perhaps she'd fallen asleep with a candle burning? Would that not risk a potential fire?

Although it made his pulse hum to do so, he entered the hallway and walked toward the patch of light. First he listened at the door, but he heard nothing. Next he knocked very softly.

There was no sound, but it was as if the air around him stilled. As if the woman inside had heard the knock, but didn't know what to make of it. Or perhaps his knock had awakened her.

"Lady Celia?" he said in a quiet voice. "Is everything all right?"

He waited. And then he heard it. A rustle, followed by the turn of the doorknob.

When she opened the door a few inches, he saw that she hadn't been crying—or at least her blue eyes looked clear enough. But she was dressed for bed, wearing a long, flowing night rail. Most remarkably, her red hair cascaded over her shoulders like a shimmering waterfall, ending at her waist. He doubted he'd ever seen anything so magnificent.

"I am sorry to disturb you," Aaron whispered, regretting that he'd had the gall to knock on Lady Celia's bedroom door in the middle of the night. "I saw the light and worried that you'd left a candle burning."

"I wasn't sleeping," she whispered back. "I'm a . . . night owl." She kept the door open only a handspan, and he could see that her fingers were stained with drops of ink.

"Are you writing letters?" he asked, wondering why he was still standing here. If someone should come upon them . . .

Her eyes widened, and she removed her hand from the door as if she wanted to hide her fingers. Aaron took a step back. He'd already invaded her privacy enough, and there was no neglected candle to be concerned about.

Before he turned and left, he had one more question to ask. "I trust you are feeling better?"

She lowered her lashes. "I am."

"That's good to hear. Good night, then." He took another step then turned. The door clicked shut before he reached the top of the stairs. Aaron wasn't sure what to make of Lady Celia's late hours, but it did make him wonder who she was writing to at such a late hour. Perhaps it was just as she said. She was a night owl.

Apparently he was one too, *tonight*. He held onto the banister as he walked down the stairs in the dark. When he reached the library, he lit a couple of candles and set to reading through the most recent ledgers tied to the estate. The ledger on the desk was half blank, and the most recent entry had been made more than two years ago.

Aaron searched around the library for more ledgers.

Finally he found several volumes neatly organized by year, but nothing that was recent.

Perhaps the ledgers had been moved? Had the solicitor of Banfield Estate taken them to his office? Aaron didn't think he could knock twice on Lady Celia's door in the middle of the night. He put the ledgers back in place and looked about the library. Then he crossed to the cupboards behind the desk and started to open them one by one. In the final cupboard, he found a box with stacks of receipts inside.

Using one of the candles for light, he held up the receipts one by one. They were the receipts and bills that should have been recorded in the ledger. Yet here they were. In a box in the cupboard.

Aaron sat back on his heels and rubbed his forehead. He was afraid that no accounting had been done since Bartholomew had traveled to the colonies. Apparently Aaron had his work cut out for him.

Morning found Aaron waking up in one of the library chairs, a severe crick in his neck. He stretched and stared with bleary eyes at the rows of books on the opposite wall as he slowly remembered how he'd ended up falling asleep in a chair.

Feminine voices came from somewhere outside of the library, and Aaron guessed that Lady Celia and Miss Kate were breaking their fast. He stood and made his way to the hallway. He should really change before encountering the ladies. And Stanley likely needed to be let outside. So Aaron hurried up the steps, taking them two at a time, and entered his bedroom, then stopped cold.

A man stood in the middle of the room, spectacles perched on his nose. He was close to Aaron's age, but he looked like he hadn't eaten a full meal in his life.

"Hello," Aaron said.

The man executed a curt bow. "Lord Banfield, I'm Mr. Ferall."

Aaron blinked.

"Your new valet, my lord."

My new . . . Oh. "Mr. Ferall. Thank you for coming. I appreciate your willingness to . . . serve me."

The man straightened his thin shoulders and lifted his chin. "It's my honor, Lord Banfield." His gaze flitted over Aaron, who was surely an eyesore in rumpled clothing. "Might I assist you? I've sent your dog into Mr. Garner's care and laid out your morning clothes."

Indeed, the man had laid out clothing on the bed.

Aaron swallowed, and tried not to think too deeply about the fact that he was a grown man and was about to have someone help him dress for the day. But he thought about the new expectations of his position, and how this job would likely put some meat on Mr. Ferall's bones. "Very well. Thank you."

The process wasn't quite as painful as Aaron had thought it might be. In fact, Mr. Ferall was quick and efficient, and Aaron was dressed much faster than he would have been on his own. Mr. Garner brought Stanley to the bedroom just as Aaron was about to go downstairs.

The dog gave an approving woof. It seemed even Stanley was impressed.

The dog trotted by Aaron's side as he walked down the steps to go to the dining room. The prospect of food always lightened the dog's step. By the time Aaron reached the dining room, the two women at the table were nearly finished with their meal.

Miss Kate saw him first and smiled. "Good morning, Lord Banfield."

Aaron wished everyone would call him by his Christian name, but it couldn't be helped. So he smiled and said, "Good morning, ladies." Before he reached the side table, his gaze shifted to Lady Celia. Although her hair was pinned into a smooth coiffure, he couldn't help but remember the way it had tumbled over her shoulders, reaching her waist.

Her blue eyes connected with his. "Good morning," she said in a quiet voice, then she picked up her fork. "I hope you like what Cook's prepared."

"I'm not finicky," Aaron said. "And neither is Stanley."

She narrowed her eyes slightly, then nodded. She looked down at her half-filled plate. He didn't miss the flush that crept along her neck; his own neck felt warm.

He picked up a plate to serve himself. "I met Mr. Ferall."

Miss Kate clapped her hands together. "He's such a devout man. My father, who's the vicar, you know, says that he's always helping someone. When Lady Celia said he would make a good valet for you, I couldn't have agreed more."

Aaron finished piling eggs and ham onto his plate, then took his seat.

"Are you pleased with Mr. Ferall?" Lady Celia asked.

Aaron met her blue gaze. "Yes. Although I am sure I have much to adjust to here at Banfield."

Lady Celia set down her fork. "I'd like to offer you my brother's clothing. You are about the same build as Bart, and there's no reason to let his clothes collect dust." The flush returned to her cheeks.

Aaron wondered if redheads blushed more readily. He was also aware of how this gesture was not to be taken lightly. If hearing her brother's favorite music played could reduce Lady Celia to tears, then offering her brother's clothing to him was a grand gesture indeed.

"I don't mean to insult you," she continued, "but a man in your position is expected to dress according to the current fashion. I should be the one to tell you so that you don't find yourself in any uncomfortable situation."

Aaron felt his mouth quirk. "I will not take it as an insult, then."

The edges of her mouth lifted. "Very good. If you'd like, we'll start with a tour of the upper rooms, then work our way throughout the house."

"That sounds agreeable." Aaron glanced over at Miss Kate, who was giving him a brilliant smile. Goodness, he hadn't had this much female attention in, well, ever. He turned back to Lady Celia. "I do have a question before we start the tour. Do you know if there are ledgers for the estate financials that cover the last two years? I can't seem to find anything current in the library."

It was not in the least comforting to see the color drain from Lady Celia's face.

Chapter Seven

HE ALREADY KNOWS, Celia thought as dread pooled in her stomach. She had not been exactly negligent with the finances. She had kept all the receipts. But she supposed she had let her temper get the best of her when the estate solicitor visited in her brother's absence and made her feel like she was a dim-witted female.

The solicitor had given her a talking-to about her sticking to her pin money for extra expenditures. Then he'd insisted on coming every quarter. Instead, Celia wrote to him and said that she had been instructed by Bart to retain the receipts and wait until he returned home before meeting with the solicitor again.

She'd turned down all inquiries from the solicitor as the months went on.

"Perhaps I should explain things later," Celia said, feeling her face warm up. Why was she blushing so much around this man? She only had to show him the box of receipts and let him sort it out. But this morning, she was noticing all kinds of things about his appearance.

The brown of his eyes reminded her of the color of a dark brandy. His hair had been expertly combed, unlike the ruffled look of yesterday. She hadn't paid attention to his hands until now, when he was sitting across from her, holding his fork. He had long, elegant yet strong fingers, made for playing the pianoforte, as he'd so well demonstrated.

Kate had mentioned more than once how handsome she thought Lord Banfield was. Perhaps Lord Banfield wouldn't marry a woman of Kate's station, but that wouldn't prevent a man in his position to take his pleasures. The very thought of intimacies concerning Lord Banfield should have never entered Celia's mind, and she looked down at her half-eaten food before she could be caught blushing at her very unspinster-like thoughts.

"Very well, then," Lord Banfield said, and even though she was no longer looking at him, she could feel his gaze on her.

It took Celia a moment to remember what they'd been talking about. *Oh, yes.* The receipts. She merely nodded, then reached for her teacup to take a sip. The tea had cooled considerably, and now it was much too sweet. She took the smallest of swallows, then set the cup down on the saucer. Porcelain clattered against porcelain, drawing Kate's attention as well.

Celia needed some air. Space and air.

"If you need a private conversation, I can wait in the drawing room," Kate said.

Celia snapped her head up. "Oh, no, we should keep our promise to give Lord Banfield a tour of the estate. Finances can always wait."

Lord Banfield cleared his throat, and Celia heard the disagreement in the sound. But she refused to look at him.

"All right," Kate said with a pretty smile that any man would be dazzled with. "If you're sure."

"I am sure," Celia said with much more confidence than she felt. "If the rain holds off this afternoon, we can tour the grounds as well after lunch."

Kate clapped her hands together. "And ride horses?"

Celia couldn't help but smile. "Yes, of course."

Kate turned her charm onto Lord Banfield. "We only have two carriage horses at the vicarage, so I don't get to ride nearly as much as I'd like to."

Lord Banfield smiled back. "Then I hope the rain holds off."

The knot that formed in Celia's stomach had nothing to do with the cold tea or thick ham. Would the next fortnight be full of flirting between the earl and the vicar's daughter? Was she to watch the pair fall in love, and then be witness to Kate's heartbreak?

"Well," Celia said abruptly, scooting her chair back and rising to her feet. "I am finished. I will let Mrs. March know of our plans so that if there are any morning callers, she will know to put them off."

Lord Banfield had risen to his feet as well, and his brows arched at her comment.

Celia didn't wait for any reply from either of them before she hurried out of the dining room and continued toward the kitchen. Air and space.

Chapter Eight

AARON COULD NOT fathom collecting receipts week after week and not writing anything down. Not one line in a ledger. Nothing. Lady Celia's embarrassment had been clear, and he didn't wish to make her think that he was upset, but he was worried about the state of finances for the earldom.

Lady Celia's quick exit from the dining room had made Aaron feel like he'd received a blow to the gut. He hoped to the good Lord that he hadn't caused her to cry again. *Blast it all.* As Miss Kate talked about her favorite horse in the Banfield stable, he inspected the food he'd piled onto his plate. He couldn't get the image of Lady Celia's flushed cheeks out of his mind. Or how her open neckline had exposed a smattering of freckles across her collar bone.

He took a bite of food, not tasting it at all. He had to refocus on matters of the estate. He'd worked with enough solicitors to know that sometimes an inheritance could be more of a curse than a blessing. If an estate wasn't profitable, or at the very least could not support itself, then it became subject to parceling off land to the auction block.

Aaron gave up on eating and set down his fork. He realized Miss Kate was still talking about a particular horse. *Laws, the young woman could chatter.* "Might we join Lady

Celia?" he said, hoping that his interruption wouldn't be perceived as rude.

He felt as if he already had enough strikes against him at Banfield.

Miss Kate smiled. "Celia is like this. She disappears sometimes." She shrugged. "She did it as a child too. Would be gone for hours."

"Does it have to do with her poetry writing?"

Miss Kate looked surprised. "Lady Celia doesn't write poetry." Then she wrinkled her brow. "Although it would explain the ink stains on her fingers that I've spotted more than once. How did you know? Did she tell you?"

Aaron couldn't elaborate that he'd seen the same ink markings on Lady Celia's fingers in the middle of the night.

Just then, the woman herself came into the dining room. Her complexion hadn't yet returned to its creamy paleness, and Aaron wondered if she was still upset. Aaron rose to his feet.

Lady Celia gave him a quick glance, then said to Miss Kate, "Are you ready?"

"I am." Miss Kate pushed back her plate, so Aaron reached over and helped her up from her chair.

Aaron followed the women out of the dining room and up the grand staircase. Lady Celia gave a very thorough tour, telling him of each room and former occupants. When they reached the corridor of paintings, they stopped before each one as Lady Celia spoke of each relative. She was certainly well-versed in her family history.

Miss Kate interjected with small tidbits of village lore, and Aaron found himself smiling at a tale of Lady Celia's father when he was young and was known to be found asleep in the strangest places. "My father said that once he'd found the young lord asleep in the vicarage stables when his parents were on a visit."

"He always was a night owl," Lady Celia. "Read through half the night."

The fondness in her tone was unmistakable, and Aaron had to stop himself from saying, "Like father, like daughter." It was clear she'd cared deeply for her family, and he couldn't help but think that a woman like her would be a caring mother. Was it too presumptuous of him to think she'd dearly value each child?

The final suite of rooms they entered on the upper floor had been Bartholomew's.

Lady Celia walked the perimeter of the room, touching items lightly as she passed by each one. She paused near the bed and rested her hand on the deep green coverlet. "My brother said that he didn't want to move into the master suite until he was married. So he continued to occupy his childhood rooms."

Miss Kate walked over to the window and looked out, while Lady Celia described some of the changes the suite had gone through over the years. The emotion in her voice was unmistakable, but she kept her chin lifted and her gaze focused on the opposite wall. Aaron found that he was paying attention to Lady Celia's tone of voice and mannerisms more than he was hearing her describe things.

Aaron knew he had to stop staring at her, so he walked about the room a bit, reluctant to touch anything. It was an odd feeling to be in the room of someone who'd passed away. He felt a distinct emptiness, almost loneliness. A boy, then man, had once occupied this space, living here and breathing here.

"And you are welcome to my brother's clothing," Lady Celia said when he paused in front of the wardrobe.

Aaron turned to look at her. Her eyes were bright with unshed tears as she kept her hands clasped together. He had the sudden urge to cross to her and take her hands in his. To tell her that he wouldn't wear one stitch of her brother's clothing if she didn't want him to.

Aaron didn't answer for a moment, then he simply nodded his head. Lady Celia blinked, but it didn't clear the sorrow from her eyes. He hated seeing her sad.

Miss Kate turned from the window. "Someone is coming along the road. It looks like my father's carriage."

So Aaron was about to meet the vicar, and while they headed down the staircase, he wondered how much comfort the vicar had brought to Lady Celia in her time of mourning.

When Vicar Jones stepped down from his carriage, Aaron greeted the portly man with shrewd green eyes. Jones practically wheezed his way up the steps. Miss Kate must take after her mother, because there was not much to compare between father and daughter.

"Won't you stay for lunch?" Lady Celia asked when the vicar arrived in the foyer.

"Of course, Lady Celia," Vicar Jones said, regarding her with a pitying look. "I hear your days are numbered."

Aaron furrowed his brows, thinking the vicar was quite abrupt for a man of the cloth.

"I will travel to my aunt's after Christmas," Lady Celia said.

Her tone spoke of determination, yet Aaron detected a forlorn note as well.

The vicar had already moved his attention to his daughter, his tone significantly softening when he asked, "Kate, you are well?"

"I am, Father," Miss Kate said.

Again, the vicar surveyed Aaron. Would everyone in the county come to inspect him?

"Wonderful," the vicar said. "Now, I've business to discuss with Lord Banfield. We will see you ladies at lunch."

Aaron thought the vicar was being too dismissive of his daughter and Lady Celia, but he didn't know the vicar well enough to argue the point.

"Come to the library," Aaron said. "Would you like refreshment?"

Vicar Jones nodded. "Refreshment would be welcome."

Stanley followed along.

"This is a . . . house dog?" the vicar asked, glancing with distaste at Stanley.

"He is," Aaron said.

It seemed that Mrs. March was already fully aware of their guest and almost as soon as they sat down, she bustled in with a tea tray.

"Thank you, Mrs. March," Aaron said.

Vicar Jones barely gave the woman a nod.

What a strange vicar—one who was meant to be serving those in his realm, but certainly didn't have much in the way of a kind word.

The vicar picked up one of the scones and took his time spreading on butter, then jam.

Aaron had to wave away Stanley more than once. Aaron suspected that the dog had enjoyed a scone or two in the kitchen.

After a rather large bite, Vicar Jones chewed, then said, "Lord Banfield, I've come to warn you."

"Warn me?"

"Gossip has already spread that you are an unmarried man, with young women always in attendance."

"I only arrived two days ago," he said. "Since Lady Celia was here, alone, we sent for your daughter to be her companion. I don't see anything untoward—"

"I am not saying I agree with the gossips," Vicar Jones said with a wave of his hand. "I wanted you to be aware.

People—women especially—will say the first thing that comes to their minds, accurate or not."

Aaron wondered if the vicar drank brandy and if it would be rude to pour a glass in front of him. "Surely you can explain if the need arises," he said. "I'm happy to explain as well, but I can assure you—"

"All the assurances in the world won't make a difference." The last bit was a mumble and Vicar Jones took another hearty bite of his scone.

When the man was finished chewing, Aaron said, "Then what can be done? Should I go door to door—"

"Nothing of the sort," the vicar said, picking up a second scone, then fixing his narrow, green eyes on Aaron. "You must marry as soon as possible. It is the only solution."

Chapter Nine

One Week Later

THE COLD DECEMBER air tugged at Celia's riding cloak. She couldn't help that she'd pushed her horse faster and faster until the wind had pulled the pins from her hair. Celia found the ride invigorating, plus it was the first day this month that there'd been no rain in the morning. That didn't mean the sun was out, but clouds and no rain were fine with Celia.

In one week, Celia would be leaving Banfield Estate, perhaps forever. In one week, she'd say goodbye to her childhood home and all hopes of things turning out differently. When she returned to the house today, she and Kate would begin to fill the Christmas baskets that they'd deliver tomorrow. Kate had opted to stay at the house instead of go riding since she had the beginnings of a cold. And Lord Banfield had already pledged his help with the deliveries. As he well should.

Celia had to admit that he'd been nothing but a good student, learning all about the estate. He spent the evenings shut away in the library updating the ledgers and leaving Kate and Celia to their own devices. This usually consisted of Celia making some sort of excuse to escape to her bedroom for the rest of the evening and continue writing her story. It had taken on a new shape since the arrival of Lord Banfield.

"Whoa there," someone called, and Celia looked over her shoulder.

Lord Banfield was riding only a few paces behind her. He wore no hat, and the wind pushed through his hair and against his clothing.

She nearly reined her horse in and turned fully around. She and Lord Banfield hadn't been alone since that first night that he'd knocked on her bedroom door. Kate had been an excellent companion, even though it had been painful to watch her endless flirting with Lord Banfield and to listen to her compliments of that man each night.

"Why the hurry?" Lord Banfield said over the wind, flashing her a smile.

Celia wouldn't let the smile go to her heart, or her mind. He smiled that way at Kate too. There was nothing special in it, not for her at least. Because of her apparent emotional state around Lord Banfield—as had manifested more than once—keeping in Kate's company at all times had been most helpful.

Even when he'd had questions about receipts, Celia had brought Kate. And when he told them the purpose of the vicar's private meeting in the library with him, Celia had had Kate with her. Kate had exclaimed over the gossip, but then quickly agreed that Lord Banfield should search for a wife.

Which was why, when the invitation to a Christmas ball came from the Foxes, Kate had encouraged Lord Banfield to accept on all their behalves. Of course, Celia had cried off. She was still in mourning for her brother. Besides, a good deal of her belongings had been packed into trunks already, and . . . well, truthfully, Celia could have attended the ball and sat out the dancing, but she didn't want to watch the women flock to Lord Banfield's side.

He was beside her now, his horse keeping pace with hers. He didn't try to speak anymore, just rode. Celia's destination was the hill overlooking the row of tenant houses, but perhaps she'd ride farther today to lose Lord Banfield. After all, he only went for short rides since he'd been so caught up in the ledgers and management of the estate.

Visitors had come and gone each day, and in truth, the only time Celia had spent with him had been at mealtimes. It was enough to see him wearing bits of her brother's clothing. A vest here, a cravat there. Never an entire ensemble, which made her wonder if he was just waiting for her to leave Banfield before he donned more of the borrowed clothing.

Today, she couldn't help but notice, he wore a new coat, one that his valet must have ordered. But the riding gloves had been her brother's. She'd given them to Bart several years ago as a gift. She tore her gaze from the gloves and swallowed back the building emotion. Soon she'd be gone from this place full of memories, and soon she'd be able to build a life anew.

As her horse thundered up the hill, she eased off the reins, and the horse slowed. Lord Banfield adjusted his pace to hers. When she stopped at the top of the hill, Lord Banfield joined her.

Out of breath, Celia said nothing for several moments as she looked over the tenant housing and the land that stretched before them. A few days ago, Celia had brought Kate and Lord Banfield out here and introduced him to each tenant.

Now that she was no longer racing through the wind, the cold, damp air settled around her and seeped through her clothing. She tried not to shiver, but her body had other ideas. Before she could protest, Lord Banfield slid off his overcoat and set it around her shoulders, then returned to holding the reins of his horse.

Still, they didn't speak. There was too much to speak of, yet Celia didn't want to speak at all. She didn't want to discuss the ledgers she'd neglected, or the distribution of the

Christmas baskets, or her impending departure, or least of all the Christmas ball that she'd be missing the next night.

"I could not sleep last night," Lord Banfield said.

The statement surprised her, and she glanced over at him. His gaze remained on the land below.

"I ended up pacing the house and saw that your light was on again," he continued.

Well, Celia had nothing to say to that. Fortunately, he hadn't knocked again on her bedroom door. So she simply nodded.

"Do you ever let people read your writing?" he asked.

Her breath hitched. "I . . . of course people read my letters."

"Is that all you're writing?" He reached for her hand and slipped her glove off.

Celia didn't have to look down to know that ink stained the edges of her fingers. The warmth of his hand holding hers was a stark contrast to the cold wind.

"Is it poetry?" he asked.

She met his gaze, wondering why he persisted with his questions. What did it matter to him? "I'm writing a novel." The words had slipped out, unheeding. Instantly, she wished she could take them back.

The edges of his mouth lifted into a surprised smile, and she tried not to notice how the shadowed appearance of whiskers on his jaw indicated the lateness of the afternoon. "Tell me more," he said.

And in those brown eyes of his, she saw that his interest was genuine. And perhaps it was because in another week, she might never see this man again, that she told him about her writing. She told him how she closeted herself in her room late into the night to write her story. How it had been a story of a young woman traveling to India, and all the adventures she encountered. Adventures she'd never see in her own lifetime, but had read about and overheard at dinner parties.

Lord Banfield had released her hand, and she'd pulled her glove back on while she told him about her manuscript. "Of course I could never have it published," she said. "I'm already enough of a blight on society as it is."

"Because you're not married?" he said.

She looked away. "Because I'm not married."

"Damn society, then," he said in a soft voice, and he didn't even apologize for his curse. "Publish anyway."

She felt a smile working its way to the surface, and she sneaked a glance at him. "Perhaps under a pseudonym."

His gaze was intent on her, and she had to focus on her breathing.

"I, for one, would be honored to read your manuscript," he said.

Celia wanted to laugh; surely he was jesting. But his expression was in earnest.

"I am glad we have this moment alone, Lady Celia." He moved his horse closer to hers. "I have done a poor job of expressing my condolences for the loss of your brother."

She did not know what to say. Many people had expressed similar sentiments, but coming from the new Lord Banfield, it felt different. More sincere somehow.

His hand reached for hers again, and she watched his fingers curl around hers. She was utterly breathless. What was he doing? What were his intentions?

"Lady Celia, I have a proposal to make."

Her pulse shot up. He couldn't mean what she thought he was saying, but when she looked up at him, she saw his mouth move with those very words.

"Marry me and stay at Banfield."

Chapter Ten

THE SHOCKED LOOK on Lady Celia's face probably didn't bode well. Aaron had never proposed to a woman before, but he didn't think this was how it was supposed to go. Lady Celia gasped, then jerked her hand away. And... her eyes filled with tears after said shock melted away.

"Is my offer really so distasteful?" he asked, trying... *hoping* to lessen whatever intense emotion Lady Celia was going through. Marriage to Lady Celia made sense. She was most certainly marriageable age, she loved Banfield Estate, she watched Aaron when she thought he wasn't noticing—which he hoped indicated her interest in him—and she was... intriguing. Her physical features were pleasant, and as the days passed, he found himself drawn to her even more.

And he didn't want passion to make this decision for him. So he didn't let his mind wander in that direction, and instead he focused on the practicalities. Which he thought she'd at least consider.

"I cannot accept your offer, Lord Banfield," she said in a trembling whisper. "I cannot let you marry me out of pity."

Before he could answer or refute her accusation, she spurred her horse down the hill, heading away from him as fast as possible. As he watched her go, he wondered if in fact he had asked her out of pity. He *had* felt the guilt of his survival over her brother's, and he'd seen the changes in her life happening firsthand.

There was nothing to do but return to the estate and set about his obligations. Whoever had penned the idea that women were a mystery had never met Lady Celia. Not only was she a mystery, but she was an enigma.

But as he rode toward the estate, he wondered at her point of view, or more accurately, her viewpoint of him. Had he misinterpreted the sidelong glances from Lady Celia? Had he been so off the mark that she wouldn't even consider a proposal by asking for time to think about it?

Surely she could see the wisdom in the arrangement. Men and women had married for far less, yet here was the opportunity for her to remain at Banfield Estate the rest of her life and raise her children here. As for Aaron . . . he would feel the weight of guilt lift. He'd be able to wholeheartedly throw himself into managing and running the estate. This time next year, they'd host the Christmas banquet at the estate that Lady Celia had so fondly spoken about. Together.

And then Aaron would be able to dispel the sorrow from her countenance. Once and for all.

He arrived at the stables, and Lady Celia was nowhere in sight. She'd ridden at a fairly fast pace, and he'd taken his time. Once he'd dismounted, he left the horse for the stable master to care for, and he strode to the front doors. Candles had already been lit against the disappearing light that a bank of storm clouds had darkened.

He strode into the hallway and Mr. Garner met him there to remove his coat. Then Aaron made his way to the kitchen, where Lady Celia and Miss Kate worked to fill each gift basket with preserves, bottles of oil, loaves of bread, and pulled candy.

"You've made it ahead of the storm," Miss Kate said when he came in.

He didn't look at Miss Kate when he replied, "Yes, I survived. I hope the weather will be agreeable tomorrow for delivery."

Lady Celia didn't look up from her task, but her cheeks pinked.

Miss Kate smiled. "It will all keep an extra day if needed. What I'm really worried about is the travel to the ball tomorrow night. What if the storm turns to snow?"

Again, Lady Celia said nothing.

"We shall have to bring rugs to fight off the cold."

"That would be wonderful," Miss Kate said. "As long as we don't miss it."

"We've plenty of rugs," Lady Celia said in a quiet voice. "You can use as many as you like."

"Oh, thank you," Miss Kate gushed. "But won't you change your mind about coming to the ball? Having you along will make all the difference."

Lady Celia gave her friend a quick smile. "It will make no difference," she corrected. "My mind is made up. I will hear all about it when you return." Without any acknowledgement in Aaron's direction, she returned to her task.

"But everyone will want to see you," Miss Kate persisted. "And to wish you well on your move." She turned her gaze to Aaron. "You must convince her. I don't like to think of her alone in this house while we are dancing the night away."

Aaron swallowed, but before he could reply, Lady Celia said, "Lord Banfield will be busy dancing with every lady in the county." Her gaze focused on Miss Kate. "And I don't doubt you'll be so busy fending off suitors that the time will speed by. You'll be back here before you know it. If it makes you feel any better, I'll wait up for you to return so you can tell me everything immediately."

This seemed to mollify Miss Kate.

It did nothing to ease the knot of unease in Aaron's stomach. Miss Kate was right. Surely the neighbors would want to give their good wishes to Lady Celia.

"You must help Lord Banfield in my stead," Lady Celia said, lifting her head at last and meeting Aaron's gaze. "He's decided to take your father's advice and find himself a wife. The ball will be the perfect place for him to meet such a person."

Miss Kate clapped her hands together, and Aaron couldn't move.

He'd never felt so insulted in his life.

The next day proved to be fairer weather, and the basket delivery went smoothly. The carriage got stuck only once, and with the help of the groom, Aaron was able to get it free. He didn't see any sign of Lady Celia upon his return at the appointed hour of departure for the ball; Miss Kate was the only one who came down the stairs.

They'd be stopping at the vicarage to collect the sister just younger than she. Mrs. March accompanied them, and Aaron wondered what she'd do all night.

Aaron barely survived the chatter on the way to the ball, and once there, his first assignment was to procure a glass of wine. Once he'd drunk that, he was ready to find a wife. Well . . . he didn't expect it to happen in one night. Especially not with any of the ladies he danced with. One thing was made very clear right from the beginning. Not one of them had the same shade of blue eyes as Lady Celia.

None of them had a stray freckle on her collarbone.

The only redhead he danced with had a laugh that sounded more like a cackle. He danced with blonde women, brunettes, women with green eyes, brown eyes, two with blue eyes. He danced with women who smelled of roses, of oranges, and of something sharper. But no one smelled of lilacs.

And he realized as the final dance was announced and he knew his feet would be sore for days . . . there was not one woman he'd wanted to kiss.

Not that he'd considered kissing Lady Celia. Well, he *might* have considered it, but he hadn't let his imagination get past the first brush of his lips against hers. Or what it might feel like to press his body against hers. Or to have her delicate fingers thread their way through his hair.

No.

"Lord Banfield," a man said. Aaron recognized Vicar Jones's voice before he turned. "Everyone is speculating on which lady you might call upon tomorrow."

Aaron held back a yawn. Perhaps everyone should just sleep tomorrow. "I have not decided," he said at last because it was true in part. He had decided, but the woman wouldn't have him.

The vicar nodded. "You do understand the urgency, do you not?"

"I understand," Aaron said. "And I cannot argue against the idea that the decision of a lifetime is most important."

The vicar looked pleased. "Very well, then. I hope to hear good news soon."

On the carriage ride back to the manor, Aaron let the conversation around him drift away. He had no interest in recounting the events of the night where he was introduced over and over—assessed as if he were a sheep or horse at a town fair—or in speaking of any of the dozen women he'd danced with.

No, he could only think of one thing—or one person. And what he needed to say to her. Mostly an apology, but also an explanation.

Chapter Eleven

CELIA HAD BEEN watching for the approaching carriage from the drawing room for what seemed like hours. She knew that balls could continue into the early morning hours, so when she finally saw the shape of the carriage come into view, she was startled to see it so early. Celia checked the large clock on the fireplace mantel. It wasn't even 1:00 a.m.

She hurried from the drawing room, not wanting to be caught waiting there. She didn't want to see the glow of Lord Banfield's face because he'd met a beautiful creature he desired to marry. Celia hadn't been able to forget his half-hearted proposal from the day before. And she marveled at how she had been able to gather her wits and tell him she would not be pitied . . . Yet she found herself wondering if being married out of pity was favorable over not being married at all.

Celia exhaled as she reached her bedroom. As hard as it would be to leave her childhood home, she didn't want a loveless marriage either. And once the heir was produced, she didn't want to watch her husband enter into a dalliance. Celia had seen the way that Kate looked at Lord Banfield, and now he'd been in a room full of women who would be more than happy to accept an offer of marriage from a practical stranger.

His new position and inheritance would be recommendation enough.

Celia lit two candles. Kate would be able to see she was still awake when she came into the corridor. Still, Celia kept her door open a crack so she could hear the voices of Lord Banfield and Kate as they entered the hall.

The voices were only a murmur, and Celia couldn't distinguish one word from the next. She shut her door without a sound and waited for Kate to knock.

By the time Kate did knock, Celia had already imagined the entire night. She opened the door, and Kate swept in. It was just as Celia imagined. Her friend had stars in her eyes.

"You look like you had a wonderful time," Celia said.

Kate grasped her hands. "It was truly magical. I danced nearly every dance, and Lord Banfield was on the dance floor almost as much as me. Dancing with one woman after the other." She sighed and released Celia's hands, then sat on the bed, her gown billowing about her.

Celia sat next to her, and for the next hour, listened to detail after detail. She had refrained from asking more questions about Lord Banfield's experience. When Kate left after wishing her a happy Christmas, Celia's mind wouldn't stop racing.

Still, she blew out her candles and drew her curtains open to let in the moonlight. Then she climbed beneath her covers. Her eyes would not close and her thoughts would not quiet. It was then she noticed a folded piece of paper near her door. She didn't recall it being there before. She didn't think it was an errant manuscript page from her book since she didn't fold the paper.

Celia climbed out of bed and picked up the paper. She opened the note and read the single word in the light of the moon.

Library?

It had to be from *him*. There was no other message, nor a signature, but it could be from no one else besides Lord Banfield.

For a moment, Celia stood still, debating what to do. What could he possibly want? As the minutes moved slowly by, she realized she did want to meet him. Perhaps for a final conversation. Christmas was upon them, and Celia would soon be leaving. They could part on congenial terms.

With this resolve, Celia drew on her thicker robe, then pulled her loose hair over one shoulder and secured it with a ribbon. She opened her door, deciding to forego a candle so as not to attract any attention should Kate still be awake or a member of the household staff take to wandering about.

Celia wasn't sure what she expected when she reached the library, but it wasn't to find it dark. The drapes had been pulled aside, and the same moonlight that had been in her bedroom now filtered across the library rug.

Lord Banfield stood at the window, turned away from her, his hands behind his back. He'd shed his overcoat, but he still wore his evening finery, and his broad shoulders were a formidable shadow in the moonlight. Celia had caught a glimpse of him before he'd left, and she had no doubt he'd been considered the most eligible bachelor of the night.

Stanley was laying at Lord Banfield's feet, and it seemed the dog was too tired to lift its head and look over at her.

She hesitated in the doorway, second guessing her decision to come into the library for a private meeting. Would Lord Banfield renew his offer, and she'd be forced to turn him away again? Or would he announce his infatuation with one of the women he'd met tonight?

Lord Banfield turned and saw her. It was now too late to disappear. He said nothing for a moment, then he crossed to her. Celia watched his dark form moving closer. The dimness of the room made her heart race—surely it wasn't anything else. She wasn't afraid of this man, and whatever he wanted to meet about, she could manage it in a dignified manner.

But when his hand grasped hers, her resolve to be dignified melted. His gloveless fingers were warm and strong, and her mind became a whirl as he led her to the window. For once, the dog didn't seem to mind her presence. There was no growling or barking. Stanley simply closed his eyes. The moonlight was brighter next to the window where Lord Banfield stopped and looked down at her.

His eyes were hooded, and without letting go of her hand, he leaned close enough that she could smell brandy and musk.

"You were missed this evening," Lord Banfield said in a low voice.

"Oh." Celia exhaled. Her heart was thudding so loudly that she wouldn't be surprised if he could hear it. "I heard it was a wonderful ball."

"I supposed it had the makings of a wonderful ball," he said, and Celia wondered why he was still holding her hand.

"But you weren't there," he continued. "And I realized something..."

When he didn't continue, Celia said, "You realized what?"

His intense gaze was making Celia feel a bit lightheaded. And when he touched the ends of her hair with his other hand, she thought she might sway against him.

"I realized that *I* missed you," he said. "I realized the only woman I wanted to dance with wasn't at the ball. She was home at Banfield."

Celia swallowed.

"I want to try something," he whispered.

"What?" she whispered back, although she was fairly certain what he was about to try.

When his lips brushed against hers, she decided she must have fallen asleep and was now dreaming. But then his hand tangled in her hair, and his other hand wrapped around her waist, and he pulled her closer. His kissing was slow and urgent at the same time, and Celia definitely knew she wasn't dreaming because she'd never been kissed before. And she could have never dreamt that she could feel this way—like she was both floating above ground and swimming in a deep pool of warm water at the same time.

She kissed him back, although she was only following his lead since she wasn't sure she was any good at this. Yet every part of her tingled, and she grasped onto his jacket to hold herself upright. And the way his kissing turned deeper and more urgent, told her that she might be doing something right.

She didn't want this to end, didn't want him to release her. When he did draw away, she wanted to pull him toward her again. She'd never be the same. No matter what happened after tonight. And even though she now knew what it was like to be kissed, she doubted she could capture the right words or right description in her novel.

"I need to tell you something," he said, his hands at her waist, his smell all around her. "I don't pity you." He lifted a hand and ran a thumb along her jaw. She felt the sensation reverberate through her body.

"You told me you would never marry," he continued. "I want to know why."

Celia had hardly caught her breath, but she stepped away from him, because as lovely as it had been kissing him, she wasn't his intended. He dropped his arms, and she felt the loss of his warmth as if a blanket had been pulled off her on a cold night.

"I didn't want to be married for my dowry. With this

hair"—she touched her hair—"and these freckles"—she touched her neck—"I have heard the whisperings of how a girl as plain as me would be lucky to get one proposal."

She held up her hand when he took a step closer. "You can't think you want to marry me, Lord Banfield. I don't want your charity, and—"

"It's not charity, Celia," he said, grasping her hand.

She pulled her hand away because she'd forget herself again. "You can't love me. We've only just met, and a marriage should be based on more than pity."

He didn't try to take her hand again, but he did move closer. "I am sorry for your losses," he said, "but it's not the pity you're thinking of. I lost my parents as well, and even though I never had a sibling, I understand loss."

"I know," Celia said. "And I thank you for your compassion."

"As for the question of whether my proposal is one of love, I can only say that tonight at the ball I realized I only wanted to be with you."

She let those words sink into her heart and felt the small flare of hope.

"Maybe I can't give a pretty speech about love right now," he continued in a quiet voice, "but me missing you has to count for something. And . . . that kiss . . ."

Her cheeks heated. That kiss had been quite divine. "You don't mind my freckles?"

He moved even closer and lowered his head. When he kissed her at the base of her neck, a warm shiver traveled through her. "I don't mind."

She wanted to cling to him, melt against him, let her hopes soar . . . "Our children would be redheads."

He chuckled, and the rumbling laugh made her feel light.

"My grandmother was a redhead," he said. "I suppose it runs in the family."

And then he was kissing her again, or perhaps she was kissing him. The second time around was even better, she decided.

"So . . ." he said when they broke apart.

"So . . ." she echoed.

He smiled, then said, "I have a present for you. I was going to wait until Christmas, but since it's now Christmas Day, I think it would be all right."

"It would definitely be all right."

He left her then, by the window, and Celia wrapped her arms about herself as she waited. She looked down at Stanley, who'd been witness to everything that had happened tonight. It seemed that the dog's nonchalance was his approval.

When Lord Banfield came back into the library, her heart leapt at the sight of him. How could she have missed him in such a short amount of time? He carried a wrapped rectangular package.

"I didn't get you anything," she said.

He only smiled. "Call me Aaron. That will be gift enough."

She returned his smile. "Aaron."

"Open it."

So she opened the package on the small side table near the drapes. Inside she found a long, narrow wooden box. When she opened it, she saw two quills, and a small ink bottle, along with another bottle of clear liquid.

"It's not much, but I thought you might find use for the quills."

For her writing, she knew. She turned to face him. "Thank you."

"The clear liquid is supposed to clean off ink stains from fingers," he said.

"When did you get this?" she asked, looking up.

"Before you turned down my proposal of marriage."

She hid a smile. "And you would have kept it if . . ."

"I still would have given it to you," he said, leaning down and kissing her cheek, and lingering. "Maybe I would have sneaked it into your luggage or something." He lifted his head, his gaze locking onto hers. "Celia . . . I don't want you to leave."

"Because you want me to stay?"

He nodded, then smiled.

"And you still want me to marry you?"

Aaron's smile spread. "Of course."

"So you can learn to love me?"

He slipped his hands about her waist and drew her close. "That will be the easy part." He leaned his forehead against hers. "Please tell me you've changed your mind."

Celia closed her eyes, reveling in his hands at her waist, the sound of her thudding heart, and how she felt as if life had become sweet again. "I've changed my mind," she whispered. "But I have one demand."

His lips curved upward. "Anything."

"The dog can't sleep in the bedroom."

Aaron chuckled. "That's your demand?"

"Stanley is nice enough, I suppose," she teased. "At least he no longer growls at me. But I want you to myself at night."

"If you're going to put it that way, then I must agree," he said.

She wrapped her arms about his neck. "Good. I'm pleased."

His hands moved up her back and pulled her closer. "I want to please you, Celia. Now and always."

"Then kiss me again, Aaron."

And he did.

Heather B. Moore is a *USA Today* bestselling author. She writes historical thrillers under the pen name H.B. Moore; her latest are *The Killing Curse* and *Breaking Jess*. Under the name Heather B. Moore, she writes romance and women's fiction; her latest include the Pine Valley Novels. Under pen name Jane Redd, she writes the young adult speculative Solstice series, including her latest release *Mistress Grim*. Heather is represented by Dystel, Goderich & Bourret.

Join Heather's email list: hbmoore.com/contact
Website: HBMoore.com
Facebook: Fans of H. B. Moore
Blog: MyWritersLair.blogspot.com
Twitter: @HeatherBMoore
Instagram: @AuthorHBMoore

www.ingramcontent.com/pod-product-compliance
Lightning Source LLC
LaVergne TN
LVHW021755060526
838201LV00058B/3106